Believe

(A Christmas Tale)

By Walter Pyne

Merry Christmas….

The Tale of the Spirit

Dedicated to my son, Arthur, and to all my Family and Friends...

Author's Note

I had a very difficult time in writing this author's note, because of many different sentiments that were going through me while I was writing this novel. Originally, I intended to put this at the end of the story. I realise now, that even though I shouldn't finish this note until after the story has completed, it is still something that contains my hopes and dreams, which should always be at the beginning of any tale.

I had a dream not too long ago, where the younger version of myself and I sat down and talked with one another. We spoke of regrets, misunderstandings, as well as all the wonderful things that have gone on throughout my life. You see, I have always been a storyteller, more so than a writer or artist. My words and pictures are a way of expressing who I am, who I was, and of whom I hope to one day become. They are a compilation of everything that makes me whole. However broken and lost I may be during any given time, I know that in my words I can find truth and hope once again. And it truly is a horrible thing to be lost in this vast never-ending universe. To feel alone and without hope, to forget all that we once were. These are the things that destroy worlds. My younger self told me thus, which was something that I had forgotten. He also told me that there would only ever be a very few amount of people, if any, on this world that will ever truly understand me, but there will be many who care about me.

So, we both continued to sit and stare at the setting sun together. He explained to me that even the way that I perceive the sunset will be different to those around me, and that I will have to live with knowing that our universe is not the same as the one that others see. My universe is a universe of limitless words and ideas that hold an infinite number of possibilities. It is one with no hope of ever truly bringing all of them to this world in one mortal lifetime. My beliefs, my dreams, all that makes me what I am; they are all within this universe that I see.

To describe this in words would take me an entire lifetime and beyond. But, if you could imagine an ocean filled with boxes. And each one containing something wonderful and undiscovered to me. Knowing that I will never be able to open all the boxes before me, one could begin to understand what my younger self was trying to tell me.

I am a simple person, and a storyteller. These words that I write, this simple story that I have to tell; these are my gifts to you. They will not change the world. They will not bring people to their knees, or cause nations to war. These words are simply a piece of who I am, who I was, and who I wish I could become. And if you are one of the few that can understand me, that sees the same sunset that I see, that hears the same voices in the wind that I hear, that can feel the universe breathe in and out as I do. If this is you, then take comfort in knowing that you are not alone, nor are you mad, but if anything, you are one of the privileged few who may get to dream of the universe as it could be and not just as others see it. Take care to believe when you have no hope, to see where others fail to look and dream beyond all other dreams.

And so, with these few simple words I have written, I give to you this story. To you, I reveal a part of my universe. May it reach your heart, and bring you all my hopes and dreams, for this is all any storyteller can hope for.

Chapter 1

Snow in Seattle

The children are singing again. The lights are twinkling throughout the streets, in a hope of catching the feeling of goodwill toward men. The people are adorning their hats and coats, and the winter has now taken full hold. What wonder and awe are we to expect, when this time of year unfolds. When the sun draws close to the unseasonable night, so the children dream of spirits and tales of men in red and white. And even though the day may bring a simple unabashed love of all things close and dear, somehow, someway we will find that special thing that brings that special morning's cheer. Oh, what shall we find for them, something grand or something plain? Yes, my friends, the day draws near, for you see, it's Christmas time again.

Wonderful, is it not, this special thing that comes to all of us, at least once in our lives. I know of no man who has not felt the touch of such innocent joy at least once. And yet, how is it we become so easily distracted and forgetful of these moments. We fill ourselves with monotony, meagre ideals, and pride. Life itself, even she seems to swallow us whole and drown our pleasures in deep shameless sorrow and loss. And why may you wonder, do I speak of such sorrowful things, upon a time of such happiness for so many? Well, you see, it is in this darkest dreariest of places that we must go to begin this tale.

Our story begins with a simple honest man, sitting on a simple, but rather uncomfortable chair, drinking from a simple plain white coffee cup. He by no means, to no fault of his own, thought himself, wished to be, or would ever call himself a simple person. But we sometimes cannot see what lies before us, staring at us day to day. Indeed, even as he reads from his undemanding, unoffending magazine about boat life, he seemingly misses everything that passes him by. With every passing sip from his cup of coffee, plain and unflavoured, he looks even further away from the world around him. His cares and wants are but only to fade into the background of life, as silent and unnoticed as can be.

It is here, at this moment that this tale begins, with such a subtle entrance that many will not even have noticed it.

"Do you believe in Santa Claus?"

The gentle brown eyes of the soft-hearted man look up from the photo of the latest nautical navigational tracking system. At first, he sees a family sitting but a table away from him. Another family draws his attention, though, just beyond the first. They are rushing about trying to gather their bags. "Hurry," he hears repeatedly. "Plane leaving," is another phrase that catches his ears. He looks off to his side, where he sees the planes rushing by and the frantic amounts of cargo trucks passing in every direction.

The sun is setting, causing the cold clouds of the north to burn the skies a wonderful rainbow of lavender and pink. Although so beautiful, it is so far different than what he is familiar with, where the oceans burn the skies red, and the clouds break the lights over the ground.

It may be a world away, and yet somehow it is always close to him. The smell of the pine trees rolling down from the Cascades, filling your lungs with cool fresh air, unlike anywhere else he had ever been. He can hear the calming sound of the raindrops falling on the ferns, as he sits on his back porch listening to the sound of waves methodically stroking the beach's edge. All the smiling people covering themselves and complaining about the weather, but somehow knowing that it's a good thing. "It keeps the trees green," is a familiar term he has grown to love. But even as the world around him is always green, it doesn't take but a second to look up to the poetic mountain ranges in the horizon, seemingly always dusted with the milky covering of white.

As he looks down to his coffee cup, reflecting softly in his own thoughts, he suddenly sees a pair of small hands at the edge of his table. His eyes follow the tiny set of fingers upward, which lead to an innocently angelic set of the purest azure eyes that he has ever seen. There is even a glow about them, just around the iris; a colour just beyond the deep blue that already dominates.

"Hello," he responds softly, with a somewhat startled look about his face.

"Hello," the girl responds cheerfully, as she brushes a single lock of her golden hair from her brow. She then looks at his cup of coffee, stretching her toes to their limits in order to see above its rim. "You haven't answered my question. But then, I suppose you didn't hear me. People your age rarely hear me. Perhaps they think I'm somewhat insignificant."

The words are spoken crisp and clearly, with a slight hint of an accent of some nature. He has travelled the world before, and has come across many different dialects of English, including the many within the boundaries of England itself. It often amazes him that in such a tiny little plot of land, that so many different dialects of the same language can arise in such vast tones and variations. This one's voice, though; she has the accent of one that has not developed fully, but is still distinguishable. He is certain that it must be a type of British accent, with a gentle well-educated infliction. Perhaps Surrey or Berkshire....

"Well??" she questions, bringing him out of his thoughts.

"I'm sorry," he replies. "Did you ask me a question?"

"Yes," she returns bluntly, with an innocent looking face overcoming her as she pulls his cup toward her. "Do you believe in Santa Claus?"

At this stage she looks at him. Her gaze pierces through him, as if to see what truth will come from the mouth of the man she stands before. And to him, there can only be one answer.

"Of course, there is a Santa," he replies quickly and promptly, without hesitation or waiver. A smile overcomes him that even he could not have feigned.

A small draft comes from behind the man; gentle, but noticeable. It flows softly over the table and blows a few strands of the child's hair back. This is enough to cause her to lift her head and face him once again, if but for a brief moment before turning her attention toward the coffee cup once more.

"I knew you did," she states looking at the chair next to her now. In one quick motion she leaps up and seats herself down in front of him.

"Don't you think your parents are going to worry about where you've run off to?" he questions, looking about to see if any sign of a panicking parent has arisen. The family that was once directly behind him has left no trace of itself, and is now replaced by three young businessmen and their laptops. Just beyond them there is a single man looking somewhat lost in thought. A brief glimpse upwards, though, almost gives way to a glimmer of hope as to the origins of the child. This is quickly dashed as the would-be hopeful lays his head forward in his arms and closes his eyes as if to sleep.

"You didn't answer my question, you know." He looks back at the young girl before him.

"I'm sorry," he replies softly, now looking around once more to see if he can find the child's origins. It is here that he feels a soft touch of a hand upon his fingers. An electric essence unlike any other that he has ever felt before passes through him, and all at once he feels an incredible calm.

"The question was do *you* believe in Santa Claus. Not is there a Santa Claus," she speaks softly to him, almost in a whisper. She then sits back in her chair, almost disappearing within its depths. "That question would be irrelevant. Almost as if one were to ask someone is there God or the Sun? The answer is neither yes nor no. By definition if something is to exist, it must simply be. Like a myth, or a legend, or perhaps even a painting, to be more precise. It is not the question of whether or not it exists, because in truth, it will exist whether or not you or anyone else knows or believes in it. If it exists, it simply will. And the same goes in our case. So the question at hand, is not whether or not there is a Santa Claus, but rather do *you* believe in him?"

A glaze overcomes him, more so even, a look of utter bewilderment. As the astonishment settles in at the overwhelming directness and depth that a child has just stated to him, he begins to smile and realise that he is dealing with no mere absent minded being. It is also at this moment, he thinks momentarily about the sorry state of affairs that forces him to compare different education systems.

"In either case," she continues, seeing his head slightly tilt to one side. "I know the answer already; otherwise you wouldn't have even heard me. That fact is undeniable, amidst any other words or phrases that will come between us, I'm sure. But for now, let us settle with this first meeting as it stands."

The child reaches to her side and removes a small elongated box, deep blue in colour, with a red ribbon tied elegantly around its centre. After she places it on the table, next to his cup, she stands from her seat and looks at him one more time before turning.

"I came across this in my travels," she states crisply. "And if I'm correct, I believe it is for you."

With her words spoken, she runs off like a small animal entering a forest. It is only as she does, that he sees her full attire; the flow of the small snow-white silken dress drowning the air around her. A matching set she adorns stylishly. A red ribbon around her waist, as well the red shoes prancing about as if she were a quiet fawn-like creature crossing the wood. Even now, her hands did not swing about as a normal child's, but remain firmly behind her as a sea captain would as he headed the helm of his ship.

All in all, he is quietly taken aback. He barely notices the surge of people that cross in front of his view, blocking out where the little girl vanishes to. At this moment he takes a breath and looks at the team of sports players, a tennis team he believes. They seat themselves not too far away from him, and their voices overpower the false silence in his mind.

His fingers brush the box next to his coffee, almost startling him; his smile fading from his face at this stage. "What a strange child," he says quietly.

He begins to inspect the gift box more thoroughly. It is soft to the touch, much like silk or velvet. Long and rectangular in length, he begins to ponder what it holds. Perhaps a pen, he thinks, much like the one his son gave him not too long ago. He turns it over to see a long slender piece of paper folded carefully and placed cleverly between the ribbon and the container. With care he removes the parchment and unfolds it precisely twelve times. Upon the last fold he turns it over and begins to read.

Snow in Seattle

242 NW Pike St.
Seattle, WA
(555) 623 – 4129

To replace 1 x Platinum pc,
To repair 1 x Diamond (inc. Fold)
To reset 5 x Diamond Saphhire

Dont worry, Ill have it all done by X-Mas

-D xx

Thoughts begin to flow through his mind of many things, including the origins of this tiny box and what it holds. Suddenly the realisation that he is actually holding this gift in his hands becomes overwhelming to the point the he has to put it down and close his eyes. As he does this, all he can see is the little girl's eyes staring back at him.

His eyes open quickly, as if they were overcome by cold water. He knows Pike Street. He has grown up with the market, and all the stores that surround it. All the memories of his childhood come flooding into his head, as he remembers with such fondness the joy and happiness that the streets within Seattle brought to him. He pushes them aside, though, and tries to think clearly.

"*Would passengers on flight NW105 please report to Gate S15 for boarding*," he hears through the mesh of mind numbing thoughts. It is only then, that he begins to clearly realize that his plane is boarding. Still in a haze, though, he calmly folds the piece of paper up and puts it carefully in his wallet, as he stands. Without thought, he then slides the box into the side pocket of his black sport's blazer as he picks it up from over the back of his chair. He then reaches down underneath the chair and pulls up his leather laptop case, with a red Santa cartoon tie dangling out of the side.

He passes through the airport without thought or observation. Everything and everyone seem distant and somewhat unreal. The voices are merely echoes of time that he cannot seem to capture. Everything and everyone seem to be rushing past him at incredible rates, moving to an unearthly music that resounds in his head. Until suddenly, everything and everyone come into focus all at once.

"Would you like a drink, sir?" he hears, suddenly focusing on the pleasantly faced lady standing in the middle of the airplane aisle. She's wearing a light blue top, with a dark blue skirt. It's the strange cloud floral pattern that catches his eye, then the bright coloured fingernails as the place a drink of water in front of the lady next to him.

"I think I'll have a whiskey and cola," he replies softly. That'll soon calm him down, he thinks.

"There you go," the nice lady says as she places the small plastic cup with a can and a small plastic bottle of whiskey on the tray in front of him.

"You look a bit frazzled dear," the woman next to him says softly, as he pours himself a drink.

"Sorry," he replies, pouring out the last of his whiskey into the ice.

"Well, I was just looking at your hands," he hears her say. "You might as well have asked for a whiskey on the rocks, hold the ice." He hears a gentle laugh over the numbing sounds of the engine. It is only then that he turns and looks at this lovely lady staring back at him. She is quite a bit older than him, but has the most striking smile and eyes, which again have a calming effect on him.

"I'm not sure why, but I'm a bit edgy today."

"Are you scared of flying?" she asks in her mild accent of the Carolinas, sipping from her water. He in return finishes the last of his drink, and then begins to pour out the cola from the can. She laughs at his actions.

"Not really," he thinks aloud. "I used to be, but I've learned to overcome it. I suppose it's just coming to the realisation that I can't control everything."

"My daughter was afraid of the same thing," she states. "She went to see a hypnotherapist. Now whenever she thinks of flying she has to draw a picture of a dog house. Something to do with that little dog who dresses up like a pilot and flies around on his dog house." She laughs at her own words, and looks over to see a small smile cross his face.

She begins to ask him the usual questions, which he answers with a gentle politeness. It is in the small conversation that he realises that he is touching the box in the pocket of his blazer. Finally, he pulls it out and looks at it carefully on the table in front of him.

"OH!" the woman declares. "Is that for someone special?"

"I'm not quite sure," he replies.

"Do you mind if I look?"

Without thought or decision, the box is taken from him and the ribbon pushed carefully aside. And in one fell motion he looks over to see the glittering of the diamonds and sapphires in the light from the skies behind him.

"What an incredible bracelet," she states, closing the box once more and handing it back to him. "It must be worth a fortune."

"I suppose so," self-effacingly he retorts his short statement.

"You look as if you don't know what to do with that," he hears her say. Then, "What's your name?"

"Patrick." He cringes as he says the name. He's not sure why he ever tells anyone that name, as no one he knows calls him that. It sounds so formal and starched, like a lawyer or council-man. And he considers himself to be anything but a formal person.

"Well Patrick, I tell you what you need to do." That name drives a shiver down his spine once again. He can hardly concentrate as she tells him how he should approach the woman he loves. "Just walk straight up to her and put this in her hand. She'll know what it is, trust me. Every woman knows what it is. We have a sense for these things."

"Right," he replies. He listens on about how he just needs to do things, and in which way he should do them. Finally, he puts the jewellery box in his pocket once more and nods his head to her. He can barely keep his eyes open, now, from all the talking the lady does. But somehow, he manages to be polite and smiles, before finally a brief pause allows him to look out the window.

Something inexplicable in the terrain of the Northwest, makes it a wonderfully beautiful sight to behold from the air. Snowcapped mountains are always abundant in the Cascades, even into the depths of summer. Even the vast great river of the Columbia stretches into the depths of the land, carving out vast canyons and rocky curves that one can recognize easily. At least one who has been raised there would know, in any case.

"Looks like Rainer is covered in cloud," he hears from behind him. He hadn't realised that the trip had gone by so quickly. Usually four hours takes an eternity, and he'd just sit and listen to the people around him. "Are you doing anything nice while you're here?"

"Might try and find Snow," he replies.

"Good luck with that here." He hears another laugh again, but he ignores it. He simply focuses on the distant mountain, and smiles to himself. "All we seem to get around here is rain, and even when it's not raining, it's thinking about it."

"I prefer to think it snows here all year round," he says softly, smiling to himself. "The people here are just a bit warmer than everywhere else that snows."

"What?"

"My grandmother used to say that it always starts off as snow," he begins, "but by the time it reaches us, it's turned to rain because of how warm everyone always is here. That's why everyone wears t-shirts and shorts in the winter."

The pilot comes on again, reminding everyone that they will be landing shortly, and that it is raining. Patrick smiles and shuts his eyes, as he lays his head back in his seat once more. He takes a deep breath and sighs softly.

"Home."

Chapter 2

Pancakes and Syrup

The drive down from the island usually takes about two hours, but on this usually calm time of day, the traffic was already beginning to slow down to a crawl. It was nearing the three-hour mark when they passed the turn towards U-district and now started heading into Seattle. Rain wasn't forecast, but that was nothing unusual either, even as at times it was so thick that he could barely see through his windshield. And the people driving around him were either maniacs or just plain blind. As one car goes forward, the car in front stops because he can't see beyond his headlights.

"At least you don't have to worry about a speeding ticket," he has said to himself more than once over the past decades. But somehow, for some reason, he puts up with it all, and smiles about it.

It takes him about another hour before he pulls into the airport car park. "Wow," he thinks as he picks up a ticket to park. "It never used to be this expensive. Seven dollars for half-an-hour." And he suddenly recalls the days when he could buy three cheeseburgers for under a dollar.

"What's wrong, Grandpa?" he hears from behind him. He looks in his rear-view mirror to see the two sleepy eyes of his grandson opening and looking at him.

"Nothing much," he replies and drives on.

"We're still a bit early, little bear," he says to the young boy sitting on the back seat. "Did you have a nice rest?"

He stops the car and immediately the young boy yawns out loud without a second thought. Ben, the grandfather of little Thomas James, watches as the *little bear* crawls out of the pickup truck as if he were awakening from a long winter slumber. Another yawn, followed by an unavoidably long stretch is followed only by the gentle laughter of a proud grandfather.

"We're a bit early, even though we sat in all that traffic," he says to young Thomas, putting his hand over the tiny shoulder over the boy.

"Traffic?" questions the child, earnestly.

Ben shakes his head, and the two walk toward the elevators. "Level 3, Row F," he quietly tells himself. It has all changed since the first time he came to this airport. Parking was free then, and there were no letters or numbers everywhere dictating to you which way to go in five different languages. Now there's security at every door, and barriers on every turn. "Still, though, it is a changing world," he tells himself confidently, trying to justify his own rationality for the surroundings. Inside it bothers him. The world he once knew has changed, and he can't tell if it's for the better or worse. What frightens him most is when he looks into the big brown eyes of his grandson and thinks about what the world holds for him.

The two of them walk hand in hand into the elevator. Thomas looks up at his grandfather, who holds up three fingers. The young boy with the fawn coloured hair runs over and pushes the appropriate button, then takes his grandfather's hand once more. His hand seems so tiny still, even though he's just turned eight years of age not two months ago. It seems not so long ago though, that he could pick the boy up with just one hand without trying. Then again, it wasn't that long ago he could do the same thing with his own son.

No, it wasn't that long ago at all, he thinks to himself. He remembers quite clearly standing there with his son sitting on his shoulders, as they walked down the waterfront and watched the Christmas lights dance across the bay. The air was as crisp as if you were standing on top of Mount Baker, herself. And the music in the air filled his heart with something that could only be described as unforgettable. He remembers a man playing a saxophone on the street corner, with three women and two men singing a Christmas ballad. Someone was barbequing hotdogs on a boat, just anchored off shore. Even the fresh taste of pumpkin pie on his lips, just snuck out of the kitchen while his wife wasn't looking; he can still taste it even now. It didn't really matter too much though, because she always made two just for the occasion. He remembers looking into his son's eyes on the day of the Christmas parade, even though it was freezing outside, and seeing the look of innocence that can never be replaced once it is taken away. It is the very same look that his grandson has every time he looks into his eyes around this time of year.

The two finally settle near the baggage claim. It's usually here that they are met by Pat whenever he returns from one of his business trips. This one was longer than the usual, but nothing uncommon. Luckily Pat doesn't go away too often, his father thinks to himself. His grandson needs his father, just like he needs his grandson.

"Hey, you two!" they both hear from the escalator off to their side.

"DADDY!" Thomas exclaims in his usual manner. He tries to run, but is held back by the enormous hands of his grandfather, at least until his father reaches the top of the escalator. After that, nothing can hold him back.

The two meet and collide with an enormous clash of arms, in one frantic overdue hug that has been building up for three weeks.

"Gosh you're getting heavy," Pat tells his son happily, putting both his laptop and his son down in the process. Then, "Hi pop. How was everything?"

"Okay, kid. Traffic like usual," Ben replies in the usual manner. "Little bear had a nice snooze on the way down, though. I'm not even sure if he got to see the stadium. How bout' you? Was the flight okay?"

"You know, I don't even remember much of today, let alone the flight. Funny, huh?"

The three of them carry on and fetch the two bags of luggage after a brief wait. It's the part his son likes best, as he always seems to get presents for some reason. This time, though, the young boy's father tells him that he'll have to wait a couple of weeks until Christmas. With a deep sigh, and feign of sadness, Thomas puts on his mighty arms and tries and lift one of the bags with little success. He then feels his father's hand on his head, brushing his hair in every direction. "Sometimes it's not how strong you are, but how you look at things," his father tells him, pulling out the lever from the side. He then gives the handle to his son, who pulls the bag along as if it were as light as a wagon filled with candy.

As they find the elevator, there is a parking machine next to it. Ben scrounges around to find the ticket and hands it to the very eager hands of Thomas. He has to be lifted, but is done so without hesitation. Ben merely wraps his arm around the boy's waste and lifts him up in one fell swoop. It takes a bit of adjusting but he manages to get the height just right and furthermore, the ticket in the machine.

"Can't believe these prices," Ben says putting his money in the machine.

"I know," Pat says frankly. "You can remember when they were free, and hamburgers grew on trees. You were even there when the glaciers started to melt, weren't you?"

A stern look from the oldest of the three causes the two others to laugh. "Laugh now, but wait until they start charging you for that privilege too." He then gets a glimmer in his eye and raises his head toward Pat. "Did you know they tore down the Cows?"

"Cows?" Pat replies. "You mean that old hamburger joint at the top of town?"

"My favourite place in the world," Ben says with vigour. "They're turning it into some bank or something. I guess the old man died off, and the kids don't want anything to do with it."

"Well it's a different world, dad."

"Yeah, I suppose so. But I've noticed that we've sure been saying that a lot recently," he replies pulling the last of the luggage on to the elevator.

It doesn't take long until all three are loaded up in Ben's pickup. Even that is a subject of debate for Ben. He had his old pickup since the latter days of his Navy years. But after constant bickering from his son, and the fact that it took a screwdriver to open the tailgate, he finally relented a couple years ago. It was more about young Thomas than anything else. With everything that went on back then, there was just no room for him to fit in the old pickup. So, one Christmas morning he woke up and walked outside and his old pickup was gone. And in its place, was a new truck; this time with a king cab. Still only a pickup, but a decent sized one, with better safety features he tells everybody. "A changing world indeed," he whispers to himself as he starts the vehicle.

"You hungry?" Ben questions everyone as they pull out onto I-5 north. "Thought we might stop and have a bite to eat, or something."

"Sounds good," Pat replies.

"Can we have pancakes?" enters Thomas.

The sun is setting over the backdrop of the Puget Sound. As they enter Seattle, the skyline is filled with shadows that dance across the magnificent towers of Seattle's city centre. Even as they pass the Space Needle, looking down across the bay, the sunburn light begins to flow across the waters into the horizon breaking through the fiery clouds who try as the will to hold the light back. It's a beautiful sight to behold, Pat thinks to himself.

"Look at that! Is that a pancake place, Grandpa?" Pat then hears, laughing to himself quietly as he shakes his head. One day he'll see what he sees. "No, Thomas," he replies in his father's stead. "That is a coffee factory, not a pancake restaurant."

"Well it smells like pancakes."

"What pancakes smell like coffee?" the grandfather asks.

"The way you cook them, dad. It's no wonder he gets confused."

"Hey!" Ben exclaims. "You'll be happy to know that I didn't burn his cereal this morning."

"There's a feat."

"I didn't have cereal this morning, Grandpa. I had leftover pizza, and orange juice." Ben coughs softly, lifting his hand to cover his mouth. Pat merely rolls his eyes and shakes his head.

"No wonder you want breakfast this late."

"Yeah, I suppose we'd best find this starving boy a pancake restaurant *internationale*," Ben says happily. "There's one of those all-day places up ahead. We'll pull in there and grab breakfast and some coffee. Traffic *will've* cleared up by then, I hope."

A calm silence seems to fill the car, for a moment in any case. As young inquisitive minds are, they can most certainly never truly stop, as so much needs to be done, learned, and asked. In this case, most of the remaining time between Seattle and finding a nice pancake restaurant is filled with questions about flying and why does it seem to take so long.

After a short while, they pull into a small little place just outside of the small town of Arlington, just beyond the Marysville turn off. What was earlier a torrent of rain and cloud, has now cleared to reveal a cold crisp night. The luminescence of the moon converging with the winter skyline of the Cascades lit the backdrop of the restaurant and the surround buildings.

"We'll have to be careful going back," Ben tells the others. "That rain earlier is going to make those roads slicker than a greasy pig in a pole dancing contest."

"Dad," Pat replies.

"Sorry, I meant slicker than wet ice."

With that the three go in, followed only by the soft yawn of a tender child as he walks backwards through the doors. "I smell pancakes," Thomas whispers, trying to keep his eyes open. He turns around when forced by the two large hands on his shoulders and faces the usual greeting of a young waitress standing behind the cashiers table.

"How adorable," she states caringly, in a mothering sort of way. "How old are you?"

"Pancakes please," he replies, not awake enough to hear what the question was, but opening his eyes once more after the following laughter and a slight tap on the back of his head.

"He's eight," replies Pat. "And I think he wants pancakes, but I wouldn't swear to it."

"Boys and their pancakes," she replies, picking up three menus and a writing pad from her side. "Follow me then."

Pat looks over and nudges his father, who is smiling quite contently as he watches the young waitress walk toward the window in front of him. It's her low-cut skirt that catches both the men's eyes, but more so Ben's. And when his son shakes his head in disrepute, Ben merely shrugs and raises his eyebrows a couple of times.

Christmas lights dance about the restaurant windows, and silver tinsel dangles from the ceiling. Thomas is the first to notice the Christmas tree near the corner with all the presents underneath. Also, there is a sock dangling from the back of the register where the lady returns to. She gathers a few things together and returns quickly with a pot of coffee, as well as a piece of paper for young Thomas and a cup full of crayons and markers.

"This is for the cute young man," she says, placing the sheet of paper in front of him, which is promptly followed by a 'Thank you.' Even Pat is impressed at how quickly his son replies. Then, "Make sure you make your list out before you go, so Santa can get you everything you want."

Pat looks over his son's shoulder to see the drawing on the paper, which has a white picture of Santa Claus in the corner, holding a long piece of paper which states, *My Christmas List*. The way his son writes, he knows that he won't be able to get but maybe five items on the list, but it's enough to keep him amused in any case. At least while the older James' order their meals, as well as a glass of milk with the pancakes for Thomas.

Thomas ponders to himself about many things, during the course of the traditional first cup of coffee that his father and grandfather have together. He has become accustomed to their infinite conversations about meaningless things, such as rising costs of houses and how much a cup of coffee costs. At eight, he is a bit too old to be colouring a picture of Santa Claus, but he does it because he enjoys drawing in some fashion or another. His teacher, Ms. Baker; she adores his drawings. And he would draw her anything she asked him too, because of how nice she is all the time. But for the time being, he is quite content at this picture of Santa, and the small Christmas tree in the corner. The green marker is dry, and the only other thing green seems to be melted at the bottom of the cup. Somehow, he makes do, though, because it doesn't really matter too much what colour the tree is, as long as he's neat. His father always tells him how sharp his colouring is, and his grandfather always pats him on the head and smiles. What else is there, really? "Well, I've never heard of a blue Christmas tree, but if someone can have a blue Christmas, then there has to be a blue Christmas tree for them," he says to himself, listening to the song being played in the background.

"Dad," Thomas begins, another thought wandering into his head as the song begins to change. It takes a minute for the two men to stop their conversation, but he is patient and waits. His father hates it if he interrupts constantly. Sometimes, it seems to be the only way to get them to stop talking long enough to hear him. But occasionally they actually listen, and there is a slight pause as an acknowledgement and understanding that he is going to eventually get to say what he's thinking, if he can manage to keep it in his head long enough.

"Yes, Thomas?" Pat responds, finishing the last sip of his coffee. No sooner does he put it down, then Darleen comes over with the pot again and fills it. He smiles and says thank you accordingly.

"Umm," Thomas thinks aloud, trying desperately to think what he wanted to say while with another hand still colouring the last bit of red in on Santa's cap. It is here that he hears the chorus of the song again and it comes to him. "Oh! I remember," he speaks quickly, seeing that the other two are turning to face one another again.

"Right then, little bear," Pat states firmly, turning and giving his full attention to his son. He smiles as he sees the look of concentration on his young son's eyes.

"Do they have Christmas in Heaven?" he queries earnestly.

Pat tries with great difficulty to not show his consternation and astonishment at his son's question. He knows instantly what will come next, but he knows that he must answer wholeheartedly.

"Of course, they do," he replies softly, but with confidence. "Why wouldn't they?"

"I don't know," Thomas replies, unsure at what is causing his father to react strangely. He notices instantly that there is a strange look within both his grandfather and father's face, but it isn't clear enough for him to know if they're angry or not. He treads lightly and says, "I just wanted to know if Mom and Grandma will have a Christmas tree like ours?"

Silence follows, and Thomas is suddenly frightened by the lost stares that the two men across from him have. But his Grandfather, as quickly as a bolt of lightning strikes, smiles grandly and laughs as he puts his hand on Thomas's cheek. A wave of softness and comfort overtakes him once more.

"Of course, they do, little bear. Theirs will be bigger and better than ours," Ben assertively states loudly and with precision.

"I should have asked her when I saw her the other day," Thomas replies, tilting his head and looking at the Christmas tree. There is a bulb on one of the branches that seems to be glowing a brighter colour than all the rest, and his eye draws itself to it.

"Asked who?" Ben returns, his voice retaining its vigour.

"Mom," he states without hesitation. Then, "I saw her in my doorway the other night, while I was saying my prayers before bed. She was smiling and said she loved me very much."

Silence enters the James' table once again, but Thomas is still staring at the bright blue light dancing on the presents pleasantly, when they are all interrupted by the arrival of their food. Thomas is the only one that speaks, though, again saying thank you to the lady as pleasantly as he knows. Then, as he picks up the pot of warm Maple Syrup, "She said to tell you not to be lonely, dad. What does that mean?"

"Lonely means that someone is by them self," his father says, his tone going soft and insipid.

"Come on, now," Ben says loudly, patting his son on his shoulder, and rubbing his grandson's head. "Let's all eat up before our food gets cold."

No sooner had Ben had spoken, then Thomas had already started cutting his pancakes carefully around the edge. He always enjoys cutting around the outside, and eating the middle first. It was something his Grandmother showed him when he was what he considered to be a baby, but in reality, he was more or less three years of age. It was the last year he would have his grandmother around. He doesn't remember much, but he remembers the hospital ladies were nice, and that his grandfather said that she was going to a better place to be with his mother. His other grandmother he doesn't get to see much of, as she is very busy in New York taking pictures of famous people. But she always sends him the most interesting things from all over. Most of the time he doesn't really know what they are, but he still thinks they're interesting. Not as fun as a toy, though. But it's always nice to get a great big box in the mail, no matter what it has in it.

It is a slow careful ride home, after they all finish their meals and pay. Not much is said between them, and everyone seems to be mostly tired, except Ben. Thomas falls asleep almost instantly after getting into the pickup and finding himself a nice cosy pillow to lay his head on. He knows to bring something on long trips, otherwise his neck hurts when he wakes up afterwards. Even Pat closes his eyes after what Ben could see was his usual morbid thinking style had set in once again. It usually takes a few days, though, but with the circumstances, he wasn't surprised.

It isn't until later that night that Ben has time to speak to his son about what transpired at the restaurant. He himself has been thinking about what Thomas was speaking about, but keeps quiet until he can sift through it. It has been very hard for him these past few years without Beth, his wife. They would have been married for four and a half decades this year. And not a single day goes by that he doesn't talk or speak to her, think about her, or feel her next to him in some way shape or form. He still considers himself one of the luckiest people in the world to have been with her for so long, and to have three lovely children together. But Pat is something entirely different to himself. Ben was married at eighteen years old, in the times that people seemed to do that sort of thing without thinking. Pat married in his early twenties, and lost her in just two years. "It isn't fair on him," he thinks to himself most of the time when he sees his son hurting, as any father does when they see their children in pain.

just finishes wrapping Thomas in his blanket, covered with superheroes and villains battling each other, when he sees his father cross the living room to head outside. He gently leans over and kisses his son on the forehead, and whispers to him to sleep well and dream about everything good in the world. He knows Thomas will rest easy as long as he has his long-eared dog, and is wrapped up in his blanket enough to where even a worm cannot escape.

The Christmas lights that decorate the house flash against a crisp icy lawn of green. The bay, shimmering the light of the moon upon its waters, is calm enough to reflect the stars and the passing clouds. Even the gentle sound of the passing waves, calmly and patiently crossing upon the sands of the grey beach; they too reflect the silence within the wintry north-western air.

"The neighbours have their lights on still," Ben hears from behind him.

"So do we," he replies matter-of-factly.

"Sure is different than Carolina," Pat states softly, pulling up a seat next to his father. "And a lot colder."

"Yeah, they say the winds are changing from the west to the north. We may get some Alaskan weather coming our way soon." Ben stops looking at the moon and faces his son, who is caught in a trance with the ocean.

"I know what you're thinking, dad," Pat interrupts, sensing the frustration in his father. He has been at odds with himself since Thomas was born. His father and all of his friends have constantly tried to find him a perfect match, or at least a match of some sort or another since *that* day so many years ago. Inside though, he doesn't think about it so often anymore. If anything, it is almost as if it's a cut that has healed itself over.

"You know the problem with cuts, Pat?" Ben says, turning and facing the moon once more. "The deeper they are, the more of a scar they leave behind."

"Maybe dad," whispers Pat to the western wind.

"You have a very smart son, who loves and adores you with all his heart. And I think that you shouldn't dismiss him so easily."

"I don't think he's lying dad, but it was more than likely just a dream." After Pat finishes his words, he sees his father begin to shake his head in disapproval. He knows that his father believes in everything of that nature. He still talks to his mother at night, as Pat hears sometimes. "It's not that I don't believe in those things dad, but it's easier for me to think that he's probably just dreaming about something that he saw on television. You know that they are always showing these Christmas movies this time of year."

"Your son speaks from the heart, Pat. Maybe you ought to listen to him. Even if it was just a dream, I think he's trying to tell you that it's okay to go and find someone else."

"Life just isn't that easy, dad. You don't just wake up one morning and find the woman of your dreams. And believe it or not, if you do, you don't ever get to do it twice." Pat takes a deep breath, feeling the inside of him beginning to quell inside. He stands and begins to walk forward toward the beach. "I've been lucky enough to wake up once and find someone smiling back at me who wanted to be there with me for the rest of her life. It's not her fault that--"

With his words cut short, finding he cannot speak, he feels the supporting hand of his father on his shoulder. It is the same hand that has always been there for all of his life, through everything that has ever gone right or wrong.

"I know you can't or won't understand this son," Ben begins, "but sometimes all you have to do is believe in something enough and it'll happen. And I know you can't believe right now, but it doesn't matter because your son does. He believes enough for the both of you. And whatever you do, don't ever take that away from him."

Chapter 3

Higher Education

Thomas James is currently the youngest member and still holding within the James clan of men. At least that is what he is told by his grandfather whenever he does something too silly or child-like. After all, he is eight now, and he has standards to live up too. His friends wouldn't dare let him bring a lunchbox with a train on it to school anymore. The days of the cartoons that he watched not so long ago are gone as well, filled instead with television heroes and villains, and the odd occasional sports hero. But life is not as difficult as it can be. After all, he still has his Christmas wishes and dreams. He still believes in the wonderful world of magic and mystery, just like most of his friends. There is of course, the odd one that can't or won't believe in Christmas, but overall, it's still widely accepted as truth. He's hears often from the television and other places that as he gets older, becomes a grown-up, that Christmas will change, and Santa won't exist anymore. It worries him, not so often, but enough to where he thinks it deserves thought.

"What's this?" asks Pat as he feels the brush of his son's hand on his.

"It's my Christmas letter to Santa," Thomas says matter-of-factly. "There's only three weeks left, so I thought I'd better get it too him as soon as possible."

"I thought you and your dad wrote one together before Thanksgiving?" Ben announces, sitting down to the table with his coffee.

Pat takes the sealed envelope from his son, looking at the very tidy handwriting that is spread across the front. It amazes him at how quickly his son's handwriting improves. Just between his trip to Europe, and his return, Thomas's writing skills have improved almost double.

"Nice writing," Ben says, noting the red ink on the front, next to a hand-drawn picture of Santa Claus.

"It's not a list. It's a letter to Santa I wrote while you were away. I just figured he already knows what I want, so I didn't want to bother him with stuff like that," Thomas says happily, picking up a piece of toast and pulling his bowl of cereal close to him. "I just had a few questions, and I wanted to ask Santa before Christmas."

The two older men look at one another and then return their gaze on to the young boy who pours his milk into his cereal.

"Well you know you can always ask us," his father says in his normally fatherly way.

"Yeah, I know." Again, Thomas speaks with a care-free tone that causes even more curiosity in the air. Then, "Don't worry, dad. You wouldn't know the answer anyway."

"Oh?" his father queries. "Okay."

"You'll make sure that he gets it won't you, dad?"

"I promise it'll get into the right hands, little bear."

And with that, and a rather wry grin from Ben, Pat puts his son's letter into his inner pocket, as not to lose it. As he does so, he notices the jewellery box in his left pocket. Startled by the discovery, his mind begins to wander briefly, until his son taps his bowl with his spoon.

"Don't forget that we have our Christmas concert this Friday, dad." The words take a second to enter his thought pattern, and then he returns a nod to his son for acknowledgement.

"I won't forget, Thomas. My memory isn't that bad."

"My teacher said that her husband's memory is like a fossil," Thomas said quickly in return.

"Fossil?" queries Ben, finishing the last of his coffee.

"That doesn't sound right," Pat replies looking at Thomas who is happily eating his cereal. "Do you know what a fossil is?"

"Yeah," he says shoveling the last bit of his spoonful in his mouth. "It's like something that is dead, or really old."

"You mean extinct," replies his father.

"Yeah, the older it is, the more extinct it is."

The two men look at one another, and then shake their heads in unison.

"In any case, I won't forget about Friday," Pat says getting up from his seat.

"You won't miss it?" questions Thomas.

"No."

"Not even if there is a storm?" insists Thomas.

"No."

"What if there's a hurricane that sweeps the school up into outer space?" Thomas interrogates. Quickly, he picks up his toast and shovels it into his mouth as much as possible.

"We don't have hurricanes in Washington, Thomas. And stop eating like a horse."

"My friend David said that horses have really hard feet that make it hard to go on sidewalks, and that when they get older they go to a special place where they put glue on them, so they stick better, but they have to eat dog food to make it work."

Ben clicks his tongue on the roof of his mouth, and Pat grimaces with a tender smile for his son. "And with that, I think I will take you to school."

"Don't know why," Ben replies half-heartedly. Gathering the plates from the table, he shrugs towards his son, and laughs slightly as his grandson runs out the door toward the car in excitement.

"I'm probably going to head down to Seattle today, do you need anything?" Pat asks, half out the door already.

"Seattle?" Ben questions, a slight sound of concern but not enough to turn his head away from the washing.

"Yeah, long story. Don't ask," he replies quickly. "You want me to pick anything up for you?"

"Nope, I think I'm good." There is a slight pause as Pat turns and begins to close the door. "It doesn't have anything to do with that jewellery box in your pocket, does it?" Pat hesitates for but a second then closes the door behind him. His father smiles softly, as he continues washing the dishes.

Pat notices the thick frost covering the car, and his faithful son trying his hardest to reach up over the windows enough to scrape it off as best he can. His breath comes out almost as heavily as the morning fog that rolls off of the hills in Tuscany. Even his son's gloves tend to stick to the windows at times when he breathes too heavily on them.

The sun is crossing upwards over the tips of the Cascades behind the car, casting the long shadows seemingly endlessly outward. The skies are filling themselves once again with the painted clouds, which hover carelessly in the air waiting for the winter to decide on which type of rain it wishes to fall this day. This is the Pacific Northwest, after all.

Pat watches for a few moments longer, just enjoying the innocence of his son, as he struggles with gloves and the ice scraper. It only takes a few seconds before Thomas spots him and runs over for the keys. He likes the sound the car makes when the doors are unlocked, and the engine starts. It is a tradition, for at least the last year that he has had this car. Although, it is somewhat disappointing for Thomas that the car remembers exactly where he likes to sit, and how his seat needs to be adjusted just perfectly, so that he can see clearly over the dash. He especially likes how it keeps his legs warm as the seats heat themselves up, almost in time for the morning cartoons to start on the television.

It is a very silent trip to Saint Aldrend's School, as per normal since the invention of in-car entertainment. Though, there is a convenient switch that will disable the televisions should he desire, Pat revels in the silence for a bit. Thomas is a very talkative eight-year-old, and has a tremendous amount to say. And when he speaks, Pat listens to every word like a doting father should. When questions are asked, he always answers, as a father should. When difficult questions are asked, he always changes the subject, as most fathers should. When thoroughly perplexing in-depth and thought-provoking questions are asked, which are few and far between with children of eight years old, (and yet are seemingly always there lurking in the background) he uses the time honoured tradition of relying upon the one thing that has seen him through all the difficult times with Thomas thus far; the short, but very sweet and tender-hearted attention span that all eight-year-olds hold.

Thomas is quite surprised, as he usually is, at how quick it takes to get to school. He barely has enough time to finish watching the latest battle between good and evil before they are rounding the corner and his father taps him on the head. This time he was actually a little earlier than usual, interrupting the very last scene between the evil green guy, just about to conquer the planet. "Oh well," he thinks to himself, "I'm still here, so I guess he didn't do it." It's much more calming to think in simple terms like that. Less nightmares occur if he doesn't think that evil has conquered the world. It does make him wonder at times, why no matter how evil or bad someone is in the cartoons or the movies, that someone on the playground will want to willingly be that person.

"Okay, Thomas," his father repeats, pulling the headset from the ears of his son. With the usual moan of discontent over, he leans over and kisses his son on the forehead as he tries to jump out of the car as quickly and unseen as possible. "Grandpa will probably be picking you up today."

"Okay, see you later," Thomas replies waving as he runs off through the school grounds. There was a time not so long ago, where he would have to stand and watch his father leave. They didn't have a bus in the area, so he's always been driven to school, usually on his father's way to work. But now he is eight, he doesn't really have time to pay attention to what his dad's doing. After all, he is just going to drive off, and there are only so many minutes before the first bell rings and he has to go to class. Addy, (short for Andrew) his best friend, will be waiting and wondering why he isn't under Old Dawson, the big pine tree in the corner of the playground near the slides.

As usual, Pat watches Thomas adoringly run off with the enthusiasm that only an eight-year-old can have. He follows his son's course to the tree for a few moments, watching as the children gather around and begin to play. He sees Andrew, the son of Farrell Patricks a prominent journalist for the Seattle area. A nice enough guy, and his son and Thomas are the best of friends. Nevertheless, he's just one of those guys that you can't seem to put your finger on, but something's just not quite right. Too opinionated perhaps, about the military and government, and other issues; all these things just don't interest a guy who just wants to enjoy a nice cold drink and watch the ocean waves.

If it is one thing that Pat has always known about himself, it is that he is never going to be a general in the army, the president, or a political rights activist. He met one once, trying to convince him that his world was deteriorating around him because of the corruption in the government and the lies that he was told. A laugh escaped Pat when Ben said, "Well, that's all good and fine, except everyone lies on this world young lady. But I've come to know two kinds of people since I've been on this planet. Those who lie, and those who bull. People who lie have to know some sense of truth, otherwise they can't be lying. On the other hand, people who bull other people are usually just trying to cause commotion or get away with something that doesn't really mean anything anyway. So, which are you, a liar or a bull artist? After all, little missy, if the guy you're talking about is so bad that we should all be worried about it, just remember one thing. It's not *how* you lie, it's *who* you lie with that counts."

Pat hears the bell ring and the kids running for the doors. He smiles as he sees his son run in amongst all the other children, carefree and happy. They all have Christmas in their minds. Even the school windows and billboards are covered in Christmas tidings. Paper snowflakes dangle along the halls, filling the spaces where artworks of painted hands and faces usually hang. Even the office, seen from the front has a tree fully decorated, blue and green lights chasing one another to and fro. If nothing else, at least the children can still feel Christmas inside. If all the world changes around them, they will never forget Christmas, no matter how many people try and take it away from them. It is their hopes and dreams of an entire year rolled into a single moment that will either fill them with happiness, boredom, or sorrow.

With a sigh that even the children in Alaska might hear, he starts his engine again and begins the drive south. It is ten minutes before he comes to his usual corner Espresso station, the Bean Oyster Café. Cheryl has come to know him as a regular, over her past four years of working at the coffee hut. It has grown as well, spreading out from a single coffee stand, into a three window, full drive thru, on the go breakfast café, service with a smile espresso restaurant. But somehow Cheryl still stays the same. He keeps threatening to take her to dinner one day, and she keeps accepting, with the exception that her husband may have some objections. "Rightly so," he replies often, as he takes his double Mocha with a twist. He's not sure what the twist is, but she assured him four years ago that he wanted it, so he keeps getting it even though he hasn't a clue of what it contains.

It doesn't take but a few minutes until he's on the Interstate, merging surprisingly easy with the somewhat empty road. Rush hour seems to have come and gone, strangely leaving the roads fairly mobile. Although he isn't in Seattle, it is still an unusual sight to behold where there are little to no cars on the road. As it is though, the roads are fairly icy, even with the grit freshly laid. His father mentioned that the weather could change to a cold spell, although from looking at the sky, it will probably rain given enough time for the ice to melt.

His hands touch the soft leather of the steering wheel, his thoughts drifting just slightly to a time not so long ago, yet at the same time such an age ago. He looks next to him, seeing the empty seat and recalls a feeling inside him that he has not known for quite some time. With a deep breath he opens his mouth and whispers to himself, "I don't know what I'm doing." His eyes turn back to the road, carefully watching a cloud up ahead starting to fill the sky with a dark misty look.

Deep from the corner of his eye, he sees a figure in the seat next to him. It is a figure that once soothed his every thought and desire, and at the same time infuriated his every breath. She was the strength within the soul that held him together during the darkest of hours. Her words filled him with hope and laughter. Her touch healed even the deepest of wounds. As much as he wished that he could do without her, he knew that it was an impossibility to even conceive. She was his heart. But she is merely a thought; a whisper in the back of his mind that no matter how much he longs for, or desires its return, can never be joined with him again in this life.

It is here that a light burst comes through the clouds in a moment that seems to happen often, but is always a breath-taking view to behold. Like the hands of the heavens reaching down unto the earth, bringing with it warmth and a healing touch, these breaks of light fill the land with a much-needed look of life once again. They begin to wash away the icy fields of grey and shadowy green and fill them with a luminous sense of life once more.

A light comes down over the road, reflecting brightly on the wet cracked pavement, causing him to look away just briefly. Suddenly his eyes catch the jewellery box once again, having fallen out of his coat pocket onto the seat next to him. Thoughts once more enter his mind of the little girl that brought it to him. He remembers her eyes filling his soul with a curiosity and patience that he has never before felt. The touch of the child's hand upon his, was as if he were touching something ethereal; an unexplainable compelling force of the combination of both influence and serenity. He thinks little of heaven or hell, or of the inexplicable mysteries of the universe. He tries not to think of death, or life in general for that matter. He doesn't allow himself to fill the void of the day with the philosophies of the unknown. It is not down to him to decide the fates of the universe or its creator. He is more in tune with the smile of his son, and the warmth of his morning coffee. He wishes for nothing more than to make sure that his son is happy. He has friends to keep him focused, and to pace the days in the order of the seasons. As most men go, simplicity and the lack of complication in most manners of thought and progression keep him happy enough.

He pushes the thoughts from his head once more, as quickly as he can in order to focus on the road. He clicks the button behind the steering wheel in order to turn the radio on and flick through the stations. He finds the desired station of choice, and a smooth soft saxophone begins filling the car with a Christmas song that seem to soothe his nerves. A brief look down at the cup holder tells him that he needs another coffee, but it'll have to wait until he gets where he needs too.

He spends the next hour or so listening to various types of soft non-intrusive music, of which a few turn out pleasantly to be Christmas songs. Before he realizes, his destination appears on the car monitor in front of him, interrupting the pleasant tones of the morning woman and her daytime love songs. Pat suddenly looks around him for what seems to be the first time on this expedition, and sees the full scope of traffic upon him. A friendly man in an old 73' pickup looks at him and smiles before slowing down enough to let him in and exit. He suddenly thinks to himself how few and far between the actions of one man are becoming. In this though, he raises his hand to the man behind him in thanks.

Parking has always been the same in Seattle since the dawn of the modern city. It entails a series of long hills and roads, and endless patterns of repetitive driving met with only disappointment after disappointment. But occasionally, much like the gift of a scratch card that actually wins something more than the value of a value meal, you find that one space that makes life inexorably easier. Just outside the Space Needle there is a small parking lot that lies within a block of the Monorail. A wine merchant just finishes loading his van up and sees Pat looking for a spot. He waves him down and says the he is done for the day, then offers him his. It is nearly a miracle upon another miracle given to Pat. Or at least that's what he feels as he finishes parking.

As he steps out of his car, he looks around briefly in order to gather his bearings. There are a few people about, but mostly just businessmen walking here and there. He looks down before he shuts the door and gathers himself enough to pick up the jewellery box and put it into his side pocket once more. As he does so, he feels a burst of cold on his nose; a wintry raindrop falling from the sky. Then, within a few steps the heavens unleash their hold, filling the air around him with an almost overpowering rain, so cold that it is nearly ice. Suddenly everyone and everything is rushing about at an incredible pace. Even he begins to move slightly faster, moving a short distance to stand with a mass of others underneath a building's cover. Amidst all of the chaos, though, he manages to see a bewildering sight. Staring at him with the same eyes that he saw not but what seems just mere moments ago, are the two eyes of the child that bestowed upon him the jewellery box. She is dressed in a slightly different dress, this time blue and white, but other than that almost undistinguishable from one another.

The girl turns and begins to walk away toward the monorail, slowly at first, then a carefree sprint. He watches for a moment, unbelieving in the way the rain seems to not affect her in any way. He begins to walk out into the rain once again, crossing the street and nearly getting hit by a car in the process. His heart rate begins to race, but calms once again when he sees the child entering the building just beyond him. She is headed most definitely for the monorail. In an instant he forgets the fact that he was nearly killed, or that he is completely soaking wet.

It takes a few minutes, but he manages to board the monorail, after missing the previous one and the one before that, due simply to the weight of passengers passing this particular day. It's been years since he's been on the monorail, but he doesn't allow any sentiment to enter his mind. Somehow, all he can manage to do is think about finding this child.

Once the monorail stops and he enters the main mall where it exits, he notices the crowds of Christmas shoppers filling the shops. Frantically he looks about in a vain hope of seeing something of a resemblance, if nothing else to just ease his mind of the pressure that this figure he saw is in fact not the same child he met. He walks about slowly for a bit, somewhat lost at which direction to take. He tries finding anything or anyone at all that will ease his mind, but comes to realise that whoever the girl was he has missed her.

He begins to head down to the lower floors, only to see a glimpse of the child once again, just leaving the northern exit. He is still two floors behind her, but he knows that the exit leads down to Westlake Avenue. The crowds are too busy to push people aside, or to try and rush in any manner. All in all, he begins to reside himself to being unable to do anything until he gets away from the shops.

As he finally exits the shop he looks around him and sees the girl standing clearly outside a shop looking into a window. He heads in her direction, then stops himself quickly, suddenly realising that she is alone. He looks about in every direction and begins to wait to see who else she is with. Perhaps he can talk to her mother or father and explain that this girl gave him this jewellery box in error. But time passes, and she remains alone, staring into the window before her. Carefully, and with diligence, he approaches her in the most unobtrusive way he knows.

"Hello," he begins, finally reaching her.

"Hello Patrick," the child replies, still looking at the window in front of her.

"How do you know my name?" he questions, looking about, still in hopes of finding some signs of adults about.

"I knew you would come," she speaks pleasantly. "Not many people would have, but I knew you would, if I asked you too."

"Come?" he responds, now focusing on the girl.

"Patrick," she states, turning and facing him. She begins to smile softly, her eyes glittering as the sun begins to break through the clouds. "Make me a promise."

"I'm confused," he returns softly. "Where are your parents?"

"Make me a promise and I will answer every question you ask as best I can," she replies. She looks deeply into his eyes. He can feel her entering his thoughts, he thinks. If he lied, she would know it. He isn't sure how he knows this, but he does.

"Alright," he resides, nodding his head slowly. "What do you want me to promise?"

"There is a letter in your pocket that is not meant for you, but you want to read it. I want you to promise me that you will not open that letter and read it until I say it is alright."

His thoughts begin to cloud once more, the clarity vanishing with every second. He manages to look into his pocket and he sees the letter that his son wrote to Santa Claus. He then looks back at the young girl and takes a small breath. He tries to talk, but somehow cannot manage the words. It takes a few moments for him to recover, but before he can speak she takes his hand once more.

"Promise me, Patrick," she states firmly.

"Okay," he whispers in return, his thoughts clearing instantly. "I promise."

"Good. Now we don't have much time, so I want to explain a few things to you while I can."

"Alright," he responds, looking at his hand as she releases it.

"The box I gave you belongs to somebody. You will have to give it back to its rightful owner when the time is right."

"Okay," he speaks, his eyes slightly closing in confusion again. "To whom does it belong?"

"I trust you'll know." A whimsical smile breaks across her face at her words.

"That's sounds as clear as mud," he returns, his strength beginning to return. He hears a gently laugh from the child in front of him. "And where will I find this person?"

And with his question, he sees her small hand point to the store across the road from both of them. There before him is a tiny fine jewellery store, with all black doors and gold trim. In the middle of the window is a light frosting-like colour that forms a border for the small delicate goods that are on display. On the sign above the store is a wonderful snowflake filled painting with the words, *Snow In Seattle*. He looks back and sees the girl smiling at him again.

"I know you have a lot of questions, but you don't have the time right now to ask them. Don't worry. We'll talk again when the time is right."

He watches as the girl turns and waves goodbye at him. She turns without another word spoken and begins to walk away. He tries to speak, but finds himself unable, still in a state of mild confusion. All he can do is watch and behold the Christmas crowds flow to and fro like waves upon waves in a malicious storm, battering against one another in a puzzling synchronicity. Without hesitation in her step, she walks into them, vanishing instantly as if by a long-lost magic seen only upon a movie screen in a fantasy from decades ago.

It takes a few moments, of which he suddenly realises that he is staring at a mass of ant-like people in a place not truly befitting of standing. He turns finally, after reminding himself that he needs air in his lungs to survive, and faces the store across the street. He opens his sports jacket and looks at his pocket and sees a letter, just as he was told. His finger touches the smooth fibres on the envelope, and remembers the moment he promises his son that he would make sure that it would be delivered into the right hands.

'Why isn't he allowed to read it?' he thinks to himself quite smugly. The temptation comes and goes, literally with the wind, as a cold biting wind comes across his face and fingers. It's not strong, but enough to cause him to close his jacket up once again. His eyes turn once more to the store, and he finds himself pulling upon the jewellery box with the tips of his fingers. He takes a deep breath and then steps forward toward the store. As he moves forward he pulls the box out of his pocket and holds it firmly in his hand, his grip tightening more and more as he comes closer to the door. He can't understand why he's so nervous. He can even feel his hands beginning to shake.

Every thought that comes through his mind is pushed away as quickly as it begins. He forces himself as best he can to not question the actions or thoughts of what transpired moments earlier. Somewhere deep inside him he knows the insanity of it all, but for his own sake he chooses to ignore everything. Another step and the closer he comes to the reality of this entire ludicrous trial.

As he comes before the black glass door with the golden trim, he sees his reflection in the large pane before him. Suddenly the man before him isn't the man he remembers himself being. He can't quite understand it all, but something is different; an unrecognisable but significant change in his being has been undertaken without him knowing. It is the strangest of feelings, not knowing why the man in the mirror isn't the same anymore. At what stage did he change? When along the many days of the past did he become the man that stares at him now? The most worrying question of all and the one which haunts him the most is the one that he has never asked himself.

"Who am I?"

His hand slightly trembles as he reaches for the handle, carefully and with great caution. Pushing aside all his thoughts, worries, and the last tiny piece of sanity left within his mind, he lays his hand upon the handle of the door and pushes forward. And yet, as he pushes the door forward, it seems to be pulled away from him, enough so that his hand falls away from the grip he once held. His weight shifts too fast forward, enough so that in order to stabilise himself he steps back to regain control, only to find a small patch of wet icy pavement underneath him.

"Oh!" he hears as he stumbles about. He recovers quickly, with the help of a hand who quickly grabs his arm in order to stop him from falling. "Are you okay?"

Pat looks up after bringing himself back together in a somewhat normal stature. As he looks up he sees a long balmacaan style twill coat, black and full length.

The hand that was on his arm, covered in a soft gentle brown suede glove, comes up and covers his other hand.

"I'm so, so sorry," he hears. It's a soft voice, but soothes his ears. He doesn't have time to react to it, or think about it. "I didn't see you there. I was talking to my friends in the store and— "

"It's okay," he manages to say. His eyes finally come into focus. It can't have been but a brief moment in time, perhaps a second at most. Suddenly, as if the universe stops in order for him to understand, he sees her. At first, he sees the worry in her face, but then he begins to understand; realise. He watches her lips move softly, slowly, with such gentle caring that he has no choice but to smile. As he does so, she follows suit. It's only then, as the world seems right, and the fear and strangeness begin to vanish that he looks into her eyes. They are lightly azure coloured, almost grey, with a beautiful clear fresh white that reminds him of the snow filled clouds passing over head. There is an unmistakable amount of life flowing through them. It is almost of if he were staring at his own son's eyes, save the colour.

"It's more slippery out here than I thought," she says to him, looking at him in order to make sure that he's alright.

"Yes," he replies, suddenly realising that he is standing in her way. "I'll have to be more careful which doors I go into."

His response is greeted with a gentle earnest laugh, to which he raises his hand and returns a small laugh to its origin. In doing so, he notices her eyes are drawn to the jewellery box in his possession.

"Oh!" she begins, completely startled by the box. "Are you bringing something to David?"

"Oh," he exclaims, "um, no. At least I don't think so." He raises his hand slightly, and looks at the jewellery box one last time. Then, with a confidence that he has never showed before, he takes her hand of which she is somewhat perplexed at first, but doesn't draw away, and releases his grip upon the box for the last time.

"I'm not sure, but something tells me that this belongs," he pauses looking up from the box and into her eyes once more, "to you."

It seems as if it is an eternity that passes before she begins to examine the ribbon, then the note, pulling them apart and unfolding the piece of paper. He can't understand why, but his heart is strangely calm. He watches intently as she reads the contents of the letter, then folds it once and opens the jewellery box. He can hear her breathing stop instantly, and he watches as her eyes begin to change. She looks up and faces him completely. Without warning, she jumps completely at him and kisses him fully and completely with nothing but pure joy and love in her. It takes him by surprise and nearly causes him to fall backwards.

"Thank you," she repeats over and over again, kissing him repeatedly as she does so. "You don't know what this means to me."

Suddenly, she turns and runs into the store, then returns as quickly as she goes. "Don't go anywhere," she commands, wiping her eyes and somewhat giggling in the process.

As hard as he tries he cannot get the feeling of her lips against his off of his mind. His heart is racing faster than he has felt in a terribly long time. It feels almost like a horrible pain filling him, but he knows it isn't. Everything inside him is unsure and lost, completely and utterly. His body is still recovering from the impact of this wonderful feeling that has overcome him. His legs are still weary and heavy, unable to move even if he wished them too. His breath is shallow and slow, overcome by the sound of his heart screaming inside him. Then, as quickly as it all started, it comes to a grinding halt.

That inexplicable moment when the universe and time stop just for that brief instance in order for him to see just her and nothing else; it comes just as she appears in the doorway. She engulfs his vision, from the long waves in her hair stretching down over the mid of her back, to the way she moves with such a fluidity as she turns and closes the door. Her eyes, still full of the life that he saw before, he can now clearly see how they fill her face. They are large and child-like, with an almost angelic innocence about them. Her nose is lovely, he thinks, with a small round bend at the end. Her lips, the top somewhat thinner than the bottom one, fill her perfectly shaped mouth just right. Even her cheek bones seem to be just flawlessly placed upon her.

"Come with me," she says, taking his hand quickly and pulling him in the opposite direction. He doesn't have time to react to her gesture, but simply follow or fall.

"Where are we going?" he manages to ask her, slightly recovering and beginning to walk in his own stride next to her. As he joins her side, she takes his arm and wraps hers around it firmly.

"Sorry, I'm not quite thinking like myself," she replies slowing her pace somewhat. "I'm just dying for a cup of tea, and I get a bit jittery without one. There's a quaint coffee shop around the corner and they serve actual tea. And not the horrible American stuff either. Proper tea."

She leads him quickly around the corner to a shop called the T-breeze, a small coffee house with a few outside seats. Without hesitation, she walks in with him through the double doors and takes him straight up to the counter, straight in front of the long queue of people. One of the men on the espresso machines sees her, and waves to her, calming the discomfort of the customers around her. He comes over and smiles, saying something, but the background music and noise of people overtake everything else.

"Hi Kate," the man says louder, this time making himself heard. "I've got your tea ready for you over here." Without another word said he brings over a cup and hands it to the woman on Pat's arm.

"Thank you, Pete-iss" she replies, leaning over and giving him a kiss on the cheek. The man smiles and looks over at Pat.

"Can I get you anything?" he asks Pat quite loudly, still smiling.

"I'm sorry!" she exclaims in return, turning and looking at Pat with a sorrowful smile. "Pete makes the best coffee in Seattle. Ask him for anything, and he'll make it happen."

"That's me," he replies with a smile and two hands pointed outward. "Anything you want."

"Uh," Pat expresses, a bit overwhelmed. "A mocha?"

"Anything for a friend of Kate's. I'll bring it over to you," he replies turning quickly and returning to the machine from which he came.

Pat follows his companion to an empty table in the corner, facing outward toward Pike St. As she sits down, she lets his arm go and she grasps her cup with both hands bringing it to her nose and allowing its aroma to fill her senses. He watches as she closes her eyes and seemingly disappears into a trance, followed only by small tiny breaths as she brings the plastic lid to her mouth.

"Mmmm," she moans, almost erotically. She opens her eyes and suddenly sees him looking at her, to which she smiles. "Sorry, I sometimes lose myself when I get my tea. I just don't understand why coffee is such a big thing here. Perhaps you can explain it me?"

It comes to him suddenly, as clear as the windows he sits next to. The accent is faint, but it still remains. "You're British," he exclaims, leaning forward.

"Not really," she replies. "I was born in Cody, Wyoming but lived in Montana for my first few years. My mother was English. She was born in London, raised in Kent. My father an intrepid stubborn cowboy. My mother however, wanted to move back home after I was born. It took a few years of convincing, but my father finally relented. We moved to a beautiful little place in the New Forest in Hampshire."

"I've been there a few times," he enters, hanging off of every word that she speaks. "But your accent is fairly soft. Have you been back here long?"

"My mother passed away when I was sixteen, and my father brought me back with him here to Seattle. But I went back to stay with my grandmother in Cambridge, while I attended *Uni* there. After that I travelled Australia and a few other places for a while, then went and worked in New York for a bit, until my father asked me to come back here. I've been here for the last four years."

"Wow," he replies, once again overwhelmed with an incredible amount of information from a woman he doesn't even know the name of. As he thinks of asking her this, Pete taps him on the shoulder and hands him a large cup of coffee with a large straw.

"One tall mocha, with whip cream and chocolate dusting for flavour." Pete winks with his right eye as Pat takes the cup from him.

"Thank you, Pete, babe," he hears from the prodigious woman in front of him.

"Anything at all. You know that," he replies turning and walking off.

"Well?" she questions then, sipping from her tea and tilting her head slightly.

His blinks his eyes slowly in all the confusion as he tastes the coffee, to which he nods. "Very nice," he replies.

"No," she states firmly. "Not that. Are you going to tell me your name, or not?"

"Oh!" he exclaims, putting his coffee down quickly and reaching forward with his hand. "I'm Patrick."

She reaches forward and takes his hand as if to shake it, but quickly pulls him forward enough to where she can kiss him. "Well Patrick, that is for bringing me my grandmother's heirloom."

"Oh," he exclaims again, leaning back and sitting himself down once again. He blinks twice and looks a bit stunned by it all, where he receives a tender laugh in return.

"You're incredibly sweet, you know," she states firmly, taking another sip from her tea.

"Thank you," he returns, his brow coming together somewhat. "I think."

"It's not an insult. Not many people would bring back something worth as much as that if they had found it. It's Russian you know."

"Really?" he says, again trying not to interrupt her.

"17th century," she begins, "given to my great great ancestor by the Empress of Russia for saving her life in a great fire that spread through the city."

"Incredible."

She pauses herself and looks at him for the first time, studying him and his posture. Her eyes follow him carefully over his facial expressions down to the way he seats himself. She covers herself and her actions slightly by sipping at her tea, but watches to see what he does and how he acts. She follows his hand as he lifts his cup of coffee to his lips, and the way he winces, but tries not to show it as he forces himself to drink the coffee even though it is obviously scolding his tongue. It makes her smile suddenly, just to see this strange man before her acting in way that reminds her of a teenage-like boyfriend.

"Are you going to ask me my name?" she queries, still smiling at him.

"Um," he stumbles, putting the coffee down before he spills it over himself. "Alright."

She shakes her head and laughs. "It's Katherine, but everyone calls me Kate. Katherine Elizabeth Ashton."

Pat looks at her, a smile filling her face as she amuses herself by watching his antics. He's aware that he must look an idiot sitting in front of one of the most beautiful women he has ever seen, and he's acting like a thirteen-year-old.

"May I ask you a question?" she enquires, reaching over and mouthing to him that it's okay. "My friend is having a party in his house on Lake Washington, on Saturday. Will you come?"

"Me?" he questions in return.

"Yes, you." She puts her finger on his nose. "Please. I'd really appreciate it if you would."

"But you don't know me," he replies, suddenly realising he said the words out loud.

"Sure, I do," she states confidently. "You're Patrick. You're an honest, kind-hearted man who believes in doing the right thing when he can. And I would really like to get to know you better. So if you can— "

"Alright," he interrupts, somewhat eagerly.

"Good," she laughs finishing the last of her tea off. Then, "I know, come with me to lunch. I know it's kind of early, but I know a place by the waterfront which has the best pasta you can get, and the sweetest pink door."

"Okay," he replies without hesitation, still following her words.

"Brill," she says, "we can walk there from here."

Kate is completely captivated by the man in front of her. She's never really met anyone or anything like him, except maybe some of the younger boys from her youth. She knows what's she doing, but cannot understand for the life of her why. He completely captivates her, on every level of her thousand levels, (as her friends say to her.)

"Come on then," she says, standing and taking his hand. "Jean-Pierre will have a seat ready for us next to the window."

"Okay then."

He is beginning to smile, his confidence recovering slightly. It's all a bit confusing to him, but exciting and fun in the same right. Kate's confidence exudes from her, completely brash, and full of life. She is everything that he has kept out of his life since before he wishes to remember, and had hoped to keep it that way.

"You're quite right, you know," she utters quietly after a moment. Suddenly, she then looks to the sky and closes her eyes, taking a deep full breath through her nose. She takes his hand and pulls him quickly, crossing the street and heading down the road. The two head past another café and then another, until suddenly she stops and pulls him under the cover of an entrance way to a building.

"What's wrong?" he begins, but is only met with her shaking her head slowly. She raises a single finger and puts it on his lips, then motions to the street with her head. The sound of the people walking along the sidewalk is all he can hear at first, but then the first drops of rain begin to fall. At first it is soft, blending gently with the sudden surprise that the people express as it begins. After the brief warning from the heavens, suddenly the rain begins to pour to its full extent, drowning not only the coats and jackets of the people underneath it, but also the sounds of the world around. It leaves only a simple roar, reminding the world of its power and majesty.

Carefully, Kate brings her hand down to his and leans forward bringing their hands out to meet the rain. The rains fall upon her hand with such force that even he can feel it through her. Slowly she turns their hands over, the water now falling upon his palm and gathering before making its way down through his fingers unto hers and then to the ground. The cold of the rain suddenly makes him aware of the warmth that her palm is generating against the back of his hand. It's a moment that causes him discomfort, but incredible excitement inside. Kate can feel his heartbeat moving faster, and as she leans closer to him, she can hear his breath begin to slow. It's enough to cause her to smile as she watches his eyes gaze at their hands with such awe and wonder.

"Remember to breathe," she whispers in his ear, feeling the rain start to dissipate. He looks at her slowly, her lips just inches away from his. He doesn't know this woman, and yet she already seems as if she is part of something deep inside him. He wants so dearly to kiss her, to have the ability to pull her closer and feel her heartbeat. But he doesn't.

Kate releases her hold on Pat and steps backward. He watches as she begins to walk into the middle of the road, holding her hands as wide as her arms will take them as she feels the last bit of the rain before it disappears. She turns and faces him, motioning for him to follow with her head.

"So," she begins, taking his hand once more. "As I was saying earlier, you were quite right, you know."

"About?" Their pace is much slower now, a relaxing tension somehow lifted in a few moments of rainfall. It is as if they had been together for decades.

"I don't really know you," she tells him, playfully brushing aside the hair from her face. She releases his hand and places both of hers behind her, taking a few steps in front of him and turning to walk backwards. "But I suspect what you will tell me will be something like this."

Kate stops, putting her hands on both his cheeks, moving his head from side to side. She looks at his eyes, but not with great emotion or wonder, but more of discovery. Then, she steps back once more, turns quickly and begins her descent down the hill toward the waterside. He has no choice but to follow. She skips playfully, completely carefree and uncaring of the conditions of the road. In fact, the sunlight has now completely broken free of its grasp upon the tops of the clouds and has now unleashed itself once again upon Seattle. The warmth changes instantly, although the cold wind reminds everyone at what time of year it truly is.

She doesn't speak to him until they reach the restaurant, but instead hums pleasant Christmas songs that she hears in the background. Once they reach Pasta and Pâté she stops humming and looks at the sky again. She turns to him and takes his hand once more, the two continuing into the restaurant together.

Just as with the coffee house, a man comes over and instantly greets Kate, kissing her on both cheeks, then insists on showing her and Pat to the best table in the house. He mentions something about a Michael and how ridiculous he is, and then takes a look at Patrick and kisses him on both cheeks. He laughs at the stunned look on Pat's face, not because of the kiss, but because of the ridiculous smile of the man.

"J'aime celui-ci, Kat'rine," he states, taking both their jackets and motioning for the waiter to bring over a bottle of wine.

"I do as well, Jean-Pierre," she replies to the dark-haired man.

"I will bring you both the *cours cinq*," he informs them, taking the bottle from the youthful waiter and quickly handing it back to him, slapping his shoulder and whispering in his ear. Only after the young man returns with a new bottle, opens it and pours a small taster just for Jean-Pierre, does he seem satisfied enough to pour each of the two guests a glass. He places the bottle on the table and kisses Kate on the cheek before disappearing without another word spoken.

"You look a bit overwhelmed, Patrick," Kate mentions softly, lifting the glass of wine to her nose and smelling its deep rich scent.

"Just trying to make heads or tails of what just transpired," he replies, taking a sip of the water next to the red wine in front of him. He picks up the glass immediately afterward and takes a taste from the edge of his glass. It instantly reminds him of the wines that they so fluidly poured in Italy, very light and easy to drink. He isn't a wine connoisseur by any means, but he does drink the occasional glass of California wine. It wasn't really until he went to the United Kingdom that he began to drink anything else. This was definitely a familiar wine to him, though.

"It tastes Italian," he states, finally sure that he has the country origin right.

"I doubt it," Kate replies. "Jean-Pierre only serves French wine to me, even though he knows I hate it. But it's something that he's been doing since I was first able to drink."

"Oh," he replies softly, sinking a little further into his chair. She laughs and puts her hand on his in comfort.

"I wouldn't worry, though," she begins, "Giancarllo, the owner usually keeps some Italian in the back if you really want some."

"No!" he states quickly. "No, it's not that. I just thought it was nice, that's all."

Their youthful waiter returns at this stage, placing in front of them a plate of lettuce with white slices of buffalo mozzarella and balsamic vinegar laid neatly over it. Pat looks down at the meal before him and returns his gaze at Kate.

"Don't we get a menu?" he queries, followed by a gentle laugh.

"Not really. Not with Jean-Pierre in any case. He likes to surprise me with whatever concoction that Giancarllo has cooked up. Why? Don't you like mozzarella?"

She watches as Pat begins to eat, just as she begins her question. She shakes her head and folds her hands under her chin.

"So, let us see," Kate starts. "What do we know about Patrick?"

Patrick stops chewing his cheese and looks at her, to see if she wishes him to speak. But before he can swallow his mouthful, Kate leans her head slightly to her side, as if she were an inquisitive child.

"Well, firstly we know that you don't know much about wine." She giggles at her own words, lowering her hand and toasting him as he tries and finishes his cheese quickly in order to respond. "But you've been outside of the states, so you must travel, or have travelled." She looks at his face carefully, folding her hands under her chin again.

"No, you don't have the eyes of someone who travelled young," she states firmly. "So, you're a business traveller. Quite recent, as well."

"Last few years," he replies. "It—"

"Don't tell me," she states defiantly, as she interrupts him and then leans back in her chair. "You work a lot, but not too much that it drags you down completely. I can't see why, though. Something stops you from that."

"My— "

"Don't tell me," she interrupts leaning forward and coming as close to him as she can from across the table. There is a long pause as she continues to stare at his eyes, then her face drops, and the smile fades away. "Oh," is all she manages to say.

"What?" he questions.

"No, nothing," she returns, looking out toward the sound.

Pat doesn't press her, even though he is unsure of what has changed between them. Still, it isn't long until the next course is brought out, and the two begin to eat once again. Kate doesn't say much in between the servings, at least until the pasta is brought out.

"Can I ask you a question?" she suddenly casts aloud, almost catching out Pat as he tries and lifts a difficult length of pasta up to his mouth.

"Um, sure," she hears from behind the fork.

"Why did you bring the bracelet to me?"

There is a pause between them, as he lowers his fork and sips from his wine to clear his mouth. "I'm not quite sure, really. I saw the name on the note and just thought I would bring it down here."

"It never occurred to you that it may be worth a lot of money?" she queries.

"Not really," he replies carefully, "I just knew that it needed to come here, so I brought it."

Kate begins to smile again, and nods at his response. "I'm not sure when or where it was lost. David was going to repair it for me, but said that it had to be sent off to a specialist. Somewhere between then and now it was sent away to the wrong place, and lost in transition. No one knew where it was."

"How horrible," he says, seeing the sadness in her face.

"I honestly didn't think that I would ever see it again," she tells him, her eyes focusing aimlessly on his fork. Then, she lifts her head and faces him once again with a smile and the shine returning to her eyes. "So, you can see why I'm so grateful to you."

"I didn't bring it back for a reward or for gratitude," he speaks.

"I know," she says, placing her hand on his once again. "I just wanted you to know, in case you decide that you—" Kate stops herself before she says what she feels inside. Something inside his eyes has told her something that she hadn't seen before. She looks at him again, lost at her words and actions. He doesn't understand what she sees, or how she feels. The next few words, the next decision, the next breath she takes will decide everything inside her. And so, she takes it; a deep soft silent breath that is so unnoticeable that her chest barely moves. But she feels it. She feels her stomach tighten against the silken fabric of her dark blue Hacoux smock.

"You know something Pat," she states, "have you ever been to the zoo?"

"The Woodland?" he returns slowly, somewhat confused.

"Yes, that one," she returns, the life entering her face once again.

"I remember going there on a school trip," he replies.

"I think the least I can do for you, after returning something so special to me is to take you to the zoo."

"Right," he states somewhat bewilderingly, his word spoken almost as if in song.

"Okay, it's settled then." With her words spoken, she begins to eat once more, quickly going through and eating the bulk of her pasta.

"Est-ce que tout est bien?" the two hear from behind Kate, as Jean-Pierre suddenly appears again.

"Oui, mon amour," Kate replies as Jean-Pierre leans in and kisses her on her cheek once more. "Tell Giancarllo that everything is absolutely superb as always."

Jean-Pierre seems subdued and pleased with her response and returns back to the kitchen with the news. Kate turns her attention on the dessert that is placed in front of her by the young waiter again. Between the two of them, she and Pat have managed to finish most of the bottle of wine, although she is suddenly feeling that she could easily finish the bottle herself. But the thoughts and doubts in her mind are pushed aside and she regains her bright smile once more as she begins to eat her Savarin dipped in rum syrup with coconut infused whipped cream and blood oranges.

Kate watches Pat struggle with his pudding, and holds herself from laughing at his numerous failed attempts at trying to eat it with dignity in order to impress her. Somehow, though, he manages to finish and still breathe out from behind his belt.

"What would you like to do after lunch?" Kate asks him, "Or do you have to be somewhere?"

"No!" he replies, again far too eagerly, causing Kate to hide her smile slightly with her glass of wine. "Nothing really, or I mean, anything really. I'm pretty free for the day."

"Wow," she replies, lifting her eyebrows. "Someone would almost think that you planned to spend the day with me."

Kate watches with suspense as Pat begins to blush at the statement. It's all far too easy, and yet still great fun. Pat reaches inside his pocket and pulls out his wallet, carefully pushing back the letter from his son as to not lose it. Kate stops him before he can fully remove it, though.

"This is my godfather's restaurant," she states. "He'd be very offended if he saw you take your wallet out."

"Okay," he replies with a nod, but looks nervously at the waiter just by the bar.

"Don't worry about Alex," she informs him. "He's still figuring out what is up and what is down."

As she finishes assuring Pat, she spots Jean-Pierre appear from the front of the building, coming from the kitchen entrance. She loves how he has changed the interior of the building from a simple rustic seafront diner, to a seemingly large picturesque bistro style Italian pasta restaurant, rated one of the most desirable places to dine in all of the Northwest. Its light blue interior designed by Heme Durauxe, an Italian designer, are absolutely a perfect match with the rest of the blend of Italian/French atmosphere.

"Est-ce que tout était bien, ma belle fleur?" Jean-Pierre questions. He helps Kate to her feet and kissing her on the cheek motions for the young waiter Alex to bring their coats.

"Il était absolument parfait, amour," she begins, smiling happily at Jean-Pierre, "even the wine. Wasn't it, Patrick?"

Pat stops half standing from his seat. He looks at Jean-Pierre, his head somewhat light from the wine. He tries quickly to think about what Kate and Jean-Pierre have been saying to one another by remembering back to his days of French class in high school. Suddenly, all he can remember is the young blonde girl with the big blue eyes that was seated across from him. He comes to a complete stand as best he can and shakes Jean-Pierre's hand, nodding his head as he does so.

Jean-Pierre laughs with a deep full breath, much like a cartoon that Pat watches in the morning with his son. He then feels Jean-Pierre's hands on both his shoulders, and him kissing his cheeks.

"You are a good man," Pat hears, deciphering through the French accent. "My Kat'rine, she's brighter when she is with you. She reminds me of when she was a little girl, running carefree in the river nudité. Kat'rine was always a beautiful girl, and now she is a beautiful woman, don't you think?"

Pat looks over and for the first time sees a timid rose colour come to Kate's cheeks as she smiles. He can't help but to feel a bit nervous at the question, but doesn't think or hesitate in his response. "Yes," he whispers, feeling Alex put his arms into his sport's blazer. "*Absolutment.*"

As the two depart, they both take in the crisp air as it touches them fully when the doors open. Pat is amazed to see the amount of people that are waiting for a table in the room as they leave, and that more are on their way in.

"What?" she asks, seeing the confusion in his eyes.

"Nothing really," he replies, looking up and seeing the clouds fly past at such quick speed, leaving behind the blue skies hanging over the sound and the islands. "It's just that I've been part of the Northwest all my life. I know almost everything about Seattle, and all its little quirks and dark secrets. I know about the waterfront on the 4th of July, and the Christmas lights on the water."

"But you're amazed that even you find that it changes so much every time you come into the city," she interrupts, finishing the words for him. "I know how you feel. But you learn to roll with it. The thing is to try things that are new and different, otherwise you'll never know.

"People love routines. They love simplicity and things that remind them that they are safe. The more familiar something is, the more they like it. Most of them just love the ability to be able to complain about it, and you cannot complain about something you do not know about. That's why it is so important to discover things, both new and old."

"An interesting insight," he replies, offering his arm to her. Kate stops, tilts her head in surprise, and accepts.

"You know Patrick," she whispers in his ear, "I think I scare you just a little."

Pat looks carefully at her, as they continue down to the pier, then he begins to smile at her words.

Chapter 4

The Unanswered Question

"So, you're telling me that you met this incredibly hot woman, and she takes you to lunch, then to the zoo? You!? My Muttly?"

"Shut up and listen, will you, please Joseph?" Pat tries not to show his hidden delight or his slight frustration with his friend's childish nature. Instead, he grasps his long glass of lemonade and sips from it. "I just want to know what you think this about this little girl?"

Joseph brushes his hands through his hair, still smiling at his friend's news. But in truth, he is a bit perplexed at the question that he asks. Who is this girl that initiated everything?

"I don't know, Mutt," Joseph speaks, his deep voice towering in the port-a-cabin. He runs his hand over some paperwork, which lays scattered over some architectural drawings on his desk. "Maybe she's just a figment of your imagination."

"Oh, don't start that. I already think I'm going crazy as it is. You're supposed to be the expert at all of this type of stuff," Pat says, leaning back and shaking his head. "What if she's some ghost or something?"

Joseph laughs at the question. "I don't know Mutt. Why is it I am always the one that is supposed to know about strange things? I'm a friggin' architect! All you crazy people think that I'm some genius."

"Oh boy, here we go," Pat starts. "Every time I ask a question you don't like, it's because you're a Native American."

"I really hate that term," he replies, squinting. Before he can say anything else, he gets a pencil thrown at him quite hard.

"So anyway, what do you think, *Indian man*?"

"Do I look like a telesales guy from Bangladesh, thank you very much?" Joseph continues to banter. "Look," he then states, picking his pencil up. "Don't think about this too much, Mutt. You've met somebody nice. Everyone knows you deserve it, so for your sake and mine, don't analyse it."

"Maybe you're right," Pat replies pulling his cheeks back with a grimace.

"We have been friends since we were eight. I was there when little bear was born, and puked all over you for the first time," he says, leaning forward in his seat. "It's a good thing, my friend. Just leave it at that."

"You still coming to poker tomorrow?" Pat replies, changing the subject slightly.

"I'll be there, after I check this latest build stage at the site though."

Pat stands and walks over to his friend, putting his hand on his shoulder. "I just don't know, Joe. I can't stop thinking about her, but everything in my mind says this is all just a bit too weird. People don't do this."

"Pat, you're a good friend so I'm only going to say this once, then I'll deny it to everybody," Joseph says, forming a fist and putting it against the abdomen of his friend. "You're not a freak. You're not a murderer. You don't go chasing little girls in the school yard. You're a good father, and a loyal friend. It isn't so impossible to think that someone out there in the world may find you a half decent find."

Pat laughs slightly and accepts the answer as it comes. He waves to his friend as he opens the door to his portable office. Just as he does, though, he hears, "It's just a shame about your nose hairs...and your shoes. Oh! Did I mention the coat? I mean, who wears a blazer in winter? Oh man, is that your cologne I smell, or is something that you picked up at a fumigation someone was having?" With that Patrick closes the door behind him.

Patrick feels a bit relieved, even if he doesn't wish to admit it to his friend. He has always believed that they were more brothers, rather than friends. Joe has the uncanny ability to give him a true piece of an untainted non-judgemental listening ear when he needs it, and the same goes the other way. At the same time, making sure that neither one of them gets too big for their own good.

Pat looks at his watch, seeing the time is going quicker than he thinks. He's already called his father, and said goodnight to Thomas. It's somewhat hard on him inside, to not be there to say goodnight and kiss his son on the head. Except for when he's physically not within the state because he's away on business, which is exceptionally rare, he has always made sure that he would make it home in time for Thomas. Inside, though, he's not sure who he does it for more, himself or Thomas. Thomas didn't seem phased at all when he spoke to him. He had more to say about what his friends were doing, what movie that they said they had watched over the weekend, and which one he was going to have to see with him. But still, he loved listening to his son, even if he couldn't understand half of what he was talking about because of the speed and incredible ease at which his son has at losing his train of thought as he rambles on.

Pat gets in his car and drives quickly out of the building complex, gets on the road back toward the U-district, and from there joins the never-ending length of cars once again. He begins to head toward Seattle's famous Union Bay, his heart beginning to beat faster the closer he gets to it. The sun's set already, and the moon is nearly full, but very low, just over the horizon of the city. It looks as if it's nearly part of the city, this large overpowering globe of light engraving itself into the skyline. Even the row of cars running across the interstate look like one long string of Christmas lights, flowing and wrapping the city streets in a festive look.

It doesn't take as long as he thinks to reach the restaurant near the Arboretum, just as he's been asked. He's not even sure quite why he agreed to all of this. Suddenly, an incredible doubt fills him, both at whether she will be there, or whether he should even go. Pat stops to think for a moment, trying to make sense of what he's doing, and why he's doing it. All he has done is spent the day with a very beautiful lady of whom he had returned a bracelet too. She merely asked him to dinner in order to be kind. And the day they spent at the zoo was a bit strange, but it was very nice looking at all the lights and the big Christmas display that they had done.

"Whatever you're thinking about cannot be good for you, if it forces you to make that type of face," he hears from beside him, as Kate suddenly appears. "But as long as it's not about money, taxes, or accounting in general, I suppose it can't be that bad. You're not an accountant, are you?"

His surprise is apparent, but he suddenly can't remember what was bothering him a moment ago as Kate kisses his cheek. She takes her arm and puts it around his, motioning him forward. "It's okay if you are, really." She only says her words because of his silence, but smiles at the sight of him blushing with her touch.

"No, I'm not an accountant," he says to her trying to step forward but finding his knees somewhat weak. With ardour in his heart and soul, he somehow begins to move with her, and together they enter the restaurant. Immediately the man tells them that there will be a brief wait before hand, and they can have a seat at the bar if they wish.

"Shall we go for a walk?" he finds himself saying suddenly. So much so, that he surprises himself.

"What a nice idea," she replies, taking the pager from the host.

The two exit and head down the pleasantly lit street, looking at the lakefront off to the distance. He motions to the street lights, each covered in a red and green bow. The Christmas lights themselves light the streets down to the local shops, and a large tree is fully lit just outside the last of the light run. The wind is but a gentle winter breeze, cold, but not enough to do more than make the reflection of the moon dance across the lake. The two say little to one another, but walk in a soft silence, listening to a faint Christmas song in the distance. Kate stops just in front of the tree, looking at its beauty and stature, leaning herself against the wooden fence that goes around it. There is a closed Christmas village, with a padlock sealing its entrance near the both of them.

"I can imagine the kids coming here in droves," he says to her, looking at the bulletin board and seeing the local events.

"A kid is a young goat," she corrects him. She looks at him unexpectedly realising her outburst. Then, "Sorry, it's a habit that my mum gave me."

Pat stands and watches Kate, looking at her as she smiles away, lost in some distant thoughts. She is wearing an overcoat, this time a cream colour. He knows from the touch that it has a suede feel, which matches the feeling of her hands. She's done her hair in the short while that he left her from earlier in the day. If he were a confident person, he would be thinking that she had done all of this to impress him. And yet, inside he cannot entertain that belief, if even for but a moment.

"So, Patrick," she begins, turning and leaning fully against the fence. "What do you want to know?"

Pat looks at Kate strangely after the question, as his brow begins to curl slightly in a mild state of confusion. She laughs at his silent reply, and shakes her head. Her arms reach out and put themselves on two posts, just enough to give her balance.

"You have a look on your face that reminds me of a twelve-year-old school boy entering the girls' locker room for the first time and seeing the showers in the corner. You're not sure what to expect, but you know that there's something in there that you have to see to understand," she tells him, her teeth flashing a light blue with the twinkle of a Christmas light. "So, go on and ask me what you need to. Absolutely anything at all. I promise I won't lie." She crosses her heart afterwards and holds up her hand.

"It's not often I'm presented with such an interesting opportunity," he begins, almost shrugging. A breeze blows through the street, causing one of his hairs to fall into his eye and blink slightly. "I don't know what I'm supposed to say."

"Patrick, you have obviously gotten something in your head about me," she states, leaning forward and brushing the hair from his face. "What is it? What do you want to know about Katherine?"

"I'm not—" She interrupts him by putting her hands on either side of his face and turning his head to face directly into hers.

"Asssk," she says forcefully.

"What's," he starts, becoming lost in her eyes with every passing second. "What's happening here?" he manages to whisper.

Kate smiles at the question, and steps back once again. Suddenly the beeper on her side goes off, and they both look down at the flashing lights. She looks back at him and shrugs and laughs, then motions with her head toward the restaurant. Pat sighs and nods in reply, taking Kate's hand as it is presented to him.

It seems a quick paced dash back to the restaurant, as they see a hostess come out and look around for them. She sees Kate wave at her, and nods her head in acknowledgement. Another hostess seats them immediately, stating that they were very lucky that the table wasn't given away. The hostess mentions the fact that they are listed in the top two recommended places to eat in Seattle. They have even made it into the Northwest's most recommended wine restaurateur in the last months wine guide by *Decantuers*.

"Interesting," is all Pat replies to her statements, taking the menu from her. He looks over at Kate more than once as she is given her menu, seeing only an unreadable expression. He opens his menu shortly after the server leaves and goes to a table on the other side of the restaurant. From over the top of the menu he tries to catch a glimpse of Kate, who is sitting quite contently looking back at him, having not even lifted her menu.

"She was a bit abrupt, wasn't she?" he asks her.

"Mmm," is the reply, her hands lifting themselves from the table and folding themselves underneath her chin. She continues to watch him as he tries hard to not look as if he is watching to see how she reacts. Finally, after the third or fourth attempt at looking over the menu, he puts it down and folds his hands on his menu.

"Alright," he announces, succumbing to his own insecurities.

"Yes?" she queries politely, still looking at him.

"What are you doing? Have I done something moronic?"

"No," she replies, shaking her head slowly but once.

"Well then?" he returns immediately afterwards. "Why are you looking at me like that?"

"I'm trying to see whether or not you really know the answer to the question. Or, were you just asking me a question that you thought I wanted to hear you ask."

Pat raises his eyebrows, his eyes opening wider at the question. He tries not to notice her clothes, but his eyes begin to follow the scarf and coat as she stands up to remove them. Her long elegant satin dress looks like someone has bottled the night itself and poured it across her. He notices for the first time her exquisite physique, and the incredible smooth gloss to her skin. He cannot help but to follow her with his eyes, as he tries to embed her into his memory. Even the silver-coloured necklace with the princess cut diamond, fills his eyes with a pleasure that he could not have hoped to have seen before. Everything moves so slowly, even though it is a simple motion for her to put her coat on the rack behind them.

"Well, now," she states, seeing the expression on his face. "At least now we can eat."

The night begins at this point, as the two begin with some wine. They speak about very little things, like the weather and the wine. She even goes as far to ask him about his tie at one stage, with a picture of four cartoon characters running across it. He explains that it is the only thing that he had lying in the car, and that he wasn't expecting to go to dinner, even though he suggested it. They ignore the strange overbearing mood of the server and the lack of continuity in the food. She continues to ask easy questions, none of which pressure either of them during the dinner. And as the meal ends and she insists that she can pay for her own meal, he reminds her that it was entirely his idea and as such she was his guest.

As the two leave the restaurant he asks her one more time if she would like to go for a walk, this time around the lake. She agrees, although he notices her slight hesitation this time. He doesn't mention it though, and the two begin their walk, this time her hands neatly placed inside her overcoat. The two speak of the stars, and the Christmas lights, and even a passing bird as it flies overhead. Finally, though, she stops him and looks at him just before the water's edge.

"Do you really want to know the answer?" she states, then.

"What answer?" he returns, trying to think of the last conversation that they had.

"I'll tell you what," she begins, pulling her coat together in the front with her hands in the front pockets. "I am going to ask you one simple question, and if you tell me the truth, I'll answer anything you ask me. Deal?"

There is a hesitation in his answer, but eventually he manages to reply, "Deal."

Kate approaches him and leans as close to his ear as she can. "If I asked you to come back to my apartment, what would you say?"

She hears his breath stop instantly. She removes her hand and places it on his chest, feeling the incredible rush that his heartbeat is undergoing. When he tries to answer, she covers his mouth with her hand and steps back. "You don't need to say anything, Patrick. I just wanted to see if it was still in there. And it is."

"I don't understand." His words are somewhat broken, and he needs to clear his throat before he can say them.

"Patrick," she begins, "you are a wonderful man, even if you don't believe that. And I think that, just in the short time I've spent with you. But— "

"Will you come and meet my son, tomorrow?" he interrupts, taking hold of her free hand. She begins to smile and nods in return.

"I'd like that," she says, a glitter coming over her eyes.

"He's eight, and a bit of a hand full, but he's great. I think he'd like to meet you," Pat says, his chest somewhat deflating with his words. He takes a long breath and continues. "I pick him up from school just after three o'clock, give or take."

"Yes, that would be nice," she repeats softly, her breath becoming softer as he speaks.

"His name is Thomas, but we call him little bear," he tells her, watching the light return to her eyes. His mind is strangely clear, he thinks to himself. It is only then that he realises that he is still holding her hand, and both of them look at their hands. She moves hers slowly, though, and intertwines her fingers with his.

"It's getting a bit cold. Do you think we should head back?" she asks, lowering their hands to come between them.

"Maybe you're right," he replies.

"So, is your son smart?" she asks, the two beginning to walk back around the lake.

"Well he told me today over the phone, that his friend said to him that he couldn't wait to be eight like my son. Evidently you get to have better presents at Christmas and his father said he could have a bike when he becomes eight. My son said that he loves being eight, because it's the oldest he's ever been in his entire life, and he wouldn't want to have to go back and play with the kindergarten kids again, because it was *sooo* long ago that he can't remember if he liked it or not."

Kate laughs at the statement, even though it doesn't really answer her question.

"Well he surprises me at times," Pat states, looking up at the sky. "He just asked me the other day if Heaven celebrates Christmas."

"How sweet," Kate coos. "He sounds a very intelligent thinker."

"I suppose. Inquisitive if nothing else," he says, looking at Kate as he walks. "Stubborn, most definitely."

"Pat," Kate begins, stopping and facing him as they approach the exit to the park.

"Yes?" he queries, seeing the look of intent on her face.

"I just want you to know, that I really enjoyed being with you today."

"I— " he stops himself.

"I love that you have a wonderful economy of words," she tells him. "Say what you think, Patrick."

"What I think?" He looks at her again, his eyes trying so hard to look away from her, but finding they can't. And before he can think, before his mind overrides his words he says, "I think that you are the most beautiful woman that I have ever met."

"There," she sighs pleasantly, a smile breaking across her face once more. "That wasn't too hard."

"No, it was not," he replies. "And the more I think of it, the more I can't find a reason for why I haven't told you that sooner." He takes her face in his hands and kisses her, unlike any other kisses they have shared before. He tastes her soul with his breath, filling the incredibly deep void within him with the life that she breathes into him.

Finally, she steps back, her face somewhat flushed. She takes his hand into hers and lifts it to her lips. Then, carefully she places his hand on her heart. "I don't give this away to anyone, Patrick. I think you need to walk first, before you run head on into something you can't control."

"I'm sorry," he replies. "I—"

"You didn't do anything wrong, Patrick." She lowers their hands and they begin to walk once again. "You'll figure it out, don't worry. I'll make you a promise."

He looks over to her and sees that she is looking at the large decorated tree in the distance. Then he hears, "I'll be here as long as you want me to be."

Pat takes her to the door of her car, and receives a kiss on the cheek for his trouble. Then, as she just about closes the door, "You really don't know the answer, do you?"

"I'll see you tomorrow?" he replies after a brief pause.

"Tomorrow."

Chapter 5

The Tubby Man Who Always Smiles

The sounds of ocean water melting into the sands of the beach begin to fill the ears of the young Thomas James. His eyes remain closed, though, as he continues to listen to the sounds around him. He can hear the ticking of his superhero clock that his father bought for him the last time they went to Florida to see the big castles and roller coasters. The sound of the neighbour's dog catches his ear, as it begins to bark after its long run down the coast. He can hear the thick spray of water begin to fly through the air as the dog shakes its coat after being in the ocean. He thinks how cold it must be, remembering how he went into the water once chasing a kite that had fallen and how blue his legs had become. His father said that it was because his legs were so cold that the blood had slowed down and couldn't reach the places it needed too. He still thinks that it has something to do with the fact that toilet cleaner is always blue when his father puts it in the water, and God must have to clean the ocean sometimes too. It makes sense, he thinks. Besides, his blood is red, not blue. He doesn't like blood that much. His friend started to bleed through his nose and they had to take him to the nurse's office, where they put these furry things up his nose and he had to hold a towel over his face for a whole hour because they couldn't turn off the faucet in his brain. His father didn't believe him, though. But he really didn't like it much when he got one during the summer. He thought he was going to die like his guinea pig. His grandfather said it died of a nose bleed.

Thomas opens his eyes at the smell of pancakes, and the sounds of his neighbour shouting at Henry (the big golden dog) as Henry soaks her by shaking off too close to her. She is a funny lady, always running by the house in the morning, and waving at his father and grandfather. She must be the only lady in all of the state to wear shorts near Christmas. Maybe even the whole world, he thinks. He heard from one of his friends, Jonathan Henry, that his mom and dad go to Hawaii every Christmas while he stays with his grandparents in Alaska. Jonathan said that it always rains in Hawaii, and that's why he doesn't go with his parents. And evidently, he overheard them saying that the drinks never stop running there in Christmas. He didn't know that drinks could run. He wonders how fast they go, and if you have to catch them before you can open them? He starts to think about presents also, wondering if they run during Christmas as well. Jonathan said that Santa doesn't ride a sleigh in Hawaii, but rides a surfboard. How do the reindeer stay dry, he ponders? Do reindeer swim?

Thomas arises quickly, running into the kitchen and seeing his grandfather drinking his coffee and reading his newspaper. His father is just finishing making the last of the pancakes, and hasn't seen him yet.

"Dad!" he exclaims. His father turns to him, his eyes looking strangely quite pleasant and lively for this early. "Do reindeer swim?"

"No, Thomas," Pat states in his fatherly tone.

"How do you know?" queries Thomas's grandfather, from behind the folds of the paper. "Have you ever seen one? If they can fly, why can't they swim?"

"I'm pretty sure that they don't swim," Pat states once more, rolling his eyes as he flips the last of the pancakes. He pours the boiling water from the pan that has been holding the maple syrup out into the sink, and removes the jar.

"I was watching a documentary the other day and it showed several reindeer migrating across the north. They had to cross rivers and small lakes together. They looked like they were swimming quite happily to me," explains Ben as he continues reading.

"How about under the water?" Thomas questions further, sitting down and looking intently at his orange juice. "Maybe they can breathe under water."

"I've never heard of reindeer diving before, but I'll be sure to ask Santa the next time I see him," Pat tells Thomas, staring intently at the newspaper as if to wait for the next outburst.

"Okay," Thomas says happily, satisfied that his father will handle the rest of it for him. His father usually knows everything. His grandfather knows a lot, but tends to keep it a secret, just in case his dad finds out. And he doesn't bother asking his teacher anymore, because she just makes him look it up on the internet. Everyone knows that everything on the internet is just something that librarians invented so that they don't have to sit in the library all day. His friend Michael Turne said that his father told him that the "www" stands for Washington is Wet and Windy. But when he looked it up on the school's computer it said something about waiting for the world's web and somebody who spiders things. He supposes that has something to do with someone like the superhero or something. It's probably how he knows when things go wrong. Suddenly he wonders if the other superheroes use the internet to find bad guys. He'll have to try himself when he gets to school.

Thomas ravages through his pancakes, all the while his father constantly telling him to slow down and breathe properly. He doesn't breathe badly, he thinks to himself. His grandfather breathes really badly when he's sleeping, and he isn't anywhere near that bad.

"Did you get your homework done last night?" Pat asks his son, as he finishes the last of his coffee.

"We didn't have any," Thomas replies, putting the last of the pancakes into his mouth, along with the last bit of syrup from his plate.

"What did we do last night, then?" his grandfather says from behind his paper.

"Oh! You mean my math? That wasn't homework," Thomas emphasises.

"That was something my teacher said that we had to do so we didn't get in trouble and couldn't watch the Christmas movie today."

"I see," Pat begins, "and did you get it done."

"Oh yeah," Thomas states, somewhat pushing his chest out. "Grandpa got three of the questions wrong, but I told him how to do it right."

"He sure did," his grandfather tells Pat.

Thomas watches his father put the last of the plates in the sink, and begins to wash. He knows that by the time he finishes that it'll be time to go to school. Only twelve more days until his Christmas vacation begins.

"Thomas," his father begins, continuing to wash away the last few plates. "After school today, I'm going to bring a friend home to see you. I want you to behave and be on your best manners."

Pat hears his father lower the paper after his words. He waits for the words to come out, but nothing reveals itself to him. Finally, Thomas begins. "Okay, dad. As long as I don't have to wear my tie, though."

"Okay, it's a deal."

"Do I have to clean my room?" Thomas questions, "Or is it just going to be Uncle Joseph who messes it all up anyway?"

"No, it's not Uncle Joseph," Pat tells his son, unsure at how to answer the next question that he's sure to ask.

"Is it somebody that is going to teach me something?" Thomas queries. He suddenly remembers the time that his father enrolled him in the art club. He really wants to play the piano, like his friend Addy. His grandfather teaches him guitar on the weekends, but it isn't the same really. Addy's piano takes up a whole room, and his guitar is only half the size of his grandfathers. Just isn't fair.

"A lady named Kate will be coming to meet you tonight," Pat begins, seeing his father raise his eyebrow even though he is facing out the window. "Kate is someone that daddy...well," he pauses, "she is a friend of mine."

"Oh. Okay," Thomas says, "as long as I don't have to learn anything too hard. Does she play the piano?"

"I'm not sure," Pat replies.

"Do you think she might bring a piano?"

"No," Pat returns matter-of-factly.

"How about a saxophone?" Thomas says brightly, opening his eyes really wide, as his father pulls him up from his chair and hands him his lunch.

"I sincerely doubt it, Thomas." Pat guides his son to the door, quickly going through and closing it behind him.

"I wonder if she'll bring an acronym, like that man we saw in Friday Harbour that one year. He only had four fingers and played with his sunglasses on."

Pat replies to his son by opening the door to the car and seating him. "It's pronounced, *accordion*, little bear." He further replies to his son by putting the headphones on his son and closing the door before he can say anything else. He closes his eyes for a moment and takes a deep breath. Shaking his head, he looks up to see the crooked smile of his own father looking out from the kitchen window at him. Ignoring him, he gets into the car and the two drive away.

Patrick drops Thomas off as normal, approximately twenty minutes before the bell goes off. He watches his son until he meets Addy underneath the tree along with the other children. Pat cannot help but to let his mind wander once again, his heart suddenly thinking about his son and his future. He wonders if he is the only father in the world that worries if his actions are completely destroying his son's future, perhaps even his happiness or dreams.

With a heavy heart, he takes some comfort before driving off at seeing one of the mothers running in with her son's lunch, what looks to be homework in her mouth, and a pair of shoes thrown over her shoulder. If nothing else, at least his son will be punctual.

As Pat drives away, his thoughts turn heavy and weigh him down slightly, figures and actions filling every corner of his mind. He looks into the mirror and sees his own eyes looking back at him, full of confusion and ambivalence. He can hear his heart inside him, a thing that he has set aside for only one creature; his son taking the only part of it that still remains. His mind tells him repeatedly that his actions the previous day were nothing more than a simple matter of conjoined actions and circumstances that he could not have predicted.

And yet, here Patrick is driving down to the heart of Seattle once more. No matter how much he looks in the mirror, or stares at the world around him, it does not resemble anything that he has seen before. It is changing uncontrollably, in ways that his heart and mind cannot comprehend.

Pat pulls into the private complex just outside Elliot Bay, following the directions that were given to him the previous night. As he steps out of his car, his body seems to fade away from his control, moving without reason. He can feel the intense desire inside him; a curiosity that overtakes thought and reason.

He does not take the elevator, but instead begins to climb the stairs, every step echoing throughout the chamber. He tries to stop, but somehow, he cannot. He can feel the muscles pulling in his legs, but he does not feel pain. He knows his heart is beating, harder and faster than it should beat, but he does not feel it. His entire body begins to numb, becoming heavier with every passing step, until he finds himself standing before apartment 3006. If someone asked him how he had gotten to where he is standing right now, he probably wouldn't be able to answer them. He does not see the violet crystal glass vase underneath the window at the end of the hall. He does not notice the limited-edition prints of the snow-capped mountains on the wall, nor the fine Chinese Fou Shou rug.

Before Pat realises where he is or what he is doing, his hand is on the door, knocking four times exactly. His eyes suddenly focus, and his entire body begins to shudder as the doors opens. Before him, standing in the partly opened doorway, looking over his shoulder, stands the figure of a man, well dressed, although slightly casual for winter. He is overcome with the sound of Christmas music filling the inner apartment, and of the other voices within. The man before him, he seems lost within a conversation about different colours of ornaments, and the size of the tree that lies within. It is only after he hears the silver blue colour announced, that he laughs and turns to face the doorway.

"Oh my—" he begins, covering his own mouth. "You must be the new bit of spare that Katey has been talking about all night."

"Oi!" Pat hears in the background, a clearly female voice. Suddenly a pillow smashes against the back of the man before him, continuing to spin and carrying itself over his head and into the grasp of Pat.

Pat hears the laugh of a woman, who opens the door and pushes past the man and grabs Pat's hand.

"Hi," a woman begins, her green eyes flashing a dark glare over at the man who is now walking back into the apartment. "Don't mind that bogtrotter, he's just an Irish ignoramus. You must be Pat, the new bloke that Katherine was telling us about. Come in. She's in the shower. I'm Tara, by the way."

"Hello," Patrick replies following the young lady into the apartment. Her British accent is undeniable, and at first is very hard for him to decipher. She leads him past the kitchen, which is off to their left. He looks briefly at its contents, seeing an incredibly immaculate silver and black cosmopolitan style kitchen, almost untouched to the naked eye. He does notice that upon the fridge though, that there are a couple of hand cut paper snowflakes with children's names on them.

"Is it true, what Katie said an' all?" Tara queries. As she speaks she stops and faces him from over her shoulder, then continues on into the main living room.

"What did she say?" Pat returns softly, somewhat awe-stricken by the overwhelming presence of Christmas decorations and icons spread throughout the main living room. He can see a main patio door in the distance, covered with flashing blue and green lights, followed by a banner of paper snowflakes that are strung together and carefully placed along the coving in order to form a beguiling array of childhood crafts. Each one looks as if it was done with the care that only a child could ever hope to capture, and what look to be children's names laced upon every snowflake. The large main window which overlooks Seattle and the sound, is covered in hand drawings of Santa, with pieces of cotton balls spread across his face in order to make his beard.

Patrick hears a noise from his side, and thinks he hears Kate's voice. He turns his head from the window and faces one of the rooms off to his right, where he is greeted by the sight of Kate stepping out of the bedroom with a towel wrapped around her, and another in her hands as she dries her hair.

"Is that Patrick?" she speaks, stopping as she sees him.

Pat is awe-stricken one again, completely overwhelmed at the undeniable beauty of the woman that he had just met the previous day. He has to force himself to close his mouth, and breathe through his nose, just to keep from gaping at her.

"I'm running a little behind today, sorry," Kate apologises. "I'll just be another few minutes. Have a look round, while I dry my hair off."

"Okay," Pat replies, unable to take his eyes from her as she turns and disappears into the main bedroom. He looks back at the woman in front of him, only to see her smile wryly at him.

"Would you like a drink?" she replies. "I've just boiled the kettle, and was going to have a tea. Ol' Kieran over there is going to make it for us." She kicks the sofa with her words, forcing the man sprawled on the sofa to stand and smile, waving his hands in the air.

"Don t'worry. I'll make it, love," he tells her, his voice rolling like a song. Not quite like the leprechauns he heard in the fairy-tale movies as a child, but enough to remind him that he was most assuredly Irish.

"Is it true, then?" Tara enters again, walking over and seating herself in front of the half-decorated Christmas tree. "Did ya really bring her nan's bracelet back to her n'all?"

"Yes," Pat says, walking around the sofa and seating himself. He picks up what appears to be a candy cane shaped cookie, only to find that it has a metal loop on the top of it, and as he turns it over, sees the name of a child on the back.

"Oh," Tara begins, laughing slightly as she puts another decoration on the tree. "That's from one of the children at school. I'm a teacher in primary....er... elementary school here. The children made them for me before I go home for Christmas."

"When are you going home?" Pat asks politely, placing the cookie ornament carefully down upon the glass coffee table once more.

"Not for a fortnight, when the children break," she returns to him, picking up a bit of blue tinsel. "Kieran and I are on an exchange program, visiting Katie an' all."

"Oh? Are you going back for good then?" Pat enters, again as polite and attentive as he can.

"Aye," he hears from behind him, "And not soon enough. I'm just not used to t'dis damn politeness n'all." Kieran places a cup of tea in front of him, to which Pat stares as he pours milk into it. As much as he does not mind tea, he has never had it with milk before.

"Kate and I are bezzies from Uni," Tara tells him. "When the opportunity to come over for a few months arose, I jumped at it."

"Very nice," Patrick returns, picking up his tea and sipping from it, nearly burning every taste bud in his mouth. He's not quite sure what she is saying, but nods politely while she speaks.

"Let it cool, love," Tara tells him, as he wipes the dribble from his lips. "So, tell us about yourself, then?"

"Okay," Patrick says softly, watching as Kieran seats himself next to him on the sofa. "What would you like to know?"

"Are you married?" Kieran starts, folding his arms on his leg.

"No," Patrick replies, "but I do have a son. He's eight and very effervescent, which keeps me busy."

"They are at that age, and cheeky like monkeys," Tara says with a smile. "How about family?"

"I have a younger brother and sister who live in different parts of the country. And my father, who lives with my son and I," Pat says to Tara with a smile. "My mother died of cancer a few years back, and we've been together pretty much since then."

"Wow," Tara announces. "Just the lads, then?"

"You could say that," Patrick concurs, although somewhat hesitant.

"Forget all that wish washy nonsense, love" Kieran interrupts. "Have you ever been to Ireland? That's the most important question."

"You'll have to forgive, Kieran," Tara says, rolling her eyes, and throwing a plastic ball decoration at him. "He's only considers people human if they drink Irish Whiskey and play golf."

"Well, I'm not really a drinker at all," he informs Kieran, then to Tara, "and I'm lousy at golf, although I do play occasionally. I have been to Ireland before, although not as extensively as England and Scotland. I've been to Wales a few times as well, but like I say, mostly just England and Scotland."

"Where'd you go in Ireland? And don't tell me Dublin, neither. I don't consider that Ireland." Kieran's voice, although distinctively musical in tone, carries a somewhat harder accent to it with his change in attitudes.

"I landed in Shannon," Pat replies. "Just for a couple of days, though."

"Ah," Kieran begins, suddenly interrupted though with the pelting of glass orbs from Tara. "Okay, love. I'll shut m'trap."

The three of them go silent as the sound of Kate's door opens. Patrick immediately stands up and turns, watching the small corridor to her room as he waits for her to emerge.

"I like this song," Kate says as she walks out from the corridor, humming pleasantly to the Christmas music. As she comes into sight, still trying to fit the last of her left earring into place, she stops and stares at the three figures staring at her intensely. Patrick takes a breath the instant he sees her, causing her to smile once more and continue forward. She rubs her hands on her light blue faded jeans after fitting the backing piece of her earring into place. Her hair is exquisitely combed, flowing as beautiful as the waves of tree tops within a brisk spring wind.

"These two aren't hassling you, are they?" Kate questions, coming forward and taking a cup of tea off of the kitchen counter. "They grill everybody I bring home, in hopes of taking something interesting back with them to tell everyone."

"I like this one," Tara says, somewhat shouting over the bells within the music. "He's much more interesting than that Daniel plonker."

"Shush, you," Kate replies, grimacing to her friend.

Kate tips the last of her tea into her mouth and rushes over to Patrick, taking his hand and pulling him away from the other two. She grabs a wintry black woollen jacket off the back of the door, as well as a pair of keys hanging on the wall.

"Shall we wait up?" Kieran questions, receiving only the sound of the door shutting for an answer.

"I thought I'd better get you out of there before they started the inquisition," Kate replies, somewhat laughing at her own remark. "They are sweet enough, just a bit nosey."

"I thought they were nice," he replies to her, watching as she calls the elevator with a push of the button. The doors open instantly, meaning only that the elevator was simply waiting for their beckoning before opening for them and them alone.

Kate is fiddling with her hair, trying to adjust her necklace, until finally she asks if Pat will clasp it for her. It is the first time he has the opportunity to touch her hair, feeling its incredibly soft silken waves brush over the tops of this hand and she pulls it aside for him to reach her neck. His fingers cannot help but to feel the immense satin-like skin as he undoes the clasp and puts the necklace around her, easily fastening it together once more.

She turns toward him once more, lifting the light blue gem into her palm and staring at it slightly. "My father gave this too me when I graduated from University. That's where Tara and I met."

"It's very nice," he speaks softly, clearly pronouncing the last word.

"I don't wear anything nice anymore," she tells him, looking up once again. She puts her scarf around her neck, and bundles herself once again as the doors of the elevator open and reveals the main car park. "I'm afraid somebody will take it, or I'll lose it somewhere."

"Like your grandmother's bracelet?" he questions, stepping out from the elevator with her. "It is only jewellery, after all."

"You obviously don't know women, do you?" Kate replies to his answer, laughing at him afterwards. "Come on, then. Take me somewhere, before you say something else idiotic."

"Alright, where would you like to go?" he returns opening the door for her and allowing her to seat herself in his car completely before shutting the door.

After Pat closes his door, the seat automatically adjusting for him again, he turns and faces Kate. She is still admiring the interior of his car and all the buttons and electronic displays that are spread throughout.

"It's like being in a spy car," she states, pushing one of the buttons that moves the flow of air to point specifically at her. "It makes my little toy look like a push car."

"My company paid for it, as a bonus for some work I did last year," he states, trying to be as unboastful and modest as he can.

"Let's go for a drive, then," Kate says excitedly. "Somewhere near the water."

"We can take a ferry if you like," he queries, trying to find the general direction to take.

"Okay, as long as we can sit on the beach," she informs him.

With a brief nod, Pat starts the journey, heading north towards the interstate. Kate amuses herself in the meanwhile by trying on Thomas's headphones and listening to the television, while trying to watch it from the front seat, somewhat haphazardly and mostly unsuccessfully. Before she knows it, they are on the interstate headed north, pleasantly going away from the large amount of usual traffic that is headed south. They head north for a bit, turning off just as she asks him about his media player.

"I'm not sure," he responds, "my friend set the whole thing up for me. He's a wizard with everything to do with cars. In exchange, I help him with anything technically business minded."

"Sounds fair," Kate says, seeing the car come slowly down the road to the ferry and parking in an extraordinarily empty car park. "So, is that what you do?"

"What?" questions Pat, turning the engine off as he hands his credit card to one of the ferry operators, who notifies him it'll be about fifteen to twenty minutes before the next ferry arrives.

"Technically business something or other is what you said," Kate says, opening the door and jumping out. Pat somewhat surprised by the move, somewhat comically follows stumbling a bit as he forgets to unbuckle. He tries to follow her, but she moves quickly, almost gliding across the pavement until she reaches the car park end, jumping up onto the large wooden rails that separate her and the rocky bank that holds the sea at bay.

"Do you even know what that is?" he questions, smiling at her childish actions.

"Nope," she replies, "but I'm sure that you'll tell me."

"It's nothing exciting," he says to her, seeing her jump down and come up to him.

"Pat, there are few things in this life that are exciting when it comes to work," she says, seating herself on one of the large boulders that are situated near them. "You seem to do well, and you're not screwed up inside. I can see that in your eyes you enjoy what you do, and it allows you to spend time with your son."

"You can tell all of that by looking at my eyes?"

"You'd be amazed, Patrick," Kate says pleasantly. "The point I'm trying to make though, is don't feel as if you have to impress me if I ask you a question. The chances are that it is just a question, not an underlining way of finding out some deep dark secret that you've been hiding all your life which has turned you into a secluded hermit that has withdrawn from all humanity in order to protect himself from the failings of life and love."

He blinks twice at the statement, somewhat lost for a moment at the words that Kate expressed. Kate responds to him by standing up and tapping him on the face. "Relax, it's just my way of flirting."

"Oh," Pat begins trailing off into a bland silence.

"So, forget about all the technical business talk, and my mindless dribbling," Kate says to him, walking away towards the car once more. "Tell me what the single most important thing in your life is."

"My— " he tries to speak, but is interrupted.

"Besides your son," she states, waving her finger at him as she continues to walk in front of him.

"I don't know," he returns to her, "I've never really thought about it."

"So, think about it," she replies instantly. Kate stops and turns around placing her hands behind her back. "Patrick, you cannot tell me that there is nothing important in your life besides your son. You must enjoy something? Beer? Wine? Lasagna? Pizza? Cars? Motorcycles? Gaming?"

"I enjoy poker," he replies, "but it's not important to me. My friends and I play once a week."

"It's a start. But surely you must enjoy other things." Kate steps forward, putting her face up against his, so that her lips are close to his left ear. "If something important to you comes into your mind you'd tell me wouldn't you."

"Yes," he replies.

"Promise?" she whispers softly.

"I promise," he returns to her, hearing the fog horn of the ferry off in the distance.

"Personally, I have a lot of things important to me," Kate tells him stepping back once more and turning toward the car. "Pretzels, for example. A girl cannot live without pretzels. Not the crunchy type, either. I love the soft gooey freshly baked ones, with garlic butter spread across in ample amounts."

"Interesting."

Kate laughs at his reply, shaking her head at the statement.

It takes a few minutes for the ferry to dock, in which time the two return to the car and watch as the other cars are shuffled off like children in a playschool. Minutes later they are on board, and decide to go up to the main deck to watch the sea roll by. It's another cold day, but somehow Patrick doesn't seem to notice it so much as he stands near Kate. He can smell the fresh scent of a rose lavender roll through the thick sea air. He watches her, bundling herself closely in the scarf and jacket that she is wearing. She can see him out of the corner of her eye, but does nothing to encourage or stop his actions.

"So where are you taking me?" Kate announces as the ferry begins it journey outward once more.

"Whidbey Island," he returns. "Have you ever been there before?"

"I don't believe so," Kate replies, shaking her head.

"It's a nice drive from the south end, with some nice quiet places along the way," he says, seeing Kate turn and face him, placing her back against the rail.

"Quiet, huh?" Kate light-heartedly voices, lowering her head ever so slightly, in somewhat of a seductive manner. "What are you planning, Patrick?" Pat can only reply with the charming colour of his blood entering his cheeks.

Kate leans over and kisses Pat on his left cheek, patting the other with her hand. She then turns and holds her hands up as a brisk wind brings the cold spray of the sea up onto the deck. She turns around and sees the look of awe in Patrick's eyes. She knows that look, as she has seen it on many a man's face before. Each of them had the same look of hunger as Patrick, but the others would not hesitate where Patrick does. Something holds him at bay. Something innocent lies within his eyes, unlike any of the others that she has known. He amuses her with his simplicity and ignorance; much like a puppy or a child finding their way. It is his sincerity and lack of aggression that draws her interest in him as she spends more time with him. It is the deep sincere honesty that his whole nature holds that causes her desire to understand him to grow.

"Patrick," she begins, walking past him and seating herself on the partly wet bench just before the window. He in return joins her, seating himself not too far from her, but in the same right making sure that the distance between them is enough not to make her uncomfortable.

"What may I do for you?" Patrick returns. He doesn't understand what is going on between them. He does not understand why he feels so incredibly at ease like he has not done in years. He only knows that he does not wish it to stop.

"So," she begins, "do you believe in love at first sight?"

Silence follows, his expression of confusion and shock overcome him. Then, "I'm not sure."

"How can you not be sure? Haven't you ever seen something before and just knew that you loved it?" Kate presses, enjoying the unease that she is putting Patrick through. Kate pretends that she is slightly frustrated, and sees Patrick struggle a bit at her impatience.

"I'm not sure," he replies again. "I've never been in love with someone like that before."

"Really?" she returns quickly, turning and seating herself fully on the seat by crossing her legs in a somewhat meditative fashion. Then, closing her eyes, "I fell in love with chocolate the first time I ever laid eyes on it. Not the plastic stuff that we get here in this country, either. This was the kind of love that lasts a lifetime. It was the first time my mother took me into the local *chocie* shop and bought me one chocolate truffle from the luxury range. It was absolutely love at first sight. I'd never seen such a beautiful perfectly shaped sweet before. And the taste was something that I still dream about at night."

"That's slightly different than what you just asked me," he explains.

"But it's not!" she insists, her eyes bursting open. "Love isn't something that just describes what people feel for each other Patrick. It's the feeling that puts you in a state of mind that makes you completely insane. Something the makes you uncomfortable and squirm about like a fish out of water. Something that makes you act completely and utterly idiotic and childish, just to have that feeling be inside you."

"And you're like that with chocolate," he returns, raising an eyebrow. She laughs in reply and nods.

"And pretzels."

"So, we've established that you love pretzels and chocolate," he tells her with a somewhat satisfied look on his face. "Is there anything else that you fell instantly in love with at first sight?"

"Ah, now you would want to know that wouldn't you?" Kate can't help but to almost purr her reply, devouring every syllable as it rolls out of her lips. Patrick can't help but to smile at her, a true earnest grin that he cannot remember doing before.

A gentle silence falls between them, where Patrick feels Kate slowly come closer to him. As she does so, he carefully holds out his hand, where she returns the gesture by taking his hand and putting her head on his shoulder.

"I don't know what you're turning me into, you know," Kate tells him, sighing slightly afterwards. Patrick doesn't reply in words, but merely watches the white caps dance behind the ferry as they press along through the sound.

The two sit in silence, although a thousand words fill the air between them. Questions that so dearly want to be asked, things that need to be said, thoughts that need to come to light; all these and more go unspoken, but are there hanging between them as clear as the sky above them. Neither one of them let it bother them though, as they sit happily next to one another. They are just two people who happened to meet a day before, and are spending a day together.

There are very few people on board, but what little there are pass before them methodically, each testing the cold to see if it is bearable enough to enjoy to clear skies. Inevitably, the deck remains empty except for the two who sit upon the cold iron bench, watching the waves break against one another, and the seagulls dance over the islands of seaweed in the water. Kate spots an eagle overhead, flying near one of the island coast lines. She watches as the majestic beast circles the air, looking for something that neither one of the mere mortals cannot see from below. Without thought or recourse, it turns as quickly as it comes and heads back into the dense forest of fir trees just beyond the beach.

"Tara likes you," Kate says suddenly, breaking the silence. "I can tell these things."

"Does she? Well she is nice enough. I like the way she decorated your apartment, with all of the children's decorations."

"Yes, the children and I had fun that day," Kate replies, to which Patrick looks down at her questioningly. "Oh, I substitute every now and then. Tara wasn't feeling well so the school district called me in. I do it every now and then, when I feel like it. They were supposed to make decorations for the school, but they wanted to make something for Tara, because she was sick. So we made Santa Claus heads out of paper plates and cotton balls. The usual stuff. Anything to keep them away from all that electronic babysitting that seems to have overtaken the classroom."

"I'm familiar," he says in reply, returning his gaze outward once again.

"Christmas is a wonderful time of year for the children," Katherine states. "I bet your son is excited."

"Only since last January," Patrick responds sarcastically.

"Well, that is just in their nature," she tells him. "You'd be surprised at how much they love the idea of it all. You could take every toy and present away from them, and they would still have a brilliant time. It's just the spirit of it all; the hope inside of Christmas itself that appeals to them."

"But superhero action figures help," he states softly.

"My mother used to tell me that Father Christmas is something more than a man in a red suit," Kate explains. "Like Christmas itself, he is something that we can't explain with words."

"I think I like the idea of a jolly old tubby man who still has all his hair and can manage to remember everybody's names. It's a testament to human resourcefulness."

"Uh huh," Kate returns with a smirk. "Mock me if you want, but I still believe in the spirit of Christmas. I see the children and the incredible love that they give unselfishly without want or desire in their hearts. I think the only reason why they want presents so much is because it's the only way that modern day parents know how to show their love for their children. It's not a bad thing, but it's been mistaken by so many as being commercial, when really it's just another form of something that has been around since the first Christmas."

Patrick looks into the eyes of the woman next to him, seeing the unquestionable sincerity that they hold for her words. Kate looks up from the seas and their two gazes join. Kate sees only admiration in his eyes, as much as hers hold sincerity.

"So, what do you want from Santa?" Patrick then asks.

"Something that he can't give me," she returns looking out at the waves once again.

"Well, you don't know if you don't ask," Pat says with a note of a silly familiarity. Kate closes her eyes and sighs, suddenly pulling herself slightly into his shoulder.

"When the time's right, I just might," Kate says softly. Then, shaking just slightly, "It's getting a bit cold, isn't it?"

"We're almost there now, anyway. Why don't we head back inside?" he tells her, standing and helping her to her feet.

Chapter 6

Cold Red Wine

Kate realises that she should be nervous for some reason, but can't seem to bring herself to be. Even though Patrick said that he would have to go and pick Thomas up from school, and leave her at the house with his father, she seemed all too willing to undergo the normally gruelling experience. Under any normal circumstance, she would have most likely called for a ride-share. But from the instant that she was introduced to Benjamin, or Ben as he insists, she has been completely at ease. And the moment that he came up to her and gave her an enormous hug, so unconditional and loving that it reminded her of her own father; the entire experience all seemed to add to her pleasant state of ease. He even offered to make her a cup of Earl Grey, which he said that Pat brought home the day earlier for some reason.

The ocean waves call Kate, pulling her to the sea's edge, where she can't resist the temptation to take her shoes off and step into the cold sand. The bitter cold bites the bottom of her feet, almost as if she were stepping into a bucket of ice. She cannot help but to smile and jump around, trying to find her way back to her shoes. As she does so, she catches a glimpse of Ben laughing at her as he brings two cups down to the shore.

"I should have warned you," Ben starts, waiting until she manages to brush off her feet and slip into her shoes once again before handing her the cup of tea.

"You must think I'm crazy," she tells him, clinging to the cup of tea as if it were a blanket.

"Nope," he states, "everybody does that when they first come to the house. Admittedly, most of the time it's Thomas's friends, and it's in the middle of summer, but I wouldn't worry. I've heard it keeps the skin tight."

Kate laughs as she sips from her cup of tea. It's not bad, but a bit strong by her standards, which is usual for the people who don't make tea often. Kate is wearing a thick sweater, but is shivering due to the cold. Ben suggests that they should head inside, where it's a bit warmer.

"I'm okay, just overcoming the cold feet is all," Kate explains.

"Okay, but don't let yourself get too cold," Ben returns, placing his hand on her shoulder. "Pat would never let me live it down if you caught a cold."

Kate looks at Ben briefly, seeing his honest face, somewhat similar to Patrick's. Pat has his father's gentle eyes, but the nose is different. The strong chiselled chin is the same in both men, though.

"Are you from England?" Ben asks, seating himself on one of the pieces of large driftwood. He sips from his coffee, the stream of heat rushing across his face like a cloud.

"No, not really," she replies, leaning against the end of the driftwood. "I lived there for most of my teens, though. My father sent me back for university as well."

"Your accent is nice," Ben tells her, sipping his coffee once more. "It's nice to hear, compared to the usual people that drift by from day to day."

"That's the thing, though," Kate says, "here in the states people drift in and out from all over the world. You can meet someone from just about anywhere, but you can never predict where it'll be from. I think that's what I love most about life; the chance that it will bring something different my way."

"Or someone," Ben enters, his deep scratchy voice even more accented in the cold. Then, "Is that how you and Pat met?"

"How does anyone meet for the first time?" Kate's reply is nonchalant and whimsical. Her face changes slightly at the thought of it all, to which she pauses slightly in her reflection. "Actually, he came to me specifically."

"Really?" Ben questions. "That doesn't sound like Pat. He's not someone to search someone out."

"Patrick just came up to me and said that he thought he had something for me," Kate explains, lifting her eyebrows in reflection.

"He likes you," Ben states firmly, watching the wind flow across the water. "You'll have to forgive him for being so damn pig headed, though. He gets that from me, unfortunately." Kate laughs at the statement. "Pat hasn't been open with people for a long time. But you've probably gathered that already."

"I did notice," Kate replies with a nod. "But it adds to his charm."

Ben doesn't press the girl, seeing that there is quite a bit that needs to be undertaken between Pat and her before he can say anything further. His first impressions of her are of a woman who is one very large handful, but in the same right, very well-mannered and undeniably striking. All in all, not what he imagined Patrick ever being with. But he thought the same thing when he was first married.

"How long have you had this home?" Kate questions, standing and coming over to sit next to Ben.

"It belongs to Pat," Ben says to Kate, looking up to her. "Shortly after Thomas was born, he gave up his job and moved back here to the Northwest. He bought this house because Thomas liked the sound of the waves. It helped him sleep at night. Probably still does."

As he finishes his words, the car pulls into the drive, causing both Ben and Kate to turn and face the house. Kate's first sight is that of a very bright-eyed young boy, whose enthusiasm and eagerness exude from his big brown eyes. Almost before the car can come to a complete stop, Thomas is out of the car with his lunchbox in hand and on the way down to his grandfather. He is carrying a large piece of paper in his hand, with bright red and green leaking through to the back of it.

"Hi Grandpa!" he shouts, almost running but not fully as he sees the lady whom he is standing next to. "Look! I won a ribbon!"

"Very cool, little bear," Ben says taking the piece of paper and seeing a ribbon attached to it. As he is looking at it, he sees Kate kneel down somewhat, to match the height of Thomas.

"Hello," Kate says cheerfully.

"Hi," Thomas says first, then, "you're very beautiful. Are you a virgin?"

"Sorry?" Kate replies, going somewhat red all of a sudden.

"Thomas!" Pat interrupts, "That's not something you ask people."

"Sorry," Thomas replies softly, then quite cheerfully, "It's only that we were talking about Italy in class, and the teacher mentioned Mike and Jelloe who made pictures of a very beautiful lady. One of the prettiest pictures of them all was a virgin called Mary, who we saw photos of in this big art book of paintings."

Kate tries very hard not to laugh, but manages only to hold herself back to a giggle. Pat kneels next to his son, trying to comfort him, unnecessarily as the look of innocence spreads to a bright smile from Thomas. Kate nods to Thomas and touches his cheek.

"That is very sweet of you," she explains.

"Does that mean you're not a vir—" Thomas cannot finish his question as his father covers his mouth with his hand.

"Kate, I'd like you to meet Thomas," Pat says, removing his hand as Kate brings her hand out in order to shakes Thomas's.

"Hello Thomas, I'm Katherine, but my friend's call me Kate," she explains.

"Hi," Thomas repeats, "I have a friend and his name is Adrian but everyone calls him Addy. And I call my daddy, daddy, but other people call him Pat, except for Grandpa who calls him son sometimes, but mostly he calls him Pat too."

Thomas feels his father's hand over his mouth again, and then his other hand wrap around his stomach and lift him up. "Come on then, mouth. Let's hush for five minutes, and maybe go into the house with Grandpa and get a cocoa."

"That sounds like a bright idea," Ben announces, taking Thomas's hand. "We'll go on ahead and start the water boiling."

"But we make cocoa out of milk, don't we?" questions Thomas.

Kate watches as Ben shakes his head and tries to explain to his grandson that he is trying to be discreet. The last words that she manages to hear is Thomas asking what a 'screet' is. Her train of thought is interrupted as she sees Pat sit down on the driftwood next to her.

"Sorry I took so long," Pat begins, "but the school traffic gets heavy sometimes."

"I'd tell you I didn't notice, but—"

"I'm sorry," he repeats, this time with a smile. "My father can be a bit daunting at times."

"He's super sweet," she states, looking at the water. "He has a quality in him that you don't see very often. And he cares about you."

"Would you like to go inside?" Pat questions, seeing her slightly shiver. Kate shakes her head, but Pat immediately takes off his coat and puts it over her thick sweater. She can't help but to smile at the outdated gesture, but warming either way.

"Your son seems really sweet," Kate says softly, looking at the waves as they swell before they enter the beach.

"Well, he's something anyway."

Kate smiles at the statement, turning from the waves and looking at the gentle man next to her. She can't help but notice his warming smile and the glimmer of light that reflects in his eyes. He's not the typically styled man that she is used to, with the perfectly chiselled face, and the styled hair and designer clothes. He is not as witty as some others, but when she looks at him; when she sees his eyes, she cannot deny the undeniable gentleness and kind nature that he holds. It is rare, and something that she has beheld rarely in her life.

"I love my son, but he is a little too honest at times," Pat says, seeing her smile at his words.

"A quality he must get from you," she responds. "You'd miss it if it ever went away. After all, there are worse things for a child to be than honest and sweet."

Patrick looks at Kate's face and sees suddenly for the first time a side of her that he has not noticed until now. It is a realisation that the woman next to him is something more than he expected. She is something more than just a superficial beauty. He's truly unsure of what she holds, and how it is affecting him. However, whatever it may be, he is willing to seek it out for what it is.

Pat returns her look of affection with his continued smile and in turn she places her hand on his. With a brief hesitation, he turns his hand over and accepts the gesture by entwining his fingers with hers.

The two sit for a brief moment, allowing the sounds of the world around them to form a wonderful orchestra of nature that dances around them in a way that brings comfort to the two.

They are both awakened by the sudden figure appearing before them wagging his tail frantically. The golden retriever turns around as he is called back to his owner, who carries on jogging along the beach.

"Shall we go in?" Kate asks, looking up and seeing the young boy opening the front door.

"We had better, before someone decides to ask more questions about Mike and Jelloe," he states, standing with Kate. Kate giggles slightly at the statement, taking his hand once more and walking with him up to the house to greet the anxious little curiosity that awaits them at the doorway with two cups of hot cocoa.

As they reach the house, the three stand on the porch and listen as young Thomas points out that the sounds of a choir are drifting across the water, sounding almost as if they were right next to the house. Kate notices the Christmas lights beginning to come alive one house at a time, almost methodically across the bay. Even the boats that go by join in the festive season, decorating themselves in arrays of brightly coloured lights and ornaments. One even has a brightly lit Christmas tree at its bow.

Winter in the northwest brings the night as swiftly as the rains, as within a few short moments, the sky darkens and brings the true colours and effects of the Christmas lights out across the bay. The sounds of the Christmas choir continue to fill the air, and the pleasant sky brings a timid joy to those standing on the outside deck porch of the house. Even the sound of a phone ringing in the background seems to be drowned out by the spirit of Christmas.

Kate cannot help but to enjoy herself, standing next to the young Thomas who is singing pleasantly to the many Christmas songs. But the song soon ends, and the three are interrupted by Ben who opens the door and comes out onto the porch.

"Sorry to break up this picture moment, but Joseph just called to see if you're still going around tonight," Ben explains, smiling politely as he does so. "He said that there's a change of plans and it'll be at his place tonight because Darren had to pull out. Do you want me to tell him that you're a bit busy?"

"Do you have plans?" Kate asks, turning and looking at Pat. "Don't cancel anything on my account. I'd be mortified if you did."

"It's daddy's poker night," Thomas explains, before Patrick can speak. Without warning, Kate's eyes immediately light up immensely.

"I have always wanted to go to a genuine cigar smoking, beer guzzling, guy's poker game!" she exclaims. Her enthusiasm unmistakably exudes from her, as she waits for an answer to the unasked question.

"Would you like to go?" Pat asks Kate trying to contain his laughter, mercifully relieving her of the few seconds of doubt within her mind. "I could cancel, you know. They're only a bunch of adolescent delinquents."

"Absolutely not," she says stringently, shaking her head in direct opposition to the statement he made.

"Are you sure you're willing to put yourself through a night with his friends?" Ben questions, shaking his head with a laugh. "You obviously have never seen what a bunch of monkeys trapped in a toy store can do."

"They can't be any worse than a group of poor young British university students on a working holiday, picking grapes for a winery with free wine for payment."

"I'll give you that one," Ben replies, seeing Kate return her look of excitement back to Pat once more.

"Uncle Joseph is really nice, you'll like him," Thomas says confidently. "He shows me how to play poker all the time. He says that you have to have a face like an ice cube."

"I think he means that you need to have an ice-cold face," Kate explains to Thomas.

"Oh," Thomas pauses. "I had a friend once who got an ice cube stuck to his tongue and nose at the same time. When he sneezed, his boogers couldn't come out of his nose straight, so it went all over his face and down his chin."

Kate laughs at the statement, seeing the disbelief in Patrick's face. She then leans forward and kisses young Thomas on his cheek. Thomas rubs his cheek with a grimace and an equal sound of a timidly disgruntled child. Ben interrupts once more, informing them that they should all retire to the dining room. Grumbling, Thomas is the first to go, following soon after by the others.

"You have a couple of hours before Joseph is expecting you Pat," Ben states. "Are you two going to have dinner first?"

Patrick looks over at Kate, who says, "I would be honoured, of course."

"Can we have pancakes?"

"Absolutely," Ben begins, "tomorrow morning. Tonight, we're having fried chicken, baked beans and cornbread."

"Nice," Patrick says with a notable hint of sarcasm. "Do you pick that up at the drive-thru?"

"Are you kidding?!" Kate says excitedly, "I haven't had baked beans in ages. I used to eat them at my granny's in Hampshire."

"This one is definitely a keeper, Pat," Ben states, patting him on his shoulder as he turns and stirs the beans.

"I'll bear that in mind," Patrick responds, going to the end of the room and opening the refrigerator in order to pull out a bottle of wine. He motions to Kate with the bottle, who smiles and nods silently. He then walks past his father, removing two glasses from the oak cabinet as well as a corkscrew still sealed in its original redwood case. Without pause, he begins the process quickly, although somewhat clumsily, somehow managing to remove the wine opener from its box. As he does so, he looks over to Kate, who lifts the bottle and smiles, twisting the cap off and pouring the wine into the glasses.

"You're kidding me." Pat shakes his head in disbelief again, looking at the tool in his hand. "Don't you always need a corkscrew for wine?"

"They haven't used corkscrews for a while now, for most new world wines at least. Almost all the problems that occur with the wine are because of the cork, so they have eliminated the need for them. You only see them in certain wines now, and older wines."

Kate sips from her glass, still smiling at Pat, as she hands him his glass. "And generally, most people don't refrigerate red wine. Although, saying that the French like their red wines cold. But they are French.

"But it is a very nice wine."

Kate walks over and enters the living room, where she notices Thomas sitting and reading to himself. She's quite taken aback by the sight, and somehow manages to overcome the taste of the red wine, which actually isn't as bad as she first assumes. Still, it makes her giggle slightly. As she does, she notices Patrick join her out of the corner of her eye.

"He's reading the latest pirate book," Patrick explains. "He loves pirates."

"Most boys do," she replies. "But it is very impressive to see someone reading instead of playing on a tablet."

"He does that too, but we always do it together. Mostly though, he reads his thousands upon thousands of books that we have scattered everywhere."

"It's nice," Kate says softly, sipping from her wine. She looks about the room, seeing the large Christmas tree with a few presents scattered carefully around it neatly. There are large green ribbons decorating the trimming across the coving, with handmade snowflakes dangling from each few feet. Even the tree itself now contains a giant painting of Santa Claus that she managed to see as Thomas exited the car with it along with his award. She notices the pictures on the mantle of the fireplace, with all three members of the family standing together in various places and stances. There are more photos of Thomas than of any other, but only one has a picture of a young woman, standing with Patrick. It catches her eye, and she is drawn to it, enough to where she approaches the mantle place cautiously. As she reaches the fireplace, she somehow stops herself from staring and diverts her attention to Thomas's reading book. She kneels beside him as he reads softly to himself.

"What are you reading?" Kate asks softly.

"Pirates of the Boneskull Island," Thomas replies confidently, showing her the cover with the skull and crossbones on it, with a snake and various amounts of blood dripping across the picture for effect. "It's about a young boy who becomes a pirate and starts out on an adventure across the deadly seas."

"Oh," Kate exclaims, feigning surprise. "It sounds really scary."

"Not really," Thomas speaks brightly. Then as he sticks his chest out, "I'm not scared of anything."

"Wow! You must be very brave then," Kate says. "I was always scared of monsters."

"My dad says that monsters are usually more scared of us than we are of them," he explains caringly. "And my grandpa says that I don't ever need to be scared because I'll always have my angel around me to protect me."

"You are a very lucky young man."

"I know," he replies nonchalantly, opening his book once more. Kate smiles and stands once again. She notices Pat motion to her as he walks to the far side of the room, opening the door to his den.

"This is nice," Kate comments as she approaches Pat, seeing the beautiful oak flooring. Even before she has a full view of the room, she cannot help but to notice the large collection of books along the visible wall.

Pat allows Kate to enter first, explaining that the room is his hideaway from the world. He points out the collection of literature that he has, varying from fiction novels to detailed workings of ancient history. Afterwards, he offers her a seat in one of his leather side chairs, seated carefully around his covered gaming table.

"We rotate poker games from time to time, and this is where we come when it's my turn," he explains, as Kate removes the leather cover of the table to reveal a beautifully hand-crafted gaming table. "My best friend Joseph gave this to me for my birthday. He somehow managed to get it from one of the casinos he was contracting to build."

"It's very nice," Kate exclaims softly, feeling the smooth edges of the deeply coloured redwood. "He must be a very good friend."

"We have been friends since the second grade," Pat divulges. "He's," he pauses momentarily, "my spirit guide, I guess."

"A guru, huh?"

"Nothing like that," Patrick laughs.

As Kate smiles, she cannot help but to laugh along with Pat as he stands behind her drinking from his wine. She looks at him then seeing a painting of the same woman that she noticed on the mantle.

"He's just been there during some rough times, that's all."

Ben calls out for Pat, to which he excuses himself, also sighting that Kate has finished her wine and he will refresh it for her. Kate cannot help but to look at the painting, the deep blue eyes staring back at her. A beautiful woman, somehow talking to her as she traces the contours of her face with her gaze; their eyes finally meeting as if by a magic that she cannot deny.

"Her name was Lisa," she hears from behind her. Kate immediately turns in surprise, seeing the young boy standing in the doorway with a picture in his hand. "She is my mother." His words are clear and defined with such an amazing clarity and emotional detachment, that she is even more surprised. Then with the intensity and innocence that only a child can give, "I think my father misses her. And not like when you turn on the TV and see that you've missed your favourite cartoon. My friend said that his dad lets him watch cartoons for eight hours a day!"

"Wow," Kate exclaims softly with a smile.

"Do you know what lonely means? I asked my father, and he didn't really tell me, but I think that's what he is."

"Lonely is when you miss something so much that you hurt inside," she replies methodically, without thinking. Then, catching herself, "Very similar to missing your favourite episode of the Superkids."

"Oh!" he cries out. "My dad doesn't watch Superkids. When he's not reading with me, he likes to come in here and think. I see him looking at that picture like you did. He doesn't say anything, but he looks at it a lot. My mother is very pretty."

"She was very beautiful." Kate leans forward as Thomas comes up to her.

"This is for you," he says, handing her the picture.

As Kate turns the picture over, she sees a wonderfully drawn picture of a cartoon-like woman standing in front of the sea, with the sun setting behind her. It is very well drawn out, and much more advanced than what she would have expected from a boy of his age.

"It is a really nice drawing," she states. "Did you draw this yourself?"

"Yup!" he says confidently. "Dad and I sit down once a day and draw together. He told me that I need to see the picture in my head first, and carefully put it on the piece of paper so that they look the same. I'm not as good as him, though, but he says I am."

"You are very good," Kate explains, pulling the picture to her chest. "I'll keep this somewhere very close, so I can always think of you when I see it."

"Can I ask you a question?" Thomas asks cheerfully.

"What? Another question," Kate returns, smiling at the young man. "Go ahead then, if you must."

"My school is having a school Christmas concert. You are very pretty, and I think that it would be very nice if you could come so I could see you. You remind me of Ms. Baker my teacher."

"Do I?" Kate replies. "Is she really pretty then?"

Thomas nods happily in return. "I think she is very pretty."

"Well then, I will try and come to your concert so that you can see me. How could I resist such a handsome man?" Kate leans down and kisses the young man on his cheek, to which he pulls his hand up on covers it immediately afterward.

"Okay," he shrugs, turning and walking back into the other room, unsure of why she just kissed him.

Not long after Pat returns with two more glasses of wine. He sits himself next to Kate, handing her the glass as he does so. A timid silence enters the room; the sound of cooking in the background fills the space between them. Kate ponders many things, her face showing signs of unease. Then she looks up from her wine and sees the pleasant smile of the innocently and placidly unaware man seated next to her, trying to drink cold red wine that chills the glass enough to cause it to condensate.

"I don't know, cold wine seems to be kind of nice," she informs him, raising her glass to him. "I think I could get used to it, I suppose."

"To cold wine, then," he toasts, to which they touch glasses. "Sorry. I'm not much of a drinker, as you probably surmised."

Kate cannot help but to smile as she looks at the portrait of herself done by Thomas. When Patrick asks, she shows him, and places it on the table in front of them.

"He is really talented, you know," Kate comments. "You must spend a tremendous amount of time with him."

"Not as much as I could," he begins, "but I think every father says that."

"You can see he cares about you and your father. And he has one of the brightest smiles that I have ever seen when he is with you."

Pat stares at his son's portrait of Kate and he smiles as he listens to Kate's compliments. He has never been complimented on the way he raised Thomas before, besides the general compliment here and there from his teachers. He has never really thought about what others thought, or what they said about him before. And yet, somehow, he cares deeply about the few words that Kate has given him. As if they are something to be treasured.

"I'd be lost without him, I think," he says, releasing the words from his lips. "It scares me at times."

"It's a good thing, how you feel. Don't ever think otherwise, Patrick," she tells him, placing her hand across his cheek.

Pat wants to kiss her, his heart beating as if it were going to come bursting through his chest. He can feel the want and desire burning inside him so loudly that it is almost pulsing though every nerve in his body, right to his fingertips. He hasn't felt this way in such a long period. But before it controls him fully, he breathes deeply and puts his hand over hers, pulling her hand slowly down into his other hand. It is here that the two hear the call of the young man in the other room, calling aloud for them to come to dinner. Kate laughs at the piercing call, as she can only imagine what must have been asked of Thomas. Pat shakes his head in disbelief, but Kate pats him on the back as she stands up picking up her glass of wine.

The two of them enter the dining room, seeing the full display of the large array of food spread evenly throughout the table. Pat is somewhat overwhelmed at the amount of food that Ben has prepared, with Thomas's help, as his son so willingly points out over and over again.

"Is there any room left on the table for us to eat?" Pat asks, seating himself in his usual place next to the wall, only after Thomas offers her a seat next to the window, even holding the chair for her. Thomas tells her that he saw someone do it on the television once.

Ben finishes the table centre piece off by placing a large cast iron pot in the middle of the table, pulling the lid slowly upward to reveal the immense aroma of the baked beans that he had prepared all day. The scents of all the food fill the air, from the corn bread, to the deep-fried southern styled chicken.

"I hope you like good eats," Ben says, seating himself and grinning in satisfaction at the look of awe on those at the table.

"You must have been cooking since breakfast," Pat states, looking at the table.

"It looks absolutely wonderful," Kate replies. "Do you always cook?"

"Grandpa always says that grandma burned water," Thomas says happily.

"Yes, I cook most of the time," Ben explains, placing his hand over Thomas's head. "But Pat is pretty good too."

"I can make pancakes," he states, "and cold red wine."

Kate laughs, "and cold red wine."

Thomas asks if they are going to say grace, in which Kate leans over and says she that she wouldn't have it any other way. So, he takes her hand, and Kate reaches over and takes Pat's. As their fingers meet, she feels a slight warmth in the tips of her fingers. It's enough to cause her to look up and see the others bowing their heads as Thomas says grace. She cannot help but to stare at him, his eyes not waving or opening for one brief second. She is listening to every word that Thomas says, and the thanks that he is giving for everything, including pancakes.

The dinner goes quickly, much too much quickly for what Kate desires. Throughout the dinner she listens to the wonderful stories of Ben, and the innocent tales of Thomas. She learns of the wonderful love that is shared between all of them, and how lucky she is to have witnessed it. And when it ends, as they are all finished, and the young boy is put to bed, she begins to think how wonderful a life these three have. But the burning question inside her; she holds this back. Every chance, every glimpse of opportunity comes and goes, and she cannot bring herself to ask the question. Instead, she holds her tongue and enjoys the moments as they pass by, drinking from her glass of cold red wine.

Chapter 7

Poker Lights and Christmas Chips

"Tonto!"

Joseph looks up as he hears two men walking through the front door of his house. The two go immediately over to his kitchen; the sound of his stainless-steel refrigerator doors opening and closing fill the house. He stands at the sound, readying himself for the next few seconds, and lifting his hand at the expectant moment that the two walk through the kitchen into the main living room. As the two emerge into the room, the taller man with glasses tosses him a can of beer. All three of them turn as they hear the front door go again.

"That you Pat?" Joseph calls out.

"It's me Joseph," they hear in reply.

"Hey Joe," the one with glasses says, slapping his friend on his shoulder.

"Hey Prof," Joseph replies, opening his can of beer.

"Hey Tonto," the smaller olive-skinned man says. His bright green Hawaiian styled silk shirt flows about him, almost as if it were a dress.

"Hey Chicano. Guess they haven't deported you yet, huh?" Joseph says, leaning forward with a fist.

"No, they didn't," he returns, "too busy building your latest Casino."

"Oh....ouch," Joe grunts, tugging at his chest. "I guess I'm just lucky that my momma wasn't crated into the country by a—"

Joseph stops speaking as he sees Kate enter the room. All of the men turn as they see the strikingly beautiful woman enter the room, followed soon after by Pat.

"Do you boys talk to each other like this all the time?" Kate questions, seeing the usual look of awe on the men's faces.

"Actually, this is somewhat tame," Pat replies immediately afterwards.

Joseph stands at Pat's comments, the first to come up and take her hand. "The ugly one shaking your hand is Joseph."

"So, you're the one that Pat was talking about," Joseph enters. "His description of the most beautiful woman he has ever seen does not do you justice. From a guy who only reads Boating Monthly, you can imagine that we don't usually rate his statements very high."

"Thanks," Kate says, "I think."

"Such a charmer," Pat announces. "The ugly looking one in the corner with the funny accent and Spanish beer is Richie."

"Enrique Martinez Vasquel Delavegas," he rebuts, raising his beer to Kate.

"And the quiet one hiding behind the glasses is Brent, but everyone calls him Prof."

"Oh," Kate says smiling and waving at the man as he stands in reply.

Joseph offers Kate a seat at the poker table, next to the larger table with the boxes of pizza and the bowls of snacks. He offers her a beer, to which she gladly accepts, although stipulates that she would like a glass.

"So why do they call you Prof?" Kate asks Brent as he is shuffling a deck of cards.

"I'm a Professor at University of Seattle," he replies, his quiet, yet deep voice resounding over the table.

"Prof teaches experimental physics," Enrique says, patting his friend on the back. "He's one of Seattle's finest geek of geeks."

"Ah," Kate acknowledges despairingly. "I kind of like intelligent men. It shows that they're mature and dependable, and most of the time quite handsome."

"Then why are you here with Pat?" Joseph states, with the two men seated laughing at the statement. Joseph then hands Kate her light lager neatly in a chilled glass, as requested.

"Well, he just happens to be the sexiest man that I've ever seen," she replies, leaning over and kissing Pat on the cheek, to where the others can't help but to laugh at the statement.

"Are we going to talk all night, or are we going to play poker?" Pat interrupts, counting out the chips. Kate looks at his face, seeing the slight red cheeks, and the timid embarrassment that has filled him. She lifts her glass to her mouth at the sight, in order to hide her grin.

Pat continues to count out the chips for everyone, and Joseph passes out beer, as well as snacks. Within moments, Brent begins dealing cards, tossing them out as if he were professionally trained. Kate watches the others intently, trying to recall her terminology of the game as Brent calls the game out. Pat leans over and asks if she needs help, but she shakes her head and explains that she's been to Vegas to play the electronic slot machines, and it can't be that different.

Time passes quickly, as does the beer and the pizza. Kate manages to keep some sanity with the jovial men, who somehow remain polite within her presence. She realizes though, that they are mostly likely holding back quite a bit on her behalf. Still, the gesture is taken to heart, and she can see the gentleness in each of them. Brent is the quietest and most uncomfortable, but he is friendly enough to her, as best he can be. He reminds her of the one of the all too familiar quiet boys against the wall at a school dance. Joseph does nothing but speak about Pat and his past together, and all the fool hardy things that they have accomplished together. It is utterly impossible not to notice the depth that their friendship has taken, and the time that it must have taken in order to do so. Enrique is something unlike the rest; a foolhardy, childish, utterly vein, and yet somehow charming in many ways character. He seems the most open out of all of them, especially when compared to Patrick. But Enrique is most definitely obsessed with his looks, constantly regaling in his own self pronounced beauty.

"I remember one time Pat and I were coming down the side of the upper base at Baker and the snow was coming down so heavy you could barely see two feet in front of you. The powder was so fresh, and the conditions were somewhat icy from the day before, which made skiing absolutely fantastic. We both were coming down really fast, following one another. Next thing I know, he's nowhere in sight, and I'm going too fast to see where he went. Thinking he took off left to avoid a tree, I stopped and couldn't see anything, so I took off back to the main lodge where we said we were going to meet. About a half hour later here Pat comes in on one ski, following this sixteen-year-old girl who just about has him laid out over his shoulder. It turns out that the tree I thought he went around, he didn't."

"What young Joseph is forgetting to mention, is the fact that the young girl was trying to snap photos of her friend while snowboarding, and ploughed headlong into me in the process. Thus, causing one of my skis to fly off into the great abyss.

"I take great console in the result of her losing her precious phone."

Kate laughs at the story, as do the others, picturing Pat hobbling into the ski lodge on the shoulder of a young girl. Afterwards, Kate stands from the table, excusing herself in order to 'free herself of tonight's liquid festivity'. Pat stands as well, heading into the kitchen as the three continue to play another hand.

Pat reaches into the fridge and pulls out a bottle of clear spring water, along with a glass from the side, finally finishing the drink off with some ice out of the automatic ice maker built into the front of his freezer. Out of the corner of his eye, he sees Joseph coming into the kitchen. He doesn't say anything but comes and leans against the counter next to him. Patrick without hesitation takes a drink from his glass and joins him.

"Thomas won an award for a painting of Santa Claus today."

Joseph responds with a silent nod of the head, lifting his bottle of beer and taking a drink from it. The two remain silent momentarily, just staring through the open doorway into the living room where the poker table lays.

"I don't know, you know," Pat enters, breaking the silent discussion the two had been carrying with one another.

"The question isn't whether or not you know, brother, but whether or not you want to know."

"I knew you'd say that." Pat chuckles slightly at the statement, sipping from his water again. "Some spirit guide you are."

"I'm not—"

"Oh, shut up, Joe. If you're not going to be helpful—"

Joseph smiles and puts his hand on Pat's shoulder before going out of the kitchen once more. Just before he fully leaves the room, though, he states, "I like her. She's definitely full of spirit, and other things."

Pat just manages to shake his head as he sees Kate walk through the doorway. She looks back into the room, glancing at the three men sitting and playing another hand without them. Kate walks straight up to where Pat is still leaning, and joins him where Joseph once was. She asks him what he's drinking, to which he responds by shaking his empty bottle of water, asking if she would like the same. With but a slight gesture of consent, Pat stands and goes over to the refrigerator and pulls out a bottle of water.

"Do you want to take off?" he asks her, holding the door.

"What about your friends?"

"They'll be at this all night," he says, "so I wouldn't worry about them."

The door shuts slowly, revealing Pat and a pleasant looking smile on Kate's face as she returns his gaze. "Actually, I have someplace I'd love to take you."

"Really?" he starts, slightly accenting the word. "Now I'm intrigued."

"We'll see."

Kate stands and walks over to Pat, taking the unopened bottle from his hand as she walks out into the living room. Pat quickly finishes his glass of water and follows her out.

"Hey guys, we're going to take off a little early," he explains to his friends as he comes up to the side of Kate.

"Come on, man, I haven't had a chance to win back everything that she's taken from me," Enrique says, standing and reaching forward with his hand. "It's been a pleasure, though.

"Asegúrate de cuidar a mi amigo," he finishes in very subtle Spanish.

"Me aseguraré de ser amable," she returns with a wink.

"An absolute delight to have met you," Brent says politely, standing as well and shaking her hand. "I hope we get to see more of you soon. Well, not more of *you*, but more of you. I mean, more of the physical you. Not what I really mean is—"

"I understand," Kate interrupts, seeing the poor man's face go completely red.

"Don't mind our intellectual friend," Joseph begins. "Alcohol makes the poor man slightly stupid."

"I'm not that inebriated," Brent rebukes.

"It's been a pleasure, and all of you have been absolutely wonderful to be with," she says, still smiling gleefully at their childish angst with one another.

"I'll catch you guys later," Pat says, motioning Kate with his hand on the small of her back toward the front of the house once again.

"You two be good now," Enrique finishes, as they depart into the kitchen and out through the front room.

The sun has set since they've first arrived, and air has turned into the freezing chill of winter once again. Pat doesn't say much as the two go out the front door of Joseph's house. And yet, even though she is cold, Kate still stops and pauses long enough for Pat to join her side as she looks out over the beautiful lake behind Joseph's house.

In all her visits to all the places she has been, she has never been on tribal land before. Even though there are houses all around them, and the roads don't differ from any other, or the buildings for that matter, she cannot help but to think that she is privileged at being allowed to see into the private part of this world. As she takes Patrick's hand to walk to the car, she continues her thoughts silently, thinking how lucky he must have been to have all of this part of his life from childhood.

"I like your friends," Kate announces happily.

"I think they like you too," he replies, unlocking the car.

"Can I drive?" Kate queries suddenly, stopping before the driver's side.

Pat squints slightly, but without another thought he hands her the keys. Excitedly she jumps into the driver's seat and he walks slowly around to the passenger's side and enters. He has to explain to her how to adjust the seat positions, but she soon figures it out easily enough. Within seconds the seat warmers begin to do their duty and warm the two cold wintry souls.

"So where are we going?" Patrick queries.

"Can't tell, it's a surprise," she explains, tapping her phone with her finger and making a call. "Hi Phillip, is it alright if I stop by tonight? Oh, great. Okay," she pauses, "About twenty minutes or so, I'm guessing. Okay. Yes. He will? Thanks Phillip. You're a sweetheart, and I owe you a kiss. Bye now, and I'll see you Saturday. You too."

Kate taps her phone again and puts it back into the inner pocket of her long cashmere overcoat. Within mere minutes they are almost on the interstate again, headed south towards Seattle. As time passes, and the journey continues, Patrick persists in enquiring over and over again, like a child, but Kate does not pander and remains silent except for moments of weakness where she cannot help but to laugh.

"Can I ask you a question?" Kate finally starts.

"You just did," he states, to which he receives a grimace in reply. "Sorry, just a habit my father taught me."

"What is your Christmas wish?"

Pat is somewhat taken aback by the question, unsure of what to say or how to act. Then, "I don't know. I haven't really thought about it much."

"But I bet you know exactly what Thomas wants," she responds quickly.

"Of course," he says, still unsure at the path of the conversation.

"And you never think to yourself, *It sure would be nice to have,* I don't know, *whatever for Christmas?* Everybody thinks about themselves sometime. Surely you must have an idea of what you'd like for Christmas."

"Not really," he says shaking his head.

"Don't you ever think, *if I only had one wish?*"

Pat notices that they have exited into Edmonds, just before North Seattle as Kate asks her question. He raises an eyebrow, still reeling inside over the question, as well as the destination. Kate silently pushes the question, nudging him every now and then, but remaining silent. As she looks over at him, she sees the honest look of confusion in his eyes, unsure at the answer to her question. She returns her gaze back to the road, pulling into the large empty car park.

"You've brought me to a mall," he states.

"Never state the obvious," she informs him gently. "Firstly, it is most certainly never the whole answer, and secondly, it only shows that you think narrow-mindedly."

"Oh," he replies. "But this is a mall, isn't it?"

"Noooo," she whines, shaking her head as she parks out in front of the main entrance. "It's only a mall during the day."

"And what is it now then?"

Kate turns the engine off and turns herself fully to Pat, and hands him the keys, a grin crossing her face reminding him of a child in a toy factory at Christmas time. She turns quickly and jumps out of the car before he can open his door. As he manages to get one foot out, she grabs his arm and pulls him to his feet eagerly. Kate doesn't hesitate but leads him straight to the entrance, where there is a security guard waiting for them. He doesn't say anything, but waves to Kate as they approach.

"Hello Paul," Kate says as they walk through the doorway.

"Do you see the money?" she questions, pointing out the tremendous number of pennies scattered around the base of the fountain, where the water runs down the stones spread evenly throughout.

"Yes," he replies with a nod, "they go to charity if I'm not mistaken."

"Every penny," she begins, "every coin, is someone's wish; a dream that someone placed in faith to the universe."

"Okay."

"I guess what I'm trying to say is that with all the problems that we have, all the over the world, we still somehow manage to find a little faith within us," she explains, leaning back on both her hands towards the water. "All the confusion, the pain, the worry; everything melts away with the water. I don't think the wish means as much as the faith that we put in it. Much like a child's Christmas list to Santa Claus, it isn't so much what's in the list, as much as the list itself."

Kate looks up at the skylights, the Christmas decorations now fully lit for the two of them. The theme in the mall is blue and silver; the ceiling filled with enormous blue and silver balls, with illustriously beautiful lights that sweep throughout the mall as if they were stars. Although Paul had turned some of the electrical features of the building on, for the most part everything remains silent and unlit, only adding to the beauty of the Christmas decorations.

"I love Christmas," Kate announces, still looking at the lights.

"Not many people I know dislike it," Pat returns.

"That only means that you have kind, loving friends," she tells him looking down from the ceiling. "For me, it's the memories that I share with those around me. I love the way my father still sets out a Christmas calendar just for me, with little chocolates."

"My grandmother and I used to bake all the Christmas cakes, and chocolates," Pat says, smiling as he recalls the memory. "Now, Dad and I try and spend as a much time with Thomas doing the same things that my grandmother and I used to do."

"Isn't it funny how we try and hold on to the memories that mean the most to us, by trying to relive them through others, knowing that they will never truly be the same?"

"Maybe," he replies, "or maybe we're just trying to make new memories to keep inside for later when it's not so nice outside."

Kate strokes his cheek, and smiles. She can sense that he is changing, and she can see his confidence with her increasing with every word spoken. She knows that she needs to be careful, and she forces herself to avoid the things that she wishes to ask. She can sense that he wishes to hear the words she wishes to tell him, the questions that he wishes her to ask. But Kate remains silent, and instead removes her hand from his face and looks to the ceiling once more.

"I enjoyed tonight," she says to him, "and your friends were adorable."

"I'm just glad they didn't get you to try the pizza dipped in hot sauce and beer."

Kate cringes at the thought, but doesn't look away from the lights. "I hope we can do it again."

"I'd like that," he reveals to her.

The two remain silent momentarily, both staring at the array of Christmas flowing around them. The sound of the water falling into the pool as it flows from the fountain is the only sound that they can hear between them.

"How is it that you managed to get unrestricted access to a mall whenever you want?" Patrick suddenly thinks aloud, looking over at Kate who smiles in return. "Not many people I know can just pick up their phone and make someone open the mall up just for them."

"I didn't, and don't," she says to him. "I just know a few people. That's all."

"Some people," he replies to her. "Know anybody at the football stadium?"

"Yes," she speaks without hesitation.

"Should I start being intimidated now?" Pat begins to smile and shake his head, seeing Kate smiling wryly at his question. She turns and looks at him adoringly, crossing her feet as she seats herself more comfortably in order to face him fully.

"Well if you do, just tell me and I'll make sure that I show you my Ferrari parked in the garage," she replies, "or my 200-foot yacht parked in Elliot Bay."

"Okay," Pat responds. "Point taken."

"Come on, then," Kate announces as she stands and pulls Pat to his feet. "Let's go find a drink somewhere."

"Sounds good."

As the two walk out toward the entrance once again, Kate turns to Pat and says, "I do have a friend who has a yacht, you know."

"For goodness sake," he laughs.

"It could be worse, Pat," she tells him.

"How's that?"

"Maybe I'll tell you one day," Kate says, waving to Paul as they approach the door.

Chapter 8

Songs of Christmas

Winter mornings in the Northwest are relatively cold and wet or a dolorous melody of drizzle and sleet mixed together resulting in the former. This morning is nothing if not reliable in the pattern of history, at least in the mind of young Thomas James, as he leaves his father's car heading for his usual spot just underneath the tree where he somehow remains dry until the bell rings calling him in once again. Addy and he have been at this tree for nearly two years now, since the older children decided that the new basketball court was the best place to stand around before school.

Thomas is carrying his backpack over his shoulder, as all the older kids do, when Addy comes up next to him. Addy's always a pleasant sight, as he is reliably the one person in the entire world that you can count on to look the silliest out of everyone, and blissfully unaware of the fact. Today his bright green sweatshirt with its picture of the Christmas grump character is only contrasted with the bright red winter coat that has a picture of a reindeer across its back. This is rounded off with his pleasant Christmas themed winter hat and dark blue snow gloves.

Addy and Thomas are joined by several other children, all of which are shivering and waiting patiently for the bell. Thomas, noticing the array of Christmas dress around him, cannot help but to be somewhat envious that he didn't choose something more spirited and festive.

"What have you got for lunch today?" Addy questions Thomas, through the chattering of his teeth.

"PBJ, and hot spaghetti," Thomas states, wiping his face dry with his coat sleeve. "You?"

"Usual," Addy replies, "wanna trade?"

"Okay," Thomas agrees. Andrew's grandmother is a British born lady that spent all of her life in Hong Kong until it was relinquished to China. As with most of the European descendants who returned to their families around the world, so Andrew's grandmother came to live with her daughter Allison and her grandson Andrew. Since his father the columnist is away travelling or locked away writing, Allison welcomed her mother who assisted in the day to day care of Andrew and the new baby girl Maddie. The end result of all of this, of course is the welcomed fact that Thomas would get to indulge in Addy's sweet and sour meatballs.

"I went to go see Santa Claus last night at the mall," the two hear from their side. It's a familiar voice who comes to join them, squeezing in between them as per usual. Terri is a young fawn haired girl that moved to the area earlier this year, but had taken it upon herself to befriend Thomas and Andrew the very same day.

"He's coming to the school for the concert," Addy reveals. Suddenly the three are smiling at one another, and looking pleasantly warmer.

"Did he ever write you back?" Terri asks.

"Not yet, but I know he's busy," Thomas explains.

"Maybe you should just e-mail him," Addy states.

"Or just message him," Terri says, pulling out her phone. "Letters are so yesterday; my mother always tells me. Grandma says they used to have to do it all the time before I was born."

"Santa's really old though, and I bet he doesn't even have a cell phone," Thomas announces, handing back Terri's phone. "Besides, I'm sure he'll get it."

"Barry, the fifth grader said that he's not real," Addy says, suddenly feeling a piercing look from everyone standing under Old Dawson. "Well he did."

"What does he know?" Terri says to everyone, punching Addy in his arm. "He's just a bully anyway. I saw him take Melissa's chocolate pudding yesterday."

The sound of rain clearly overtakes all the others, causing a united squeal from all the children as even the shelter of the tree cannot help any longer. With one great rush, a migration is undertaken into the playground as the monsoon of water falls upon them almost drowning out the sound of the bell.

As they enter the classroom, each of the children takes their seat after carefully removing their drenched outerwear as best they can. The room seems somewhat steamy and filled with lovely dense warm air that hangs on everything it touches. The fresh smell of the teacher's coffee is waving across the noses of the children, to remind them that her presence is near, even though she is not there in the room. The class board which is normally filled with things that explain the day is empty, and instead filled with pictures of Santa Claus and other Christmas related items. The windows that are normally bare and usually reveal a view of the playground outside are instead covered with the paper snowflakes that the children have been making over the last few days.

Thomas loves coming to school, although his father assures him that will fade with time and that his father should really cherish the statement. For Thomas, though, the love of coming to school is stemmed from good memories of friendship and joy. From the earliest he can remember he has always enjoyed school. He cannot seem to recall the time that his father reminds him of, when he was scared and afraid of leaving home. Thomas only recalls the times that he and Addy had together, and the inseparable bond that they share even to this day. In fact, they often share these moments of thoughts and recollections together while pondering the mysteries of their vast universe while sitting faithfully underneath Old Dawson the tree. So long ago, they say to one another.

For Thomas the best times of school are always Christmas time. Without a second thought, he would choose this time of year over any other, and have itself repeated every day until the end of time. He loves the scent of the Christmas cookies that roll into the classroom from the kitchen cafeteria, and the freshly made Christmas cake that Mrs. Salmon always brings in for them. (Mrs. Salmon is of course the aid of the teacher Ms. Baker, who is the most beautiful person that Thomas has ever seen. Although, his father's new friend is very close as well.)

Yes, Christmas if given, would be the most perfect season for any of the children around Thomas. He has never known one person in his entire life of eight years that did not like Christmas, except for that grumpy cartoon.

Thomas's thoughts are interrupted as Mrs. Salmon comes in, carrying her wonderful cake in her arms. The children remain silent and watch her as she pleasantly greets them with a hello.

"Good morning, Mrs. Salmon," they speak in unison.

"Mrs. Salmon's probably the single most nicest person in the whole universe," Thomas thinks to himself in his own wonderful descriptive way. She is the oldest lady that he knows, although she does not have grey hair, so she could not be a grandmother. She often speaks of her grandchildren, but none of the children really believe her. They do love her stories, and the funny little ways that she makes each and every one of them smile.

As the children watch Mrs. Salmon unravel her Christmas goodies, the door to the classroom opens slightly, with the familiar young hand of their teacher holding it slightly closed as she talks to an unknown figure on the other side. Slowly the door opens, and Thomas watches Ms. Baker walk across the front of the class, his adoring eyes glued to her with a beloved innocence. Some of the other children are talking in the background, and others are still watching Mrs. Salmon as she begins to carefully unpack the cake that she had made earlier that morning. Then, without notice, the children hear two taps on the desk, and all goes silent.

Ms. Baker had to install the tapping system after one young boy, Marcus Darl, wouldn't stop talking and shouting one morning. Thomas remembers that he was always a bit loud and not very nice in general. He was the type of person that most of the children didn't like because he was a bit of a bully. When he argued that one fateful day with Ms. Baker, the principal came in and took him away, and the children have yet to have seen him since. So now when Ms. Baker taps her desk twice, all the children listen attentively.

"Good morning, class," she begins, the class remaining silent. They used to say good morning to her, but she thought it a bit too childish, so she requested that they not say it to her. "I have a surprise visitor for us today, who has volunteered to come and explain about where some of the Christmas songs we are going to sing originate from."

Mrs. Salmon comes over as she sees Ms. Baker motion to her politely. The two whisper between themselves and a look of glee somehow escapes Mrs. Salmon's face. She then carefully walks over and opens the door to the room once again and waves in the figure that has remained hidden behind it for the duration of the introduction.

"You should all know this person, and I want you to remain quiet as he speaks, so that he can hear you when he asks questions later. He's a bit of an older gentleman, so be nice and very polite." Ms. Baker looks across the room to see the reaction of the children. She enjoys the look of confusion and worry that spreads across their faces. Then as the person emerges from the shadows of the hall, their faces fill with utter delight and incredible joy as they try and contain their excitement.

"Children, may I introduce, Mr. Claus," Ms Baker says, to which all the children burst out into cheers. Even Ms. Baker can't help but smile at their reactions, as the elderly gentleman in his dark red and white attire enters the room. The light glitters across his carefully sown buttons of gold that are neatly folded down his jacket line. His blue white beard glistens as he moves, almost as if it were freshly fallen snow. All stare at the blue of his eyes; eyes that could match the innocence and purity of a new-born child. Even the sound of his steps reflect a tranquillity and calm across the floor, almost as if he was not touching the ground upon which he walked with his large black leather boots, carefully laced and belted with a golden buckle.

Thomas and the others cannot help to fall silent as the man before them enters the centre of the room and seats himself just slightly upon the edge of Ms. Baker's desk. Ms. Baker walks over and joins Mrs. Salmon near the doorway.

"He is amazing, really," Mrs. Salmon states in a whisper. "But what happened to George Eccleson, the local composer that was supposed to be coming in?"

"I don't know," whispers Ms. Baker. "All I know is that George didn't turn up, and this guy said that George sent him in his place."

"Hello children," Santa begins, to which all his audience listens. Santa Claus begins his tale of German soldiers during a great world war dug deeply in freshly made trenches. He then tells of how during this great war, the British laid not too far away from them in the same types of trenches. The children gasp as he explains how bombs and destruction occur all around them even though it is the time of Christmas.

Santa looks outward and sees the dismay as he explains the sadness and emptiness of war, and yet, somehow, for whatever reason, the two sides who were both taught nothing else but to hate, kill, and destroy one another, managed to put aside their differences for one brief moment to come together and take part in the spirit of Christmas. He explains how the men sang songs and shared gifts with one another, and how for that short time, they were just brothers in a single spirit with one another. He tells the story with vigour and an honesty that only children can appreciate. And when he finishes, the children truly look at him with awe and wonder.

"So you see, even the darkest times of the world are filled with some light, if we choose to find it. The power of the Christmas spirit, the kindness inside of men, and the ability to lay aside your own desires is what makes men and women, and little children all around the world better people."

From the back a little girl raises her hand and asks, "When is your birthday?"

The room fills with his powerful laughter that magically fills everyone that it passes through, erupting like a cannon. The laugh is one that echoes through one's soul, making even the usually coldest people smile.

"What a very smart question," he states, nodding his head. "It reminds me of another story."

And so, the next passing moments went, with the large finely dressed man of Christmas telling the children different stories of many of the songs that they are going to sing at their concert. Every story the children gasp and let loose their emotions of joy and ecstasy. He makes them laugh over and over again, filling each of their minds with tales of Kings and Dukes, and tiny reindeer that are trying to grow and find their place in the world. And when he is finally finished, the children are completely appeased. Just as he stands to leave and all the children sigh, he smiles and gives them one more laugh, which is instantly followed by the lunch bell.

Thomas watches as the children rush out, each of them shaking Santa's hand as they leave for the playground. For some reason, he can't seem to stand, and he's somewhat at odds with himself. But before he knows it Addy and the others are gone, leaving only Santa and he remaining in the room.

"Do you have a question for me, young Thomas?" Santa asks coming over to his side.

"You know who I am?" responds Thomas in awe and wonder.

"Yes," Santa returns. He sits himself on one of the children's desk next to Thomas and folds his hands across his lap. "You look as if something is bothering you."

"Not really," Thomas thinks. "Should there be?"

The familiar laugh catches the youth off guard.

"No. But I want you to know that I am very grateful that you sent me that letter. As soon as I have an answer, I will let you know. Sometimes these things are more difficult than they seem. I will try my best though. I promise you that, Thomas.

"I apologise that I cannot stay and talk with you more. I know you are a very talkative young man who loves good conversation, and who is doing very well in his English classes. So keep that up."

Santa stands and walks out the door without Thomas able to say a single word. His state of wonderment finally passes enough for him to intake all that has been said, and he seems at ease. But then he notices suddenly that he has missed some of his precious lunchtime, where the sun has overtaken the rain, which makes it even more precious than just precious.

Chapter 9

First Love

The sound of the waves rolling across the rocky beach seems somehow different today, then yesterday. Their sound seems to fade away and leave only a picture, and a sad love song that sounds its melody in his heart over and over again. Pat hasn't been this far up the beach before, and it looks completely different than his little patch of ocean. There are no runners here, or people in general for that matter. Even the birds stay only on the ocean top, quietly laying there as the waves roll underneath them. They do not move, or make any sounds, but listen to the ocean as they float upon its waters. The sun is in its winter low off to his side, but his dark midnight blue sunglasses hide its light from his eyes. It could be night or day to him, though. It could be any day, of any month, of any year. It wouldn't matter, because to him, there is only day; the same day that repeats itself over and over in his heart, each and every day. For years he has drowned it out and stopped listening to it or anything else.

In his mind he thought he was healing, but there is no such thing. Time may glaze over the truth; it may hide the fact that it hurts so deep that he can't breathe, but the fact remains that it is there. It will never leave. Things like this never fade away completely, really. The heart goes cold, and it tries to build walls, and shields itself from the outside world. Like anything in life, if you cannot face something, you turn away from it. It is only the foolhardy or the brave, or perhaps a combination of both that face it head on, in the face of danger to themselves and others.

What alternatives does he have, though? He has the most beautiful son that the world has ever produced, and although he is with him daily, and he sees him every day, he is a constant reminder of what was taken from him.

Patrick has done his best, though, and raised Thomas as best he could, in the only way he knows how. He is a fine, kind-hearted innocent young child, which any man on earth would be proud to have as his own. And he does not hesitate to tell him this. He does love his son, with every breath that is left inside him.

The sound of a wave crashing against the rocks in the distance awakens him. He looks over to the cliff side and watches for a moment as the waves explode with such ferocity into the rock beds. The anger of the ocean is peaceful, soothing the hatred that has built up over the years inside him. And he does hate. Oh, does he hate. Life itself would be stripped away from every living creature if he was given the chance. Why should they have a chance to live, whe—

When. He cannot bring himself to even finish the word, let alone the sentence. And so, he adds another brick to an already impenetrable wall. He is proud of his wall. There are only so few people that know of it or have seen it. Joseph always laughs when he talks about the walls he has built, saying that he should be in construction. Pat needs this wall, though. At first, it was just something to block out the pain, but over time is has helped him stand and hold himself together. If not for the wall, he would have died a thousand times over by now. And there are still the times that he feels as if he were.

The ocean draws his attention once more, as a bald eagle flies across his head and swoops down not too far from where he is. He sees another eagle in the distance, and he wonders if it is his mate. Within seconds the two seem to be together and fly off into the tree line behind him. He remembers a nature program that told him that eagles are one of the few types of birds that mate for life. Well, there are crows as well, he suddenly remembers. Questions begin to fill his head, and he begins to wonder why animals are the only creatures that can stay together without fear or remorse.

The song returns to his mind once more, and he struggles so hard to hold back the tears. It isn't fair, he thinks to himself finally, bringing his hand slowly to his chin for strength. He knows he must be cringing like a baby, but somehow it doesn't really matter. Life, destiny, whatever you want to call it; it had no right because it was his. She was his.

"YOU HAD NO RIGHT!" he shouts, standing from his log and clenching his fists as hard as he can. Every muscle in his body is aching from the strain that he is putting on them. Every heartbeat is pounding harder and harder with an anger that a thousand men in battle couldn't hold. His strength knows no bounds, and he can crush the world in one single stroke.

And then he breathes once again. His body falls lifeless downward to his knees, and lands on the little bit of sand that lay underneath him.

"You were my destiny," he whispers, his eyes filled with tears that he believes he is unable to shed. Instead, he finds solace in the rain that begins to fall. "You were mine...."

"I was never yours," he hears in his mind. "I was part of you, but I was never yours."

"You were—" he stops, then, "you are what makes me whole."

"And I always will, Patrick. But you have to live without me," the voice says.

He feels her soft hands around him. He can see her face staring at him with the smile that she gave him a thousand times before. He sees eternity in her eyes, and his breath stops.

"God, you are so beautiful," he whispers to her. "I didn't tell you that enough."

"I didn't matter," she replies.

"It does," he insists. "You were my first love. You were the woman that I took on my first date. You were the first person that I held hands with on the beach. You were the first person that I flew across the world with. You were the first person I brought home to see my parents, however strange they may have been. You were the first woman that I let into my life, the very first woman who I introduced to my friends. You were the first person that forgave me for not being perfect. You actually liked my stupid imperfections."

"I love them," the voice says.

"I didn't know what love really was before you. You were my fantasy; my dream. I looked into your eyes for the first time and I knew that you were going to be the one that I spent the rest of my life with. I knew that you would be the woman that would make life worth living."

"Only you can do that," returns the voice.

"No. You did. You were the reason I woke in the morning. You were the reason why life meant anything to me. I may have lost sight of that, but I know it now. I lived so that I could feel you with me, to feel you in my arms, to feel your lips against mine."

"That isn't what life is about," he hears her tell him softly.

"It may not be, but it was for me. I knew that from the first time you touched my hand. You were going down some steps, and I was going up, and our fingers touched. I knew it that instant. From that minute forward, I was going to be everything you wanted me to be. I remember walking miles to the store early in the day so that I could bring home a bunch of flowers for you. I remember that old beat up car that you used to drive, and how much I loved fixing it because it made you think I was so manly. I could fix anything in the world as long as you wanted me to. You gave me the strength to do the impossible."

"The strength was always there. I just helped you see it," she tells him.

"No. My strength came from you. My life came from loving you. Before you there was nothing, only childish dreams. With you, life began and ended. I got my first grown-up job because of you. I wanted to give you something that you could feel safe in. I wanted to give you a real car, and a house. You and I had to rent at first, but it was our first real house. I wanted so badly to make everything perfect. I probably made more mistakes doing that, then just letting things happen."

"It was a bit cramped, but we were together," she tells him.

"I miss you so much, you can't believe it," he announces suddenly, the pain filling him once again. "You were the first person that I ever held in my heart completely. I never told you how much you meant to me. I never had a chance to tell you that I was sorry for acting like such an ass. I didn't mean to block you out. I didn't mean to hold you away. I just wanted to be the man that you wanted me to be. I wanted to give you everything you wanted and deserved. I wanted to give you the perfect life, with the big house, the big cars, and the money to buy whatever you wanted."

"You know those things don't really matter," returns the voice.

"I know. I know, but everyone wants to believe they're special. I know you told me, but I guess I was too stubborn to hear it. All I could hear was the bills, the bank, and the world; all of which crushed me with every passing day. I ignored what was important, and I turned away from the people who loved me the most," he says softly.

"I knew you still loved me," the voice says with a tender compassion.

"I should have told you more often. I should have held you in my arms each and every day and told you how much you fill me with strength. I should have been more than just a man in your life. I should have been the husband you deserved. I should have spent every waking moment with you, instead of—"

"You cannot change the past, Patrick," he hears, feeling her soft hand stroking his head.

"No. But I should have told you all of this when I could," he sighs. "You were the last woman that I ever wanted to kiss. I remember leaning over the table nervously and touching my lips against yours. You were eating octopus."

"Calamari," the voice corrects.

"Calamari, and not very good calamari either. Food was always so important to me before. I used it as a way of masking myself from you, and I suppose trying to connect with you in a way that was easy for me. I thought I was doing something special with you, but it turns out it was just another place for me to hide."

"You're still hiding," she informs him.

"I know. But what choice do I have? Without you this world seems so insignificant and empty. Everything I see, everyone I meet; it all just fills me with memories of you. I need you. You were supposed to be the last woman I ever held, the last woman that I ever loved."

Silence falls upon him as he feels the rain cover his face, and he is forced to open his eyes. The sky is dark and filled with clouds as far as the eyes can see. For a moment, he doesn't move, but instead kneels there engulfing himself in a memory that he has not felt in years. He lifts his hand and touches his chest, his heart hurting him so much that he can't swallow or speak. His mouth feels dry and empty, even though the rain continues to pour over him. Eventually, he manages to gather himself enough to push himself into a seated position.

"You were my first; my only love."

His tears are hidden by the rain, as he stands once again. His chest still feels as if it were just ripped open by something. He remembers the last time that it did this, so many years ago. He remembers the last time he saw her. He remembers touching her hand, and holding her so close that he believed that she was with him. He remembers when he kissed her for the last time, tears so dearly wishing they could fall but not being able to because he wanted to be strong for his son and family; for her. She was so cold. She wasn't there with him any longer, but still he held her. The woman that he had promised his soul to was no longer there. The soul that was entwined with his had been torn away by some force that he could not understand. He refused with all his heart to let her go. He rejected the idea, and still does to this moment. But his heart does not lie to him, and he knows it. She is still here with him, beside him, inside his soul, but he cannot touch her any longer. She is still his strength. She still speaks with him, although he has not listened to her for so long. She has been trying to talk with him, and he has refused to listen. But today she was there with him again. If but for one fleeting dream, she was there.

Patrick takes a deep breath, not bothering to wipe his face because of the rain. The song that haunted him earlier is gone from his head again, and he is thinking about Thomas once more, and how he forgot his umbrella. He remembers that he was asked to have pasta and steak ready for the young man for dinner. And with that thought he turns and begins the long journey back to the house.

It takes him nearly an hour to reach his home, of which the rain did not stop once. After a while, he forgot that it was even raining, because his clothes were so wet that he could no longer tell the difference. As he approaches the drive he can see his father pull up in the pickup. He can see him laughing even before the engine stops, and he gets out of his truck.

"What on God's green earth are you doing out here? You look wetter than a soaked tea bag," he somehow manages to say between the laughter. Ben doesn't stop to help, though, but reaches in and pull out two bags of groceries. "Well come on then. Let's get you dried off before the neighbours think we're putting in some sort of new age Zen water feature or something."

Pat refuses to rise to the bait and ignores the remark as he follows his father in. By the time he crossed the threshold of the doorway he can hear that Ben's already put the coffee on and has gone off to grab some towels. When he emerges from the bathroom he tosses two towels to Pat and says not to get the floor wet.

"Wouldn't want nice looking guests getting the idea that we are pigs or something," Ben states, returning to the kitchen.

"You didn't even tell me whether or not you like my haircut," Patrick retorts snidely.

"I didn't realise that you had any hair left to cut?" Pat hears in the background. And with those words his throws the towel down and begins to undress. Once he is completely bare, he ties the second towel around his waist and walks over to the kitchen which Ben is already heading out from with two cups of coffee.

"I hope you're not going to leave those lying on the floor over there," Ben announces. "I just mopped this entire house yesterday."

"Oh shut up you old woman," he tells his father, heading up the stairs to fetch some more clothes. "You're beginning to sound like mom."

"Well, it could be worse," Ben starts, "I could be your mother-in-law."

The comment is followed by a towel which lands across Ben's face. He laughs as he pulls it off, walking over to the couch and seating himself comfortably before throwing the towel on the pile of wet clothes by the door. He hears in the background the start of a shower, and it makes him laugh. He thinks how funny it is to just get absolutely soaking wet in the rain, and then to take a shower. "Obviously didn't get enough of the water," he whispers to himself.

A knock comes at the door which surprises him, and he stands a bit hesitantly. There is a tiny little car in the drive that he doesn't recognise and he isn't expecting anybody. In any case, he pushes aside the soaked pile of clothes and opens the door. Huddled under the porch way, somewhat soaked herself from just the walk from the car to the door, is Kate.

"Gosh girl, you're soaked," Ben states, motioning for her to come in. "I've just boiled the kettle, and we've got fresh coffee."

"Thank you," she replies softly, her teeth chattering. She's wearing a large winter sweater that hides almost all of her neck and the bottom of her chin.

"You're freezing," Ben announces, guiding her to the sofa.

"I guess I'm just not used to these Northwest winters, after all" she replies seating herself. Ben immediately fetches a cup for her and stops himself before pouring coffee, then makes her a tea instead.

"Here you go," Ben says coming before her and handing the tea to her by the brim. She takes it carefully and wraps her fingers around it for warmth.

"I don't know how it can be so cold outside, and still rain?" Kate says, smiling. "There's just no other place in the world like here."

"That is true," Ben laughs. "My father used to say to me that here in Washington you could wake up to snow, then have rain by lunch, hail in the afternoon, and just before bed have the most beautiful sunset in the world staring at you."

"Growing up in England, I remember the winters having so much snow that you could walk across the tops of the hedges to school. I don't think they get much snow anymore. At least not like that."

"It must have been wonderful growing up there," Ben says politely.

"It was. There is truly no other place on earth like it. Living in a small village, everyone knows each other, and you watch people grow up around you and stay around you. I was raised in the country, but I remember walking for hours through apple orchards and strawberry fields. My best friend and I used to pick them in the summer, and make ourselves sick eating them so much," Kate says fondly. "But it's all changing now, like everywhere in the world. I suppose it's like anything, people grow up, and new people come. Families spread further and further apart, and life goes on."

"That is true," Ben acknowledges. "But no matter how much it changes, or what people do, it is still home."

"Yes," Kate says with a surprise, looking at Ben with a fond smile. "It will always be a part of me, wherever I am. Just like Montana, I suppose."

"You were a lucky child," Ben tells Kate.

"I suppose, but I never really thought about it like that. I just know that my parents loved me. Everything else, well it just fell into place."

The two are interrupted by the sound of the door opening and shutting upstairs. Ben calls out to Pat, explaining that he has a visitor. Silence ensues for a moment, then the sound of footsteps coming across the floor and then down the stairway.

Kate looks carefully as she sees Pat stop just shy of the middle of the steps. It's enough to catch his entire body, covered only by a towel that is around his waist. She can see the look of disbelief on his face, but waves to him nevertheless, just to make him feel a bit more uncomfortable. Her eyes engulf his body, as she cannot help but to let her eyes stray. He is in rather good shape, considering how much he must work. She doesn't know why men have such nice legs all the time, but they do. It makes her cross to think how easy it is for them to look so good, when she puts all that effort into hers just to keep them like they are. But he does have a nice chest, and his round little tummy that he is hiding makes her laugh. She can see he is holding it in on her behalf.

"Hi," he says, extremely startled by the entire situation.

"Hello," Kate replies with that tender smile. "I didn't mean to interrupt your shower."

"No!" he exclaims, suddenly self-aware of the fact that he is only covered by a thin towel. His entire body goes red, and he takes two steps back in order to try and hide more of it. "You didn't. I mean you weren't. Or aren't. Um...let me just go and put something on and I'll be right back down."

As he turns, the towel slightly falls, and she can see his backside just appear before he disappears behind a wall, the towel falling to the steps and rolls down until it finally stops about mid-stairwell. Suddenly, Kate realises that she is sitting across from Ben, and she goes bright red, as she faces him again.

"Yeah, Pat doesn't get to go to the gym very often, but he does go about once or twice a week. The company he works for has one in the office complex," Ben says as he smiles from behind his cup of coffee.

"Uh huh," is all she can manage, still red from embarrassment.

"You'll have to excuse me, young Kate," Ben says standing, "but there are a pile of groceries that need attending to."

"Okay," she whispers.

"Are you warm enough, or would you like another tea?"

"I'm fine," she replies, handing her cup back to him, not even realising that she had finished it so quickly, or how strong it was, or that it didn't have milk in it.

It takes a few minutes, but Pat finally makes a decision at what he's going to wear, deciding between casual and lazy. He opts for a nice casual shirt from Pierre Carfinni and some dress khakis for a matching ensemble. His mind is racing, and he can't think straight about anything he's doing. He nearly sprays deodorant in his face, thinking it is hairspray, but suddenly catches himself, and picks up the bottle of aftershave instead. He isn't the type of man that uses many fragrances to make himself smell like all his friends, but they have been constantly buying him a variety of expensive mixes for him since before he can remember.

Pat finally prepares himself, his heart racing like a schoolboy, and he walks as calmly as he can down the stairwell. When he first sees Kate, she is looking out the window at the rain. Her hair is still slightly wet, but he cannot help but to think how amazing it looks. She has rolled down the thick sweater to reveal her neck, as well as her arms. Her hands are patiently folded across her designer black blue jeans, revealing a platinum ring carefully placed on her right middle finger, with a blue sapphire in its centre.

"Sorry I took so long," he says to her, seeing her slowly turn and smile.

"That's okay, you weren't expecting me. I'm not interrupting anything am I?" she questions, watching as he comes forward and seats himself in the love seat next to her.

"No. I just have to pick up Thomas today. I was supposed to go into work and work on some figures with the analysts, but I just couldn't be bothered today. I don't think they could either, because they haven't called me to tell me that they wanted me."

"It must be nice to have a job like that," she replies softly, still staring at him with the gentlest of faces.

"Not really. It's just Christmas and everything is sort of wound down already, so only a few of us go in to work. Since I've been out in Europe recently, and then the East Coast, they're cutting me some slack." Pat watches as she attends to his words, knowing how dull it must be for her to listen to him talk about his work. "So why are you here? Not that I mind at all."

"Oh!" she says startled, "Nothing really. Just seeing if you remember about the dinner on Saturday and if you've got a formal dinner suit, as it's black tie. If you don't, I have a friend who can make one up for you before then. He's a brilliant dress maker. He does all of the Pacific Opera's dress and costume."

"Uh," Pat stutters, "I'm not sure. I don't think so. I'd have to check."

Kate immediately pulls out her phone and makes a call. She says three words, and speaks to a man named Casey. She mentions that she needs something done for her, and then laughs, then closes the phone. "Right!" she then states. "If you don't know if you have one, then if you do, it probably doesn't fit right anyway. So grab your jacket, and let's go get one."

"But—" he starts, but Kate has already jumped to her feet and pulled him to his.

"I'm stealing Patrick!" Kate shouts to the kitchen.

"Just make sure you bring him back in one piece," is the reply. "Preferably with a new brain if you find one."

Pat grunts and the two stand under the porch together close, waiting for a break in the rain. He can smell her lotion, which smells like roses and lavender. It makes him close his eyes momentarily, because it is so heavenly to his nose. Her skin looks so soft that he could reach forward and touch her neck so easily, if not for the fact that she is holding both his hands behind her back. Even they are soft, although cold.

"We'll take my car," she states, interrupting his thoughts. "It's easier if I drive, because you probably haven't been there before anyway."

"Okay," he returns, clearing his throat.

The wind is pushing her silky hair against his cheeks, filling his nose with the smell of her peach-like shampoo. It feels as if she is brushing a feather across his face, taunting him to laugh. But he merely takes a silent breath, trying not to let her see that he is breathing her entire being into him.

Suddenly and without warning, Kate pulls him forward making a run for her car. The rain is still heavy, and every drop feels like an ice cube running down his skin. But the once cold fingers she had seem so warm now, within his. She releases him in order to unlock the car and jump in as quickly as she can, screaming like a young girl being splashed with water in the summer.

Pat seats himself comfortably in her car, as they pull away as quickly as she can. She reminds him of *her*, he finally admits to himself. She is childish, brash, and has this stubbornness that he hasn't seen in so long. But he also realises that he has missed these things much more than he would like to admit.

He doesn't say much, but listens to the strange indie-styled music that she has put on, and listens to her as she sings away carefree to its tunes. For a while he says nothing, but stares at her, watching her just enjoy life, filling herself with every drop that it holds. It is something that he is so unfamiliar with, and has not done for so many years.

Kate catches him looking at her, and hits him across the arm. He doesn't really feel it, but he feigns pain, nevertheless. "Stop staring," she laughs. "I hate it when people look at me like that. You look like a lost puppy or something."

"Sorry," he moans, ill-contentedly. He rubs his arm and looks out the window at the falling rain. The road-spray is so heavy that you can barely see two cars ahead of you. And yet, Kate speeds along happily, moving between each car and passing them as if it were second nature. She looks over at him briefly and sees his fear as she is driving, and smiles.

"Does my driving bother you?" she queries as she passes a semi-truck fully loaded with eight brand new cars on its trailer. Patrick doesn't reply, but merely shakes his head 'no' in response. "I learned to drive in England. Well kind of. If you don't count the old beat up 1979 pickup that my dad used to let me drive on the ranch."

"Is driving in England different, then?" Patrick asks, watching her move in between two cars without looking. "More aggressive perhaps?"

"I don't know, really. Faster if anything. I still feel like I'm crawling across the floor here, but I'm used to it now. I've slowed down quite a bit," she explains. "And the rain doesn't bother me, either. When it rains there, it's like gravy. This is like bottled water coming down compared to the muck that's thrown at you on the motorway."

"Oh," Patrick replies, closing his eyes as she comes up quickly behind another truck, and then changes lanes quickly to pass another. "Does it rain a lot there, then? I thought it was pretty sunny."

Kate laughs, looking at him funnily. "I thought you said you've been to England."

"Yes, but I don't remember it being like what you've described," he informs her. "I remember travelling through the countryside and seeing nice little villages and meeting friendly people who helped me find where I was going."

"Uh huh," she says with a smile. "And I bet you didn't drive, either."

"Not really."

"That's what I thought," she responds, nodding her head. "You'll never get the true experience of England unless you sit on the roads for six hours in traffic, then speed to 95mph just to keep up with the person in front of you, only to slam your brakes on again and sit for another half hour. It's all about timing, love."

"Like LA, then."

"Similar. I think LA is much more stressful, though," Kate replies. "Like LA, only without the guns."

A song comes on that Kate likes, and she turns up the radio quite loudly, beginning to sing away as loud as she can. Pat can't help but to stare again, smiling at her singing and the pleasure of her beauty. She is a wonderful creation of life; a part of something that he has forgotten. He cannot help but to watch her wonderful essence exude from her soul, full of an energy and being that cannot be denied. It is only then that he finally admits to himself; she is undeniably beautiful.

"What?!" Kate exclaims, awaking him from his short-lived daze. "I hate it when people stare at me like that."

"Sorry," he replies. "I'll try not to do that, but I won't swear to it."

"Is there something wrong with my face?" she enquires, lifting her hand to her cheek and rubbing it.

"No, nothing like that. You just are probably one of the most beautiful people I have ever met," he says.

Kate roars out with laughter, passing yet another car. "I've heard that once or twice." She looks over at him, to see his face and what reaction he holds. When she sees his eyes, she knows instantly that he did not mean it the way she took it. And she lowers her laughter to a mere smile. For whatever reason, she believes him.

"Sorry," he returns to her, looking forward once again.

"It's okay. It's just that I've had more than one person tell me that, and they weren't really trying to tell me that because they were being nice, either."

"Oh," Pat sighs. "I can imagine."

"Probably not, but we'll leave that there," she tells him, then hearing another song she likes, turns the music up loud once again to sing.

The singing continues for some time; Pat enjoying the atmosphere. She repeatedly tries to get him to sing along, but to no avail. Although, Kate does manage to get him to move his body somewhat to the music, waving his arms back and forth at times. Enough for him to realise that he is not a dancer of any shape or size.

"We're just going to make side trip really quickly, okay?" Kate informs him, to which he acknowledges with a quick nod.

They pull into Kate's apartment complex and she stops the car, opening the door without hesitation or thought. "Are you coming, or do you just want to wait here?"

"I don't know," he responds slightly confused. She motions for him to follow, and he begrudgingly gets out of the car and follows her. She can see the confusion on his face, and she puts her arm around his for comfort.

"Don't worry, my friends aren't that bad," she whispers into his ear.

"I never—" he starts, but she covers his mouth and laughs.

"They've been dying to see you again, anyway. I think they're trying to find something 'gossy to take home."

"Gossy?" he retorts.

"Gossip, love," she tells him with a pat on his cheek.

The two enter the apartment only to hear the sounds of weapons firing and Kieran shouting abusive comments profusely over and over again. As they continue in further, they spot Tara standing over Kieran who is seated comfortably on the sofa, holding a white wireless game controller and bouncing about back and forth as he continues his eloquent verse of profanity. Tara is laughing away as she continues to sip from her cup of tea, (Patrick assumes in any case.)

"I'll only be a minute," Kate tells him, as the two walk into the living area. Tara sees Patrick and Kate, and instantly comes over. Tara smiles at Pat, but takes Kate's hand and walks into the bedroom with her.

Patrick takes Tara's place behind Kieran, who is completely oblivious to his surroundings and probably wouldn't hear him even if Patrick said something. So he resides himself to standing and watching the match between Kieran and the alien onslaught, of which it seems the aliens are winning. It is almost like watching a space movie in action, only the hero who faces insurmountable odds, is losing badly instead of winning, hence the ongoing profanity.

Kate returns with Tara shortly after, and the three of them walk into the kitchen, leaving Kieran to save the universe as best he can.

"I just needed to pick up some things," Kate informs Patrick before he can ask, pulling a bag over her shoulder.

"So, are you looking forward to this dinner on Saturday?" Tara asks Pat.

"I don't know," he returns, slightly confused at the question. "I don't even know what it's for."

"He doesn't know?" Tara asks Kate. "That's so naughty."

"What?" Pat queries, completely lost at the conversation.

"Have you met Daniel, yet?" Tara asks, getting nudged in the ribs by Kate. "You haven't, have you? Oh, this will be fun."

"Should I be worried?" Patrick asks, look at Kate.

"No. Daniel is an old friend, and he's the one hosting the party at his house. That's all," Kate assures him, taking his hand and pulling him out of the apartment again. "Don't listen to Tara, she's just trying to scare you."

Pat blinks twice, and raises an eyebrow at the thought of the entire ordeal. Nevertheless, he follows Kate willingly and marches with her accordingly back to the car.

Nearly an hour later, the two are pulling into the streets of Seattle once again, to a place that he has never been to. It's a small street, with parking just outside the building, which is rare in itself. Kate hasn't said too much about whom they're seeing except for that his name is Freddy and he is Polish.

The building is a bit rustic at first glance, with graffiti in places, and a garage off to the side. It looks somewhat like a throwback from the seventies and in need of serious repair. And yet as they pass through the small green door, it reveals this illustrious warehouse of beauty and culture. There are statues laid carefully throughout the long corridor, and paintings that hang on every wall. The visible interior is painted this translucent yellow, to offset the gold and white tiled flooring that is carefully placed throughout like a mosaic.

"KATHERINE!" Patrick hears from deep within the building, a deep booming voice echoing over everything else. He hasn't even noticed the large amount of people that are moving back and forth like ants. Soon, this rather large man with what he assumes is a Polish accent, (although to him it sounds somewhat Russian,) comes up to them both with arms opened wide. He stands towering over the both of them, reminding Pat of one of the television wrestlers he used to watch as a child.

"Hello, my darling," Freddy speaks to Katherine, leaning down to kiss her on the cheek as he gently holds both of her arms with his enormous hands. "How are we today?" His thick accent is hard for Patrick to understand at times, and continues to remind him of a Russian spy rather than a Polish person, but as he has never been to either location, he couldn't really tell the difference.

"I am wonderful, sweetie," Katherine says, "but I need your help. This beautiful man next to me needs something to wear to one of Daniel's annual Christmas dos."

"Ohhh!" Freddy roars, again reminding Patrick of a villainous spy, straight out of a movie. "No problem. I will have one of my babies look at him and we will have him something within minutes."

Freddy shouts out a name that Patrick can't understand, snapping his fingers in the process. Within seconds out from one of the office doors to their right, appears this incredibly beautiful young lady. Her hair is tied neatly behind her back, and she is wearing a very tiny black dress that reveals more than most women would dare. She brings with her a clipboard, and glasses, which dangle from her fingers like a pencil.

"Achsania will make sure that the measurements are right, and I will have David take care of the rest," Freddy speaks to Kate.

"Is David back from Prague then?" Kate questions politely, somewhat excited at the idea.

"Oh, he has been back for weeks now, so don't go on," Freddy speaks roughly, shaking his head. "He has won so many awards that his head has grown so big, that he probably won't remember who you are any more, my beautiful."

"Well tell him *simple*, sweetie," Katherine explains, the words hissing somewhat as she emphasises it. "Patrick is merely a virgin and he won't know how to cope."

Pat stands silent as he is spoken about and not too. He tries not to look uncomfortable as the beautiful young lady begins to look at him up and down, touching him on his shoulders and other places as she circles him. Kate tells him to relax, and that 'Achi' doesn't bite. He sincerely doubts the sincerity of that comment, though, looking at her.

Moments pass, and measurements of every part of him are taken, after removing his coat and his outer pants, which he felt extremely uncomfortable doing, but did knowing that he was wearing somewhat long boxers underneath. Afterwards, he is ordered to put his clothes back on and follow Kate to meet David.

"Who is this David?" Pat whispers finally, after seeing the young lady disappear with her clip board and glasses.

"He is an old friend of mine, from years ago. He is a designer," she informs him, struggling for the right word. "It's hard to pin who David is, and easier to say what he is."

"Okay," Patrick replies, squinting in confusion. Kate shakes her head and kisses him unexpectedly on the cheek.

"Don't worry, love," she tells him. "He's gentle."

Kate leads Patrick through a maze of corridors, passing what seems to be hundreds of people who are walking calmly back and forth throughout the building. The corridor that they turn into has display cabinets resting carefully against the walls, each holding a masterpiece of clothing and art. He manages to catch some of the names on the plaques that are placed carefully underneath each display. Most of the names he can't pronounce, and the others he cannot recognise. But in one display, in which he cannot help but to stop and look at it, he sees the name David L. Malchovo. Its design is something that he has only pictured in magazines, and not in real life. It reminds him of a peacock, with a lion's tail trailing down its side. He is unsure how to describe it, only that it is an absolutely hideous creation that he cannot understand nor has any desire to.

"Yeah," Kate begins, "he is a bit wild at times."

Patrick holds his opinion to himself, and resides to keeping himself in Kate's good books by keeping quiet lest he be duplicitous in his words. But he cannot help but to ere on the side of caution if this is the man that is going to make him a dinner suit.

Kate continues leading Pat down the corridor, unto the very last door on the right, which is coloured three separate colours. The outer frame is pink, with a blue border, and the middle of the door is green, with a yellow painted handle. She runs her finger across the middle of the door, feeling its soft silky paint, then reaches for the door handle and opens it.

"David?" she calls out.

Out of the back of the rather large room, near a bright window, comes this shadowy figure. He emerges from behind a cloth wall, slowly at first, in which the two of them can see the figure tilt his head in curiosity.

"Are my ears deceiving me, or is that the illustrious tones of the always fashionable love of mine, Katherine?" the two hear, seeing the man emerge finally from behind the cloth. "Is that you, love?"

Pat notices the British accent instantly. Yet another person from England, he thinks to himself. He didn't think to himself that there were these many British in Seattle, let alone the country. I suppose he just never really bothered to think about it before, or try and find out.

He looks at David carefully, watching as David comes forward and puts his arms around Kate to lift her up off her feet. He stands no taller than Pat, but is much thinner. Strangely, he dresses somewhat normally for what he thought a 'designer' would look like. He is wearing some scruffy looking jeans, and a torn white t-shirt, and a pair of what looks to be leather sandals. Pat sees the glitter of a diamond in his nose, which has always made him cringe at the thought of it, or the pain one would have to undergo to put a diamond or any other thing into their nose.

"What brings the most beautiful woman that has ever worn my clothes back to his humble arms again?" David says, devouring Kate with his eyes.

"Stop," Kate says, stepping back and laughing. "I need you to get my lovely boy Patrick fitted for Daniel's party."

"Daniel? That plonker," he announces. "Are you still moving around with that self-contained egotistical git?"

"He's not that bad, but that's not the point," Kate says lowering her head as if to gesture away from David and toward me. "I'm taking Patrick, and he doesn't have anything to wear."

"Quiet, isn't he?" David replies, looking at Pat carefully. He goes over to a small laptop that's on a large white table, and begins to type. "Okay, here it is."

David looks at the computer, hitting a few keys as he scrolls through. Every now and then he lifts his head and stares at Patrick, then returns his gaze to the computer. Finally, he stands up once more and walks over to Pat.

"Hi mate, I'm David."

"Hi," Pat replies, "Patrick."

"Wicked," David says, moving around like a crazed boxer. Then, suddenly, "Come on then, let's go walk over to the trials."

"Trials?" he mouths to Kate. Kate smiles in reply and motions for the both of them to follow. As she does so, she comes and takes Patrick's arms.

The two then leave David's room and walk back up the corridor, David just in front of them.

"So Patrick," David shouts over some rather large clanging sounds in the air, "How'd you and Kate entwine yourself?"

"He means how did we meet, in his own kind of way," she tells Pat, to which she then says, "it's none of the nosey little git's business, either."

"Right, love," David replies, laughing as he does so. "Another stray cat out of the eighties then."

"Could be worse," Kate says, "he could be a bloody-minded fackin' numpty cockney bubble head."

"Ah, you still care, then," David says, wiggling his rump more exaggeratedly as they continue onwards.

"Do I sense a bit of tension between you two?" Pat whispers to Kate.

Kate smiles and shakes her head. "He's an old school friend, and we always give each other a hard time. He's been trying to sleep with me since University."

Pat is quite shocked by the statement, for more reasons than one, but doesn't say anything. Instead, he follows without question or hesitation, until they come to another room. David motions for them to enter the room. It's almost completely empty, except for a small door off in the far corner; the rest of the room is just mirrors.

"Wait here with the puppy, love," David tells Kate. "Make sure he doesn't wag his tail too fast."

Kate rolls her eyes and walks over to the far corner where the only seat is situated. Patrick follows like a child, trying to act as manly and passive as he can.

"How are you handling all of this?" Kate queries, seeing Pat pace a small corner.

"I'm not quite sure how to take all of this. It seems a bit surreal," he returns, tilting his head to one side in order to stretch his neck muscles.

"Don't worry," responds Kate almost instantly. "I used to do this sort of thing on a daily basis, and it's just a formality. It's not painful, and if you give it half a chance, it can be a little fun."

"Like playing dress up," he replies, looking over to her from the corner of his eye. "I hated dress up."

"Well, now you're just being stubborn," Kate huffs. Kate stands at his obvious pouting and walks up to him, taking both his hands. "Do you want to get your own suit?"

"Not really," he says, looking into her eyes blinking slowly. She is rubbing the knuckles of both his hands softly, swinging both their hands slightly, almost playfully. His eyes soften, and he rolls his eyes.

"Then let David sort it out," she tells him. "He is absolutely the best designer that I have ever come across, and I've known hundreds."

"Really?" Pat queries.

"Sure, didn't I tell you?" she says nonchalantly.

"No, I don't think so," he returns, suddenly seeing three young ladies enter the room, rolling large rails of clothes into the centre. David follows shortly after, his hand on his chin as he enters the room.

"Oh, never mind, it was a long time ago," she tells Pat, stepping away from him and going over to the doorway to greet David.

The three ladies come over to him, followed by the other lady that he met earlier with her clipboard again. He cannot really tell them apart, as they all seem to be dressed exactly as one another, with even their hair tied the same way. Within minutes they are looking him over, circling him like a pack of wolves. David claps his hands together once and then they immediately go and pull out several different items.

"I'm not sure if I'm comfortable with this," Patrick states hesitantly, as they begin removing his cloths, except for his boxers.

"It's alright, little puppy," David says to him, causing Pat to cringe a bit. "It's faster this way. We don't have time to sit around and watch you change over and over again. So just relax. They are professionals."

And professionals they are, as they go to dressing him in every way, including changing his shoes as they do so. Every garment except for the necessities are removed and changed over and over again, always to the disproval of David. Until nearly an hour later, and after one very disheartened Patrick begins to lose all hope and strength, David finally shouts aloud that he is happy.

Patrick did not have an opportunity to see what was happening to him, as they were moving him about like a doll. But with yet another clap, the women disappear from the room, leaving only David, Patrick, and finally Kate, who is covering her mouth with glee.

Now seeing his attire in full for the first time and looking it carefully over with his somewhat astonished eyes, Patrick gazes into the mirror with an open mind. His dinner jacket is a wonderful silky texture, with a dark blue edging around the collar and sleeve. It's just slightly different than what he would normally expect, and a little smaller than he would usually wear, but it shapes him well. His shirt is an amazingly course looking creation, that feels like it should be harsh, but is actually almost unnoticeable. Even the cuffs look like they should be slightly course, and scratchy, but are strangely comfortable. His slacks are dark black, almost a midnight blue if looked at the right angle in the light. They are cut precisely to his size, and seem to match his elegant leather shoes that he was given to wear. There are even little silver cuffs on the end of the laces of the shoe to match his silver cufflinks. Overall, he is extremely impressed at how toned and nice he seems to look.

"You look fabulous," Kate says, coming up and stroking the fabric along the length of Patrick's back.

"I know," David says smugly. "Isn't he just the cutest little puppy you've ever seen? You owe me one serious cleansing service for this."

"In your dreams," Kate replies. "But seriously, thank you. Pat really appreciates it."

Pat nods, and interrupts by repeating what Kate has already said, taking David's hand and shaking it. David merely laughs and places his other hand on top of Pat's in order to sandwich it.

"Don't mention it, Patrick. I love working with virgin puppies. You are so sweet to watch squirm."

"How much do I owe you for all of this?" Pat enters, to which Kate looks at him somewhat disappointed.

"OH!!" David announces aloud, shaking his head as the blood drains from his face. "Never....never ruin a masterpiece by corrupting it with such evil words."

David kisses Kate on the cheek and insists he has to leave before something happens.

"What did I say?" Pat enquires, completely lost at what had just occurred.

"Never talk money with David. It's insulting to him," Kate explains. "It's like you've ruined his painting or something. He doesn't think of you as a person, but a canvass he can play with."

"Okay." Pat winces at the thought.

"Don't think too much about it. David is a bit melodramatic. Go ahead and just put that stuff on the bench in that room, and they'll make sure it's ready for you before Saturday. I'll wait outside so you can have a bit of privacy."

"What for, I just had four half naked women undressing me for the last hour?" Pat grumbles pleasantly. "What's one more going to hurt?"

"I'll wait outside anyway. Wouldn't want myself to become overwhelmed by such vast amounts of manliness all at once."

"Okay, but just remember that I didn't ask for this."

Kate stops herself from leaving and turns then returns to Patrick's side. She leans up as he is trying to remove his jacket. He is somewhat startled by her, but stops what he's doing in either case. Kate just returns the gesture by placing the tip of her lips against his.

"Merry Christmas," she replies.

Chapter 10

Please Explain

Intelligence is a definition of one's capacity to acquire and apply knowledge through the faculty of thought and reason. Faith is the confident belief in the truth, value, or trustworthiness of someone, something, or an idea. Faith does not require proof. Love, the emotion or thought, regardless of statement, desire, or means, has no true definition. It is merely a composite of all one's emotions, feelings, and beliefs placed into a single word so that one may describe what one believes is an intelligent faith in another.

Patrick and Thomas are sitting at their dinner table, of which Ben is serving spaghetti and meatballs. A typical night's dinner, save for the fact that they are eating early in order to get to Thomas's concert as early as possible for a decent spot at parking.

"Are you excited?" Patrick asks his son, noticing the considerable amount of silence which is terribly unlike the usual household atmosphere of chaotic noise.

"I guess," Thomas shrugs, in somewhat of an indifferent fashion. "I'm going to be next to Molly Macguire and she's always likes to kiss me, so I'm not too pleased about that."

"Oh?" Ben questions, seating himself down. The three of them hold one another's hands and Thomas says his prayers and gives thanks for the food that they are blessed to have. It is a tradition that has been in the family since his birth, and even though Patrick has always been uncomfortable with it, he respects that his son believes in something that he perhaps does not. His love for his son, and the innocence that he holds has only ever been met with an open-minded warmth that one should give to another.

"So, who else kisses you, then?" Ben persists happily.

"Well, there's Amber, and Heather, and that new girl that plays with the dolls all the time, Charlene I think her name is."

"My goodness boy," Ben announces, patting his grandson on the shoulder. "You're quite the charmer."

"*Blech*" he says sticking out his tongue, as if he's eating something horrible.

"Are there any girls you do like?" his father asks, carefully eating his supper.

Thomas thinks about it carefully, so much so that he uses his fingers to go through in a methodical fashion as not to forget any. Then, suddenly, "Terri!"

"Oh yes, that little brown-haired girl that's in your class that lives down the street," Pat says, trying to hide his smile. "Why her?"

"I dunno," Thomas shrugs again, playing with a piece of bread. "She's just nice. She likes to play with Addy and me. But she likes to hold hands a lot. She helped me write my letter to Santa, though. Do you think he's gotten it yet? Only I saw him today earlier in school and he said that he's really glad I sent it and that I'm doing really good in English, which is good, and I should keep it up."

Ben and Pat look at one another and smile silently at one another, their eyes glittering with admiration. "I'm sure he's got it then, and that you should listen to him."

"Okay, but I don't really like English so much. Math is more fun, but I really like science. I like it when the teacher makes things blow up. Last week Mr. Finkle came in and cooked a piece of bacon in some soda pop. I didn't know that soda pop got hot enough to cook bacon. Do you think it can cook pancakes? That'd be really cool, because all I'd have to do is take a jar of pancake mix to school and then pour some soda over it......except we can't have soda in school," he pauses, "but I'm sure I could figure it out."

"I'm not sure it works that way Thomas," Patrick tries and explains.

"Oh, that's true," Thomas acknowledges happily, "I'd need a plate too, and they're too big to fit in my lunchbox. Maybe I'll just eat them when I come home. Do you think we can try and cook pancakes with soda tomorrow Grandpa?"

Ben laughs happily. "Of course," he nods pleasantly. "Now you'd better eat up before we get late. You still have to brush your teeth and get dressed."

"Aw," Thomas grumbles, "Do I have to wear a tie?"

"Yes," Patrick whines back. "Your teacher gave me strict instructions to put a tie on you, so that she has something to grab hold of if you sing wrong."

"Really???" Thomas's eyes open wide and a small amount of fear exudes from his face. Ben calms him down by laughing and rubbing his head.

The James household finishes their meal promptly, and Thomas heads off upstairs to ready himself for the long night ahead. Usually he would be asleep before the concert would finish, but his father has assured him that this is just one exception to the usual rule.

"So," Ben begins, taking the dishes to the sink. "Is Kate going to come tonight?"

Pat pauses at the question, looking at his father who is patiently washing. He can feel his father's eyes looking at him, even though he does not turn or make one-minute gesture toward him, save that of washing the dishes.

"She said that she's going to try and make it, if she can," Pat replies. "Kate has something that she's doing with her friends."

"Oh," his father replies, "I was just wondering."

"I'm sure you were." Pat finishes clearing up the last of the plates, and brings the final one to his father. He can see the empty expression on his father's face, and the question that he has yet to really answer. Then, "I gave her our spare ticket. I don't know if she'll be there, but yes, I did ask her to be."

"Right," his father says, his simple expression going unchanged.

Thomas returns moments later, with his tie in hand and his shoes somewhat half on and half off. Patrick smiles and scratches his head, then has him jump up on a seat so he can help. When he finishes, he cannot help but to give his son a large hug that he has been longing to do for the entire day. He looks at him as a father can only do. A pride that has engulfed him for all of his son's life accumulates in his mind, and he almost has tears in his eyes as he thinks how proud his mother would be to see their son now.

Pat stands from his knee and pats his son on his head, then takes a deep breath to try and compensate for the emotions inside him. Ben sees this and orders Thomas to grab his coat in order to go. He then walks over to his son and places a steadying hand on his shoulder. Pat replies with a nod, and takes another deep breath.

The three of them pile into Ben's truck and head quickly over to Thomas's school. The rain has silenced itself for the meantime, although the winter wind is creating a tremendous amount of ice and frost, which of course makes the journey a slow going one for them all. Once there, they then have to spend time manoeuvring between the other parents who are trying to find a space themselves. Ben is very careful in his wording of the situation, but cannot help but to voice his opinions aloud. Patrick has to gently remind him of Thomas and his mindful ears more than once.

Eventually the three enter the main gymnasium, of which Thomas runs off immediately after spotting Addy. Patrick watches as a little brown-haired girl comes up to Thomas and takes his hand, leading him to where the others in his class are by the stage where their teacher is waiting.

"We've still got a few minutes, so I'll go and grab our seats," Ben says, looking at the ticket number and the seats that are assigned to them.

"Okay, I'm just going to go outside and get a breath of fresh air," Pat replies softly, as everyone else around him seems to be whispering.

"Well let me know if you see her, while you're getting your air," mentions Ben as he's walking off. Patrick can only roll his eyes and turn and walk away.

The cool winter air shows his breath as he leaves the concert area, standing in the front of the school and watching the parents and children flow into the gymnasium. Patrick stands quietly by the entrance where a couple of the fathers are standing and talking with one another. He continues to look out over the parking lot, wondering inside if she'll show up. He wants her too, but in the same right, he hopes that she doesn't. His heart is torn; confused. It is just at this point that he looks over into the car park and sees the little blonde-haired girl.

Pat's heart stops instantly, and he blinks twice to make sure that it is the same girl that he saw before. She waves to him, and he looks around to make sure that he isn't going insane. The other fathers next to him continue to talk to one another, as fewer and fewer parents arrive.

Carefully, Patrick walks out into the parking lot, where he comes before the child, still in the same garments that he has seen her in the previous two times.

"What are you doing here?" he questions. "Who exactly are you?"

"Good questions," she replies. "And I'll answer those both in time. But for now, we need to talk briefly." Her words are spoken so clearly, as if she were of an age far beyond what Patrick could see before him.

"Again? The last time we talked you promised that you would answer my questions," he replies, putting his hands in his pant pockets.

"So I did," the little girl replies, "and I will. I always keep my word. But you aren't quite ready to hear the answers. I don't think you'd believe them if I told you anyway."

"Believe what? That you're some magical creature that bounces in and out of people's lives, making them think they're insane?" he responds wryly. "For all I know, you're some figment of some delusional state of mourning deep within my brain somewhere."

"Not quite," she replies. "I don't have much time, as I'm quite a busy person, you know. But I'll endeavour to make this as simple as possible."

"Alright then," Pat begins, "go ahead. Wave your magic wand and do your stuff."

"I don't have any magic wand to wave, Patrick" she explains, placing her hand on his. "All I have is a little advice. I know that it is very hard for you to believe in something that isn't real and physical; something that you can't touch or see."

"Right," he says guardedly.

"People think that destiny is a set of events that lead them to a certain point, and that no matter what they do or say, the outcome of this will always be the same. In truth, all beings of this universe are given a wonderful gift unlike any other. Destiny is real enough, and it is a powerful tool that can be used for so many things. Ultimately, though, no matter how much we'd like to believe that everything will turn out okay and right, Destiny cannot do this for us. It is in our choices, our decisions; it is in our hearts that we are led into this world. Remember, the greatest gift that you have been given, is the gift of choice."

"I'm not sure I understand," Pat replies softly.

The child takes a deep breath and steps back, looking at the entrance of the school. "Patrick, you have been given a great gift, of which you can choose to let it grow, or to have it fade. No one else in this world can help you make this decision. But you will have to make it. You cannot hide from it. You cannot turn away from it and hope it goes away."

"You're talking about Kate," says Patrick in a whisper, his eyes slowly beginning to focus upward into the dark night.

"Katherine is a beautiful, loving person."

"You gave me the necklace so that I would meet her," Patrick says stepping back. "But how did you know?"

"The question isn't how did I know, but more so how did you know to give it to her? It could have been anybody's necklace. But out of everyone, you chose Katherine to give it to."

"I don't know why I did," Patrick says as he shakes his head in disbelief. "I just knew it was for her. But this is all just unreal."

"I have to go now, but I want you to understand that this isn't magic. Not like you believe it is. When I see you next, I promise I will explain everything," she informs him, turning and walking away. Patrick looks up from the ground and tries to see where she has gone too, but cannot. Instead he turns and sees his son standing at the entrance way of the school, waving frantically to him. Hesitantly, he takes a very long breath and shakes his head once more, then returns to the school.

"Grandpa told me to come and get you," Thomas says. "My teacher says that my tie is very nice."

"That's good," Pat replies.

Thomas takes his father's hand and the two walk hand-in-hand together into the school. As soon as they're through the doors, Thomas sees Ms. Baker and runs off as quick as he can. Patrick in turn begins to look around the four hundred some seats for his father. He begins by looking at his ticket, and then follows the seat numbers until he finally comes up on a row near the front. As he does, he slowly moves about trying to reach the middle of the seats, in which he sees three empty chairs in a row. It isn't too hard to get to them, simply because many of the parents are still buying concessions and the children are still lining themselves behind the stage.

As Patrick seats himself he begins to watch the children line themselves up just beyond the three different staging areas. Like all parents he is only concerned with his own child and his class, but will watch the entire show regardless.

"Look who I found wandering alone by the concessions," Patrick hears to his side, recognising his father's voice. He looks up and sees a figure turned speaking to a parent. She is very smartly dressed, with a combination black evening dress and overcoat, with long slender gloves going up each arm. As she turns, saying excuse me politely to the young father that she is passing, Patrick recognises Katherine instantly and stands.

"You came," he announces.

"Very astute," she replies, taking his hand as she takes the seat directly between Ben and Patrick. "Sorry I couldn't get here earlier, but I was in the middle of getting Tara ready for her school's concert."

"Oh, is Tara's tonight as well?"

"I think it's possibly an American tradition that all schools have their Christmas plays or concerts on the same night so that no one can figure out a decent schedule," Katherine explains in a dull soft voice, as the crowds of people are now settling in. Ben laughs at the young lady's comment and offers her some school-made Christmas cookies, along with some warm apple cider.

"I just don't understand how you guys can drink warm apple juice," Kate announces as she takes a sip of the cider. "In England, Cider is something that men drink to keep the hairs long on their chest. Especially fresh Devon cider, just out of the jug."

The two men look at Kate, who smiles at her own statement. Then, Patrick nods and says, "Yeah, I remember going down to Devon and Somerset, and some guy offered me a cider in a pub, and I could barely see straight that night."

"Exactly," Kate nods in return. "It should be almost strong enough to make you go blind, and just weak enough to make you feel like you're standing on a boat at sea."

"Changing the subject slightly," Patrick whispers, "Why didn't you go to Tara's Christmas recital?"

"Oh!" Kate begins, somewhat startled at the question. "Well, your son invited me first."

"Did he now?" Ben enters.

"Yes, but I wasn't going to say anything," Kate says in a dull tone. "Because Patrick asked me as well."

There is a silence that suddenly overcomes the crowd of parents as the first group of children come out to the far stage. Their teacher arranges the children who seem somewhat lost. They are the youngest of children in the school, and all the parents can't help but to coo at them.

Kate smiles and places her hand on Patrick's as she laughs at the tiny little costumes that each of them are dressed in. From a tiny little Christmas tree, to the various different animals; each costume unique and full of love. They sing a lovely little ballad of a poor little girl offering a gift to the baby Jesus for Christmas, but can't afford too. One of the little girls, she is the one chosen to take a little bird up to the middle of the stage and sing to it. All the parents in the house coo again as she finishes, and some nearly break into tears. It is quite an inspirational and moving piece, that some of the older children had to participate in, but nevertheless it was well executed and performed.

It is here that the principal comes out and greets all the parents, and formally thanks each and every one of them for being their willing audience for the night. He explains each performance and how it will be done, and follows with a light comment on the refreshment stand that is located near the entrance.

The parents and guests begin to talk once more, as the principal explains that they will need a short break to set up the next performance. Ben takes the opportunity to say how good the performance is compared to the previous year.

"Do you come every year?" Kate queries loudly over the noise of the parents rumbling and speaking to one another.

"The school seems to pride itself on involving all the school children that they can. Some parents choose not to participate, but on the whole, it usually is about this size, and every year so far has been different than the previous," Pat clarifies.

Soon the concert continues, and the performances rage onwards, each different than the next. Every class, every year, has an opportunity to show its talents by singing or acting. Some of the acts even combine classes, as some of the younger children are just too young to accomplish the act on their own. From musical instruments, to dancing sugar plums, the school gives its best to impress the audience. Even Thomas himself played three various roles, from drummer boy, to an introduction to one of the younger classes plays, to finally singing solo in his classes choir. And when it came time for him to hit his extremely high note, all the parents cringed as he slightly went one octave too high, but everyone cheered anyway. It was Kate and Ben of course being the loudest of all there.

The entire concert lasts nearly two and a half hours, and the strain on some of the younger children becomes quite evident. As the principal comes out and wishes all the parents and guests a Merry Christmas, he asks that each of them exit in a nice orderly fashion by row, starting from the back. This causes Pat to look over his shoulder and see a tide of people behind him.

"I think we're going to be here a while, so we may as well sit," Pat explains to Ben and Kate.

"What did you think?" Ben asks Kate.

"Thomas was absolutely brilliant," she replies ecstatically. "He really can sing well, and you can see he enjoys what he's doing."

"Except for the one note," Pat enters.

"Aww. Bless his little cotton socks," Kate starts, "he was brilliant. He's only eight. And he sang his little heart out in front of all these people. He must have been really nervous."

"Well I don't think that anyone here will forget him soon," Ben says, seeing one of the parents just behind them laugh at the comment.

One of the mothers that is sitting just in front of Kate, turns around as she hears the comment. "Was that your little boy that was signing the solo?"

"Yes," Pat replies proudly.

"You tell him that he made this concert for me," she says proudly, nodding to him. Then, "Better that he stand up and sing his all out, then to hide behind the cows in the manger, like mine."

"I'll make sure to tell him," Pat says, to which the lady turns around once more.

"See," Kate says with a nudge of the elbow. "Everyone liked him."

"I never doubted it for a second," Patrick returns with a smile. Ben interrupts by pointing that the people are clearing in an extraordinarily orderly fashion which is making things move rather smoothly and efficiently.

"Thomas and the children will meet us outside I suppose," Pat wonders, looking around and not seeing any sign of any children anywhere.

As they walk down the aisle, Kate cannot help but to put her arm around his, and make a laughing gesture at him, as they seem to be walking in step together because of the people in front.

"Are you getting practice in for the real thing?" Ben asks the two.

"A girl can't wait forever, you know. We women have to train these men quickly," Kate replies, looking over her shoulder as she speaks.

Patrick cannot help but to yawn at the two, casting his smirk toward the people in front as they continue to walk at the slow pace. Kate just nudges him with her shoulder in return.

"Do you want me to pick you up, or do you want to drive?" Kate asks.

"When?" Pat returns, looking puzzled at the question. "Oh! You mean tomorrow. I don't know, I'll drive if you want."

"Oh good, I was hoping you'd say that. I like your car," she explains. "More buttons to push."

As the three exit the building, they are met with waves upon waves of children, each standing and waiting for their parents in an orderly fashion. The teachers do a strict job of holding tight to their classes, only releasing them as their parents come into view. Thomas, after seeing his father, comes running up to him with an excited look of glee spread across his face.

"Look what I've got!" he announces happily, showing his father a stick of bubble-gum.

"Very nice, little bear," Patrick replies. "Say hello to Kate, Thomas. She came to watch you tonight."

Thomas walks over and says hello politely. "Did you see Ms. Baker?" Thomas asks her softly.

"I did," Kate replies. "She is pretty."

"She gave me a kiss, but I didn't mind. And she gave me a stick of gum because everyone laughed when I sang my line. But she says that was a really good thing."

"It was," Kate assures him, taking his hand and whispering in his ear, "I think you sang the best out of everybody."

Thomas steps back with a confident smile and announces his usual, "I know."

"Well I guess I'd better get going. Tara is probably going to be home pretty soon," Kate explains. "It was an absolute delight watching you, young Thomas. I am so very glad you invited me."

"You're welcome," Thomas replies with the usual lacklustre.

"You're more than welcome to come back to the house with us and have some cocoa and marshmallows," Ben says welcomingly.

Kate looks at Patrick, who smiles politely. Then, "No, I think I'd better get back and let this little bear get into his bed."

"I'm not tired," Thomas immediately responds.

"I bet you're not," Patrick says to Thomas rubbing his head. Then to Kate, "It's been really nice. I'm glad you came."

"I'm glad you invited me," Kate says. She then leans down and shakes Thomas's hand. Kate then stands and looks at Pat, turns and walks into the crowds of parents again.

Pat takes a deep breath, realising the awkwardness of what had just passed. He looks down at his son, trying not to show any sign of emotion. Thomas wouldn't notice even if he had, as he stares happily at his stick of gum. Then, Pat turns and walks back to the car with his father and his son on either side of him. Ben nods his head in silence, and places his hand on Pat's shoulder.

Chapter 11

Thinking Kind

"What are you thinking?"

Silence ensues. Kate is staring out over the bay, holding her cup of shandy (a British drink composed of beer and fizzy lemonade.) When she was in England, she rarely went to the sea, except for the odd occasions when the summers were being agreeable. Even then, Bournemouth and Brighton were hardly what she considered places that she would like to live. And yet, she loves the water. She loves to stare out and watch the moonlight dance, and the city lights glitter, and the boats ferry themselves across without effort. Seattle is a wonderful place, she thinks to herself.

"I don't know, Tara," Kate finally replies. "I'm just not sure."

"Well, love, you know you're always welcome to come home with us," Tara says. "Just think of drinking a real bitter shandy again. And real tea! And Lancashire sausage with black pudding!"

"That sounds disgusting," Kate says sticking her tongue out.

"Well, you know what I mean, love," Tara says, coming over to her side. "So what do ya say?"

"I just don't know, babes," Kate whispers.

Tara comes over and wraps her arms around Kate from behind. The two stare out into the ocean and just watch the world go by for a few brief moments.

"When I look into his eyes, I only see sadness," Kate whispers.

"But you can see the way he looks at you," Tara replies, still holding her friend tightly. "It's something magical."

"There is a gentleness in that man that I have never seen in another person. I love the way he is so insecure with everything," Kate smiles and Tara laughs.

"He is sweet. I like the way you make him blush at the slightest thing," Tara reveals. "Bless his little cotton socks."

"How are you supposed to know, babes?" Kate says putting her hand on the window. She begins to trace the outline of a star that is lit on one of the buildings just down from them.

"I don't know, love," her dearest friend returns to her. "There are no answers for this sort of thing. Look at Kieran and I. We've been together for what, nearly seven years now. Is he the one that I want to spend the rest of my life with? Well, you know the answer to that. He's lazy. He's rude. He's overbearing and arrogant. He drinks too much lager, and spends more time at the pub than at home. When he's home he plays video games and is as profane as a drunk sailor."

"But you love him," Kate replies, patting her friend's hand.

"Yes, I do, love. And his accent is cute."

"And what you're saying to me is that I need to decide?" Kate replies.

"That or run away with Kia and me," Tara says.

Kate smiles once again and turns to give her friend a full hug. Then, "You know, I think I'm going to get some air. It's still early enough."

"You want me to go with, lovie?"

"That's okay, babes, I'll be fine. I just need to clear my head," Kate says softly, feeling her friend touch her on the face and moving to one side to let her go.

Kate prepares herself by taking a heavy coat from the coat rack, one of Tara's. It's a thick puffer-styled jacket that you normally see in the streets of London and the outlining cities. Her scarf is one that her grandmother gave her, a thick pashmina which she throws around her face to cover her from the cold bitter wind.

Kate begins her walk down by the complex's pool, running her fingers across the various ferns and trees that are evenly placed in a garden like setting. She is humming to herself, happily looking around her at the different ways that the various apartments have decorated themselves with all the different lights. The complex committee has decorated the area throughout with many carefully chosen decorations and lights. She remembers when they passed the fliers out for the meeting. Kate has never been one to attend those types of things, so she just sort of ignores them. But all in all, they did a fairly nice job choosing them, although a bit bland and politically correct, she thinks to herself.

It's different here, she thinks to herself. There isn't anywhere else on earth that does Christmas like the States. It may seem to be commercial, and fake at times, but there is an undeniable essence that you feel at Christmas that you don't seem to get anywhere else in the world. The malls, the buildings, people's houses, and even the parking meters are decorated in ribbons and holly. In England that just really isn't possible, she honestly believes. England is a wonderful place for Christmas, and Kate has such fond memories of it and will always love it there, but it is different somehow.

She begins to ponder her childhood days, when the snow was so high that she could walk along Mrs. Hobson's stone wall on her way to school in the morning. She remembers fondly going down to Kent and visiting her aunt and uncle for a big Christmas dinner with fresh lamb and Christmas pudding. Her uncle doesn't really like turkey, although her aunt makes one for everybody else. And there was always just enough left over to make sure that all the dogs were well fed and had their Christmas supper as well. And then, after the pudding, they'd all pull the crackers, (these wonderful little presents that pop when you open them.) Each person would take one end and the person on their side would take the other, crossing their arms as they did so. So, your right hand would hold the cracker on your left, and vice versa. Then you pull, and they would make a large bang and the cheapest tackiest little presents would come out and fall onto the table. Then there were the worst most pathetic jokes that somehow always made you smile. Not to mention the most idiotic looking paper hats that the entire household would wear. And yet, everyone laughed and smiled, and when the Queen came on, they listened with widened ears with fondness, admiration, and love.

"Christmas is supposed to be a time of fond memories," Kate hears, startling her suddenly. She looks around and cannot see anyone, but suddenly sees movement from a man situated in the shadows of a tree, laying comfortably and very relaxed on a lounge chair meant for the poolside.

Kate watches as the man sits up, coming into view. He looks at her with a tender smile, his hands and his body somewhat tanned, almost as if he's been in the sun for days. He is wearing a long pair of Californian board shorts, which hang just beyond his knees. They are bright red, and crisp white, with white laces running up and down their sides. His sandals are dark black with silver lining, and he's wearing a red ball cap with a white rim bent slightly upwards.

"Hi, I didn't mean to disturb you, I was just walking through here," Kate says, somewhat hesitant, but still feeling a degree of safety because she is still within the complex.

"You're not disturbing me, I was just commenting on the look you were giving," the man says to her, seating himself more comfortably but not standing. "You had that look of deep reminiscence. Christmas has a way of doing that to people when they are struggling to find answers. We look back at the times that we cherish the most."

"That's true," Kate says, somewhat surprised at the conversation. "How did you know I was thinking about Christmas?"

"Most people. Not all, but most, find solace in the happy times that they had in their lives. The happiest times of all are during the times that we remember and feel the most safe. It helps us work through the problems that we have, and by remembering things that we cherish the most, we find ourselves again when we are lost," the man explains. "I've seen so many faces that held the same expression as yours, and only Christmas does that."

"Wow," Kate says. Then, with a slight grimace on her face, "You're a man. Can I ask you a question?"

"It would be my pleasure," the man says, watching as Kate comes forward and seats herself on a lounge chair near the pool. "Question away."

"Do you believe that people can change? Men, I mean," Kate questions.

"A very interesting question," he returns, with a pleasant smile absorbing his face moving his bleached goatee upwards. He removes his thin golden aviator sun glasses, with the light blue tint, to reveal amazingly clear blue eyes. "The answer to that is that people change every day, and don't even realise it. We become lost, heartbroken, elated. We become lovers, friends, and find ourselves in places that we never knew existed. I think the answer you are looking for, isn't whether or not someone can change, but can they change in a way to make you happy."

Silence follows, and Kate looks carefully at the man's soft eyes.

"If you ask someone to change, or force them to change, then they will because it is just another part of life. But the force of the change that *you* are seeking must come from the heart, and not from any other superficial means. For example, if you wish to change yourself to impress another, you will find that the change will only fade over time, because it is natural to become what we were most comfortable with. But if you look at yourself and see the world around you and feel the heart beating inside you, and see the change you wish to be from within, it will happen because it was meant to happen."

"Like a butterfly," she whispers.

"Like a new-born baby," he replies. "Change isn't something that anyone can do overnight. It isn't something that can be handed out and given on a whim. It has to occur within before it can be seen outwardly."

"So then tell me, why would anyone choose to lock themselves away from the world?" she queries. "I just can't understand why someone would want to voluntarily keep himself locked inside this shell when there is a world out there just waiting for him."

"As I said before, we find ourselves looking for solace in the places we feel the most safe." The man takes a deep breath, smelling the cold air that surrounds them. "Sometimes when we are angry, when we are blinded by the hate, we cannot see the world around us. We put on masks to hide the pain and suffering that the world has put us through. And the only choice that we believe we have, is to lock ourselves away in place where we feel safe and content. We do not risk, or try, or believe in anything or anyone. It is not because we cannot love, but that love and being loved only brings more pain and suffering. It is at times like this when men can do nothing but just breathe and live day to day, month to month, year to year, waiting for life to finally give way."

"I just don't understand," Kate says, shaking her head. "Life is so beautiful and precious. Why throw it away?"

"Why indeed," returns the man. "Why love? Why put your faith in something that inevitably will go? When you fall in love with someone, you know that sometime, somehow, that person will leave you."

"That's a sad way to look at it," she comments, crossing her arms.

"Sad, but true. The universe gives and takes as it pleases, and life moves back and forth in a never-ending cycle that cannot be controlled by you or anyone else upon the mortal plain. Eventually everything dies. So why live? Why love?"

"Because I believe that true love survives everything, no matter what happens," Kate explains, nodding her head.

"Because you believe," he returns softly. "That is faith. And it is in faith that we exist and live. The undying belief that we place in something or someone else; this is why we try."

"Faith," she replies. "So, he doesn't believe."

"I don't know," he replies. "Perhaps you should ask him, instead of a strange man sitting on a lounge chair in shorts during winter."

"Well, I didn't want to say anything," she announces with a smile, standing up again. "But they are nice shorts."

"Thank you," he replies. "It's a fashion thing."

"Cracking!" Kate gives the man a wink and turns and to go back to the building.

The cold winter wind catches her as she tries to move forward, but finds herself suddenly stopped. It almost pushes her back, but then relents enough for her to move once more. She cannot help but to look back to see if the man that she was speaking to is still in the lounge chair, but finds that he's gone. She gives it no second thought and enters the building once again, filling herself with the warmth as the pressure releases when the doors open.

Kate begins to wonder even more as she walks up the stairs, each step seeming more difficult than before. She ponders why and how you can make someone believe in something that they cannot see or touch. And why should she try? Why is this one different than all the others before? What it is that makes him so special? Why does she keep thinking about him?

Kate stops herself, and sits down quietly on the staircase. She takes a deep breath and smells all the various perfumes and cleaners that are pulsing in the air in order to sanitise it. She can't help but to twitch her nose, but still leans her head back as far as it will go and closes her eyes. Suddenly she can hear the dogs running in the snow, chasing her across the fields behind her mother's house. She can see her mother smiling through the little Edwardian styled wooden paned windows, washing the dishes from lunch. She can remember waving so frantically, and jumping backwards into the snow to make snow angels, only to have the dogs come up and lick her face. She hated that bit. Dog germs and other things of such nature have never pleased her, but she did love those dogs with all her heart. She didn't care if she was cold or wet, because inside the house she knew there would be a warm fire waiting for her.

Kate remembers going out that evening in the cold weather, dressed impeccably and freezing her toes off, in the hopes of getting a warm mince pie from old Mrs. Tompkins, along with some warm mulled wine. The church choir was always the dread of every child, because of the cold long nights and the sores that the shoes always put on their toes. But when they had their mince pie and mulled wine, the only time of the year that they were allowed anything like that, it made everything worthwhile. And the vicar always made sure that when they went back to church on Sunday, all the children would have a special treat for the Christingle service.

Kate slowly opens her eyes as she hears one of the tenants open the stairwell doors. She takes a deep breath and can't help but to smile. Then, in one swift motion she stands once more and begins the walk back up to the apartment.

As Kate opens the door, she shouts out to Tara, "I think I know what I'm going to do!"

Kate walks around the corner and sees a man standing next to Tara, who has a very bemused look. Tara rolls her eyes as the man turns around to reveal himself.

"Daniel," Kate exclaims, almost startled. "I thought you weren't in town until tomorrow night, for this party."

"I got back early, and I wanted to come over and surprise you," the man replies. He is a tall man, well built with a very devout chin. His hair is perfectly blond, which matches the light sports coat he is wearing that accents his broad shoulders perfectly.

"Oh," Kate returns, walking up to him slowly and giving him a confused half-hearted hug.

"Look, Kate," Daniel begins, somewhat stuttering. He looks down at a box he is holding, with a perfect ribbon tied around it. "I know that you couldn't find your—" he pauses. "Well, anyway here. I flew over to Russia and I had someone make one up for you exactly the same as the other one. We even had to go into the Russian State Library in St. Petersburg and find pictures of it. Even then they were sketchy but the jeweller promised me it should be as close to the original as possible."

Kate looks down and opens the jewellery box that Daniel hands her. She carefully pulls the ribbon off and opens it to reveal a similar piece of jewellery to her heirloom. She gets somewhat teary, and closes the box and hugs Daniel.

"This was so incredibly sweet," she says. "It must have cost a fortune."

"Well, it's not like I don't have enough," he says, shrugging when Kate steps back.

"I can't accept it, though," Kate says putting it back into his hand.

"Don't be silly!" he exclaims. "Why wouldn't you?"

Kate takes a deep breath and puts her hand on his chest. She then lifts a single finger up, motioning for him to wait while she goes off to her room. Within seconds she returns with the box that Pat gave her days earlier, opening it and showing Daniel. Daniels face drops at first, but then a smile overcomes him, and he nods happily.

"Wow," he shouts in exasperation. "Where? How? When?"

"A few days ago, a friend of mine found it," she explains softly. "He said that he just knew it was for me. Isn't that funny?"

"Yeah, really!" Daniel replies happily. "Well, it doesn't matter. I had this made for you, so keep it for a spare."

Daniel puts the other box in Kate's coat pocket and kisses her on the cheek. Kate shakes her head and tries to grab hold of it with her hand, but he has already begun the walk toward the door in order to leave.

"Stop, Daniel!" Kate proclaims, following pathetically behind.

"Forget it, Kate," Daniel says. "Can't anyway, have a meeting in fifteen minutes. I'll talk to you more tomorrow about it."

"Blimey Daniel, you silly plonker!" she says in frustration, then stops and sighs as he shuts the door behind him.

"Bloody twat," Tara says, folding her arms across her chest. "For such a rich bloke, he sure is bloody-minded."

"Yeah, but he's sweet," Kate replies, plopping herself onto the sofa.

"I don't know what it is about him, but he just winds me up. I don't know, I guess rich bloody Yanks just think they can buy their way into everything. Money isn't everything."

"Well, it can help," Kate laughs.

"But it can't buy the one thing that counts the most," Tara says.

Kate goes silent, and nods her head.

"So?" Tara returns, walking off to the kitchen. It only takes seconds, but she brings back two cups of tea and hands one to Kate. "What were you saying you think you know what you're going to do?"

Kate holds the cup of tea in her hands, warming her fingers as she stares at the box on the table. "Never mind, babes. It doesn't really matter."

Tara walks over behind Kate and puts her arms around her, resting her chin on top of Kate's head. The two sigh and look at the empty screen on the television. It is only then that they hear a huge belch come from the bedroom. The two wince at the sound, then laugh at the same time.

"Do you wanna kill some alien scum?" Tara says suddenly, looking at the game console on the floor.

"Yeah!" Kate returns happily, watching as Tara leaps over the back of the sofa with her tea.

"Have you ever noticed how all the alien bad guys are British?" Tara says curiously. "Then again, I guess we are a bunch of hooligans at heart."

"And I wouldn't have it any other way," Kate says, grabbing a controller and seating herself next to Tara on the floor.

Chapter 12

The Thing About Spirit Guides

"How was the concert?" Joseph asks, sipping from his beer, putting his feet up on the coffee table he bought six months ago. The sound of a pizza box opening barely can be heard over the inane amounts of Christmas music that's playing on the television while they wait for the sports game to start.

"Yeah, the boy did good," Pat replies, seating himself at the other end of the couch. "He kinda hit a wrong note, and everybody laughed, but you know Thomas."

"He didn't even notice, did he?"

"Not one bit," laughs Patrick. He reaches over and Joseph hands him the box of pizza, setting it back down in between them after Pat finds himself a piece. The two then sit and drink their beer, watching as the cheerleaders on the television dance about in their Christmas style outfits and wave happily at the cameras.

Moments pass, and the announcer comes on television, showing pictures of the snowfall that is rapidly coming down on to the field, and the seven feet of snow that surrounds the outside that is constantly being cleared away. They show pictures of beautiful ice castles and sculptures that people have made, which always impress all who behold them.

"So," Joseph begins.

"What's that?"

"Do you realise that this is the first concert that you haven't given me a ticket to?" Joseph looks over with a sombre face at his dear friend, as he raises the beer bottle to his lips. "So."

Pat chuckles a bit, slightly going red at the thought, and takes a drink from his beer to mask it. He merely shrugs in reply, reaching over and getting another piece of pizza.

"Did she like it?" Joseph says, turning and facing the enormous wall mounted television again.

Patrick coughs slightly, spilling his beer down the front of his shirt, and his piece of pizza falls back on to the top of the box, cheese side down of course. Joseph just takes the opportunity to laugh and take another drink.

"What's wrong with you, Muttly?" Joseph asks.

"How do you mean?" Pat seats himself back down after wiping some of the beer off of his shirt. He then grumbles to himself as he peels his pizza back off the top of the pizza box. He decides to just fold it into a sandwich shape instead and eat it this way.

"Kate's incredible," Joseph says calmly. "And far be it for me to say anything, being your best friend and all, but you are the biggest jackass in the universe if you can't see that."

"Thanks," Pat replies with half the slice of pizza in his mouth.

"Seriously, Mutt," Joseph insists. "That woman is probably the best thing in the world, and she for whatever miracle you mustered actually thinks you're the ball. So, you'd better wake up and do something about it before she's gone."

Silence ensues, to which Pat just takes a few sips from his beer. Joseph stands and goes into the kitchen, bringing out two more beers for them. He tosses Pat one as he seats himself.

"Mutt," Joseph begins, "I know things feel like they're just going lego on you, but you can't keep holding on to her. You can't keep suffering inside just because you think that you should be punished."

Pat continues to remain silent, finishing his beer and starting the next. The game begins on the television and the roar of the crowd overtakes the announcer's voice. He is staring at the television, but he is not watching it. He merely continues to listen.

"You didn't do anything wrong, bro," Joseph says softly and clearly, pronouncing every word slowly and crisp.

"I did, Joe," Pat finally says. "I ignored her. I turned away from her. I wasted the time that I should have spent with her."

Joseph reaches over and puts a hand on his friend's shoulder. The two sit there for moments, just listening to the empty words of the announcer, and the Christmas music they are playing in the background at the stadium.

"Believe it or not, you didn't do anything that any other man on earth hasn't done in their lives. So you lost track. So you forgot to pay attention to her. No one on this planet is perfect. Not enough to suffer like you are," Joseph says.

"The last words that she told me were 'I love you, Pat. More than you'll ever know.' And I didn't know what she meant. I honestly didn't know," Pat explains, sighing and trying to hold the pain inside. "I just wish I could believe that she really knows how much I love her, and that I'd do anything in the world for her. I'd sell my soul to have her with me again."

"I know," Joseph replies. "But you can't sell something that doesn't belong to you. And even if you could, do you really think she would want you to?"

"No," Pat whispers.

"You have a chance to build something wonderful with someone else," Patrick hears. "All you have to do is open your eyes and look at her. I mean, ***just look at her!*** The woman thinks that the world revolves around you, and you can't even see it."

"It just doesn't happen twice," Patrick says.

"Maybe not. Maybe you're right," Joseph confesses, standing up and walking over to the wall. "It will never be the same as it was before. It just isn't possible. Life changes, people change, the world changes, the universe is constantly changing with every second that passes. So why would you possibly think that it would be like before? Why would you want it to be? You're absolutely right when you say it just doesn't happen twice. But it can happen again, differently. All you have to do is just give it half a chance. Open up that gate inside your brick wall and let this person in. For goodness sake, Muttly, all you need to do is just say three words to her and she'd give you her soul. I'm no expert, but even I can see that."

"I don't know if I'm ready," Pat replies, slowly looking up at his friend. Joseph instantly comes down to his knees before his friend and shakes both his hands at him in frustration.

"YOU DON'T KNOW???" he exclaims. "Have you looked at this woman?"

Pat laughs at the statement. "She is beautiful."

"She is a goddess," Joseph corrects. "And she likes YOU!"

"I don't know, Joseph. Maybe she's just being nice," Pat returns.

"Don't make me slap you with the pizza. Afterwards, I swear I will take down my television and smash it over your thick skull. And believe me you don't have that much hair that it's going to shield the blow."

Pat can't help but to smile. He closes his eyes and nods. "I'll say something to her."

"Thank Christmas for that!" Joseph shouts, standing up once again. "I was afraid of how I was going to clean the cheese off my couch."

"I'm not sure what, though. But I'll say something."

"Okay, fine, now we can at least sit down and watch some football," Joseph announces, slapping his friend on his knee. "Like civilised humans."

"Right," Pat returns with a nod, drinking from his beer. Joseph picks up a piece of pizza again and begins to take a bite from it. "But I'm still not sure she likes me."

Pat is met with the slice of pizza across the side of his face. He closes his eyes, quite unsurprised at the tactic his friend has used. In fact, he removes the pizza slowly, somewhat surprised at how much sauce is remaining on his face, then proceeds to eat the rest of the slice.

The two continue to laugh, and be friends, just enjoying one another's friendship throughout the game, as they have done so many times before. But Joseph can feel his friend is changing. His soul is turning. His heart is beginning to beat once more. It may have stopped for so long, and it may have shrunk and become cold to the idea of many things except his son, but it is beginning to warm and breathe life into him once again.

The two reminisce for hours, remembering times together throughout their lives and the many idiotic things that they have done. They remember their many puppy loves throughout school and the stupidity they had when trying to show them how much they loved these girls. They have been part of one another's lives for so long, that they cannot remember life without the other. The one would only ever wish the best upon the other, no matter what the consequence.

Eventually the night comes to a close, the game finished, the endless conversations complete, and Pat stands once more. He has been drinking coffee for the past few hours, but has enjoyed the company of his dear friend. The two when together seem to escape the mundane realities of their existence. It is just how it has always been.

The night has turned later than he has expected. The concert took much out of him, and then watching the game on television with Joseph as well hasn't helped either. He does everything he can to keep his eyes open, and knows that he shouldn't drive, but he needs to get home to his son.

The drive takes an extraordinarily long time, and he should have taken Joseph's advice and just slept at his place. They sat and talked for hours, about life, about women, and their past relationships, and about Kate. Joseph really likes Kate, and makes no attempt at hiding the fact that she may be the best thing in the universe for Pat. The words echo throughout his mind, over and over again. He knows inside he feels something for Kate, but what he isn't sure. He knows that she is probably something that will change his life forever, make him stronger and a better person. And yet, he still hesitates. He is comfortable and happy. Or at least he believes he is. There is so much emptiness inside him. Joseph says that it is because he feels betrayed by life. But it is only he who is betraying himself. He is taking the long empty road to self-destruction. It may not happen today, or tomorrow, but the time will come when he has no choice but to sit in a room with himself and say that there is nothing left on this planet for him. One day his son will leave him, and if he carries on this road, he will hate his own son for it. And his father will leave him, just like everyone else that he has cared for. One day, he will be alone. He will be alone because no matter what he does, or who he is with, they will never fulfil the one thing that he needed most in life. The anger will build, and it will merely be a defence against life and the people in it.

Pat pulls into his drive as slowly and quietly as he can, knowing that it's late and that the others will be asleep, although he can see the kitchen light on. He has been thinking so much, that he can barely remember the drive, which would normally scare him, but the hour is too late, and he cannot be bothered to be scared, only tired.

As he steps out from his car, he takes a deep cool breath from the wintry night itself filling his lungs with as much as he can. The thoughts melt away, and for just a single moment he doesn't seem to be thinking about anything or anyone. It soothes him, even if it is only until he opens his eyes once again and walks into his porch way. As he enters the house, he can see a figure sitting at the table, waiting for him. At first, he thinks it may be his father, but then, as he approaches, he can see that Kate is sitting at the table waiting for him, sipping from a cup.

"Kate?" he queries, slowly coming into the kitchen.

"Patrick!" she says excitedly.

"What are you doing here so late?" he says, coming in and sitting down next to her.

"I'm not sure," she laughs, almost in tears. "I guess you could say that I was passing through, but I'd be lying. Your father told me to come in when he saw me pull into the drive, and he made me a cup of cocoa with marshmallows, because he ran out of tea. He's just gone upstairs to check on Thomas." Pat smiles, and he cannot help but to put his hand on her back comfortingly.

"How long have you been here?"

Kate looks up and looks at the microwave to see the time, and covers her mouth when she sees how late it really is. "I'm sorry, I didn't realise how late it was. I think I should probably go."

"No!" Pat returns, putting his hand over hers. "Stay. Please, you're here now. At least have another cup of cocoa and sit and talk with me for a while."

Kate looks into his eyes, and she can't help herself, but just smiles and nods to him. Patrick stands and walks over to a pan and heats some water for her, as the kettle seems to have disappeared. He looks over and sees the shadow of his father walking back up the stairs as quietly as he can.

"What did you think of the concert?" Patrick asks Kate cheerfully, mixing the cup of powdered cocoa with a bit of cold milk. The same way he makes it for Thomas in the mornings to drink with his pancake.

"It was wonderful," Kate coos. "I'm so glad that I could go."

"I think Thomas really appreciated it," Pat explains to her, leaning himself comfortably against the counter while he waits for the water to boil.

"I think that he has a crush on his teacher," Kate reveals, smiling as she watches him. "She is really quite a pretty teacher."

"Do you really think he has a crush?" Pat is quietly surprised by the statement, but is interrupted by the steam coming over from the pan of water. He turns and pulls the pan off and tries his best to fill her cup while stirring it with a spoon. He is rather unsuccessful, which causes Kate to giggle slightly, but he still manages to make two cups of cocoa which he then tops with tiny little marshmallows.

"Thank you," Kate tells him as she takes the cup from him.

"Wow," Pat says to himself, looking up at the picture of Santa Claus that his son had drawn, and he had hung on the refrigerator. "I'm just amazed."

"Your little boy is growing up," he hears, suddenly awakening him from his daze. "I think you've done an excellent job with him, you know."

"I don't know about that, but I did what I could," Pat returns.

A silence ensues as Kate looks at him, and watches the reaction on his face when she spoke her last words. He isn't looking at her directly, but staring into his cup, carefully watching the rainbow coloured marshmallows circle one another as they melt into one giant mass.

"Patrick," she begins, to which he lifts his head and looks at her.

"Yes, I know," he replies with a nod. "The answer is nearly eight years... Just after Thomas was born. We were only married for two years."

Kate struggles to find the right words, but only manages, "It must have been hard." She closes her eyes, as she cannot believe what she just stated.

"It was at first," Pat replies without hesitation. "But we managed, and I did what I had to do."

Kate places her hand over his, to which he only closes his eyes. The words she thought would come so easily, the conversation that she had played in her mind over and over again fades and eludes her. She cannot remember her name, let alone what to say or how to say it.

"I still hear her inside," Pat reveals. "She still talks to me, telling me what I'm doing wrong with my life, and how I need to be strong...to change."

Kate says nothing, but merely continues to listen as she holds his hand as comfortingly as she can.

"I don't know. When she left me, everything inside me died, shattered into a million different pieces. I didn't know how to breathe, let alone stay alive. It was like someone had driven a stake straight through the centre of my chest and I couldn't do anything about it except just stand there and die.

"Eventually, though, I picked the pieces of my life up, choosing which ones I wanted to keep and which ones I wanted to leave there on the floor in front of me. I looked at the world around me and decided then and there that I was going to give my son the best father on earth."

"You've done a brilliant job," she whispers to him, stroking his knuckle with her thumb. "He's a brilliant little boy who smiles and lights the entire world up."

"I know. He gets that from his mother," Pat replies, his eyes remaining closed. Then, he cannot help but to open them once more, revealing the water in them as he tries so desperately to hold his feelings back.

"She must have been a very special woman," Kate says, still unsure at what to say but trying to follow what her heart says.

"You would have liked each other, I think. She was strong, and stubborn. Everyone liked her, though. Like you, people can't help it, they just seemed to fall in love with her the second they met her."

Kate hears the words, but remains silent.

"She was my universe; my everything," Pat replies, fighting with his emotions. "I just..."

His voice trails off for a moment. Pat takes a deep breath and stands up slowly, walking over to the fridge and getting a bottle of water out. Kate remains silent and watches him, seeing the pain pour from the open wound in his chest.

"I blame myself for everything. I feel I should have been more to her, while I had the chance. I regret that every day, using it as a constant reminder to do the right thing and be the kind of person that she would have wanted me to be."

"I think she would be very proud of you, Patrick," Kate whispers.

"Maybe... I'll never know. I'm only left in this constant state of confusion, wondering if she can ever forgive me for not being there when she needed me most," Pat explains, drinking the entirety of the bottle. Then, "I suppose that is what hurts the most. She would take me in her arms and just try and hold me, and I'd just push her away. We never yelled at each other, but I just went into a shell, which hurts even more. I'd go silent and cold, filled with anger and hate for the world and everything in it. And I could never say I was sorry. It was childish of me. I loved her, and I just didn't know it until it was too late.

"There was a time when I would have flown across the world just to buy her a set of pearls straight out of the water just for her. But towards the end, anything I did for her, I resented with every fibre of my being. Just bringing home flowers made me resent her more, because I couldn't stop what was happening to the woman I love. And yet, she still loved me through all of it. Through all the misery, all my pain, all the anguish and shame that I was feeling because of something I couldn't control; she never gave up on me."

Pat looks over at Kate and sees the tears in her eyes, and her hands folded across her face, the tips of her fingers just underneath her centre brow.

"Her last words to me were that she would always love me, more than I would ever know," he explains. "And I didn't realise what she meant, until now."

Kate stands, her hands still firmly in place. She lowers them slowly, their eyes locked upon one another, and she steps forward to him. In one swift motion, Kate puts her arms around his waist and pulls him close, her hands resting on his upper back. Slowly, Patrick raises one hand and puts it around her, then the other. And in one swift motion their bodies are so close that they cannot help but to feel one another's warmth. It is this moment that all humanity lives for. In this brief moment, their souls finally touch, reaching deep into one another in a wonderful amalgamation of two beings that were lost before now. They hold one another, just content at finally finding themselves.

Kate is the first one to step away, only so that she can take both his hands, and hold them in hers. She looks at his face and smiles, releasing a glow upon him that he could not see before. It is here that she takes his face in her hands and pulls him down into her, kissing him. It is as if she were kissing him for the first time, and unlike any other kiss that he can remember. Her lips are the softest that he has ever felt, and they bring a warmth and kindness to his soul that has been missing for years, decades, centuries.

"Stay with me," he manages to whisper, as she pulls her lips away.

Kate looks at him and smiles that wonderful gentle smile at him, taking both his hands in hers once again. She merely shakes her head slowly and pulls him close once more.

"I can't," she whispers. "Not yet."

Pat pulls her so close that her feet leave the ground, and she can't help but to giggle slightly in surprise. But then, he puts her back down and nods.

"I've got to go," she whispers, placing her cheek against his chest. "I've got what I came for now. But I'll see you tomorrow for the party, okay?"

Pat can't speak, his throat is dry, and his heart is racing to the point that it hurts to breathe. He feels Kate touch his chest with her fingers as she steps back away from him.

"You're trembling, and your heart is beating fast," she tells him, her words soft and gentle. "I think I like listening to your heart beating."

And with her words, Kate turns and slowly walks out the door, turning one last time and smiling to him as she does so. Then, the door closes, and she is gone.

Pat stands there in utter disbelief, unsure if what happened just really happened. He touches his chest, and closes his eyes, unsure if he is hurting or not. He can feel the immense pain flowing through him, and yet, he is euphoric and elated. He feels numb suddenly, and has to seat himself down, his stomach so tight that he feels like vomiting. Through all these strange emotions, though, he feels happy, and completely confused. For a minute, he feels like he is ten years old again.

A moment passes, and he hears the stirrings of someone behind him. Fully expecting to see his father, he turns to see Thomas standing in the doorway, his eyes halfway shut and his arm trying to block the light out.

"Little bear," Pat says, coming to his feet and picking his son up into his arms. "Did I wake you?"

"No," he responds with a deep yawn. "I just wanted some pancakes."

Patrick laughs, and takes his son back upstairs. He remembers not a year ago he couldn't even feel the little guy, and now it's like lifting something twice as heavy.

He is growing so fast, and so quickly, that time just won't forgive him the chance of missing a second.

"Daddy," Thomas whispers into his father's ear. "Why were you talking to Santa earlier at the concert?"

"I wasn't talking to Santa," Pat replies softly, stroking his son's head.

"Yes, you were. Don't you remember? At least I think that was him."

Pat merely smiles, and kisses his son's head.

After Pat finishes putting his tired son back into bed, and kisses him on the forehead, he turns to see his father standing in the doorway. His father kindly puts a hand on his shoulder as he exits and shuts the door to Thomas's room. Together the two walk back downstairs into the living room.

"Sorry about that, son," Ben says, seating himself in his usual spot that he has been sitting in for the last five years or so. "She just sort of turned up about a half hour or so ago, and I couldn't leave her out there."

"It's alright dad," Pat says with a nod of his head, also seating himself in the process. "You did the right thing."

"I figured you two needed to talk about something," Ben explains. "Do you want to talk about it over some coffee?"

"Yeah," Pat returns. "That'd be nice."

Ben stands once more, followed not too long after by Pat, to which both men head into the kitchen. It doesn't take but a few silent minutes for Ben to make them both a cup of coffee, and for them to seat themselves at the kitchen table once again. Ben wants to ask the question, but he knows that it has to come from Pat. He had been pressing him for so many years, and has learned to understand that it just pushes deeper and further away into his hole of solitude.

"The game was good," Pat begins. "The Spirit Guide and I sat and watched it."

"I figured that's where you were going. How was Joseph?" Ben replies.

"Good. He and I sat and talked for some time. Like we used to do," Patrick explains. "We talked for most of the game. You know what he's like."

"Did you find anything out?"

"Certain things, I guess. Mostly, I guess he just started me thinking about the direction I was headed, and which direction I needed to focus on most. He has a funny way of putting things, but it usually comes out in a way that I can understand them.

"He started talking to me about mountains, and things, and how everything in life if just like a mountain. Why the most beautiful animals on earth live in some of the harshest conditions. Things like that."

"Sounds like Joseph," Ben says laughing at the words.

"He's been my dearest friend for before I can remember having friends," Patrick says to himself.

"I know," Ben replies, not really understanding the context in which his son spoke.

"I think he made me realise that I'm not supposed to keep blaming myself for the way life turned out," Pat reveals, looking into his father's eyes. "I don't know why I couldn't hear it before. What happened, why it happened, all of these things; they are all in the past. I have to let it go, and open my eyes to what's standing right in front of me."

"Kate?" Ben returns softly. "She's definitely an incredible woman. Strange, but aren't they all."

Pat finished his coffee, and stands, going over to make himself another cup. Afterwards, he stares outside at the frost that covers the grass, making the world look as if it were covered in snow.

"I'm not quite sure what's going on between us, but I know it's," he pauses, "different."

"I think she thinks that as well," Ben returns, choosing his words carefully. "Is that why she came here tonight?"

"I don't know," Pat discloses. "I guess she wanted to know about Lisa. Whatever it was, I think I told her whatever she needed to know, because she left happy."

"Well, that's something son," Ben says.

"Yes, it is."

"You know, that's the thing about spirit guides..." Pat's father words trail off as he takes another sip of his coffee.

Chapter 13

The One Choice

Patrick awakens slowly, his eyes opening to the sounds of Saturday morning cartoons on the television in the living room. His neck hurts, and he realises quickly that he must have fallen asleep sitting at his desk in his den. The first thing that he manages to focus on is the painting of Lisa, and her eyes staring back at him with that gentle smile. He had dreamed of her again last night, something that he hadn't done in quite a while. He can't remember how he managed to do it, but in some way, he blocked her out. But last night she haunted his dreams, filling them with memories of the two of them together when they were most in love, and of times that they could have shared. He can feel his heart aching once again, but somehow, it's different than before.

The sounds coming from outside his den tell him instantly that Thomas is up and that his favourite show is playing. The fresh smell of pancakes rolls into the room, even through the closed door, and there is no doubt left in his mind of which day it is.

Patrick remains in his chair for a moment longer, staring at his left hand and the finger that has remained without a ring upon it for longer than he can remember. He touches his chest, and still feels the lump that lay under his shirt, hiding the ring that he carries near his heart. His breath stops momentarily, and he closes his eyes, tracing the edges of the wedding band with his fingertips. He holds his hand over it momentarily, and then takes a deep breath. Slowly, his eyes open and he brings himself to his feet.

As he opens the door, the light from the low winter sun outside nearly blinds him, and he has no choice but to put his arm up in order to see into the room. He can make out a small figure sitting completely entranced upon the floor, of whom he can only assume is his young son, and the smell of the pancakes would only lead him to believe that his father is in the kitchen.

"Morning," he says to Thomas, to which he receives no reply. He truly didn't expect one, but he always tries. Instead, he continues through the living room and enters the kitchen, where as predicted Ben is preparing the last of the pancakes and finishing off some breakfast sausages for everyone.

"Morning, kid," Ben states happily. "Did you sleep good?"

"Not really," Pat replies, stretching his arms as best he can, trying to get the pain out of his neck. "I think I must have fallen asleep at my desk again."

"Kinda figured that," Ben returns, still quite cheerful. "What kinda eggs ya' want this morning?"

"I'm okay, thanks," Pat explains, pouring himself a cup of coffee.

"Some foreign speaking guy showed up first thing this morning," his father reveals, "and left you a whole mess of stuff. I put it all in your bedroom for you."

"Already?" Pat says, yawning in the process. "Don't people ever sleep in on Saturdays anymore?"

"I was up before the sun, son," Ben states happily, tilting his head in a quick motion as he does so.

"Yeah but you come from the generation that believes that if you don't walk six miles to work, then you're not actually working." Pat smirks at his father, and yawns yet again.

"I don't know about that, but I believe that every sunrise that you get a chance to see, is better than the best dream that you may be having," he tells his son. "Because— "

"Because the sunrise is real, and a dream is just a dream," Pat finishes for him.

It is here that the two hear Thomas waddle into the room, taking a big stretch as he does so. He says nothing, but rubs his eyes and walks over to the table and seats himself comfortably.

"Morning," he whispers.

"Did they save the universe again?" Patrick asks, drinking his coffee.

"Yeah, it was wickedly cool!" Thomas says excitedly. He then proceeds to tell the two a step by step description of what happened in his show, of which both men try desperately to sound enthusiastic by it all.

Ben finishes the last of the pancakes off, and then the three seat themselves and give their thanks. Afterwards, they begin to eat, with Thomas as usual taking as many pancakes as his plate will hold. They continue to eat, in a somewhat orderly fashion, with Ben reading his paper.

"Little bear, may I ask you a question?" Pat enquires of his son, trying to gather his attention. "What do you think of Kate?"

"She's pretty," Thomas replies instantly. "And she's nice. I think she likes you."

"I do too," Pat returns. "Do you like her?"

"I dunno," he shrugs to his father, somewhat unsure at the question. "She likes pirates!"

"Yeah," Pat nods to himself. "Do you mind her being around here?"

"Nope," he says pleasantly. "You don't seem to be grumpy so much when she's around. Well maybe a different kind, anyway. I think. And she likes pancakes."

"Grumpy, huh?"

"That's an understatement," Ben says through the paper.

"As I was saying," Pat continues, "I'm thinking about asking Kate if she would like to come over more often. Would you think that's alright? I think she'd like it if you wouldn't mind."

Thomas continues to eat his pancakes, and shrugs at the question. "I guess so. Is she going to change the channel a lot? I don't like it when people do that. Mrs. Patrick does that a lot when I'm over at their house, and I don't really like that."

"I'll make sure I tell her that."

"And don't let her stand in front of the screen with the phone, either. That's not very nice," Thomas explains wholeheartedly, putting another piece of pancake in his mouth.

"I will make sure she knows that," Pat tells his son. "Finish eating, before you can think of anything else."

When their meal is finished, Thomas asks if he can return to his important Saturday duties, and Pat stands to wash the dishes. Between Ben and himself, the two finish rather quickly, a gentle silence falling into the room. There is a gentle unrest, though, and Patrick can feel his father's anxiety even through the silence.

"What is it, dad?" Patrick finally asks.

"I didn't say nuthin'," Ben grunts in return, in his usual grammatically incorrect speech.

"Just ask me already, so I can go have a shower, and maybe have five minutes rest on a real bed before the day hits me for real."

"Nothing, son," Ben repeats. "Well, maybe....I don't know. Are you sure about this girl, son?"

Patrick laughs, and slaps the back of his father's shoulder. He merely shakes his head and turns away heading out of the kitchen.

"Well, I was just asking," Ben grumbles to himself. Along with his statement he returns to putting the last of the dishes away.

Patrick climbs the stairs and enters his room, his eyes still somewhat tired from the lack of sleep. He heads over to his bathroom, but suddenly stops when he sees the multiple boxes on the floor and the fabric suit cover hanging on the door. There is a note on the main suit cover addressed to him. As he opens it to read it, he notices the soft velvety silk Pat of the paper. He inspects the words, noticing that they are step-by-step instructions on how to prepare the garments, and in which order they are placed on him. He rolls his eyes as he sees the signature of D. Malchovo, to which he crumples the paper and tosses it on the floor, then proceeds to the bathroom for his shower.

"Instructions," he mumbles begrudgingly, feeling the warm water begin to come out of the shower tap. "It's not like I've never worn a suit before!"

The water pours across his flesh, and he continues to turn the heat up slowly every few seconds, the steam so heavy that he cannot see anything except himself. He continues this process, grumbling and speaking angry insults and sarcastic statements aimed at David, until finally he realises that the water is coming out too hot and he has to jump backwards in order to keep from scolding himself. It takes nearly all his strength to reach through the shower and turn the heat back down to a reasonable level. Finally, he finishes rinsing himself off, still shaking his head, he dries himself off as best he can.

As he walks back into the bedroom, towel around waist, he walks over the boxes and past the piece of paper crumpled on the floor. He cannot help himself, but to pick it up and look at it once again. Then, without hesitation he crumples it again and throws it over his shoulder.

Pat hears Ben calling up to him as he finishes putting some jeans on, and he steps out into the hallway to hear more clearly. He hates it when people shout profusely, as Thomas now does as well. So, without answering, he walks down the stairs and into the kitchen where Ben is looking out into the garden, not even noticing that Pat is standing behind him as he continues to call out his name.

"Yes, dad?" he asks quietly, causing his father to jump. As Ben turns around he notices that he is holding up and waving his cell phone.

"Kate is on the phone for you," Ben explains.

Pat sighs and takes his phone from his father. He can feel his heart beating faster and faster as he looks at it momentarily. Flashbacks of his high school days enter his mind, and he notices that his palms are becoming sweaty, along with his forehead. A deep breath, he takes, until he finally brings the phone up to his ear.

"Hello," he says cheerfully.

"Patrick," Kate says softly, with a gentle warmth that only she knows to give.

"Hi," he replies, his voice becoming soft suddenly. He turns as he sees the expression on his father's bemused face. Patrick decides to carry on outward into the living room, and then up the stairs into his room as quickly as possible.

"I was just calling to..." Her voice trails off. "I don't know, just to say hi."

"Hi," Patrick repeats, and hears a small laugh on the other end of the phone.

"David called me and said that you should have your clothes for tonight. You are still coming, aren't you?" he hears her ask, a slight sound of concern dancing amidst her voice.

"Yes," he manages to say.

"Good!" she exclaims with joy. "Don't worry about driving, because someone should be around to pick you up."

"Pardon?" he asks.

"Just because you might want to have a drink, or toast something, or just anything like that. Daniel is sending cars out to all the guests who don't have drivers," she explains.

Pat suddenly gets an uneasy feeling in his stomach, but manages to keep it under control.

"Anyway, I'll see you at the party. I promised David that I would go with him to see Daniel early, so I'll just have to meet you there. Are you going to be okay with that?" Kate questions.

"Okay," he says somewhat hesitantly.

"Good! I'll have to talk to you later, I'm in a bit of a rush," she explains. Then, softly, "I'll see you there, and we'll talk more. I promise."

Patrick hears a beep from his phone, to say that she has gone. He can feel his heart racing again, and he seats himself on the edge of his bed, putting the phone next to him as he falls back into his covers, both arms spread outward. He can only close his eyes from exhaustion and sigh.

Time passes, and he doesn't realise how long it's been, but he is awakened by his son as he jumps up on the bed behind him, shouting "wake up sleepy head." His entire body is shuddering and throbbing like a painful headache, but he can't help but to smile and close his eyes. Within seconds, as the bouncing continues, he sighs once again and jumps up as quickly as he can in order to grab his son's feet and pull them out from underneath him. There is an almighty squeal that he is sure that all of Seattle has heard, followed by immense laughter as he tickles Thomas until he nearly has tears coming from his eyes.

Patrick stands, his son running out of the room as quickly as he first entered. He looks over to his clock and sees that it is still morning, and he has at most of the day yet until he is supposed to be picked up to go to this extravagant event. Joseph told him that he was going to meet him at his place and they would meet the guys over at the local pizza place for lunch, along with Thomas. Thomas always looks forward to spending the day with Uncle Joseph, because he lets him have the all-you-can-eat ice cream buffet.

Pat readies himself as best he can, and heads downstairs calling out to Thomas to get himself ready for going over to Joseph's house, in which he can hear an ecstatic shout of glee from his son. It's the one day of the week where Thomas is allowed to wear what he likes and usually wears his superhero t-shirt and some sunglasses that Joseph bought for him when they all went skiing earlier in the year up at Mt. Baker.

By the time Patrick has reached the bottom stair, Thomas is bouncing on the couch, jacket on and ready to go, laughing at his sleepy-faced father. Pat can't help but to wonder where he gets all the energy from, as he picks his keys up off the side table and shouts out to his father. The two of them exit the house, Thomas racing to the car as fast as he can, and his father crawling along like an old tortoise.

"Uncle Joseph said he had a new gadget for you and him to build together," Pat informs his son, who is busy buckling up.

"Cool!" Thomas replies aloud. "I wonder if it's the new XS-B from the fighter squadron series. It just came out yesterday, and I saw it on the television."

"Sure," Pat returns, knowing full well that it most likely is, because his dear friend tries successfully to spoil his son. "Just remember to say thank you."

"Yup," Thomas replies happily, putting the headphones on and starting the television. Pat can but roll his eyes in exasperation and sigh. And with the faint exhale of air, he pulls out of his drive.

The drive itself to Joseph's has become familiar to both parties within the car. Thomas has come to learn every tree, road sign, and mile marker in between in order to know when to turn the headset off and get ready to jump out. He likes to know how much longer he can watch his programs, or program as the case may be.

Joseph is awaiting the two of them patiently on his porch, playing with the latest palm-sized video gaming machine as they pull into the drive. Thomas is immediately drawn out of the car before it comes to a complete stop, shouting familiar words such as "cool" and "wicked" over and over again. Pat can't help but to smile at his friend, who hands the machine over to the young man and shows him how to use it as best he can.

"I thought we weren't going to get him anything before Christmas," Pat says to his friend, taking his hand and pulling him into his chest as they always do.

"What are uncles for?" Joseph says in return. "Besides, one of the contractors gave it to me. His brother works down in Seattle for one of the gaming companies."

"Sure," Pat returns with a slight note of sarcasm.

"Let's go inside," Joseph says, patting his friend on the shoulder.

The two men enter the house, leaving the youngest sitting happily on the front step, playing his new gaming machine with such vigour. Joseph walks into the kitchen, while Pat finds himself his usual place along the sofa, to await his drink.

"What's this I hear you're going out tonight?" Joseph calls out, coming into the living room with two glasses of ice water. Pat doesn't reply, as he knows what's going to come next, as he reaches behind his head to take hold of the water. "Have you decided what you're going to do then?"

"Yes and no," Pat whispers.

"Well, you'll have to figure it out sooner or later."

As Pat opens his mouth to speak, Thomas comes running into the house with his new toy in his hand. The two men turn over their shoulders and look at him, his eyes looking as if the world was just about to come to an end.

"Is everything okay, little bear?" Pat questions.

"Did the game break?" Joseph then asks, seeing the look of confusion on Thomas's face.

"No," he says, "but I just saw the time on this, and I don't want to miss the ice cream buffet!"

Pat and Joseph both give a tender silent laugh, and turn back to set their drinks down on the coffee table. Joseph says that he'll drive them over, standing with Pat. Thomas loves riding in his Uncle Joseph's sports car. Pat always says that it's a bit too excessive for his tastes, but somehow it just suits Joseph completely. His reply is always the same to everyone he meets, though, which is that he didn't choose it, but a little bear picked it out for him. Besides that, how many sports cars have booster seats in the back, he usually finishes explaining.

After arriving at the pizza restaurant that they meet at every weekend accordingly, the three exit the car and head towards the door, with Pat having to remind his son to be mindful of the surrounding cars and people. Even before the two men can reach the door, Thomas is in and talking to Jenny, the friendly young waitress that has greeted him happily every time they have come for the past year. Thomas knows better than to wait for his father at this stage, as he knows that both his uncle Joseph and his father will be talking with Jenny for some time. Jenny has already told him exactly where the others are sitting, which is the same place that they always sit at, just next to the window in the corner, not too far from the ice cream counter.

"Tonto!" Enrique shouts, laughing as he finishes losing the arm-wrestling challenge he gave Thomas.

"Hey," Brent says, nodding his head once and pushing his sun glasses up with his finger.

"*Sup*, Prof!" Joseph sits himself in his usual chair, and picks a slice of pizza up from off the table. Pat follows suit, as Thomas runs off with his cup to get himself an orange soda from the self-service fountain. It is a treat he is afforded every once and awhile.

"So, what's going on with you and the *cipota*?" Enrique asks immediately after Thomas leaves the table.

"You mean Kate, I take it Richie," Joseph replies, knowing how much Enrique dislikes the name.

"Well," Pat begins, putting his hand behind his head and laughing with difficulty. Enrique merely throws a straw at him and laughs in return. Brent looks quietly at the situation, and sits himself back while he continues to eat the piece of pizza he started.

Enrique moves himself slightly over, as Thomas comes carefully back with his small cup of orange cola in his hand, filled to the very rim, as he's only allowed one. He tries so carefully to put it down on the table, with such care that nothing spills. In doing so, though, he manages to spill some on his hands, to which his father merely pats him on the head and hands him a paper napkin and tells him to go wash his hands before they become sticky.

"Gosh he's grown," Enrique says, watching him run off obediently.

"Yeah, that's an understatement," Pat replies, feeling Brent's hand on his shoulder.

"Not to pressure you, but tentatively speaking, in academic research, it's proven that children progress both socially and academically faster with a father and mother," Brent says, taking his hand from Pat's shoulder and taking hold of his glass of beer. Joseph laughs at the subtlety and pours himself a glass as well out of the pitcher, offering it first to Pat, who shakes his head.

"No, I have that thing tonight with Kate," he explains.

"Right, I forgot," Joseph says.

"OH?" Enrique interrupts. "Does that mean tonight's going to be the big love scene night; fireworks and music, and so forth?"

"Um..." Pat can only smirk at the statement his words trailing off, again lifting his hand to the back of his head and scratching behind his ear.

"No, you'd better not have any beer," Enrique persists, taking a drink from his glass. "Wouldn't want you drunk dialling her before the big event, now would we?"

"What's drunk dialling?" Thomas inquires, returning to the table from behind with his hands in front of him, still wet from washing them.

"Your hands are wet, little bear," Pat returns, trying to change the subject. Thomas smiles and wipes his hands down the front of his shirt. Pat can only shrug and smile, looking at Joseph out of the corner of his eyes.

"Well at least you know he washed them."

"So, what's drunk dialling, dad?" Thomas says, seating himself finally as his father places a piece of pizza on the plate in front of him. Thomas reaches to the centre of the table as hard as he can, but just can't seem to reach the straws. Before he can climb onto his chair, Joseph hands him the straw from across the table.

"Hmmm," Pat ponders carefully.

"It's something that your Uncle Richie does when he goes to a party and finds a girl that looks his way," Joseph interrupts, causing Thomas to look over and see Enrique start to cough slightly on the beer he is drinking.

"Oh." Thomas squints at the comment, and then decides that whatever it is, it probably isn't as exciting as they are making out, if it's something that involves girls.

Chapter 14

Moonlight and Romance

"What do you think she would have wanted?"

The light from the moon and the clear sky seems to reflect brighter than normal across the lake. Although there isn't snow on the ground, the stars that normally are hidden seem to dance like falling flakes across the heavens. The sound of a waterfall nearby drowns out some of the music that echoes in the background. Off in the distance, there is a bright light coming from a bonfire that a party has built along the shoreline. There is a single boat not too far out with a lit Christmas tree on it, which gently rocks back and forth ever so slightly, as if it were being blown in the wind.

The driver came to pick Patrick up nearly fifteen minutes earlier than he was told. And although he had ridden in executive cars before, he hadn't thought that this event would have afforded such luxury. He was already somewhat hesitant when Kate said there would be a driver, but a limo service as well, was something he was unprepared for entirely. And yet, Mike, the driver, was quite pleasant and shook Thomas's hand when he came rushing out to see the long white stretch car. It eased the tension, especially when he said that he would be the only one riding in the car on the way there, although he would most likely be riding with others on the return trip.

Pat has been out to Lake Washington a few times before, as he had some business colleagues who had taken him out once or twice on their boats. He enjoys the lakeside quite a bit, as he works there often when needed.

When the driver dropped him off at the house... No. House was the incorrect word to describe Kate's friend's place, he thought to himself instantly. The gated entrance, with the European peacock design, and the long driveway leading past the guest quarters off to the left, along with the house made especially for the labour; all of these were something that one would never describe as a mere living abode. Mike continued to point out all the several buildings and ornaments of the house as he drove up to the main quarters where the party was.

The party had yet to be fully commenced when Pat had first arrived, so he took the opportunity to walk about the grounds, as some of the other guests were doing. Somehow or another, he managed to find himself a small path lit with small rock shaped lights that led down to a terrace overlooking the lake, near the shoreline. Nobody was there, so he decided to stand there a bit, until the time came for the party to officially take place.

And so, Pat stands in silence, watching the surrounding world fade away into a blissful night. Every breath is soothing and calm enough that he could easily close his eyes and feel as if he were standing outside his own house.

"Mind if I join you?" he hears from behind him.

Patrick opens his eyes and turns his head to see the shadowy figure emerge into the moonlight. She is a beautiful lady, he thinks instantly, with a white off shoulder cut that glitters with the night. Her deep brown hair looks almost black with only the light of the moon to reveal any colour.

"Of course not," he replies, turning his body now and standing upright once again.

"Isn't it funny how when we sleep, we have no sense of time? Whether it's been five minutes, or three years, our minds can't seem to comprehend time while we sleep," she says, walking up to him. "Sometimes I wonder if I'm asleep right now, dreaming my life away..."

Pat can't help but to look stunned at the statement. He stands momentarily, unsure of what to do, or what to say to the figure approaching him. Then, for a reason that he can't comprehend, he replies. "I think I've been sleeping for far too long. But it does seem like it's been moments ago when I first closed my eyes."

"I'm Ella," she reveals, reaching out her hand to him. Her voice is very instrumental, and almost angelic, he thinks to himself.

"Patrick," he says with a gentle authority, slightly cringing afterwards at the deep tone.

Ella comes up beside him and carefully places her hands on the edge of the stone terrace. The white laced gloves are quite thick, obviously made for the wintry season, as well as the thick velvet shoulder wrap that matched her gloves. He can see she is smiling, looking up at the moon, which eases the silence that comes between them. Pat decides to follow suit and turns once again to stare at the water.

"You don't come to these events often, do you?" she asks softly, her eyes unwavering from the moon.

"Not really," he replies softly, looking over to her and seeing her lower her gaze to him. "Do I stick out that badly?"

"No," she whispers to him with a smile. "It's just you have a different aura about you."

"Aura?"

"Most men here are working hard to impress someone or another," she begins. "They mingle and move around like bees in a hive, working to achieve and accomplish goals. To them, this is just another business evening, and a chance to progress."

"I see," he returns, raising his eyebrows as he turns his head toward the water. "And how do you know I'm not one of those types of guys?"

"Because you're out here," she says simply, "with me."

"Doesn't that defeat the purpose of this party?" Pat replies softly. "If everyone is doing what you say they are, then why bother having a party to do it?"

He receives a gentle polite laugh from her as a reply, causing him to look over to her once again. Her eyes don't waver, as she looks at him carefully now. Finally, she reaches over and adjusts his coat slightly, as it seems to be just ever so somewhat crooked.

"You have a very nice dinner suit on," she begins. "Who made it, if I can ask?"

"Hmmm," Patrick thinks aloud, causing his right eye to close slightly. "David something, I think. Malcolm....Marlow...."

"Malchovo," she interrupts, trying to ease the strain that he is so easily showing from the lack of memory.

"Yes!" he shouts, somewhat too much. Then, he smiles when he sees her pleasant smile returned. "He delivered it to me earlier within the week. A very strange man, if you ask me. Do you know him?"

"Interesting," she states pleasantly with a nod, with a slight hint of curiosity lingering within her voice. "You must be very lucky. He is an extremely busy person, from what I here, and also, he is a very hard person to find. I thought he was in Russia, designing something for a film producer."

"I wouldn't know." Patrick can only shrug at the statement, comfortably putting his hand within his pockets. "He's a friend of Kate's, is all I know."

"Katherine Ashton?"

"Yup," he says smugly. "She's supposed to be here somewhere helping set up this party."

"How do you know Katherine, if you don't mind me asking?"

Patrick stops for a moment, looking carefully at the very composed woman next to him. Ella smiles softly to him, the moonlight gathering around her, as if she were an ethereal creature.

"It's a long story," he begins, somewhat chuckling at the statement.

"That's alright, I've got some time," she replies, turning her body enough to lean herself against the terrace wall. "It wouldn't happen to have anything to do with a certain piece of jewellery, would it?"

"How did you know?" Pat says, again somewhat stunned by her words.

"So you are the one," she whispers.

"Sorry?" he asks, tilting his head slightly.

"Nothing," Ella states, standing once more. "I was just thinking that you look very much like a handsome knight, standing there in that outfit."

With her words finished, she smiles and looks off towards the house once again. Ella pushes herself off of the wall and begins to walk up the path once more. She looks over her shoulder as she leaves, seeing Pat watching her intently with but only a simple look of confusion and she turns her head towards the house once more and raises her hand to wave a simple goodbye. Then, "I'll talk to you later, I'm sure."

"Uh," Pat says softly. Then, "Okay!"

He watches as she vanishes into the shadowy path once more, and thinks to himself silently whether or not this was such a bright idea coming to this party after all. Nevertheless, he looks at his phone, seeing the time is still early. He chuckles to himself as he sees the strap to his fine watch around his wrist.

"Oh, how times have changed," he thinks.

Katherine told him to meet her at the front door around nine, so he still has some time before then. Rather than risk his chances standing near the door, he thinks remaining on the terrace will be a safer experience.

Patrick closes his eyes and takes a deep breath, rolling his head back as he does so. He can feel the cold stone of the terrace wall seeping through his clothes, almost as if it were wet. The sound of the band begins to fill the air, as they are starting to warm up for the night event. He can't help but to tap his foot to the music, his eyes still closed, but the light from the moon filling his face even then. His body starts to sway slowly, the music now filling his body, a smile coming slowly across his face.

"Moon dancing, huh?" he hears, his eyes suddenly opening and his body freezing, as if every muscle in his body were clenching. He hears the laugh from the shadows and he stares intently to see who is coming down the path.

A figure begins to emerge from the path, the light gathering once again upon her as he has seen so many times since he has met her. He knows instantly that it is her, without doubt. His body is tense, and yet relaxed as well, as he watches the flowing goddess walk into the light and reveal herself to him.

Kate is pulling her dress up slightly, as not to step on it as she walks down the few terrace steps. She is careful of her midnight blue ruche tier gown, watching her step as she walks toward Patrick, and finally letting go of the satin after feeling the last step beneath her feet pass. The light dances off her beautiful diamond necklace, but Patrick's eyes notice nothing except for her eyes staring at his.

The two stand in silence, listening to the song finish. Soon after another one begins, this one much slower and more peaceful. Pat cannot take his eyes off of her, as if he has been possessed by a spell. Kate does not move in response, unsure about the look upon his face, his countenance somewhat empty. Then, she's surprised as he takes her hands and pulls her close. He says nothing, shows no emotion across his face, but the two begin to move, as he begins to dance with her. She is stunned momentarily, her feet moving on instinct, her face still watching cautiously at his unwavering gaze. Slowly though, she feels the warmth of his hands against her back, and she cannot help but to put her head against his shoulder. Suddenly, she finds herself smiling.

"I've been thinking about you," he whispers to her. Kate is about to say something, but he continues. "So many things have been running through my mind since I've met you. Emotions that I didn't think I could have. And today, for the first time, I felt guilty for even knowing you."

Kate stops, followed soon after by Pat. She wants to step away, but she feels his hand come up to the back of her head and hold her softly. His hold is so gentle and kind, full of warmth and something much more. Then, he starts to dance with her once more. The song ends moments later, all too fast. Before she can react, he is holding her face, staring into her eyes.

"What's with you tonight?" she tries to say jovially. "You're so intense."

"I feel guilty inside," he tells her, "because I'm asking myself how I would feel if it were the other way round. How would I feel if I were in her place?"

"What are you trying to say?" she whispers, a pain hitting her deeply in her chest. She closes her eyes suddenly, dropping her head as much as his hands will allow. "What do you think she would have wanted?"

Kate feels the wintry breeze flow between them, and then unexpectedly feels an amazingly warm sensation come across her entire body as she feels his lips on hers. She opens her eyes in shock, her body tensing up, and then she cannot help but to close her eyes once more and let herself just fall. That's all she can do, she thinks to herself. Just fall.

"I love you, Kate," she hears, her eyes still closed as he pulls his lips from hers ever so slightly. She has heard those words before, from so many men, from so many different types, and all somehow saying the same thing to her in the same way. But his words, the lips they come from, the voice that says them, the man that is speaking to her; unlike all the others in the world, she can't ignore those words when he says them. She can't even open her eyes, because she can feel the tears welling inside her eyes. She can't believe that she's getting this emotional over those same stupid words that haven't meant anything to her before. Why now? Why all of a sudden? Why do those words suddenly mean something? This isn't what she wanted, is it? This isn't what she had planned. And yet, it feels nice; right.

Kate takes a deep breath and opens her eyes, seeing for the first time the man that said the words that are making her cry. She feels the tears building in her eyes, and she can't understand why. Why... Why doesn't he take his hands away from her face, so she can turn away? Why doesn't he say something? Why does she feel stupid?

Pat watches as she opens her eyes; those eyes that penetrate deeper than anyone else has ever done. She is so beautiful, he thinks. He is captivated by the incredible strength that she has even at this moment. He's not thinking any longer. He cannot think clearly enough to put together any words that mean anything. All he can do is lean forward and kiss her again. Only this time, he feels her hands come to his face as well. She is kissing him.

Another song fills the air once again. This time, the two slowly step back from one another, but neither can take their eyes from the other's. Neither can seem to find the words.

Finally, Kate smiles softly, brushing a loose hair that has fallen into her face. "Well, it took you long enough."

Pat can do nothing but smile in reply, putting his hand in his pocket and leaning against the terrace wall again, trying to regain some composure for himself. He starts to laugh to himself softly, to which Kate comes to his side and taps her shoulder against his arm.

"What're you laughing at?"

"I don't know," he says, shrugging. "I had this all planned out in my head, and somehow it didn't go anything like I had pictured."

"Really?" she says, smirking and raising her eyebrows to him. "So you were planning this?"

"Eh," he starts, "not like this. Something more romantic, I think."

"Oh." Kate looks up at the moon, then smiles. "I think I kind of liked this way."

Kate leans her head against his shoulder, then feels his arm wrap around her. Then, "Nerd."

"Thanks," he whispers.

"So where do we go from here?" she asks, looking up and seeing his distant smile looking at the night sky.

"Well, I suppose it'd be a shame to come to this party and not actually attend it," he replies.

"Damn!" she says, jumping to her feet. "That's why I came down here."

"What?"

"Oh," she thinks aloud, "the princess said you were down here when I was looking for you, which is why I came down here to find you."

"Princess?" he enquires, raising his head at the statement.

"Never mind that, I'm supposed to be helping Daniel," she says, bringing both her palms to her temple in frustration. She feels Patrick's hands take her wrists and pull them down to her side. Seeing the smile across his face makes her forget whatever she is thinking, and she cannot help but to feel suddenly embarrassed at the look he gives her.

"Come on then," he says softly.

Chapter 15

The Thing About Parties

The main entrance to the hall where the focus of the party is being held, has a host of people awaiting to pass through the two large oak doors. Luxury cars continue to arrive, dropping passengers off and leaving to their designated areas. Even inside, past the three ladies who are employed only to take coats from the guests, the entrance to the gymnasium sized hall was carefully filling up with those who were having their names called aloud as they arrived and are officially recognised.

Kate tries to explain to Patrick what was going to happen, and could easily see the discomfort on his face at the grandiose and outlandish style that this party is, so she takes him through the kitchen entrance where all the catering staff are working hard to try and accomplish the impossible for the evening. Once inside, Kate has no choice but to leave Patrick behind, as she had promised to help Daniel with something beforehand. Thus, Patrick is now standing by himself; surrounded only by people he has no idea about, and of whom he has never seen not met before.

Patrick is standing very near to the stop that Kate had left him minutes earlier, holding precociously a glass of champagne that a young lady had brought him as she passed by. He can't help but to feel a little overwhelmed at the entirety of the party, and the immense size of the house that he's in, to be holding this amount of people, and watching as even more are coming in by the second. Slowly, though, he forgets about his unease, and begins to remember the words he told Kate. Nothing else matters, except for that, he thinks to himself. And soon, he finds that his hand casually finds its way to his pocket, and he can comfortably rest his shoulder against a nice tall stone statue looking thing.

As Patrick continues to look down at his glass of champagne, unknowingly smiling to himself, he thinks of nothing else but Kate. A shadow passes in front of him, causing him to raise his gaze, though, and suddenly he sees a figure approach him.

"Am I interrupting something?" Ella asks softly, her hands folded behind her regally. "My, don't we look sophisticated in the full light of the room."

"Do I?" Pat replies, moving his glass to one side so he can look down at himself.

"I was speaking of your demeanour and stance," Ella explains. "Leaning there against the piece of art, and holding your glass in your hand; you look like a carefree rogue."

"Oh?" Patrick raises his eyebrows in a somewhat jovial manner. Then, "Well, I shall take that as a compliment."

"Good," Ella replies with a laugh, bringing both her hands to her front now and folding them carefully together. "Did Katherine find you in the end? I passed her on my way back to the house."

"Yes, thank you," Pat says with a nod and a polite smile.

"I don't mean to be rude, but may I ask you something somewhat unorthodox?"

Patrick looks carefully at the very elegant lady standing before him. Already, he notices that quite a few people are looking over his way now, their faces somewhat unsure of the situation. As he looks back at the woman before him though, he notices that her eyes never leave his face, and that her expression of polite happiness never ceases.

"What do you know about Katherine?" Ella finally asks, watching Patrick's expression carefully. He is unwavering, although a bit uncomfortable. She is unsure whether this is due to the surroundings or the line of questioning that she is undertaking. "Hmm.... Perhaps that was a difficult question to begin with. Perhaps I should have asked something simpler for this. Such as, who were you thinking of when you were smiling so, lost in your daydream?"

"Um," he starts, hesitant and obviously confused.

"Were you thinking of Katherine?" she persists, seeing his expression slightly change.

"Yes," he says softly, his fingers rubbing the tip of his glass. He stands and makes firm his countenance, clearing his throat as he does so. "I suppose I was."

"Do you love her?" she says boldly.

Patrick lifts the glass slowly, trying to cover his cough. He takes a sip from his champagne for the first time, feeling its cold bubbly sweetness fill his mouth. It gives him enough time to see her face, and to hope that she is merely toying with him playfully. But her face does not change, and the timid smile that was once there still remains, almost as if she were a painting. Finally, he resides his fate and says it.

"Yes. I think I do." Suddenly, the polite smile slowly fades from her face and she steps closer to him.

"To think you do, and to know you do, are two completely different things," she whispers in his ear. "But I'm sure that I needn't explain that to such a sophisticated man as you."

"No, you don't."

"Have you told her?" she queries further, stepping away once more, and receiving a single nod of the head in reply. "I see."

"I don't mean to be rude, but I'm a bit— "

"What did she say back?" Ella interrupts, folding her hands behind her once more, and looking off to her side at some men that have just entered the room. "You see, I have known Katherine for many years. We both have been through a tremendous amount in our lives, and have seen things that neither of us would ever reveal to anyone. We are both..." Her words trail off momentarily, as she watches the men circle around and begin to speak with some others.

"I'm sorry," she announces, turning back to him once more. "I suppose what I am trying to say in my own way is that Katherine is a very beautiful woman. I have seen countless men come and try to steal her heart away, as I'm sure you can imagine."

Suddenly Patrick raises a brow, trying to hide his discomfort. Of course he didn't imagine. Why would he try and do that? Just the idea of it makes him begin to clench his hands so tight that the glass he's holding might break.

"Did she tell you about how she feels?" Ella asks, looking over her shoulder once more. "Did she say she loves you?"

Patrick can't reply, his throat has gone dry and his voice has left him.

"What do you really know about Katherine?" Ella then asks. "Do you know her favourite colour? When her birthday is? What kind of books she reads?"

For the first time since the day began, he can't feel his heartbeat. The incredible heat that had been keeping him warm throughout the cold of the winter suddenly seems to creep into every fibre of his being. Even his fingertips begin to feel numb, and his head starts to become filled with noise. It was so clear a few seconds ago. Everything was clear. Her words, they make perfect sense though. He knows nothing about her, and yet, just minutes ago he told her he loved her. He doesn't even know what her birthday is.

Suddenly, he feels a deep comforting warmth overcome his face, and he looks up to see the beautiful smile of Ella looking directly at him. Her eyes are tender and filled with kindness once more. She is no longer trying to hide herself from him, but is showing him something that he hasn't seen in her since they began to talk.

"It's okay," she whispers to him, her words clear even through the noise of the hundreds of others around them. "I didn't say those things to frighten you. Katherine ***does*** care about you. She told me so herself."

"Kate said— "

"She has never said the words to anyone before," Ella explains, interrupting him. She sighs softly, lowering her hand from his cheek and placing it over his. "The point isn't what she hasn't said to you. It isn't about what you know, or don't know,

Patrick. The point is to ask her. She will answer you, if she is going to answer anyone."

"Who is this?!" the two hear from behind them, startling both. Ella immediately turns and sees a group of three men standing behind her. They are the same group of men that she had been watching earlier. She had taken her eyes off of them only momentarily, and yet they seem to have crossed the room in such a short time.

"Daniel." Ella replies first to the gentleman closest to her, who instantly takes her hand and bows slightly to her. "Barrington," she nods her head to the next gentleman, and then in consecutive order, "Henry, and Parker."

"Your ladyship," the other three men reply in unison.

"And whom have we here?" Daniel inquires, coming to Ella's side. "You two look awful cosy together. You haven't found yourself a new friend, have you?"

"This is Patrick James," Ella says, controlling herself with ease. She has become accustomed to Daniel's arrogance of late. "She is Katherine's friend. He is the very man who found her bracelet."

Patrick is somewhat startled at the introduction, unsure about the persons before him, including Ella, who seems to know more about him than the others. The one to whom Ella called Daniel immediately brightens his expression and smiles happily towards her and Patrick. Seeing this, the others come forward and shake Patrick's hand, each introducing themselves. Patrick watches Ella and her ease with these men, and yet, somewhat obvious annoyance with them. She handles herself well, though, as if she were a politician in a debate. Finally, when the men finish their queries and introductions, they begin to turn their attention to Patrick. They begin by questioning his work ethics, and where his associations lie politically. He is amazed at how little he needs to speak, watching how each of them seems to involve themselves within their own conversations without him saying a single word. Ella smiles to him comfortingly, and then takes his hand.

"I apologise, gentlemen, but I must make my departure," Ella states softly, interrupting the conversation. "I am called for elsewhere. It was a pleasure, Patrick, and I hope we can speak further before the night is through."

Patrick can only respond with a polite nod, before the others begin their polite farewells, and return quickly to the conversation at hand.

"So, Patrick, what line of business are you in, per say?" the one named Barrington asks, with the others turning and awaiting his answer.

"Enough! You three are boring me to death already!" Daniel states, putting his arm around Patrick's shoulders and pulling him close as if they were dear friends. "Talk business some other time. Patrick and I have more pressing things to speak about, besides dreary things like politics and money."

"Of course," Barrington says with a wry smile, watching as Daniel pulls Patrick off, and begins to walk with him.

Pat is unsure of why he is walking next to Daniel, nor can he comprehend what exactly he wishes to discuss with him. Nevertheless, Patrick humbly walks next to the somewhat forceful, although quite pleasant man, who hands him another glass of champagne as the young hostess walks by.

"What do you think of the house?" Daniel begins.

"Well," Pat returns softly, looking around momentarily. "It's big."

Daniel laughs at the comment. "Yeah, I think that too. Have you had a chance to look around yet?"

"I went down to the lake," he explains to Daniel, the two walking up to a large empty wall, with a large painting and an extravagant fern in the corner. "Other than the terrace, you mean? Not really."

Daniel stops and looks at Patrick, smiling as he does so, then quickly finishes the glass of champagne in his hand and sets it on the edge of the stone pot that holds the fern. He laughs suddenly which catches Pat off guard, then looks at the wall and places his hand carefully to the side of the painting. Slowly he then pushes the wall, which gives way to reveal a doorway into another room. Without a word spoken, he motions for Pat to follow with his head, and then disappears into the wall.

As Patrick enters the chamber, he looks back to see if anyone else has bothered to notice that he was entering. For a moment, he stares at the enormous gathering, with people moving flowing from person to person, almost as if it were an entity in itself. Not one person there notices that he is watching them, nor do they notice that he is leaving. He hears a call from behind him, to which he turns and enters the chamber fully, the door behind him closing slowly and carefully on its own.

The hidden room itself is not nearly as large as the previous room, but in comparison, Patrick cannot help but to think to himself that this room alone is most likely the same size as the sum of his entire house. There are stairs off to the left, and a fireplace directly on the far side, near a large open view of the lake and a patio doorway that leads out unto another terrace. The second level is made up entirely of a library, which contains only a walkway veranda, and an open floor that shows the open skylights above. The first floor also has a library, although much smaller in comparison, as it is contained within a fraction of the left wall, just beyond the open staircase that leads to the second floor terrace.

"What do you think?" Daniel queries, laughing at Patrick's expression of awe. He walks over to the bar, which is closest to the right corner, just near the entranceway. The bar itself is tucked into an alcove, which is easily reached, should he wish to walk behind it, by the means of a slide door. "This is my home within my home."

Daniel pulls two glasses from behind the bar, and puts ice in each, then pulls out a decanter from one of the many bottles layered against the mirrored wall of the bar.

"You'd never believe this room is adjoining the party," Pat says softly, commenting on how silent the room.

"Yeah, when I had this place built, I made sure that this room was sound proofed," Daniel explains, coming from behind the bar and handing Pat a glass, as he sips from his own.

Patrick takes a sip, to which he almost coughs as he continues to try and engulf the room with his eyes. Daniel laughs, and places his hand on the Pat's shoulder.

"It's cognac," Daniel explains, seeing Patrick looking somewhat bewildered at his glass. "The finest that there is."

"Strong," Pat manages to say, which only receives yet another laugh, and a pat against the back. Then, after he can breathe once more, "So this is your house?"

Daniel pauses momentarily at the question, looking carefully at Patrick. Then a bright enormous smile breaks across his face and he says freely, "That it is!"

"I see."

"Didn't Kate tell you?" Daniel asks, more for himself than for anything. In fact, before Pat can say anything, he is already walking away from him, and heading for the desk near the fireplace. "I'm surprised really. She is always talking about you, whenever I speak to her. Hasn't she ever mentioned me?"

"I—" Patrick pauses, seeing again that Daniel is lost in thought at something else.

"I have something I want to show you," Daniel announces excitedly, opening a drawer from behind his thick oak desk and pulling something out in his hand. He then, walks over to the fireplace, and motions for Patrick to follow, once again using his head as an instrument to instruct.

Patrick obligingly follows and approaches Daniel and comes over to the desk, his eyes looking at the maple flooring and the beautiful crest that is carefully laid within the centre of the room. It is here that he notices a small Christmas tree in the corner with no lights on it, and just a few decorations. As he looks closer, he can tell that it isn't real, but is merely a plastic tree that looks as if someone would purchase in a dollar store.

Daniel comes out from behind the desk, walking over to the fireplace, and then to the bookshelf adjacent to it. Patrick continues approaching, although slows as he watches to see what Daniel is doing. As he approaches, he can see that Daniel is balancing a box in his right hand, along with the glass of cognac in the other, which carelessly dangles from his fingertips.

"Do you see this bookshelf?" Daniels asks, his voice changing somewhat from the previous tone of adolescent arrogance. "This entire bookcase is special."

Patrick finally comes up to his side, and looks at the change of expression. He can see that he is almost sombre now, which somewhat confuses Patrick. Still, he has just met this man, so what does he expect to know of him, except that which he chooses to show.

"Go ahead and choose any book," Daniel instructs Patrick, his body and countenance unchanging.

Patrick looks at him once more, and then turns to the bookcase, which is filled with what looks to be several hundred books, each with a hard leather backing. As he steps forward, he can see that there are no titles though, and it looks as if each of them is unread. He looks over his shoulder once more, seeing that Daniel has turned away and is walking back toward the fireplace. Patrick then turns and pulls out the closest book to him, which is somewhat hard to remove, as they are placed tightly together. He studies it for a moment, looking at the gold gilt that surrounds its pages, and the dark black leather binding that one only sees in the movies. He raises an eyebrow unknowingly, and opens the book to find that there one word on the first page, and that there is nothing else inside it, except for empty pages.

"That entire bookcase is filled with empty dreams," Daniel says, sipping from his glass. "Things that I was going to do, that I haven't done yet. What does it say inside it?"

"It just has a single word," Pat replies softly, questioningly.

"What is it?" Daniel returns coldly, taking another sip.

"Sailboat."

Daniel laughs, and turns to face Patrick once again. "Yeah, I remember that one well. I was seventeen, and I remember learning to sail with my father near the Hood Canal. We spent the summer sailing, just him and I, fishing and shrimping the days away."

"It must have been nice," Patrick says softly, somewhat bewildered at the book he is holding. Daniel looks at the expression on his face and starts to laugh as he leans against the mantle.

"It's not what you think," he explains. "I promised myself that summer that I would build myself a sailboat by hand and sail it around the world."

"So, this entire book is a reminder?"

"Not so much," Daniel reveals, looking down for a moment. "Money is everything in this world. I told myself that every day of my life. I can accomplish any dream, and task, and overcome any obstacle if I have enough money."

"Life is usually rather different than what we imagine or want," Patrick replies, closing the book and placing it carefully back onto the bookshelf.

"You're pretty blunt, aren't you?" Daniels voice suddenly lightens, and he begins to laugh at his statement once more, standing and coming next to Patrick. He then slaps Patrick's shoulder and puts his arm over it, as if they were friends once more. "I like that. Everyone here is trying to impress someone or another. But you seem to be just....well...just exactly how Kate described you."

"And how is that?" Pat winces slightly as Daniel pulls him closer and then releases him. Daniel smiles and reaches forward and looks carefully at the books in front of them, his fingers tracing the outline of each one until he comes across the one he is searching for. Carefully, he removes the dark blue leather book, with the gold binding, and hands it to Patrick.

"This is why I brought you here," he explains.

Patrick opens the book, seeing that unlike the previous book, this has words within it, all handwritten, unlike the other one. When he turns the pages to the front, as instructed by Daniel, he sees the words on the first page.

"Propose to the most beautiful woman I have ever seen," Patrick reads aloud. Before he can turn the page, he sees the glitter of light coming from the corner of his eye, and he turns his head to see Daniel holding up the box in his hand and looking at the ring inside it. The box itself is larger than any ring container that Pat has ever seen before, containing a private light that is strategically placed to shine upon the diamonds of the ring.

"It's all there," Daniel announces, gazing at the ring, "from beginning to the party tonight; everything about Kate. I knew the first moment that I met her, that she was the one that I was going to marry."

Patrick's heart stops momentarily. He hears the words, but somehow, they fade away from his mind. The book he's carrying begins to burn his hands, as if it were on fire. He wishes so much to close the pages, and to put the book back, but instead he stays motionless. Even his face is numb, without thought or emotion.

"Even this ring that I have here," Pat hears, suddenly coming into focus once more as Daniel pushes the ring in front of him. "I spent six months tracking this ring down. Or I should say that I had a team of heraldry specialists track this ring down. It took them seven families, spanning twelve generations, but they managed to find it."

"It matches the bracelet that I gave her," Patrick whispers, his throat dry and unable to produce a full sound.

"Exactly!" Daniel says excitedly. "It's the matching set that goes with it. Or at least so I'm told. There's also a necklace as well, which I am having shipped here. But I definitely wanted to propose to her with this ring."

Patrick closes the book, and forces himself to smile, even though he feels as if he shouldn't. Suddenly he can't think of anything to say, but knows that he mustn't show any sign of emotion. Smile, he thinks. That is what he must do.

"What do you think?" Patrick hears as he places the book back into position. He is trying desperately to remain calm; to push aside his own feelings. He is unsure of his own feelings though, so to push them aside seems nearly impossible. Smile. It is all he can do. He must smile. Then, "Do you think she'll like it?"

Patrick feels a hand come to his shoulder, and he closes his eyes, trying hard not to tense up. Luckily it is pulled away quickly, and the hand slaps his back in a happy gesture. He can hear Daniel talking, answering his own questions over and over again, and walking the room lost in his own thoughts.

"I'm glad we had this talk, Pat!" Daniel says, closing the box to the ring once more and putting it in his desk. "I feel a lot more confident now."

Patrick doesn't hear his words, but manages to nod with a smile. He places his hands in his pockets, and tries desperately to hide all emotion, although it seems to him clearly that Daniel is completely lost in his own obsessions to realise anything to the contrary.

"The problem that I have is that everyone around me is just somebody who always agrees with me. That's why I wanted to talk with someone like you. A realistic person who has nothing to gain from any of this," Daniel explains walking toward the door. "Feel free to have another drink if you want. But don't be too long. I don't want you to miss the big event!"

Before Patrick can breathe or make a sound, Daniel leaves the room. He is left standing in front of the bookcase of empty dreams, unsure of his own thoughts or emotions. The doorway itself is open still, the noise from the party rushing in as if it were a flood overpowering the silence that once loomed. For a moment, his eyes flash at a shadow standing at the doorway, to which he almost thought it was someone that he knew. Slowly the light blends, and he approaches the figure, like a moth drawn to the flame. The figure turns and runs away, the dress she is wearing flowing like the shaded outline of a cherry tree against the sunset.

He approaches the door steadily, his eyes still not completely focused due to the lights from the next room. Once he reaches the doorway and steps into the party once more, he hears the door behind him close, and the world begins to focus once more. People are flowing all about him, reminding him suddenly of the airport he was in not too long ago. And yet, this is more of a medieval ballroom, he thinks to himself again. Although very few people are dancing, it looks as if just the movement itself is a dance, as he watches the party flow from person to person.

Suddenly his eyes come to focus on a tiny girl, completely and utterly out of place. His heart stops briefly, as he knows even from this distance that it is her. He can't think straight, his heart beginning to race once again. She is near the centre of the room, standing and waiting for him. As he moves closer, she turns once again and moves like the wind, flowing past people as if she weren't seen. Patrick follows her as best he can, his mind is clear of any other thoughts or distractions.

As Patrick approaches the main entrance, he stops himself and turns back to the sound of Kate's voice. She is holding a microphone, and is standing near the band next to Daniel. He pauses for but a moment, then turns and exits.

Down the path, just past the trees, in a small clearing that has already begun to frost, Patrick comes to rest. His breath comes out heavy and the cold air bites deeply into his lungs. Even his hands that are resting on his thighs as he tries to catch his breath momentarily, feeling the frosty winter air over them.

"You really ought to exercise more," the girl tells him, standing calmly with her hands behind her back. Just as before, she stands with her dress flowing in the gentle breeze, unaffected by anything or anyone around her, glowing with an innocence that is ethereal.

"Thanks," Patrick replies, trying his best to regain his countenance. Slowly his breath begins to return to him, and he stands once again, placing his hands in his pockets as he does so. "So why are you here tonight?"

"You called me," she replies softly, stepping forward so that he must look down to see her face. "There are questions that you want me to answer."

"Did I?" he replies, blinking slowly. "And are there?"

"Truly, I must admit, you are probably one of the more challenging people I have come across recently," the girl says playfully, stepping away from him once more, and turning her back towards him. "Always complaining about everything in front of you, and constantly lying to yourself over and over. And yet, for whatever reason, you see me and hear me; feel me even. I suppose that is what brings me back to you each time."

The sounds of the party fill the air once again, the music rolling across them as if it were waves from the sea. Patrick hadn't noticed them before, his mind suddenly returning to the moment that he had left the party. He can't help but to look back at the path he took, unsure of what he will see or why he must look.

"She isn't coming," he hears. "Not yet."

"And how would you know?" he replies, refusing to turn around in a vain attempt at defiance. "In fact, how do you know anything at all?"

"Is that the question you truly want to ask me, Patrick?" she returns, coming to his side and taking the cuff of his jacket in her small hand. He looks down to see the gentle face staring up at him. "Why did you call me here, Patrick?"

"I didn't call you here," he replies softly. "I don't even know who or what you are."

"And yet here I am, and there you are talking with me," she retorts pleasantly.

As the band continues to fill the night air with its sounds of Christmas music, Patrick looks up once more to the house. His mind fills with thoughts of Kate, and their last moments together.

"You told her you loved her, didn't you?" he hears.

"Yes," he replies instantly, unsure of why he is even answering.

"Do you now regret it?" she asks, her tone changing slightly.

"No."

"Even if she doesn't feel the same way about you?" The question bites deep into Patrick, as it was intended. He can feel her very thoughts entering his mind, even before she asks the questions. "Do you regret meeting me?"

Patrick finally looks down at the child next to him, and thinks carefully about what he sees. Her face, her body, they are both childlike in appearance, but something inside him knows, and has always known that this is no child.

"Why did you give me the bracelet?" he asks finally.

"Fate is a wonderful thing, don't you think?" she replies with a smile.

"Fate?" he says pessimistically, his tone almost sneering at her.

"So many people like to believe that fate does all the work for them, and that these great events that are produced throughout their lives are because of that wonderful divinity," she explains, her smile returning the most gentle of looks to him. Her hand lowers from his sleeve, and returns to the naturally folded position behind her. "But fate doesn't really have the power to do those grand miracles. It doesn't make love happen, or cause nations to fall. Nor in the same right, does it bring peace, or tear two people apart. You see, perhaps fate did play a part in your life, but only because you allowed it to.

"Why did I give you the bracelet, you ask? You already know the answer to that."

"To bring Kate and I together," he whispers.

"No!" she returns hastily. "You could have given the bracelet to anyone. But you didn't. You could have kept it and sold it for money. But again, you didn't. You CHOSE Katherine to give it to. I didn't force you to do that."

"But you—"

"You decided every action that you have taken. I was merely the person who led you to the choice," the child insists, as she walks forward a few steps. "But these are all things you already know. Things that if you didn't know, you would never have decided on the actions you have undertaken, and neither of us would be standing here at this moment."

Patrick realises suddenly that the music from the house has stopped. He can hear voices speaking, sounding like an announcement of some sort. His breathing stops for just a moment, his thoughts clouded and jumbled. He tries to clear his head as he closes his eyes and takes a deep breath. It doesn't help. He is unsure of everything.

A feeling of ease overcomes him as he feels a gentle warmth touch his hand, which quickly spreads over his being. He opens his eyes to see her standing before him, the beautiful smile looking up to him.

"What is it your heart cries for?" she asks softly. "Why are you so unsure? What is it that you cannot believe?"

He has no answer. No reply he could say will be enough, he thinks. So he can only smile half-heartedly and lower himself to her height. Then, "I am lost."

"Isn't all of humanity?" she replies sincerely. "Whom of this entire world do you know who holds the answers? Truthfully, the answers that you seek have no words. I think this is why you struggle so hard in finding them. In which case, there is truly only one thing left that you can do."

"Believe," he replies softly. "But in what?"

"That is something that only you can answer," she whispers, reaching out with her finger and touching his nose. It feels cold to the touch, and almost makes him want to sneeze. Instead though, he finds himself smiling.

"Who are you?" he asks. "What are you? A ghost? Are you Fate? Destiny? An angel??"

The child laughs heartily, and folds her dress underneath her as she seats herself on the frost covered grass. She seems to glow almost, filling the air with an ethereal light. He cannot help but to smell the scent of roses and other beautiful flowers as he watches her. Even being near her makes him feel as if it is spring.

"Did you know, most angels don't have wings?" she replies, tilting her head slightly as she speaks.

"Does that mean you are an angel?" he returns, blinking slowly again.

"If I said I was, would you believe me?"

"Yes," he replies instantly.

"I suppose it's a shame that I'm not, then," she laughs.

"I don't understand," he says without confidence.

"No," she replies with warmth, "you wouldn't. Not yet. But soon, I promise."

"You said that before," he returns to her. "Why all this mystery? Why can't you just explain everything to me now?"

"Because," she says, touching his nose once more, "you haven't asked the right question yet."

Patrick can only shake his head as he closes his eyes in disbelief. Finally though, he finds himself smiling, then he opens his eyes and looks to the sky. Before he knows his own actions, he begins to chuckle slightly, thinking about how he feels life is sweeping him away in its current, and all he can do is stay afloat long enough to see the sun touch the wave.

"I don't know why," he begins, "but for whatever reason that my insane mind has, I believe you."

"That's a beginning, then," he hears. "I will explain, but there is something you must do for me yet. You had better return to the party for now, Patrick. Someone is waiting to see you. I will speak with you soon, I promise."

His head lowers, and he see the young girl still seated upon the grass. Slowly he sighs, then pushes his knees to bring himself to stand. Without question he begins to head toward the house once again, unsure of what lays ahead. He doesn't turn back, but he knows that she is still there.

"Don't worry so much about Katherine's intentions, Patrick. Sometimes it's better to ride the wave, as you say," he hears, causing him to stop momentarily. He wants to look back; to see what he knows is already gone. Instead, he merely smiles and slowly walks up the long path to the entrance of the main house.

Chapter 16

Fateful Night

As Patrick approaches the main entrance to the house, he can see that there are just the two porters at the front door who are left. He hadn't noticed before in haste, but people were still coming in when he had chased after the little girl. Now, all the cars have been moved away from the entrance, and the lights are turned down to a minimum. He can see in the distance a group of drivers standing and chatting together, undoubtedly waiting for some drink and food from the side entrance where the kitchen is. For a moment, he finds himself hesitant, watching the night sky as the clouds flow aimlessly about the stars.

Lost in the seamless eternity of the night sky Patrick begins to think about the events of the night; his thoughts finally beginning to take form once more. At first, his thoughts are filled with the words that he spoke to Kate, but slowly he begins to reflect upon the conversation the he had with the little girl. What is she really, he wonders, unsure of everything that has taken place since meeting her.

It feels as if he has been swept under by this vast wind, and all he can do now, what is left is to just try and keep the landing as painless as possible otherwise he'll fly headfirst into the insanity of it all. Otherwise, what would he be doing if all of this were just a dream, he asks himself. He would most likely be sitting in his den, staring at the painting of ***her.*** It seems as if it has been so long since he has last thought of Lisa, which seems sad in a way. For as long as he can remember, too long perhaps, he has spent every day thinking of her; thinking about how he could have changed things. What if he had done something differently? What slight changes could he have made, and what outcome would it have made? It wasn't losing her that hurt the most, he has told himself timeless amounts of time. No, it was not seeing her pain before she was gone.

Patrick stops himself, forcibly for the first time since his wife died and the great overwhelming loneliness overtook him. He turns his thoughts once more to Kate, and the words that the child spoke to him. Is she really waiting for him? He wonders for a moment, his feet unwilling to move forward. What lies inside the house? Why does his heart feel as if it is going to burst from his chest? He knows that no matter what happens tonight, he will regret everything if he doesn't step forward.

He must step forward. He cannot hide from the world any longer. Then, he closes his eyes, takes a deep breath; deeper than he has taken all night. He feels the cold air fill his lungs, giving him a false sense of security.

His feet begin to move forward, first the right, then the left a bit farther. He's unsure of why, or how, but somewhere he lost control of his body and he realises he's nearly running. It seemed so close, but the more he moves, the more he realises how far away the house truly is. Faster, and faster his feet move, his mind unable to control what he's doing now. He can see the two men at the doorway looking at him bewildered, but he doesn't care. He has to go through the door. He has to do this. Whatever happens, she ***IS*** waiting for him.

As he enters the house, after somewhat frightening the porters with the frantic look upon his face, he hears the soft subtle tones of a trumpet being played off in the distance. Soon the entire band begins to play, and a female begins to sing softly, a slow Christmas love song. There are a few places where people are still standing and talking, some sitting at tables, but an area near the band has been cleared where there are people dancing now.

Patrick scans the tremendous room in hopes of seeing Kate. His eyes move from person to person, place to place, as he walks down the blue carpeted steps into the heart of the party. His breath is heavy, his brow slightly sweating, but he feels refreshed and...alive.

Christmas decorations reflect back and forth as the lighting is dimmed just slightly for ambience. He wants to laugh at the situation, as it reminds him of a movie scene he once saw, but he contains himself and resides his efforts are with his search.

He stops near the middle, where the ice carved Christmas tree is stationed, along with the champagne fountain. He doesn't recognise anyone, he comes to realise, and tries in a vain effort to see into the heavy crowd of over-dressed people moving to and fro. He realises suddenly how difficult his task is, lost in the maddened sea of people. She is waiting, he thinks to himself though. He moves forward, after picking up a glass of champagne, in a small futile attempt to mask his own insecurity at being in this place. Then, he hears a laugh from behind and a gentle tapping on his shoulder.

"It doesn't suit you," he hears, turning slowly around and seeing the beautiful smile of Kate standing there.

"Kate," he whispers, unable to move.

"Yo," she replies, bringing a knuckle to his forehead. "What's with the serious look? Did something happen I'm not aware of?"

Patrick blinks slowly and then smiles as he shakes his head in reply. Kate looks up as a new song begins to play. He can see the look on her face change to a childlike expression as she reaches for his hand. Just as the first day that they had met, she again pulls him, leading him to an unknown destination that he willingly follows her to.

Before Patrick has any time to object, he is led out to the area just before where the band is playing. Then, as if he were watching someone else, he moves his hands where she guides them, and his feet begin to move with hers. She is laughing; her eyes almost completely shut as she does so, but her face is gleaming with unabashed joy. All he can see is her, all he can hear is her laugh; the only feeling is the touch of her hands. There is nothing else.

She continues to laugh even after the song ends, and the two stop dancing. Patrick suddenly realises the floor around them is clearing, while the band is going to begin another song. Finally, her eyes focus on his, and she loses her tender laugh. Her hand comes to his face, and her fingers trace the outline of his cheek.

"You are probably the sweetest man I have ever met," she tells him, a smirk coming across her face. "But you're ever so bewildering, too. I would say almost to the point of being annoying."

"I am?" he queries.

The lights dim, causing Patrick to look up from her gaze, as a spotlight comes down and focuses on the singer that is walking out from behind the small curtained area not too far away from them. He has seen the woman before, but he can't quite remember where. An image flashes in his mind, as the lady walks by the two with her microphone in her hand. She gives a small smile and an almost unnoticeable wave with her fingers as Kate smiles to her in return.

"Is she—" Pat begins, suddenly thinking aloud recognizing the famous singer.

"Yes," Kate interrupts, whispering to him.

"And you—"

"She's a friend," Kate replies, looking back at Patrick and smiling a gentle smile.

The lady doesn't speak any words, but Patrick notices instantly how the room suddenly has gone silent in anticipation. Slowly the band begins to play, the song instantly recognisable by all. It is an old love song, and Pat notices Kate close her eyes to the beginning of it, as if she were lost in a memory. Patrick responds in turn by stepping forward and pulling her close to him, causing her to open her eyes slowly and smile.

"I was watching you from the second you came through the door, you know," she reveals to him as they begin to dance.

"Enjoying watching me look the fool, undoubtedly," he says to her with a crooked smile.

"You're no fool, Patrick. You did however have a look of utter seriousness. It was as if nothing was going to stand between you and what you were looking for," she continues, "as if...as if whatever you were looking for was the only thing in the world that mattered to you."

He cannot reply to her words, but instead watches her looking somewhat lost and insecure as she stares beyond him. Before he can say anything, the song ends, awakening her from her brief twilight dream. She smiles at him, as if she is indifferent to what she had just been like, and takes his hand once more.

"I'm kind of tired, I think," she tells him softly. "Do you want to go a little early?"

"What about the party and everyone here?" he asks without conviction. She looks up to face him, and sees his gentile gaze looking down upon her. She merely smiles in return and begins to walk toward the kitchen once more, holding his hand and gently persuading him to follow as she does so.

The two exit out through the kitchen, the staff paying no heed to their movements, as they continue to move to and fro like mice caught in a maze. Patrick follows her obediently, marking his footsteps with hers, until they finally are out of the house and breathing the winter air once more. Only then does Kate stop and sigh a sign of relief. As she turns towards Patrick, she sees the look of confusion on his face.

"Sorry, I just couldn't think straight in there," she explains to him.

"It's okay," he replies, placing his free hand in his jacket pocket. "I'm not very good at parties, if you couldn't tell."

"I'm sorry about that too," she says softly, releasing his hand and turning away from him.

"What for?" he queries, instinctively placing his other hand in his other pocket.

"I invited you to this party, and I haven't been able to spend two minutes alone with you," she returns. She then feels his hand come to her shoulder, her body tensing up at his touch. She looks up at this moment, just as the clouds allow the moon to escape their darkness.

"Shall we go for a walk before we leave?" he asks her, coming forward to her side. She looks at him briefly, then smiles and nods.

They listen as another song begins to play; the signs of the party continuing as normal. Another love song fills the air. Patrick doesn't look back as they walk the path down to the lake terrace. He knows that it is a different world, one so far away from him. He is all too happy to leave it behind, and yet he feels somewhat dismayed at the fact that Kate is by his side. He realises that she belongs to a world he is unfamiliar with, and cannot help but to feel unsure about being even a tiny part of it. But for all the fear, he knows that if he truly wishes to be with Kate, he needs to be beside her whenever she needs him. He won't run away from her.

"Whatever Fate brings," he whispers, watching as she walks away from him up to the terrace wall.

Kate stares out unto the moonlit lake, unable and unwilling to say anything. Her mind is filled with so many thoughts, that even she can't understand what it is she wishes from it all. And yet, she knows that Patrick is near. Throughout all the confusion, he is still near.

"Kate," he tries to say, but is interrupted as she turns suddenly around and faces him.

"Let's go down to my friend's lake house!" she announces. "It's just a short walk from here along the shore."

"Alright," he returns, watching her as she begins to walk off again. Just as he steps forward to follow her, he feels a raindrop on his head. Within seconds the night sky turns dark once more as the moonlight fades away as quickly as it once came. He looks up momentarily, only to see the darkness and to feel the full force of the winter rain come down upon him. He is taken aback at the beauty of the night rain, glistening ever so slightly as it falls, reflecting whatever light it can catch.

Patrick is awakened quickly as his arm is grabbed by Kate, who is now merely a dark figure in front of him. She begins to run with him down the terrace unto another path, which leads down to the lake's edge. The frost that was once covering the grass seems to fade away into a muddy terrain with every footstep taken. The moonlight returns momentarily as the clouds break and the rain lightens ever so slightly, revealing the outline of a house not too far from where they are. Although he is following her, she looks back for a moment, just long enough for him to see her smiling, and to see her eyes glisten in the light.

Just as the two reach the footsteps to the porch of the house the rain begins to grow even stronger, this time a wind pushing against their side. They come up to the door, and a light turns on shining against them, unveiling the doorway to the log house. For the first time, Patrick sees Kate and how she looks since the rain started. She is shaking slightly as she opens the door, casting aside the high heeled shoes that she had been holding in her hand since she started running. She must have taken them off when the rain first began, he thinks to himself. Both of them are soaked through, he continues to realise, his own body beginning to quiver at the water that is against his cold skin. Winter rain is unforgiving at the best of times, he knows from experience.

Kate enters the house; Patrick beginning to realise it is not as small as he first thought. Its rustic look makes him think of a cabin that one might see up on the mountains, rather than here next to a lake. But it's amazingly warm, and very well kept. There is already a fire going in the far corner, and the smell of fresh plants linger in the air. As he looks around for a moment, he sees the stairs off to the left, leading to a second floor, which he deduces must be the bedrooms. The sound of the rain beats against the roof, but echoes throughout the house overpowering the sound of the fire.

"Is it alright?" he suddenly thinks aloud. He then sees Kate going into a room not too far from them, and returns quickly with two large towels flung over her should and another one that she already is using in her hair.

"This is a guest house," she explains to him. "I come here quite a bit, when I'm on the Eastside, so I wouldn't worry. I've already told her that I'd probably be staying here anyway."

"Oh," he replies, and then thinks for a moment. "Told whom?"

"Well I'm a little too tipsy to drive," she says a laugh, "and it's probably better if you don't go stomping back to the house looking like you do."

Kate hands him a towel as she walks by, heading toward the kitchen. She shouts out to him to sit down by the fire, at which he walks over somewhat bewildered. His body is shivering, although he is managing to dry his head and face with the towel. As he sits in front of the fire, he takes off his dinner jacket and the tie, placing them on the metal rail that is next to the fireplace. Soon after, he removes his shirt, and places it over his jacket, where he then wraps the towel around him like a blanket.

It isn't too long before Kate comes back into the room and comes to his side carrying two mugs of cocoa. Her dress is completely soaked through, and he can see she is somewhat pale, although her cheeks are slightly red.

"Here," she says, handing him the dolphin shaped mug. She sits herself next to him on the floor, one towel already wrapped around her shoulders for warmth. "I don't understand the northwest sometimes. It can be the coldest thing you've ever felt outside, and it'll still rain."

"It doesn't start off that way," he replies softly, looking at the fire. "It starts off as snow, and by the time it reaches us, it turns to rain. My mother always called it Christmas tears."

"Christmas tears, huh?" she replies, wobbling slightly. He catches her, and looks worriedly at her, feeling how cold she is. "Boy, I guess I had a little too much champagne after all."

"You should really get out of that dress," he returns to her seriously. "It's blocking all the heat."

"Aren't you slightly in a bit of a rush to get my clothes off? Perhaps a bit of an eager beaver?" she replies, standing. She laughs at him as she sees his face turn red. "I think she's got some spare clothes in the room upstairs, so I'll go check. But I don't think there's anything for you, I'm afraid."

"I'll..." he stutters, "I'll be fine!" His words are somewhat abrupt, filled with lingering tones of embarrassment. She continues to giggle at him as she walks away, heading up the stairs to the room furthest away.

"Why am I acting like a twelve year old?" he says to himself, unconsciously speaking aloud. He turns his gaze to the house once more, looking around and seeing the fine paintings that are on the wall. The one directly above him is of a woman, extravagantly beautiful in an equestrian riding suit. At the angle he is at, he can't fully see the picture, but he can tell from the eyes that she is very striking. He then looks down to the fire once more, his pants beginning to steam slightly from the warmth, causing him to move back. He looks down as his hands touch soft fur, and sees a large black lambskin rug laid out behind him. Just beyond the lambskin rug is a step which goes down into a recessed living space, with two large sofas and a wooden centre table.

Patrick finally finishes his cup of cocoa when Kate emerges to his side, once again, this time wearing a sweatshirt and pyjama bottoms. Her hair is wrapped in the towel she originally had around her shoulders, and her hands are clinging to the owl shaped cup that she had before.

"Well it may not seduce senators and princes, but it's warm," she says to him, seating herself next to him once more.

"You look—" he begins to say, but she covers his mouth with her hand.

"Don't say it!" she returns forcefully, then looks away from him childishly in a huff. "I've had enough people trying to compliment me tonight, and tell me how beautiful and lovely I am. Right now, all I want is a cup of tea, and we're all out, so I have to drink cocoa."

"Oh," he says, as she takes her hand away from him. "But you are beautiful," he whispers. She looks at him quickly, her eyes glaring, and he cringes away. Slowly she then smiles and turns back to the fire.

"Thank you," she whispers back.

The two sit in silence, Patrick dangling the handle of the cup from his fingers as he rests his arm over his knee. There is a strange sense of comfort between them, as they both continue to sit and watch the fire, listening to the sound of the rain fall. Patrick is the only one to look away momentarily, just to see her smile once more.

"Can I ask you something?" he says softly, looking up to the skylight.

"If you must," she returns, her gaze unwavering.

"Whose house is this?"

"You met her earlier," she reveals, "the princess."

"Ella?" He looks to her for a response, but Kate merely places her hands behind her head and lies back unto the lambskin rug. "Is she really a princess?"

Kate yawns and smiles as she closes her eyes. "I'm tired, I think."

"Why do you always smile?" he says aloud, unaware that he is saying the words.

"Probably too much alcohol," she replies without thought. "It's a weakness of beautiful girls, you know. We tend to drink too much and always smile at handsome men that come along...as long as they don't ask too many questions, that is."

"I see."

"And we're easily seduced in this state too, you know," she continues, opening her eyes and seeing that he is looking at her. His eyes are the same eyes, with the same face that she saw when she first kissed him in the coffee shop. What is it about those eyes, she ponders. She can't help it, she thinks. Then, "Are you going to seduce me, while I'm in such a vulnerable state of being?"

"I wonder," he returns, a smirk breaking ever so slightly across his face. Not too long ago he would have been horribly embarrassed. Tonight, though, he merely smiles and folds his hands behind his head and joins her in lying on the lambskin rug.

"It's been a really long night, hasn't it?" she whispers, closing her eyes and smiling at his statement. Her eyes remain shut, but she knows the touch of his lips against her own.

"I don't know," he returns, "ask me again in the morning."

Chapter 17

Cut To The Onions

Patrick's eyes are slow to open, but his senses do not forget the scent of beauty that lays next to him.

"Good morning," he hears softly, looking at Kate's eyes that are staring at him gently. Her hand covers his, her thumb moving back and forth over his skin. There is a tenderness in her touch that only comes from an honesty that he has known but once before. "Do you want to come and meet my father?"

"Yes," he replies without hesitation, sparking a smile across her face.

A silence falls between them as Kate simply watches the man next to her. His breath is slow, and his eyes are barely open. She can feel something inside that she refuses to answer, but doesn't resist. It washes through her, filling her with a warmth that she has never felt before. At the very least, it is unlike anything that came before meeting him. For a moment, she feels as if the world has fallen away, leaving only one thought.

Patrick's eyes are closed, his breath is soft again, but he feels her gaze against him. For a moment, he feels as if the world has fallen away, leaving only one thought.

"I bet you're thinking about a cup of tea," he whispers, suddenly hearing her laugh in reply. Then, her lips touch his, gently at first.

"How did you know?" she replies, kissing him once again.

"I bet you know a really good breakfast place around here as well," he states softly, her lips covering his again.

"Hungry?" she asks, kissing his nose.

Slowly his eyes open and watches as she closes her eyes and places her lips against his. Suddenly, he thinks to himself, "*Ah. This is what falling feels like.*"

The sound of the falling rain fills the air. The silence between them is only broken by a gentle laughter from Kate as she feels Patrick's fingers brush against her shoulder as he moves aside her hair from her neck. She stares at his eyes and she hesitates for a second, causing him to stroke her cheek with his thumb.

"What is it?" he whispers.

"Nothing," she returns with a gentle smile. "I'm just not used to this."

Patrick responds with a smile, kissing her once more as he seats himself upwards. He knows that he must refrain from pushing her into a conversation that he himself is unsure of. For now, he is content to simply just be in her presence.

"I must be crazy," he hears to his side, seeing her thrust her arms over her face. Carefully, he takes her wrist in his hand and proceeds to remove her arms. The first he places above her head, and the second on his shoulder as he positions himself over her. Their faces are inches away from one another.

"From the moment I met you, my life has been nothing short of this," he whispers to her, "wonderful adventure. I have never felt anything that has moved me the way that I move when I am with you.

"You are like this immense force that pulls me in a way that I didn't think possible. And I feel as if everything that has happened has been this amazing amalgamation of ethereal coincidences that have continued to lead up to this point."

Patrick leans forward and kisses her. His lips and breath intertwines with hers in ways that make every movement meaningful. Then he slowly pulls ever so slightly away.

"If you need to say that this is crazy to make it feel right," he states softly. "Then call me crazy."

She can feel it again. Her heart moving in a way that she is unfamiliar. Without moving, without breathing, she feels him come to her and engulf her unlike any other has before. She cannot describe or control it, so she simply lets it happen.

Meanwhile, back at the James residence, a young Thomas arises from his morning slumber to the smell of breakfast cooking. His eyes are still heavy, and he almost wants to close them, but he knows his grandfather is waiting for him, so he forces himself to sit upright. His somnolent feeling is overcome easily though, as he remembers that the next episode of his favourite show is being released today and he is allowed to watch as much streaming cartoons on television as he wants until Terri arrives for studying.

Ben finishes cooking the last of the morning's pancakes and stacking them nicely onto the plate when he hears the rumblings above his head. Carefully, he sets the plate on the kitchen table and seats himself comfortably and picks up his newspaper after taking a sip of his coffee. He feels the vibration on his belt alert him of an incoming call on his phone, which startles him slightly. He carefully reaches to his side and unclips the oversized mobile phone and brings it to his face in order to read it.

"Hello?" he answers, seeing that it is Pat. "Long night?"

"Hey pop," Patrick replies. "Yes. And I'm probably going to be a bit longer than I thought. I'll probably be back around lunch or so."

"Alright, but Pat..." Ben replies with a smile across his face, suddenly remembering an old Gene Autry song. "Sit tall in that saddle. Hold your head high. Don't be scared. But remember son, just enjoy the ride."

Ben laughs as he hears the groan from his son and the beep to inform him that the call has ended. As he puts the phone back into its holder, he looks up to see his very lively young grandson make his way into the kitchen.

"Morning, Grandpa!" Thomas announces, leaping into his seat.

"Good morning, little bear," Ben replies as the phone finally clicks into place. "Your father sends his regards."

"What's regards?" Thomas questions as he uses his fork to take three pancakes and place them on his plate.

Ben looks over at his young rambunctious grandson and takes another sip from his coffee cup. The look of indifference and yet a wonderful eager innocence mixed into that of a genuine request makes him pause for thought momentarily.

"Do you remember when you were upset because one of the older kids said you were shorter than that young brown-haired gal friend of yours?" Ben asks.

"You mean Terri?" Thomas pauses, then nods as he takes a sip of milk. "Yeah, they were making fun of me because our ball went into the basketball court."

"Well, do you remember what you told me she said to you afterwards?" he questions his grandson, placing his hand over the boy's head.

"She said that I wasn't short," the boy nods heartily. "I just don't realise it starts raining at the same time as she does."

"Yes," Ben replies with a deep laugh. "That son, is regards."

"Oh." Thomas pauses eating momentarily. His face scrunches up slightly as he gives himself a pause for thought, then nods to his grandfather. "Okay."

Thomas finishes his breakfast happily, still not quite sure what his grandfather was trying to explain, but not too bothered in the same right as there are cartoons to watch. He finishes cleaning the table, and heads into the living room to settle in for a good morning's adventures in space.

Ben finishes reading his paper and folds it carefully before putting it on the table. He notices that Thomas has headed off into the living room, and has made a serious attempt at cleaning the table. As much as an eight-year-old does, he thinks to himself.

"Better than his father was," he finally says aloud, picking up the utensils and the warm pot of syrup that is half emptied. He then continues to clear the remainder of the table before undertaking the cleaning of the dishes. In the background, he can hear the explosions and voices of all the different characters gallivanting on their adventures together.

Ben isn't sure when it happened, but his routine has somehow managed to consist of a morning where he makes breakfast, cleans dishes, walks through the house to turn off every light that somehow manages to leave itself on, and then enjoy the warmth and flavour of his coffee.

Although he loves his grandson, he isn't sure how it came to be that his childhood and that of his grandson's came to be so different. From the streaming of practically any show in human history at any time of day, to the mere reality that all the world's knowledge is in fact available to his grandson who seems to prefer utilising it to look up release dates on when his show will be coming out next; it causes Ben pause for thought.

After almost tripping on a baseball, Ben picks it up carefully and stares at it momentarily before walking over and returning it to the large chest where it belongs. He enjoys playing with his grandson, but fondly remembers not but a few weeks ago where he watched as Pat and his son were tossing a football around outside on the beach and Pat accidentally overthrew his son. This in turn caused Thomas to have to run off to fetch it. After his father apologised, Ben remembers clearly his grandson's response as being, "That's okay dad." After tossing the ball back to his father, the young lad then paused momentarily and proceeded to ask, "Wait. When you say something nice that you don't really mean, that's being polite. Right?"

A smile suddenly overcomes Ben as he thinks to himself that at least the boy understands what polite is. And with that thought, he turns and returns to get another cup of coffee.

The young brown-haired girl down the street, that Ben can never seem to remember the name of; her mother calls as he seats himself comfortably on the sofa with his coffee. She asks if it still alright if her daughter comes over to study with Thomas. He tells her that it's perfectly fine and that she's welcome to come as well and stay for lunch if she would like.

After speaking with Terri's mother, Ben finally manages to finish his coffee. He again chuckles at himself, thinking about the days of modern communication and how showing up at the doorstep seems like such an ancient tradition.

"Grandpa," he hears from his side. Ben turns and see the youth laid out across the sofa with his eyes still on the television screen.

"Yes, little bear," Ben replies.

"Why do people say they hang up the phone?" Thomas queries quietly, never once looking away from the screen. Ben looks over and sees one of the cartoons he is watching and notices that it is the most likely cause of the question.

"Well, I suppose it has something to do with the fact that people get older faster than the words they speak," Ben says in a somewhat elderly manner.

"Like when dad tells me to talk slower?" Thomas says, momentarily looking away from the screen to his grandfather.

"Not in the slightest, little bear," Ben states, laughing. Before he can even finish his statement, Thomas has returned to watching his show.

It isn't much after that, when the doorbell rings and Terri comes into the living room forcing Thomas to sit upright and allow her to seat herself next to him, as close as humanly possible. He looks over to his grandfather in the kitchen and sees that he is talking to Terri's mother.

"I think my mother likes your grandfather," Terri says bouncing slightly on the sofa cushion in order to test its durability.

Thomas lets out a loud groan of disgust at the statement, which receives a shrug from his friend in return. They watch as the two elders continue to converse, but move out to the porch.

"My mother and my father are divorced. She says my father is somewhere on the east coast living with some college student who isn't able to count how old she is," Terri announces.

Thomas looks blankly at Terri who takes the tablet controlling the television from him and starts the next episode of the cartoon series. Then, "Is he teaching her how to count?"

"I'm not sure. But my mother told me when he left last year that she had her coffee to keep her company. Because coffee doesn't lie about texting other women and hiding a cell phone."

Thomas blinks twice at the statement. He opens his mouth slightly, and looks at Terri who seems very matter-of-fact in her words. He begins to ponder the words, going as far as to squint and scratch behind his ear for a moment. He's not quite sure what a "divorce" is, but it doesn't sound very nice. He begins to wonder about the state of his health momentarily, as he begins to liken it to sickness. Suddenly he remembers it is a thing that seems to only happen to adults and he begins to relax.

Terri continues to watch television and then suddenly jumps and turns to Thomas, nearly startling him.

"What did Santa say about your letter?!" she asks excitedly.

"Well, he spoke to me in class when he came to visit that day, and said that he didn't have an answer for me yet," he explains to her. A look of disappointment comes across her face, but vanishes nearly as quickly as she turns toward the television once more. "He said that it might be hard."

"Yeah, crazies," she replies. "Are you going anywhere for winter break?"

"I'm not sure," Thomas says, standing on the sofa to see where his grandfather is. Upon seeing that he is still out on the porch, he launches himself downward into the sofa once again. "If it's supposed to be a break, then why do we have so much math to do?"

"It's not just math," Terri bemoans, looking over at her friend. "We have to do all the reports. Not just fractions."

"Yeah, but math is the one that makes me think the most," he replies. "I don't mind the ones that I can just write or draw and not think."

"It's a good thing I'm the smart one in this relationship," Terri states, shaking her head in disapproval.

"I'm not exactly sure what a relationship is, but if it means that I don't have to do math then I'm okay with it."

Terri looks over at Thomas, who has now absorbed himself in the cartoon once again. She reaches over and takes his hand causing him to look at her for a minute. He blinks twice then turns back to the cartoon, at which point she leans her head on his shoulder and continues to grin happily.

"Do you think my mother is depressed like your father? I'm told divorce does that."

Thomas looks momentarily upwards at the ceiling and takes a breath. He looks slowly over to Terri who is comfortably watching the cartoon while easily navigating the curve of his shoulder as a pillow. Quite honestly, it's a bit uncomfortable he thinks, but realises that there is an innate danger in disturbing her. He has learned that from the countless times he has received a fist on his arm from her.

"Does your mother cook pancakes?" Thomas finally asks after considering all his options.

"Do you always think with your stomach?" Terri replies, still unwavering from her position.

"My brain likes to sleep a lot, but my stomach is always awake and ready," he replies instantly. "I like to think of it as a defence mechanism against complicated things."

"Yes, she makes pancakes," Terri huffs. She sits up finally and pauses the cartoon. "Why?"

"Are they good?"

"Not really," she replies, moving her head and wincing slightly at the answer.

"Well I don't really understand the divorce thing very much, but I know that when my grandpa cooks his pancakes while he's happy, they taste good. But I've also noticed that if my father's in charge of cooking while he is grumpy or depressed, then it's better to make a peanut butter and jelly sandwich for myself."

"Strangely, that almost makes sense," Terri returns somewhat surprised. She then falls over to her side and places her feet on Thomas's shoulder. "So, my mother's depressed. That explains why we eat out so much."

"I guess I just don't understand grown-ups in general," Thomas returns. "I think we're just thrown into life too fast."

"Did you want a chance to preview it first?" Terri returns.

Thomas shrugs and takes the controller from her. As he does so, he hears his grandfather and Terri's mother enter the kitchen. He sighs, as he knows that it means that his cartoon time is officially over.

"Grown-ups don't understand the importance of cartoons," he tells Terri.

"What do you two want for lunch?" Ben questions, as he stands in the entranceway to the living room. Thomas eyes light up and he stand up onto the couch.

"Can we have pancakes?!" the young Thomas asks excitedly.

"Well, I suppose if you finish your homework and that it's alright with everyone else, I don't see any reason not to. But you'll need to finish all your homework first before we talk about it," Ben says somewhat sternly.

"Okay!' Thomas says looking over and seeing the disapproving stare of Terri.

As Ben walks back into the kitchen, Terri merely shakes her head as she begins to stand from the couch. Then, "You may not understand them. But they definitely understand you."

Back in Seattle, Kate suggests a wonderful breakfast place in Belltown to grab a quick bite, that Patrick agrees to happily. They have travelled back across town from the Eastside which took a bit of coordination but was accomplished. Kate, being more forthright in her ambitions for food, announces that she's going to just make a quick call to her friend to have the food ready for them upon arrival.

"So, does this mean you officially know everyone in this town?" Patrick queries as Kate finishes ordering breakfast over the phone. Kate simply laughs in reply.

"I might have a few friends scattered here or there," she states whimsically.

They are at her apartment, which is astonishingly quiet with her friends residing. Patrick does not enquire about their whereabouts, but waits happily as Kate finishes changing. As she does so, he looks down upon his attire and smiles at his formal dress. He pulls out his bow tie from his pocket, and hears a tiny laugh in the background, causing him to look up and see Kate standing in her bedroom doorway.

"You look absolutely charming," she states, covering her mouth with her hands.

It is at this moment that the two hear the door open and Kieran and Tara walk in, speaking rather loudly at one another. Pat stands somewhat awkwardly near the sofa, as the two continue their argument and head directly into the kitchen.

"Bloody twat!" Tara states loudly. "You're a right plonker sometimes."

"It's not my fault, love," Kieran replies solemnly, somewhat reserved as he sees both Kate and Patrick.

"I'm not even sure you love me anymore!" Tara iterates as she slams a cup onto the counter and prepares herself a tea. "I can't believe what a git you are!"

"Tara love, did something happen?" Kate asks softly walking over toward Patrick, leaning her upper body toward the kitchen.

"Yes! Kieran is a right pillock, that's what's wrong!" Suddenly a deep sigh comes from Tara. Then, "Sorry, love. This plonker booked the wrong bloody dates back, and now we're stuck here until after New Year's!"

"Oh! Tara," Kate says, walking over into the kitchen.

"I'm not going to see my family," Tara begins angrily. "And I'll have to mail my nieces and nephews gifts by mail. They probably won't— "

Kate wraps her arms around her friend as she begins to cry. She rubs her friend's back as she watches Kieran walk carefully over to Pat. Tara continues sobbing and mumbling incoherently into her friend's shoulder blade.

"Are you sure everything is booked?" Pat asks Kieran in almost a whisper. "Usually they can find something."

"Nah, mate. We've just returned from the airport, after two bloody hours. They're absolutely jammers until after the New Year. No point olagonin' the issue though, it only makes things worse."

Pat blinks twice and remains silent. Suddenly he hears, "And he never says he loves me anymore!"

Immediately afterwards, Kieran shouts into the kitchen, "I said I loved you when we started dating! If things change, I'll let you know!" Then, after a bit of a huff, "I know your upset love, and you can try calling them again, but it's biscuits to a bear."

"Wanker!" she replies.

"Come on, love. You know Kate has a glad eye for this bloke and you're trying to make a mountain out of a mole hill. We'll figure it out. I promise."

Tara suddenly appears from the kitchen and walks past the two of them and heads straight into her bedroom and slams the door shut. Pat and Kieran look at one another momentarily and are about to speak when the door to the bedroom opens once again and Tara reappears only long enough to throw a large rectangular pillow into Kieran's face. He doesn't bother catching it, but lets it strike him and then fall, hearing the door slam as it does so.

Kate walks over to Pat and smiles. She leans over and kisses him, then smiles at Kieran.

"Why don't Kieran and I go pick up our breakfast and let you two talk alone for a bit," Pat says softly.

"Sounds like solid idea," Kieran returns.

"She'll calm down," Kate assures Pat, kissing him once more. "Either way, I'll be here waiting for you when you get back.

Her words strike him deeper than he imagines, as he stands and watches her knock on Tara's door and go in. For a moment he can do nothing but smile as she vanishes from his sight. Then, only to be interrupted by an unfamiliar hand on his shoulder.

"Well I made right bags of that," Kieran states. "Let's be off then, before she takes ma head full off."

"Sounds like a plan," Pat replies.

Chapter 18

Red Lemonade

The sound of Irish music and laughter fill the crowded pub next to the breakfast eatery that Kate directed the duo towards. She phoned while they were locating a space to park in order to let Pat know that it was probably going to better if they stayed out for a bit longer and to go ahead and have breakfast without her. She also notified him that she would text him once the situation had calmed itself. At this stage, Kieran suggested that they head into the nearby pub to see what Seattle thinks an Irish pub is supposed to be.

"Evidently, it's haunted," Kieran explains to Pat over the sound of the music as they seat themselves at the bar. "You'll fit right proper being dressed to the nines and all."

It's just before the lunch hour, so the pub isn't as boisterous as it can normally be. As Patrick looks about him, he sees a wide array of twenty-somethings scattered throughout the building. The music has switched to more of a Celtic Christmas theme as the live band begins to play, to go along with the décor and time of year. People continue to laugh and drink as they eat their chosen brunch specials.

Patrick turns to Kieran and watches him seamlessly gain the attention of the female bartender at the end of the bar. She immediately comes over and fills their order promptly, setting the drinks down within seconds.

"Have you been here before?" Patrick queries, taking a sip of his coffee.

"Nah," Kieran replies. "It's a nice pub n'all, but it's not got the proper black stuff. It has a bit of an off taste about it over here. Then again, no one besides a Jackeen would actually drink it anyway. But they do have proper TK, so it isn't a complete loss."

"Right," Patrick returns from behind his coffee cup, trying to converse during this awkward situation. He barely understands a word the man speaks to him, let alone what he should reply as an answer. He decides at this point, it would probably be a safer choice to change the direction of the conversation slightly. "How long have you known Kate?"

"She and Tara are best mates," Kieran explains. "Tara says she's a culchie originally. But they met at uni and had a bit of a laugh together there. I've only known her for a short spat myself."

Patrick watches as Kieran looks up and watches a match that is being played on the television in the corner. Kieran continues to drink from his bright red clear-ish drink, sipping at it slowly as he seemingly becomes lost in thought. At the end of the bar, Patrick hears an elderly lady speaking in a thick Irish accent, much harder than Kieran's. She is speaking with a younger couple that are happily listening to the story of a sea merchant the lady once loved.

Kieran is methodically wobbling his chair back and forth ever so slightly, causing Patrick to look down and see that one of the legs seems to be slightly crooked.

"This chair is bajanxed," Kieran states, finishing the last of his drink and signalling for another to the lady bartender.

"What are you drinking?" Patrick replies, seeing the red liquid being poured into the glass, followed by a bit of whiskey and ice.

"Just some lemonade to warm me up," Kieran replies, wincing as he sees a play he dislikes on the television.

An awkward silence falls between them, as Kieran's focus remains on the television screen and the match being played. Patrick decides to take the time to message his father and see how things are progressing with Thomas and studying, to which he receives and heart, dog smiley and a regular smiley face as a reply. Pat tilts his head for a moment, then simply decides it isn't worth investigating.

"Mate, I made a right stink of this one," Kieran says putting his glass down empty.

"So, what exactly happened?" Patrick queries.

Kieran signals the bartender and requests two of his drinks. He places the second one in front of Patrick and nods his head. Patrick raises an eyebrow and lifts the soda looking drink to his lips and raises his eyebrows at the strange almost orange or lemon soda flavour that immediately strikes him. Mixed with the Irish whiskey, it tastes rather smooth and easy to drink.

"Booked the wrong dates is all," Kieran announces, sipping from his glass. "I was a bit racked because I'd been gaming with the mates all night. Must have just hit the wrong date."

"It happens," replies Patrick.

"I sees her point. But it makes it worse, cause I don't have much family back in Cork. She's telling me that I think she's mad as a box of frogs, and that I don't understand, which cuts straight to the heart of the matter," Kieran explains softly. "She's all my family, mate. How could I not understand?"

"What happened to your family?" Pat asks as he takes another drink. He looks down and realises that he's finished nearly half of it without knowing. The bartender nods at him, and he nods back. Moments later another drink is placed in front of him.

"It was only ever my Mammy and I," Kieran replies as he sets his drink down momentarily in order to look at the stack of coasters in front of him. He laughs for a minute, then states, "Same feckin coasters in every Irish bar in the world it seems. They probably sell them off the back of a lori at fifty to a zonk."

Kieran finishes his words and tosses the cardboard coaster back on top of the stacked pile in front of him. He looks up at the ceiling and sighs.

"Right, I'm off to the jacks mate."

Patrick continues with his drink as Kieran goes off to refresh himself. He once again finds himself staring at his phone, awaiting a message that he hopes will free him from the awkward experience he seems to have found himself in. Although, he does enjoy the drink, albeit a bit sweet.

He takes a moment to reflect, looking at a picture that Kate took of them together after snatching his phone away. It seems very representative of their entire time together. It seems a bit as if time itself is just this strange and wonderful adventure that only others seem to have. It's almost as if he has been snatched away from his life and placed into an epic fantasy that he has no control over. And yet, he doesn't want it to stop.

"Sorry mate," he hears from his side, as Kieran seats himself once more. "I think I drank those first couple a bit quick."

"This does tend to hit you rather quickly," Pat says finishing the last of his drink. "I think it's coffee for me here on out."

Kieran laughs at the words, and nods his head. "Yeah, I'd best not go back being langers and all. Probably wouldn't send the proper message."

"Probably not."

Kieran pats Patrick's back at the words and orders himself a coffee.

A few short moments pass between the two, where Kieran watches the last of a match as he finishes his coffee. Patrick continues to check his phone, as well as listen to all the strange stories that seem to swirl about him.

"Mate," Kieran announces, setting his cup down and turning towards Patrick. "I wanted you to know that I'm sorry about all this muck. I know you and Kate probably had some plans for today and all."

"Not really," Patrick returns. "She mentioned something about meeting her father."

"Oh!" Kieran states with a look of surprise.

"What?" replies Patrick questioningly. "Is that a bad thing?"

"No. No. That's a bit of a drive is all. He lives up in the mountains somewhere," Kieran explains. "He's got a bit of a posh landing, if you ask me."

"So, you've been before?"

"Just once, a couple years back." Kieran speaks matter-of-factly. His words roll easily off of his tongue, causing Patrick to pause momentarily to weigh the gravity of them. "Tara was a bit enamoured with the beauty of it all.

"She was a bit put off when I said it didn't hold a candle to the isles though."

Kieran laughs at his words, just as Patrick hears his phone ring. Mercifully, it is Kate who states that things have calmed a bit and that there probably is going to be a bit of change of plans but that they would talk about it once he brings Kieran home. Patrick cannot help but smile at the statement. He immediately notifies Kieran of the situation and motions for their exit.

The car ride back begins quite slowly, as holiday shoppers and the weather have seemingly combined to create a wonderful mixture of horrible accidents laden throughout the roads. Kieran is not much of a talkative fellow, but avoids staring at his phone as his fear of what might be on it keeps him at bay.

"I bloody hate these things," Kieran announces, staring at his phone.

"Why's that?" Patrick returns, watching as the traffic in front of him comes to a complete stop.

"Everything on this thing is addicting, mate. Me mams," he begins, "she'd watch me play for hours on it and ignore the world. Kinda wished I'd spent a bit more time talking with her instead."

"Did something happen to her?"

"She passed a few years back," Kieran says somewhat solemnly. "Just before Christmas."

"I'm sorry to hear that," Patrick says carefully.

"Tara bought me my first console that Christmas. I spent thirty two feckin hours beating that first game," he laughs as he speaks. "It was a bloody good day. A good feckin game.

"I really put this Christmas in tatters." His voice trails off, as he stares at this phone.

"Things like this always have a way of working themselves out," Patrick reassures him as the car inches forward slowly. "That's the good thing about being loved. They tend to forgive us for being us."

Kieran laughs and nods at the statement.

It takes nearly an hour to reach Kate's apartment. During which time, Patrick and Kieran have discussed in great detail the complexity of fighting aliens and fending them from different types of space ships. Patrick discovers the several different forms and styles used, as well as all the different clans that people join to do so.

As the two walk in to the apartment, they hear the comforting words of Kate being spoken to Tara. She is speaking in a somewhat excited fashion about how this will work, and it will be a great time.

Upon seeing the two come in through the front door, Tara arises and comes over to Kieran and looks at him. She has clearly been crying, and is still visibly upset, but her breathing has calmed. She speaks no words, nor does Kieran, but the two communicate easily in silence. After a moment, Tara places her forehead on Kieran's chest and he places his arms around her. The two hold one another, before she breaks from him and takes his hand in hers and leads him over to the sofa.

"I'm sorry," she whispers as the two sit.

"I'm sorry as well, love," he replies.

Kate walks over to the kitchen and grabs her purse and keys. She then comes over and joins Patrick, motioning silently that they should go out into the hall. As the two continue out into the hall, Patrick feels her hand take his and their fingers intertwine slowly. Once the door shuts behind them, she leads them down the hallway toward the window and the stairwell.

"Thank you for doing that for me," Kate says with a gentle smile over coming her. "Tara was really upset by the entire thing. I know Kieran didn't mean anything by it, but it still hurt her tremendously at the realisation that she can't be with her brothers and sisters for the holidays."

"Does she have a big family then?" Pat asks, seeing the sunlight break the clouds through the window.

"She has three older brothers and two older sisters," Kate explains. "Every year they meet at their parents' house in Kent. It's this beautiful converted hop farm. It's always a quintessential British Christmas."

"Sounds very Dickensian," Patrick replies with a laugh. He receives a glare from Kate. "I've always wanted to say that."

Kate squeezes his cheeks with her hand and kisses him.

"You're adorable," she tells him as she kisses him once again. Then, "Come. Let's go out and leave these two to have some time to figure things out."

"Right."

Chapter 19

Holly Day Farm

"I've noticed something," Kate tells Patrick, looking over her shoulder.

"What's that?" he says softly, looking at her pleasant smile once more.

"Thomas is a fairly quiet child, isn't he?" she says, waving her fingers at him to try and get his attention off of the screen on the back of Patrick's headrest. It takes him a moment, but Thomas waves back with his enormous grin, bearing all his teeth. She then turns back towards the front of the car and looks out the windows at the passing coastline.

"Just wait until his show is finished, and then you'll hear him in all his glory," Patrick replies, a wry grin coming across his face. He notices how empty the roads are, and how clear the skies have been. "It's a long drive yet, so I'm sure you'll have plenty of chances to hear from him about some loving thing that he has planned or done."

Looking at Patrick when he speaks about his son, there is no doubt about how deeply he loves him, how no matter how much or little he spoke and nothing that Thomas could say would ever fall on deaf ears when spoken to his father. It's something that she has not experienced first-hand, nor been a part of on the level that she sees before her. She is always close to her family, her father especially, but even then, there is a certain amount of distance between them. Even through childhood, there were things that she could never tell her mother, even from an early age. Simple tiny little pieces of her life that she kept all to herself; these were the foundations of her life today.

"You know we could have always taken the ferry," Patrick says suddenly, looking back over to Kate, seeing her somewhat bewildering expression.

"Oh! No, it's not that," she insists. "I was just daydreaming. Besides, this is such a beautiful day compared to the other night, so a drive is much nicer. And there's one more thing..." Her words trail off, catching Patrick's ears.

"Yes?" he says slowly, questioningly.

"I don't know how to get to the place from the ferry," she says quietly, almost childlike. "It's been awhile since I've been up there."

"Good grief. I'm sure your cell phone could have directed us."

"Where's the adventure in that!?" she exclaims happily. "Besides, I'm sure that there is a secret ploy on all navigation devices to spark the robot-uprising. It's just a matter of time."

"Um," Patrick states, raising an eyebrow. "Right."

Kate laughs in reply, and turns towards the window again, watching the clouds in the sky take on different shapes.

The drive continues somewhat peacefully, until of course Thomas's program ends, and he begins his talkative narration of the show. Kate listens in awe, amazed at how one child can ask so many different questions, and respond to anything that she says so easily, as if he has experienced everything in life. A child's innocence, they call it, she thinks to herself as she listens to him. He is a wonderful child, she tells herself with such a warm smile and small laugh as he tells her about his school friend and the fact that he got his tongue stuck to his lunchbox. She watches him with such envy, unbelieving in the fact that he has such a heart-warming ability to just speak from his heart without hesitation or fear.

Nearly an hour passes before Thomas finally stops his conversation with Kate, ending with the emphasis on how wonderful pancakes are with ice-cream on them. Even then, Kate had to promise to make him chocolate crepes at some later day because they were very similar. Soon after they stop speaking, Patrick looks into his mirror and sees Thomas has fallen asleep, where Kate then notices a very fatherly look overcome him as he drives down the now forest road.

"That's a nice look," she says softly, unaware that she is speaking.

"What look?" Pat replies, seeing the soft eyes of Kate looking at him suddenly. "What did I do now?"

"Nothing," she laughs.

Kate ponders for a moment, looking back out to the mountains in the distance. It won't be too much farther before they reach their destination, and somehow, she feels as if she has let time slip between them. There was so much that she wished to say before Patrick picked her up this morning. She was filled with much resolve, and somehow between then and now, she seems to have lost it. She can hear Tara laughing at her in the back of her mind, telling her what a coward she's being.

"Patrick," she finally manages to say, unable to look at him.

"Yes?" he responds, slowing as a sharp turn comes as they begin to head towards the mountains.

"About the other night," she begins, pausing momentarily. Kate then can't help but to look and see what his expression is. Patrick is merely smiling, though, concentrating on the corner, and the oncoming cars. "Never mind."

Patrick is listening, although is a bit more concerned about a larger truck that is over the line slightly. He looks over at Kate, thinking that although he knows so little about her, from what he does know, she isn't one to just hide things when something is on her mind. She has always struck him as someone that could say anything, loudly and clearly. The look that he sees on her face is something completely different; a child-like nervousness.

"Kate," he starts, drawing her attention. "What do you think about marriage?"

The reaction across her face is instant, and humorous to see. Patrick only sees it out of the corner of his eyes, but the sudden look of confusion is one that he hasn't seen from her before. It is a rare pleasure to see her struggle, even if but for a second.

"Depends," she returns, composing herself once again. "Are you asking me?"

"Ah, now that's an interesting reply," he says happily, a grin overcoming his entire face. "Let's say I was. What would be your answer?"

"Blimey," she says, her accent becoming quite hard all of a sudden. "Plonker."

Pat feels her hit his shoulder and he laughs, knowing that he's eased her a bit, even if she didn't answer. He thinks to himself for a moment, listening to her grumble slightly, but nevertheless smile. It's here that he decides to help her along with her original question that she can't ask.

"So, does this mean you've had people ask you before?" he presses, raising an eyebrow.

"What?!" she interjects before he can finish. "Well...maybe...yes, I suppose."

"Oh?..." he returns, trying to hide his smile. "And what was the reply?"

Kate doesn't look at Pat, but instead looks out the window. "The truth is, I think everyone wants to find that one person they want to spend the rest of their lives with."

"Probably," he replies, his voice somewhat matter-of-fact. Then, more softly, "The problem with that is, that with certain people at least, it's very easy for them to fall in and out of love. The idea being, if you can give you heart to someone so easily, then it is just as easy to have it taken away."

"Exactly," Kate responds, smirking at the thought of something or someone. "The more that people throw the word around, makes it more difficult to believe it actually exists. Not to say that I don't, but I think that I've grown a bit smarter in those who I do or don't believe."

Patrick ponders the statement, continuing along the long seemingly empty stretch of highway.

"There's the other side of that also," Patrick continues. "For some, it's something that is the hardest thing on earth to do. I mean, to give someone their heart is like giving them the most precious thing in the world. For whatever reason, it's been locked away or kept so close to them, that love is the greatest thing in the world. At the same time, it's harder for these types of people to fall out of love. The dilemma in that being, when it does happen, it can cut so deeply if it ends that it can crush them. It makes me wonder which way is better."

"I think that I would rather be given someone's heart who wanted me to cherish it forever, than to have someone give me a heart that was theirs simply because they can," Kate says, refusing to look at Pat. "If I was going to give my heart away, I don't want to believe that it'll ever be given back to me some day or that I would have to take it back."

"Hmm," is all he can say in reply. He doesn't push any further though, sensing an area that he is very weak at, and feeling the unease behind Kate's voice.

"You know, don't you?" he hears.

"About?" Patrick returns quietly. The car begins to approach an old green painted iron bridge, the rust in places leaking down as if the bridge itself were crying. The tires make a funny vibration as they cross slowly, also causing an intrepid sound of intermittent thumping of sorts. Kate tries to speak, but her voice jolts, and she decides to hold her words.

"Daniel proposed to me at the party," she then states, just as they finish crossing. "I thought he was going to do it in front of everybody, but he decided to wait until were alone. He tries to act bold, but in reality, he's quite a timid person."

"He gave you the matching ring, I take it. The one that goes with the bracelet," Patrick says, pulling the car over to a small scenic pull-out. He can see the look on Kate's face, and how she is staring at her hand. Her eyes are holding back a pain that he never had seen before. Then, she closes her eyes, smiles, and lifts her head to him.

"So, he did speak with you, after all," she says, her eyes still shut. "It must have been quite painful, especially after telling me that you loved me. Did it make you want to take it back?"

"No," he replies, placing his hand over hers, causing her to open her eyes. "At first, I didn't know what to think. I left the party shortly after he told me, I will admit. I...needed some air."

"Do you hate me?" she asks him, the sincerity piercing into him with every word.

"Why would I hate you? Because of you, I've started to breathe again. Laughter fills my world in a way that I didn't think possible before."

"I need to ask," Kate says firmly. "How do you know you love me, Patrick? What have I done that made you think the way you do? We've only known each other for such a short time." Kate pauses after each word, almost as if she is trying to find the next word within herself; to make sense of something that she herself does not understand.

"Kate," he says gently, taking her hand within his. "My world until now has been so black and white...so many variants of grey that I can't possibly count them all. The moment I saw you, the world burst into colour again. It was as if the universe rained colour into my very being.

"Honestly, I feel as if I've been standing in the dark dreary rain for too long," he states, a smile coming across him. "I don't expect you to know all the answers. I'm not asking for them. But when I'm with you, the rain isn't lifeless. It's beautiful. Life is beautiful, just like you."

Her eyes swell at his words. Kate doesn't need for him to say anything, because she can literally feel his honesty pierce deeply into her heart unlike any other man has ever done. She can hear the storm in his being beginning to change into Spring.

"Does that make sense?" he whispers to her, turning and returning to the steering wheel. Kate simply smiles as he begins to drive off once more. As he pulls out onto the road, she leans over to him, resting her head against his arm.

"I told him no," she whispers.

Patrick says nothing in return, but continues to drive down a very long empty road a smile forming across his face. Kate merely closes her eyes at his silence, trying to let her mind be clear of anything and everything.

"You have a lot of secrets, don't you?" Patrick says, encroaching on the peaceful silence. Kate looks over at him questioningly, as if unsure at how to reply. "I don't really know much about you, do I?"

"No," she whispers, still unsure of the line of questions. "I guess not. Does that bother you?"

"Not really." Patrick looks in the mirror, and then smiles as he hears the soft snore of Thomas in the background interrupting his train of thought. "He's always been like that, you know."

Kate watches as Patrick's eyes continue to watch his son. She looks over her shoulder and sees the innocent face of the young man who drew a picture for her.

"He reminds me of my puppy I had when I was a child," Kate reveals. "You're a wonderful father, you know. I think it's pretty amazing what you're doing, both you and your father."

"Not really that amazing, although Dad's definitely amazing. But, I have my good days and bad, like everyone," Patrick retorts.

Kate looks up suddenly, quite surprised and sceptical at the statement. She knows she wants to say something, but the words escape her, so instead she merely smiles and scoffs.

"It's true," he continues. "Shortly after his mother died, I wasn't in a very good place. Part of me wanted to run. I couldn't think straight at all. One day, I came home and decided I'd had enough. I didn't care about anything or anyone. All I thought was that I had to go."

"Where?" she manages to say. She winces at the statement, thinking to herself what an idiotic question.

"To the end of the drive," he replies, looking over to her and seeing her discomfort. "I got to the end of my driveway before I realised what I was doing. I realised in that short distance of a few feet, that no matter how much pain and suffering I was going through, I couldn't leave my son. I needed him. I still need him, probably a lot more than he needs me. But that's just part of being a parent, I think.

"Shortly after, I packed up and moved up here to be with my father."

"But you were smart enough to realise that you needed help, and what was more important," she replies with a serious countenance. "Most never do that."

Patrick smiles and looks at her out of the corner of his eye. "I like your smile."

There is a herd of elk crossing the road ahead, causing them to slow behind a few cars that are stopped. Kate's eyes are locked on Patrick though, who is still smiling despite the look that she is giving him. Finally, he turns to her, putting his arm around the back of her headrest. He then leans forward to become slightly closer to her.

"I have never told anyone that before," he says to her, losing his smile.

"Really? Why would you tell me?" she returns, holding the face of sincerity.

"Did you know that cows are really just slow elk?" he asks, blinking twice slowly.

"What???" She looks past him and sees an elk standing on the side of the road, looking into the car. She blinks suddenly and jumps at the sight. "That's a huge deer."

"Elk," he replies. "Haven't you ever seen an elk before?"

"Is it something like a reindeer?"

"Somewhat, I suppose. I thought you were born in the wild plains of the country," he says, squinting for a moment as he thinks back to his small amount of knowledge concerning the animal. "I think they're more like a mule with horns on it, really. At least that's how my father always explained it to me."

Kate laughs, watching intently at the elk slowly moving into the woods. They don't prance like the deer that she's seen near Seattle. Also, she cannot help but think in some minor way that they do almost look like a small horse with antlers. She almost regrets seeing the last of them cross the road and vanish as if they were never there.

As Patrick drives off, Kate looks back at the empty road behind them, as if in hopes of seeing the elk come out once more. Kate looks at Thomas momentarily and smiles as he snorts slightly, then turns around and faces the front once more. She seats herself and composes herself to a very upright position, her nose tilted ever so slightly upwards. Pat only watches her from the corner of his eye, but notices the change in her.

"That was very sly of you," she announces softly, turning her head just slightly towards him.

"Was it?" he says, a smile ever so slightly breaking across his face.

"You know, you almost managed to get me to say something mushy," she continues, folding her hands neatly in her lap. "As if I would do something like that."

"As if," he replies. He feels a sudden warmth overcome him as he watches her start to scratch her arms in a very ridiculous manner. "What's wrong?"

"It's you," she says, scratching her neck. "You're exuding too much happiness. Stop it! It's making me itchy."

"My happiness is making you itchy?" He watches her stop and cross her arms like the little girl that Thomas plays with. She's sulking, he thinks. She's cute when she sulks, he determines in his mind; his happiness continuing to exude from him.

It isn't long after that the car pulls into a long narrow road, as directed by the car navigation system, to which Kate had begrudgingly entered the address. The drive up to the main lodge is somewhat bumpy, but a welcomed change to the extravagance of the house that he attended the other night with her. This time, although he knew very little of the details, he can see instantly that it is a beautiful setting once again, but much more of a homelier looking estate. There are school buses parked not too far into the drive, and there are children running in the fields of large bushes neatly grown off to their left. As he looks further ahead he can see a man standing at the end of the drive wearing a cowboy hat and holding a coffee cup in his hand. He instantly strikes Patrick, as he stands out of the bundles of children and other adults walking about.

Patrick is somewhat surprised at the reaction that Kate has when she sees the man standing there, walking up the drive. It is a cross between curiosity, laughter, and disgust. He isn't sure which is more prevalent, but watches carefully as they approach him and the man can clearly see them.

Thomas has fully awakened now, and is looking about, albeit unusually quieter. When he sees the man with the cowboy hat come up to the car as they approach him, his eyes and interest both begin to peak, and he leans forward with utter curiosity as Kate rolls her window down.

"Is he a real cowboy?" Thomas asks, trying to lean as much into the forward seats as possible. "Does he ride a horse?"

"I didn't think children knew what cowboys were anymore?" Kate responds, looking back to young Thomas, as she waits for the man to come to the window. "Hello, William. My handsome young friend here wants to know if you are a cowboy?"

"Hmmm," the tall man replies, tipping his hat as he leans into the car and rests his arms on the window frame. "That's a very tough question, kiddo."

Pat looks carefully at the gentleman standing next to his car, somewhat older than himself, but generally he thinks about the same age at first glance. The cowboy hat definitely throws him though, as there is an unmistakable thick Scottish accent when the man talks.

"The only cows this man has seen Thomas, is the ones in the petting zoo," Kate says, leaning over and kissing the man's cheek. "How are you William?"

"Fine, lass," the man replies with his voice growling intently due to his accent. "I think that was a bit harsh on the poor lad, though. I've seen good old Aberdeen Angus before."

"In a superstore, maybe," she replies. Kate curls her nose at the man, and sticks her tongue out as she does so. "Oh! Before I forget, this is Patrick, and the young handsome man in the back is his son Thomas."

"Nice to meet you, lad," William says, reaching into the car and shaking Thomas's hand with his giant hands. "You'd best get up to the main house and get some warm apple juice while it's there. And if I get back early enough, I've got some nice cider set aside for us later."

"I like cider!" Thomas says happily.

"This cider is a bit too strong for a little lad such as yourself, but I'm sure you're going to like the apple juice that the house has." William tips his hat and steps back, telling them the direction to the main house just over the hill and around the large set of trees. He instructs them that because they'll be staying at the house for a bit, they may as well park there.

Patrick follows the instructions given him, and parks next to a large four-wheel drive vehicle that is parked just next to the front door of the large manor house. Although it is large in size, and beautiful in its own right, it is made of a much simpler design, somewhat of a ranch style manor, rather than a mansion style home.

"Wow!" Thomas says excitedly after seeing the house and the long black executive car that is parked not far off from the front of the car. "This is where we're getting a Christmas tree?"

"I am beginning to wonder that myself," Patrick responds, looking at Kate with a small grimace. "Because one would always see one of those type of cars at a Christmas tree farm."

"Well, my friends tend to travel somewhat ridiculously at times," Kate responds, trying to muffle her answer. "I'm sure it'll be leaving soon."

"Can I ride in it?!" Thomas asks, nearly leaping across to the front of the car after removing his seatbelt. "Is it one that a movie star has ridden in? Maybe the guy who invented pancakes is here!"

"Maybe, but unlikely," Patrick says, stepping out of the car.

Thomas climbs over the seat and jumps out of the car with a bound, landing happily next to his father. Kate steps out of the car before Patrick can close his door, and laughs as she sees the young boy trying to blow smoke rings with his breath because of the cold air. Her attention is caught as she sees some large Clydesdale horses that are being led just beyond the house down the path leading to the stables near the far edge of the estate, beyond the hill that they came up.

"They're bringing the horses down to the field for the hay ride," she says to them. The two turn in response, watching as eight large exquisitely maintained Clydesdale horses are walked carefully in pairs down the farm path. It is almost as if they were watching their very own parade.

"Wow, they're super huge!!!" Thomas says excitedly. "Are those cowgirls, then?"

"Firstly, those aren't cows, little bear," his father says, placing his hand on his head. "Secondly, I'm sure if you ask them, that some will most likely say yes."

"Cool," he says. "Do cowgirls where cowboy hats?"

"I imagine so," Pat says, looking down at his son's eyes, knowing what the next question will be.

"Why don't they wear cowgirl hats?"

"When I lived on the ranch with my father, I used to have a special cowgirl hat that I wore all the time." Kate's words only seem to add to the confusion of the young boy's thoughts. "Never once, did I ride atop a cow though."

"Oh," Thomas says in earnest, his eyes looking intensely upon the horses and those who are guiding them. "I wonder if Terri wears a cowboy hat. She came from California. Do they have cowboys in California?"

"Probably, but they're slightly different," Patrick replies. "And they still don't ride cows."

"Shall we go and get some apple juice to warm us up?" Kate interjects, trying to hold her laughter back.

The three walk towards the main entrance to the house, where a young lady opens the door and walks out to greet them. She is wearing a holiday sweater, with a picture of a snowman placed neatly in the centre, as well as a green Christmas hat with white trim and a white furry ball which is place neatly to one side. At the end of her long golden hair, which is tied back behind her carefully, is four bells which make a light somewhat hollow jingle when she moves.

"Hello, Katherine," she says happily, stepping to one side of the door as the three travellers arrive upon the large oak door.

"Hello Mina," replies Kate with a smile. "I see you are as festive as ever."

"Of course, Katherine," the young lady states in return, motioning for the three of them to enter the house. "There are refreshments awaiting the young master, and I believe Sampson is down with the other children in the barn area, although he is a bit difficult to keep track of. Shall I take the young master down to where the others are?"

"That sounds like a good idea. Thank you, Mina," Kate says, to which the young lady kneels before Thomas and asks him if he wishes for some Christmas cake and warm apple juice.

"It's okay, Thomas," his father tells him, although he is already holding hands with the young lady and walking off with her without his words.

"Looks like he didn't need much persuasion," Kate says, walking into the house and pulling Patrick in behind her.

"He's always been like that," he explains, sighing as his son disappears into the distance with the young servant lady.

"A sucker for blondes, huh?" Kate laughs, taking Patrick's arm in hers and walking off into the other direction. "Come on, there is someone I want you to meet."

"How come I have a bad feeling brewing inside me already," he replies softly, feeling her grip tighten.

"That could just be anticipation," she returns, "and I'm sure that the cider William has in store for you will help with that."

Patrick feels a shudder go down his spine, and he winces at the thought, although still continues forward willingly. He suddenly is reminded of the horror films he used to watch as a child, where the man goes into the room feeling the ominous air all around him, following the beautiful heroine willingly into the darkness never truly knowing what evil would befall him. Even when Kate invited Thomas to this farm, so they could choose a tree for her father, Patrick knew inside there would be no escape when she mentioned a pirate cove and bon fire with marshmallows. How any of that relates to choosing a Christmas tree he has yet to understand.

Kate seems to know the layout of the house well, although Patrick remembers clear that when he asked about where they were getting a tree, all she would tell him in detail was that it merely a friend of hers' estate. Although, admittedly she did promise him that it wasn't anything like getting a tree from somewhere he'd probably been and that people tend to dress up in costumes at times but that it wasn't compulsory, unless of course Thomas wanted to wear a pirate outfit. This took quite some time for Patrick to convince him otherwise. Why there was a pirate cove on a farm in the middle of winter was yet another question that puzzled him entirely. Then again, he knows inside he should just reside the fact that these things seem to occur more often than not since he has met Kate.

They approach a room at the far end of the left wing of the house, where two large wooden doors take up much of the wall. One of the doors is slightly ajar, of which Kate smiles as she sees the signs of a black nose poking out of the bottom of the opening. She motions for Patrick to walk quietly, but she can already tell that she has been spotted, as the nose begins to twitch fervently the closer they approach.

Within seconds the nose begins to move sideways, opening the heavy doors wider and wider, until all at once a large Siberian husky pounces through and runs over to them. The dog completely ignores Patrick, and instead seats himself majestically in front of Kate, as if awaiting her approval.

"Patrick, this is my good friend Sampson," she says, kneeling before the dog and giving the large beast a ferocious hug around the collar. Sampson wags his tail, but doesn't move until she stands once more. He then looks over to Patrick and barks once, the sound echoing throughout the house with authority. He then raises his paw, and awaits Patrick's response. "He wants to shake."

"Oh!" Patrick says to Kate, somewhat stunned at how well trained the animal is. He leans forward with his hand outward, trying to let Sampson sniff him, but Sampson merely places his paw on top of Patrick's hand. Taking notice to the response, Patrick turns his hand over with a laugh and shakes with Sampson.

"Sampson, where's Emma?" Kate asks, as if she were asking a child.

Without hesitation, Sampson comes to all fours and turns to head back into the room where he emerged from moments earlier. The two then follow him; Patrick following somewhat more cautiously than Kate.

The room is brightly lit, with windows fully surrounding the two far walls to the front of them and to the right, with a large alcove window in the centre of the right wall. There is a large round table next to the alcove, to where Patrick sees two ladies standing behind a rather exquisite looking figure, which looks as if she is speaking with another lady further in the alcove that he cannot see.

As if he had done it a hundred times before, Sampson walks over to the table and pushes the young lady's leg with his nose, bringing her attention away from whomever she is speaking with. The lady then focuses her gaze at the two who are approaching her from the doorway, causing her eyes to light up filling with anticipation. She wishes to stand, but doesn't, instead holding her hands up when the two come close enough.

"Katherine," she says aloud, her voice very soft and eloquent. "And this must be the handsome Patrick that I have heard so much about."

"Me?" he replies, looking at Kate for support. Kate merely smiles and leans forward to kiss the lady on both cheeks.

"How are you Emma?" Kate asks, her voice filled with concern, although trying not to.

"She's doing fine," another voice enters, to which Patrick looks up to see the lady standing next to the alcove window.

"Ella," Patrick says with a smile.

"Oh?" Emma says somewhat startled, looking over. "You know each other?"

"We met at the Christmas evening that Daniel held the other night," Ella says softly, smiling at Patrick and turning around once more to face out the window. "Patrick made quite a refreshing impression of what life as a commoner can be like."

"Ella!" Emma says in rebuke.

"I didn't mean it as an insult," she returns, continuing to face outward towards the large field of trees.

"You'll have to forgive her," Emma explains, "she just was informed of some bad news and she is sulking."

"There is nothing to forgive," Patrick says, coming forward and seating himself as motioned to. He looks at the two ladies standing behind Emma, both dressed in servant attire, although pleasantly wearing green and white Christmas hats, and yet both somewhat older than the three ladies around the table.

"I'm glad you both could come," Emma says, her voice still somewhat soft and timid compared to what Patrick is accustomed. "I wasn't sure if Katherine would be able to convince you to come, Patrick, but I was hoping to meet you."

"Well I'm not exactly sure why you would want to meet me?" Patrick says, putting his hand on the back of his head and somewhat forcefully laughing to hide the discomfort.

"I didn't actually invite him, rather than his son, Thomas," Kate explains, smiling at the blushing man next to her. "He's the real boss of the family."

"I see," Emma replies with a smile. "Is he not with you?"

"He's with Mina now," Kate returns, watching as the servant leans forward and pours both Emma and Kate a cup of tea.

"I see," Emma says once more. Then, after taking a sip from her tea, "I doubt we'll see him for some time then, knowing Mina."

Patrick looks confused, watching as the two ladies sip from their teas. Emma sees the distress across his face and begins to look apologetic.

"I'm sorry," she begins. "You see, Mina has a tendency to dote on young children. Don't worry, he's being looked well after, and will probably be playing with all the other children before long."

"Oh," Patrick returns, somewhat relaxing at the answer. "That does make me wonder, though."

"About what?" Emma queries politely.

"The school buses," he replies, tilting his eyebrow ever so slightly. "Why are there so many children here?"

"This is an annual event that the estate holds once a year for the local children in the area. Although sometimes it is very hard for certain members of my family and friends to be here each year, this is somewhat of a tradition that I personally oversee for the sake of the children."

"If you'll excuse me, I think I've had my fill of sunshine for the day," the group hears, turning to Ella as she silently passes behind Kate and Patrick with incredible disdain exuding from her as she leaves as quickly and noticeably as she can.

"Ella," Emma whispers aloud. Her eyes reveal the pain within her, but her mouth remains silent, unable to call out what she wishes. Then, "I'm sorry. You'll have to excuse my sister. She has been terribly worried over these past few days."

Kate looks silently into the eyes of Emma, saying nothing, but noticing all. Patrick gazes at the two, completely confused and oblivious to everything that is taking place before him.

"It has been a bit of a strain organising these events this year," Emma says softly, looking out the window as she wraps her fingers around her china cup. "When we first held these events, I was a child myself, and there were only a few children that would come. It was more a party, rather than anything. Over time, more and more children came as the towns nearby grew larger and larger. But I can't imagine not having them around. They give me such joy, watching the happiness that this time of year brings to them. Don't you agree, Patrick?"

Emma turns to Patrick, catching him completely off guard. For the first time he is caught by the intense stare of the woman before him, and the exquisite softness within her eyes. There is such pain, he thinks, and such beauty. He has only ever seen it once before. All he can do is bow his head and nod to her, knowing that whatever words he would say, would never answer the real question that she posed.

"Well, judging by the movement outside, it is almost time for the Christmas festivities to begin. Would you two care to join in and accompany the children and I on the hay ride to the Christmas lunch? I am sure that your son has already been taken down there if he is with young Mina." Emma looks at Patrick once more, this time with such an endearing smile.

"Of course, we would," Kate says boldly, taking Patrick's arm and nearly pulling him from his seat. "Patrick was telling me the entire trip over here that all he wanted to do was go on a sleigh ride with me."

"Oh, yes. How do I wish it so," Patrick says methodically in reply, emphasizing his words in a heavy western accent. He is suddenly aware of the amount of British presence he is in the company of, and feels somewhat embarrassed at his attempt at humour.

Emma can only laugh timidly, covering her mouth as she does so, watching the ease that the two share with one another. Immediately she thinks this one is most definitely different than any other that she has seen with Katherine. There is such care and comfort in her eyes. It makes Emma almost envious.

The two servants leave the room as Kate and Emma finish their tea. Minutes later they return with a fur blanket and a fur trimmed dark blue overcoat for Emma. They inform the three that they have sent word to William and that the preparations for them would only be momentary and that he would be sending someone immediately. Emma merely smiles in reply, and places her hands on the servants as an answer, who nods in return and resumes her place behind her mistress. A few minutes later William appears at the doorway with a pleasant smile.

"Your chariot awaits," they hear from the Scotsman.

Emma is the first to stand, showing her timid and elegant stature as she does so. Patrick watches as she is cared to by her servants, who see to her jacket and then a shawl over the top as well. The three are then led out into the main courtyard where they are led further up the road to where the caravan of horse drawn wagons are, each one filled with hay, and all are full of children and parents.

As they approach the first carriage, Patrick hears the familiar shouts of his son amongst the crowds of children who are merrily cheering the horses and singing various Christmas songs. Even Kate stops and waves at the fourth carriage where Thomas is seated happily atop a large hay stack next to Mina and other children.

"Is that your son?" queries Emma, who smiles pleasantly and waves as well.

"That's unmistakably Thomas," he replies with a proud father grin.

"Do you want him to join us?" Emma asks, looking at Patrick with a cheerful curiosity.

"No," he replies instantly. "He's enjoying himself where he is. And I'm sure he's made friends already. So, there's no point in spoiling his fun."

"True," Emma returns, turning and taking William's hand in order to climb into the back of the wagon. The attendant lady with the blanket waits carefully until all three have situated themselves close to one another, and then hands the two ladies a large fur blanket in order to cover their legs.

"It's a long trek up to the farm, everyone," William says quiet firmly. "Make sure you are comfortable and warm. There are blankets and mittens for anyone who needs them, as it will probably be snowing soon, and it won't be light when we get back. I heard tell from the staff this morning that the ground was already covered in a light snow."

There is a cheer from the children after hearing the word snow and even the parents cannot help but to shed a glimmer of happiness and joy at the sound of the voyage. The air is definitely bitter, but the sound of the jingling bells begins to warm all as the horses begin to move forward. The sound of their thunderous hooves echoes against the trees, and the air of Christmas dances about them all.

"Is this something you do every year?" Patrick asks Kate, as she pulls the blanket over both hers and Patrick's legs.

"I try but less often than I would like," she reveals, "but I fly back and forth, from here and there."

"Kate and Ella are quite the travellers," Emma says pleasantly. "They have been that way since their late teens."

"How did that come about?" he asks, the question more directed at Emma rather than Kate.

"Mostly work among other things," Kate replies, her voice somewhat soft and muffled.

"Didn't you travel with them?" Patrick asks, once again speaking with Emma.

Emma's countenance remains a pleasant one, whereas Patrick notices a slight change in Kate's after he poses the question. Also, he notices quickly how Emma takes Kate's hand in her own, as if to reassure her of something.

"I am not so much a traveller as a homebody," Emma explains with a natural smile emanating from her.

"Have you ever travelled?" Patrick continues, trying to make as much a pleasant conversation as he can, but maintaining an awareness of an invisible boundary that he is approaching.

"When I was younger, I travelled with my sister quite often," Emma discloses. "Even then, though, I was much more content sitting and painting, or drinking a nice cup of tea by the river watching the geese and ducks go by."

"It sounds very picturesque."

"It was, but lonely at times," she says softly, feeling Kate's hand once again she remembers to smile. "We all have those times though, do we not?"

"Yes," he replies, seeing Kate's eyes looking at him.

"What about you, Patrick? Do you travel often?" Emma looks carefully at Patrick, seeing his unsure face which makes him somewhat childlike in appearance. "Katherine has already revealed that you have been to England and Italy."

"Oh," he replies, his eyebrows rising. The thought of Kate telling others about him suddenly worries him somewhat, in a way he is unsure of. And yet, on the same token, he feels somewhat satisfied and reassured in a sense. Two emotions pulling at his brain, until he hears the giggling of Emma and Kate.

"So cute," they say to one another. "He's like a twelve year old with two pieces of candy." Kate's words cause him to wrinkle his brow.

"I am most certainly not a twelve-year-old," he replies in a huff. Then, "And yes, I have travelled, albeit for work mostly. I try and stay home as much as I can, because of Thomas, but work unfortunately doesn't always agree. Although sometimes if I'm allowed to bring him along with me, we try and go see things together as a family."

"That's nice," Emma says. "What about his mother? Katherine says you never speak of her."

Kate immediately looks at Emma, who merely laughs at the face she is given. Patrick, although stunned, simply smiles at the question and sighs.

"What would you like to know?" he returns.

"To begin with," she says pleasantly, as if to evade the severity of the question, "why is it you never speak of her?"

"I'm not sure," he pauses, "I've ever been asked that before."

"No," Emma says softly, "I suppose you wouldn't have really."

"Patrick is not the talkative type at the best of times," Kate says quickly, trying to break the oncoming silence the might ensue. "But he does say what's on his mind, which is better than most."

"Yes," Emma replies with a nod. "Ella was telling me. She was quite fascinated with you, and spoke in quite detail about your meeting with one another. You should consider yourself quite the man to leave the impression you did."

"I don't remember doing anything," he replies, his eyes raised in surprise. "In fact, she only told me that I didn't really fit in."

"That's probably her way of complimenting you," Kate informs him, patting him on the shoulder.

"Speaking of which, I was told by a little bird that young Daniel proposed to you," Emma says spiritedly, a glint of devious joy reflecting in her eyes.

"Did he? I had totally forgotten already." Kate is looking away from Emma purposely, knowing that her eyes are piercing into the back of her skull even as she speaks. Patrick is somewhat confused, but not shocked. Instead, he tilts his head slightly as to see Emma, and a slight amount of amusement crosses his face.

"And how did Patrick feel about this, I wonder?" Emma turns her face away from the others, knowing that they are approaching a bridge.

The sounds of a waterfall overtake all others as the caravan of horses and carts come bounding up to the bridge. Signs of the winter air are evident everywhere as the hay riders look onward to the long winding river and the beautiful waterfall in the distance. The rock face of the waterfall holds long slender icicles and the trees are already showing signs of light snowfall. The wooden planks of the bridge make a unique thumping sound with every turn of the wheel of the horse drawn carriages, somewhat rhythmic and soothing. Enough so perhaps, that even some of the children cannot help but to break into song as they begin the climb of the long road up the mountain.

It isn't long before the sounds of the waterfall are far behind them, leaving only the echoes of the various Christmas songs that are being sung by both children and adult alike. Talk between Emma and her two fellow hay riding companions become more conversational rather than anything promiscuous and delving as before. The further the caravan heads up into the mountainside, the colder it becomes, but the lighter everyone spirits develop.

The sound of the wheels turning against the hard ground below them begins to change along with the hard beating of the horses' hooves as they pull steadily along. With the air getting heavier with every breath, the compression of the snow begins to become more a regular tone in the background of the trail. Occasionally the backdrop of the Scottish horses snorting their noses in acknowledgement to the cold and the arduous work, that always causes the children to laugh and make a silly comment.

The group finally reaches the lodge in the early afternoon, just after the freshly fallen snow from the morning begins to grow stronger. All the children and parents are unloaded carefully from the haystacks and led into the main doors of the barn, where a warm fire and a banquet of food await them.

The festivities are pleasant, with several of the children meeting a variety of elves, pirates and other miscellaneous characters from throughout the world of imagination. Thomas is having a wonderful time, occasionally looking about to see where his father may have wondered off to, but generally unconcerned as the Christmas party seems to be too involved for him to think about anything else.

Thomas fills himself on warm apple juice and hot cocoa with marshmallows, as he meets several other children from the local area. At one stage everyone had several chances to take photos with Mrs. Clause, all while awaiting to see the man of the hour appear. He isn't much for photos, but likes to grin rather peculiarly when the opportunity is presented. His father always tends to scold him, but he has caught him laughing several times and try not to show it.

After the grand photo event, the children scatter off around the grounds to explore the different areas that are created for them. Thomas, along with a couple of the other boys head over to the pirate cove. As they do so Thomas seems a bit drawn to a strange light blue sparkle off in the distance. He slowly walks over to its origin, just nearby the Christmas Tree farm.

As Thomas looks around him, he suddenly is in awe at the vast abundance and variety of trees as well as their beauty as the snow falls around them. There are heat lamps not too far off, that create a strange illusion of lighted candy canes with their adornments. It almost reminds him of a Christmas wonderland he saw in a cartoon his father watched with him.

For a moment, he simply stands in awe and beholds the scenery around him, covered in a strange warmth that he isn't aware of. The snow continues to fall around him, as the twinkling of Christmas lights reveal the splendour of the evening.

"Hello, young Thomas," he hears from his side.

Thomas turns slowly and sees a large figure before him. It takes him a moment, but he soon realises that he is in the presence of something much grander than he first thought. His eyes begin to sparkle as he beholds the golden shine of the buttons and the dark black leather belt which contrast with the deep velvet red suit that this figure is clad in.

The figure kneels down and places his enormous hand on the young boy's shoulder, filling him with a strange instant comfort. A slight jingle seems to come from him, resonating a peaceful musical tone in the air with every movement he makes.

"Do you know why I'm here, Thomas?" The man's voice resonates throughout the trees; his deep voice echoing throughout.

Thomas can only respond with a slow shake of his head, which causes the man to smile. He looks into the man's deep blue eyes, feeling them pierce him unlike anything he has ever known before.

"Thomas, you are a fine young lad," the man speaks. "You have something that many do not. And while I normally do not undertake such grand happenings as the one that has caused me to expand my expectations a bit further than I would of this world; it is for you I have made an exception."

Thomas blinks slowly at the words, wanting to scratch his head, but knowing that he probably shouldn't. Instead he remains still and focuses on the giant before him.

"Your letter, Thomas," the man speaks with his resounding voice. "I know that there is not very much time left before Christmas, but I thought that I would come and speak with you for a bit. Would that be alright?"

Thomas nods slowly, a smile widening across his face. Then, "Of course," he manages to say pleasantly. He is almost surprised at himself.

"Do you know what makes Christmas special, Thomas?" the man queries.

"Well," Thomas begins. "Presents and cookies. Oh! And grandpa makes special chocolate chip pancakes for me!"

A loud bellow of laughter echoes aloud momentarily, as the man before the child folds his arms over his knee. Thomas looks on carefully, with a pleasant comfort that he is unaware of. It is as if this man were a member of his family. Someone that he has known his entire life, he feels subconsciously.

"Thomas, adults have a challenging time simply being an adult. They focus on everything that they believe is right, and move forward awkwardly based on that. Everything that they believe in, drives them to make the choices they make. From what they should eat, to where they should work or even how and if they should fall in love; all of this tending to get in the way of seeing what Christmas really means.

"You see Thomas, I have a unique ability to judge a person's character and generally people are good, albeit a bit confused at times. What makes this time of year special, is that most people truly do want the best for their friends and family or even dare I say, the people of this world. What makes it even more unique is how easily that message becomes lost."

The man lifts his arm and places his red glove on the boys head, pushing his bushy hair down softly. Thomas laughs a bit, as it feels as if he is being tickled throughout his body for some reason.

"What makes you special, Thomas," the man begins, "is that you dear boy understand what is truly important. It isn't the toys, or the video games, or the candy, nor is it the countless other things that someone can simply purchase whenever they'd like. It isn't about consuming a thing at all. It's the kindness from within. That's what makes us all special, dear Thomas. If only they could see the kindness around them, instead of focusing on the hate and all that is wrong; to see the world through your eyes would be a wonderful gift indeed."

The man stands, once again towering over the youth, as he straightens his thick gloves and adjusts his belt. His large hand strokes his thick white beard, and he turns to walk away.

"Thank you, for being a wonderful boy," the man says with a wink. "And I will do my very best to grant you all your Christmas wishes."

A cold wind blows through the trees suddenly, blowing up the snow and causing a moment where Thomas cannot see a thing. Once it settles, he sees the path once again. There is a small sign off in the distance pointing the direction of the pirate cove. Thomas blinks twice, placing his hands behind him, and then he slowly walks towards the sign. Somehow, he thinks, a pirate isn't quite as awesome as it was a moment ago.

Chapter 20

The Missing Words

There is gentle silence in the air. Katherine and Patrick are walking hand in hand down a gentle slope in the garden outside the main cabin. The last of the children and their parents have left for the evening, leaving only those who reside at the farm and their guests. It is just beginning to snow, small snowflakes gently gathering on the ground as they continue their peaceful walk.

Katherine changes her posture slightly, wrapping her arm around Patrick's, as she begins to smile so warmly at him. Then, "When I was younger, the sky always seemed so much closer to me."

Patrick stops for a moment at the statement. He looks up at the night sky, watching the snow fall from the heavens.

"It does seem so far away at times, doesn't it?"

"That's why I love Seattle," replies Kate. "It smells like the sky is all around you when it rains."

"I believe the term is called an atmospheric river," he returns to her with a bit of a smile. She simply looks at him and smirks.

As they continue through the woods, seeing the last of the horses being led back up the trail to make their way into their lodgings for the night, the snow begins to fall much heavier. Kate stands away from Patrick momentarily, holding her arms out and lifting her head upwards to catch the falling snowflakes. Patrick simply looks on with a look of delight as she encompasses her childhood pleasure.

Suddenly Kate stops and looks at him, her hands coming down behind her back and she intertwines her fingers. She watches him staring at the sky with a somewhat solemn face. It is here that she kneels down slowly and begins to pick at the snow on the ground. There isn't enough to do much, but a handful is all she needs to gain his attention once more.

Patrick can't help but to sneeze as the small badly formed snowball explodes like powder across his nose. A loud unadulterated laugh resounds in the air as he wipes his face and looks unamused at the woman near him, who cannot help but to continue to laugh and clap her hands at him. He looks down at the ground, pausing for a moment in order to decide whether or not to return the action. As he does so, another badly formed snowball hits his ear.

The snow continues to fall and cover the land in a majestic coat. Kate's laughter slowly seems to fade away into a gentleness that reminds Patrick of why he loves the woman before him. As she approaches, she places her cold hands on his face, wiping away the snow from his ear and his nose.

"I'm sorry," she speaks through her tender giggling.

"Are you?" he replies, merely curling his lip into a smirk as he raises his eyebrow. She replies to his words with a gentle kiss that follows with another more deeply longing one.

Kate steps back just slightly, enough for him to lunge forward and throw her over his shoulder. This causes a loud scream, followed by laughter from both parties. He spins her about, through her pleas to stop and ensuing laughter, and then slowly puts her down. For a moment she pauses to look at him, then can't help but to seat herself on the ground.

"Act like a child, and I will treat you like one," he explains to her, seating himself next to her. Kate merely laughs and kisses his cheek.

"You're adorable," she replies.

"So, while I have your attention, perhaps you can explain to me how any of this is related to picking out a Christmas tree for your father," Patrick enquires as he feels her head rest against his shoulder. "Not that I'm complaining."

"Nothing really," Kate laughs, looking up at the falling snow once more. "We'll pick one out in the morning and William will have the tree ready and prepared for us whenever we want to leave. I can't believe it's only a few more days until Christmas. Are you sure your father is fine coming to my father's farm?"

"Of course he is. But honestly, this all seems a bit much for visiting a tree farm," Patrick continues. "Was this your way of vetting me with Ella and Emma?"

Kate kisses his cheek again at the question. Then she grunts as she pushes herself upwards to stand once more. She motions for Patrick to follow with her head as she brushes the snow off of her clothes.

"Of course not. There is no vetting going on whatsoever," Kate explains, taking Patrick's hand as he rises. "What do you think of Emma, though?"

"She's nice," he replies. "Obviously from a world that I could never understand."

Kate pauses at the statement, looking first to Patrick and then to the sky once more to watch the snowfall down upon them both. A gentle smile lingers across her face in which Patrick cannot help but to wonder its meaning.

"Do you believe in Santa Clause?" Kate suddenly asks, looking down towards him once again. She then giggles slightly at Patrick's confused look. "I thought that I might get that from you."

"I didn't say anything," he replies, furling his brow.

"I think I believe in him," she replies. "And you didn't have to."

Kate begins to walk, slightly pulling Patrick along with her. She releases his hand and runs a few steps forward, folding her hands behind her back. Patrick suddenly is reminded of the little girl that began this entire adventure.

"I think I do as well," he says to her, recalling that moment in the airport that seems so long ago.

"Liar!" she says playfully, spinning around on one foot like a child. Then, as if someone has startled her, she stops and unclasps her hands. "I truly hope there is. I think the world needs him. It needs one glimmer of hope that flows innocently throughout this world. Someone who listens to all our hopes and dreams. I don't think the world is expecting him to grant them. Just to know that someone is listening is all we really need."

Kate feels Patrick's hand touch the mid of her back. It feels so strong, she thinks. As if he could take away all the world's problems for her.

"I'll always listen to you," he tells her. "Tell me all your hopes and dreams, Kate."

Tears form in her eyes, but she manages to hold them back if not but momentarily. She turns and bends over in order to put her forehead on his chest as to hide her eyes from him. It was one word that struck her above all the others. A word that most of the men that she knows would never say. It is at this precise moment she realises. She finally understands. With one word, he has managed to enter into a place deep in her soul that she has never allowed anyone before. It is almost overwhelming, and wonderful at the same time. Questions want to fill her mind, but she pushes them aside in order to savour this for just a moment longer. For this moment, she just wants to feel him. She just wants to be near him and to hear his heart beating.

"Thank you," she whispers.

"For what?" he returns to her, placing his hand on her back. This action causes her to step forward and hold him.

Suddenly, Kate turns and begins walking up the path once more. Patrick only catches a glimpse of her immense smile as she does so.

"Do you ever wonder what Santa Clause really looks like?" Kate finally queries, still not facing Patrick and continuing to walk away in a somewhat playful manner.

"I'm not sure what you mean?" he replies as he begins to follow her. "A red suit and fluffy white ball thingy on the end of a hat."

"You have no sense of imagination, my dear," Kate announces, leaning back slightly so that she can see him as she walks.

"I didn't realise that he looked different than that." Patrick curls his lip at her statement and his reply.

"Okay, think about it this way," she says. "Where do you think he lives?"

"The North— " he begins

"Oh, come now!" she interrupts, stopping in her tracks and pivoting on her feet to face him. She shakes her head as she watches the confusion come across his face once more. She can't help but to smile, then turns and begins walking again before he can catch up to her.

"I'm not sure where this is going," he says softly, receiving a motion from her hand to follow in return. "Fine. Where do you think he lives?"

Kate stops at the question, a soft wind suddenly blowing through the air. It causes her hair to move as if it were almost like water. Patrick cannot help but to stop and watch in awe at the beautiful scene before him. The snow continues to fall around them, the light from the lodge in the distance seemingly illuminating it to a wondrous blue colour. He watches her breath flow like a mist upwards in a child-like manner, as she tries to create rings with it. He can only think how amazing she is.

"I like to think that he lives somewhere near a warm beach," Kate announces softly. Then, folding her hands behind her back, "Somewhere practical!"

"The beach is practical?" he asks. "So, Santa lives in California?"

"I said practical! The taxes would kill any of his charity work," Kate laughs, causing Patrick to smile. "No... Somewhere wonderful and quiet. Where he can watch the world go by."

"So, Cancun."

Kate turns at the statement and grimaces. "You're being facetious."

"My apologies. Do carry on." Pat steps forward one step, causing her to reach backward for him. He reaches out, and their hands intertwine again.

"It doesn't matter," she replies, pulling his arm into hers.

"No. No. I'd like to hear more," Patrick assures her. "I assume practical includes the internet at least. We couldn't have Santa cut off from tweeting his daily status."

"Oh. Obviously," she replies, nodding to him.

"And I assume he'd be wearing some skimpy bathing suit to match his unique physique?" Patrick feels Kate's grip on his loosen slightly at his words. He looks over to her and he sees her staring off into the distance as they walk.

"No. I don't think so," she says matter-of-fact. "I imagine he would have long board shorts and sandals. Along with the most wonderful little cap and sunglasses."

A silence follows momentarily as they walk. Patrick watches her eyes, almost as if they are in a slight trance. Then, she blinks and begins to smile again, stopping him in order to pull him over to kiss his cheek.

"You're amazing," she replies. "Thank you for putting up with my craziness, and all of my friends and their eccentricities."

"You know, growing up my grandmother always told me that everyone is crazy," Patrick responds kissing her forehead gently. "It's finding the crazy that makes sense to me that counts."

"And do I make sense?" she laughs, as they begin to walk again.

"As the lighting is to the rain," he replies.

The two return to the lodge shortly after their evening stroll. They find that Thomas is happily sitting along the Scotsman listening to a splendid fishing tale about salmon, while wearing the overly large cowboy hat that he was given to by William. Emma is in a chair near the fire, and Ella is speaking with Mina near the far end of the room, near a small set of bookshelves and a settee.

Thomas doesn't notice that his father has returned from his walk, as he continues to speak about salmon and how wonderful they are to catch. William distracts him with talk of salmon pancakes and how wonderful they taste, which causes the young boy to listen intently.

The hour draws later in the evening, and the grandfather clock in the corner begins to chime, as if it were an alarm to awaken them from the merry moments that each of those in the room are trapped in. Patrick uses this time, to speak with Mina and the shortly thereafter pull Thomas away from his discussion with William.

Thomas and Patrick are led to a room on the upper floor, three times the size of his room at home. Thomas can't help but to stare in wonder at the enormity of it, and the grand paintings of horses that line the wall. His bed is much larger than he has ever been in, and it takes him a bit of effort to leap up into it. After he settles momentarily, seating himself on the edge, he says goodnight to Mina who excuses herself.

Thomas takes a moment to change into his night clothes that have been laid upon the bed for him before he arrived. He doesn't even notice the small detail, nor questions why or how such a task occurred. Instead he quickly changes so he can leap backwards into the bed, which engulfs him like an enormous pillow.

"Did you have fun tonight?" Patrick asks, coming over and seating himself next to his son. Thomas returns by leaping on his father's back and wrapping his arms around Patrick's neck.

"Yup!" replies Thomas, trying to climb up his father's back.

"I'm glad," his father replies, standing up and picking his son up over his shoulder. He slides forward and Patrick grabs his feet as his son stretches his arms outward to try and touch the ground. Slowly he is lowered and carefully rolls forward as his father releases him.

"I had loads of hot chocolate and warm cider!" he exclaims as he seats himself and crosses his legs on the floor. "And Santa thanked me!"

"That's nice. What did he thank you for?" Patrick questions softly, picking his son up and holding him into a standing position. For a moment he stares at his son's innocent eyes and remembers that it was not so long ago that he was able to pick him up with one arm.

"For being me, of course!"

"Of course," Pat rolls his eyes, helping his son crawl into bed. "Are you going to be okay here by yourself tonight?"

"Yup!" he replies, just as the door opens slightly. Both of them turn to see Samson come in and lay himself next to the bed. "I'm not going to be alone anyway."

"I see that," Pat returns, smiling.

"Dad," Thomas begins. "Is love kind?"

Pat was about to walk towards the door, but instead he stops and looks at his son who is crawling under the covers. It is here that he moves back towards the bed and seats himself next to his son.

"What made you ask that?" Patrick questions the boy, placing his hand on his son's head.

"Well, Terri told me that people are happy when they are in love. And Santa told me that people should see the kindness in the world." Thomas places his hand on his neck and scratches behind his ear. "I'm just wondering if they're the same thing."

"What do you think love is, Thomas?" Pat says softly, trying to carefully approach the subject.

"Well," Thomas says, drawing out the word. "I think that it's like when you're sitting in a room at Christmas and everyone is opening their presents. I think if you stop and listen, that's what love is."

Pat stops breathing for a moment and looks carefully at his son. A pride unlike any other fills him, and he leans forward and kisses his son on his forehead. His eyes almost well up, and he has to stand and turn away from his son before he can see his father's watery glance.

Pat walks over to the light and turns it off, turning back and facing his son once more.

"That's exactly what love is," he says to his son as he pulls the door just slightly ajar. "Goodnight son. I love you."

"I love you too!" he hears as he begins to walk back down the hall to the stairs.

Patrick continues down the hall and finds the stairs that lead down to the lodge's den where he finds Kate and Emma awaiting him next to the fire. Both have a cup of warm tea in their hands, and are speaking happily of the day's events. They stop momentarily when the notice him enter. He passes Mina, who informs him that she'll be bringing a nice warm adult beverage for him shortly.

"Where did everyone go?" Patrick asks as he approaches the two.

"They retired for the night. It's been a long day," Emma explains, looking over to Kate with a smile. "Will you come join us?"

"Of course," Pat replies, coming to stand behind Kate. "What were you two discussing?"

"Oh, nothing," Emma replies with a wry smile. "I was just explaining to Kate that we are short on rooms, and if she was okay sharing with you for the night."

"Oh..." Patrick raises a brow, as Kate begins to laugh.

"It's okay, Patrick," Kate interjects. "She's just teasing you."

"Ah," he returns, looking over to the door as Mina enters with a glass. "Oh! Good. I was just getting thirsty."

The two ladies laugh at Patrick's reply and immediate reaction to the question. They watch as he walks over and takes the drink from Mina and drinks it rather quickly, coughing at its strength and asking if he can have another.

Kate calls Patrick over, motioning with her hand to a loveseat close to the fire. Patrick obliges them, carefully assessing the two women who have obviously been partaking of more than just tea. The fire is pleasant though, and the atmosphere in the room make for a wonderful night.

"What shall we discuss, I wonder?" Emma ponders aloud.

"Anything you'd like," Patrick states, leaning back into the sofa. Mina returns shortly after so, and hands him another drink.

"Well now," Emma announces with a devious glint in her eye. "Perhaps it's the wine, or the various other drinks I've had tonight, but I feel like a good adult conversation is in order. Wouldn't you agree, Katherine?"

"Oh dear," Mina allows herself to slip and say, covering her mouth as she does so.

"Katherine tells me that you and your family are going to her father's estate for Christmas," Emma begins.

"That's very true," Patrick reveals. "After Kieran couldn't get the flights for he and Tara, Kate thought it would be fun to have a family event at her father's ranch."

"It's absolutely stunning this time of year. I remember seeing it years back, and thinking how lovely the snow and trees looked compared to Berkshire's rain and wind. Not that I've been in Berkshire for some time."

"You know that you and Ella are always welcome," Kate says cheerfully, sipping the last of her tea.

"I think my days of wintry mountains are coming to a close, dear," Ella responds. "I'm more concerned about the fact that you've never brought another man back there before."

"Really?" Pat says, raising his eyebrows and leaning forward in his chair.

"Katherine is rather shy when it comes to introducing members of the opposite sex to her father," Ella explains. "Isn't that true, Katherine?"

Kate squints and looks over to Ella, rising at the question. She shakes her empty tea cup and smiles pleasantly to the two.

"I think I need another tea, love. Would you care for one?" she asks instead of pandering.

"Mina can get you one," Ella returns with a devious smile.

"I'm perfectly capable of getting my own tea," she returns, walking over to the door and leaving.

"You'll have to forgive her," Ella says with a great fondness. "She is one of the few friends that treat me like a normal human being."

"Are you an alien then?" Pat questions jovially, sipping from his crystal glass of scotch.

A great sigh escapes Ella, as she turns from the door and faces Pat. She sets her tea down and crosses her hands across her laps, filling her face with a large smile. She brushes her dress slightly then straightens her back, as if to ready herself for the next words.

"I suppose I am," she reveals. "Although, only according to your government's definition of an alien. But I'm perfectly legal, if that's what's bothering you."

Patrick can't help but to laugh a bit at the statement. Ella joins him momentarily, and then looks deeply into his face.

"No," she says softly, but maintaining the pleasant smile across her face. "You see, I'm nearing the end of my time on the world."

Patrick tilts his head slightly. He struggles to find the words, but instead chooses to say nothing. Even before he can, Ella raises her hand to him in order to stop him.

"It's alright. Everyone acts that way when they find out," she explains. "Katherine was the only one who didn't. In fact, she's the only one who made me laugh."

"How so?" Patrick queries, somewhat stricken by the frankness of the woman before him.

"We were at a social function, and to be honest, I was not in very good spirits. I was acting like a child, and my sister and I had just had a rather troublesome fight over something trivial. When Katherine asked me what was wrong, I unceremoniously shouted that I was dying and that my sister needed to accept it and stop hating me because of it," Ella explains. Her words are light as air, reaching Patrick with ease.

"I can imagine that didn't go down well," Patrick nearly whispers, carefully watching his words.

"It's okay," Ella insists, her smile reassuring Patrick. "Emma was very upset at the news, and still to this day is angry at the world, and the universe, and herself, I'm afraid. But those are demons that she'll have to overcome on her own."

"What did Katherine say to make you laugh?"

Ella looks over as Katherine walks into the room once more. She stops behind Patrick as she hears the question.

"I said," Katherine begins, "that death was a dull, dreary affair and should be avoided for as long as possible. But to quote a well-known bear, *how lucky you are to have a friend that makes saying goodbye so hard.*"

"How lucky I am indeed," Ella replies softly. "Be good to her, Patrick. She is my one dearest friend that this universe has given me. And I am truly lucky to find it so hard to say goodbye to her."

Chapter 21

The Ashtons

It has been approximately three days, four hours and six minutes since Patrick has last seen Katherine. The James family is currently making their way up the I-90 Interstate toward Snoqualmie Pass, on their journey to reach the Ashton ranch just past Cle Elum. Young Thomas has been asleep for much of the journey, as they departed rather early in order to account for any unexpected traffic and the snow conditions which were due to be heavy. The elder James member, Ben, father of Patrick, sits happily next to his son who is driving the three towards their destination.

Ben thinks to himself how nice it is that he doesn't have to drive so often anymore. As much as he'd never admit it, his eyes aren't what they used to be, and his reflexes aren't nearly as quick as he tells himself. Not that he feels he is unsafe, but he no longer feels that he needs to be in control. Especially inside Patrick's glorified computer on wheels. Ben once looked under the hood, and where the engine was supposed to be, was a plastic container with some writing on it.

Yes, life has certainly changed over the years for the three. But never more so than now. The change that has occurred, or perhaps is still occurring, strikes Ben as a bit fantastical. Nevertheless, they are following along this path that the universe seems to be leading them on, which is at the moment is a ranch.

"Who am I to judge," Ben whispers aloud, looking down at his coffee.

"What was that, pop?" Pat questions his father, watching the road for ice or slush.

"Oh, nothing, son. I was just thinking that if you'd of asked me if I would have ever paid five dollars for a milky cup of coffee with vanilla, I'd probably had laughed at you," Ben says to himself, laughing a bit as he does so.

"Yes, I know. Twenty burgers for a dollar or whatever," Pat exclaims, changing lanes to avoid a rather oddly shaped car, who is slowing down to take photos of the mountain. "Twenty years ago, you'd probably be drinking your coffee black, after it had been sitting in a coffee machine for four hours. And you'd also be saying how bad it tasted, but that it made you a man."

"Now it just gives me heartburn," Ben sighs.

"Exactly," returns his son, slowing down to compensate for a large truck that he is coming near which is throwing up sludge from the road. As they enter a tunnel, Pat accelerates to pass the truck while he can still see clearly. "These roads are fun."

"I thought you could just hit a button and let the car do the driving for you," Ben asks rather humorously.

"If there was a button that made everyone else drive better, I'd probably hit that one first," Patrick exclaims as he sees the signs for the pass and the ski lodges coming up. "Once we get past the lodges up ahead, things should taper out and traffic should die down."

"I would expect so," Ben says with a nod. "I doubt many people are in the mood for a jaunt over the mountains to see the wineries in the dead of winter. Although, you never know. Maybe it's better chilled."

"I have heard ice wine is rather good," Pat says with a laugh. He pauses for a moment, looking over and seeing his father sitting next to him looking out at the snow-covered trees and mountains that paint a picturesque winter scene of the Pacific Northwest. It is here he feels a wave of gratitude overcome him, enough to where he can't help but to simply speak. "Thanks, pop."

"For what?" Ben replies, looking over at his son.

"For everything," Pat returns. "For being there whenever I needed you. For putting up with my silly ideas, and for all the unreasonable arguments that kept me sane. But mostly, just for being you, and allowing me to be me. It's taken me a while to figure out who that is."

"I think Kate has helped with that quite a bit too, son."

Pat simply replies with a nod, as he turns his signal on and takes the exit that his phone says to take. As he does so, the sound of a yawn comes from the back seat and causes Ben to laugh as Thomas immediately begins making sounds in awe at the snow outside.

"I wonder how deep that is!" the young boy exclaims excitedly. "Do you think it's taller than me?"

"Might be," Ben returns to his grandson. "Let's hope you don't find out."

"Can we have a snowball fight when we get there?!" Thomas says, leaning as far forward in his seat as possible.

"We're supposed to meet with everyone first, and then we can see what happens afterwards," Patrick replies, causing a sigh from his son.

The drive to the ranch is a bit of a drive from the main interstate road. Thomas becomes silent, as he places his headphones over his ears and begins his program. Ben can't help but to shake his head a little while stating what a shame that technology envelopes everything, including the scenery.

Kate is standing on the porch of the main house looking out as she sees Patrick's car pull into the gate. She and Tara arrived a couple of days earlier in order to get the house ready for everyone. She's quite pleased with the way things have turned out, with what the last couple of weeks have been like it's a wonder she even managed to convince anyone to come.

Kate's eyes begin to shine as the car parks next to hers, seeing the young Thomas jump out of the car immediately. She cannot help but to contain her smile as she sees Patrick for the first time in days. Her heart immediately begins racing, and her face becomes quite flush. Her father's dog, Cieral awakens her with his loud deep bark. Being a hound, his bark is much slower and less of a bark and more of a howl of sorts.

Cieral looks at the oncoming travellers, but doesn't arise from his warm bed on the porch. Being a Basset hound, he tends not to make too much of a fuss unless something is really and truly disturbing, like a cat or squirrel.

Kate laughs as she looks down at her father's best friend, seeing Thomas come running up to him almost instantly. Thomas tries and talk to the old dog, but he simply closes his eyes once more and lets out a great sigh with every stroke of the boy's hand.

"Looks like we're the first ones to arrive," Patrick says, watching as his father gives Kate an endearing hug as a greeting.

"There's hot coffee and tea in the house," Kate tells Ben, pointing toward the back of the house. "Tara's in the kitchen making hot chocolate and cookies. Thomas, you're more than welcome to go help her if you'd like."

"Cookies!" he states, running into the house. Ben is second to follow, giving only a nod to his son as he shuts the red door behind him.

"Nice wreath," Pat tells Kate, looking at the fresh pine cones and holly leaves that it is made out of.

"I made that with Tara last night, while drinking some port," she laughs, pointing out how crooked it is. "Did you bring all the gifts to put under the tree yet?"

"Joe will bring them up tonight after Thomas has gone to sleep. He has to pick up the ones for our neighbour as well. Are you sure it's okay that my dad invited her and her daughter?"

"Perfectly. I think it's lovely," Kate smile, taking Pat's hand in hers.

"Well the house looks big enough to take it," Pat says, looking at the size of the mountain lodge looking ranch house. "How big is this place?"

"My father owns roughly about two hundred acres. I want you to meet him, but he won't be back until later tomorrow. Hopefully in time for Christmas dinner anyway," she says. "He's working on the other side of the mountain with one of his neighbours, trying to get the livestock up from the valley. I guess they got loose late last night."

"I can't wait," Patrick says softly, his eyes revealing a gentle truth in the words.

"Let's go in and get something to drink. Kieran is on his way with some last-minute items that Tara needed for tonight. Other than that, I'll show you around the ranch," Kate informs him, pulling him slightly but receiving a bit of resistance.

When she looks back to see why he isn't moving, she's met with his lips on hers. His hand comes to her face, which warms her cheek to the touch. For a moment she melts, her knees suddenly weakening, but not enough to cause her to move away. Pat then lowers his hand and smiles at her.

"Merry Christmas," he says to her.

"Merry Christmas," she replies softly, her cheeks now fully red.

The morning turns into the noon hour quickly. Kate takes the opportunity to show her guests the ranch, including the stables and the byre. Thomas is overwhelmed at how many animals there are, including how many smells they have as well. The chickens somewhat wear him down, enough to where he gathers enough courage to ride a horse with Kate. By the time they return to the stables, Kieran is standing by the porch door waving at the lot of them with the young Terri and her mother there as well.

Thomas waves at Terri happily and somewhat excitedly as the two meet one another and immediately go dashing off to the kitchen in hopes of hot chocolate and cookies. Kieran explains to the others that lunch is nearly ready, but will take a few more minutes to finish up.

"Like the wind," he replies.

"Yes. Like the wind," the voice replies. "But if you let yourself sink to the bottom of the darkness, and live behind all the doors you have closed, then there is nothing that it nor I can ever do for you."

The snow begins to fall heavier, as the wind begins to blow stronger. For a moment the cold fades away and as he looks around, he sees nothing but the white snow blowing. And yet, as he continues to look about, he suddenly beholds the small girl that he met so many days before, who handed him a small box in an airport. Her smile fills him with such a warmth, that he cannot describe how full his spirit feels at this moment. All he can do is simply watch as she comes forward and takes his hand into her tiny hands.

"All the magic and beauty that this universe holds, is already in your hands, Patrick. All the gifts, the love, the happiness, the joy; these are all already yours. All I can do, is open the door to let you see them. What you do after the door opens, is up to you."

"I understand," he whispers, kneeling down to her. She wraps her arms around him and hugs him momentarily, then steps away from him.

"Patrick, tomorrow morning, I want you to read the letter that you have been holding on to for me."

She takes another step back and turns to walk away from him. As she does so, he stands and watches the snow blow all around them.

"I have truly enjoyed watching you, Patrick. You have a wonderful life. Live it to the fullest," she says as the snow begins to engulf her. "Enjoy where the wind blows you next. You really do give great hugs."

The Letter

Christmas morning is quite the event in the Ashton ranch. Everyone has gathered around the tree, which is fully decorated with silver and blue decorations. Laughter fills the air as they watch one another empty their Christmas socks full of candy and small pleasant items that bring smiles to everyone. The sounds of music fill the large room, and there is a roaring fire ablaze keeping everyone warm.

Christmas breakfast follows the socks, in which special chocolate chip pancakes are included in the feast. Pleasant conversation flows in the air, as time seems to pass quickly, although not quickly enough for the two children at the table.

Finally, the gift giving begins. Unfortunately, Kate's father is still away, so Ben volunteers to become the Santa for the day and hand everyone's gifts out to them. He enlists the help of the young Thomas and Terri to assist in delivering them to the appropriate persons as he pulls them out from under the tree.

Patrick makes a special comment to Joseph, thanking him for helping the real Santa Clause find out where everyone was, and to make sure that all the gifts arrived before morning.

With the final gift opened, with the exception of Kate's father's, which are stacked nicely under the tree, everyone begins to relax. Hugs are delivered to all, and laughter and conversations continue.

It is here that Kate asks for Patrick's assistance in the kitchen, to which he happily obliges. The two make pleasant conversation as they clean the dishes which doesn't take long and prepare for the cooking of dinner. Once finished, they seat themselves at a small kitchen table, where they treat themselves to some eggnog.

"Thank you," Kate says to Patrick, seating herself closer to him on the bench. She leans over and kisses his cheek as she sets a small box in front of him.

"What's this?" Pat responds, raising his left brow.

He picks the box up and looks at its elongated shape and the simple bow that's wrapped around it.

"Open it," she insists, her face showing obvious signs of how nervous she is becoming.

Patrick unwraps the box, and then carefully opens it. For a moment, he looks at the contents. Confused, he looks over at Kate, who nods once at him. Carefully, he pulls out the small piece of paper that is inside, unfolding it approximately six times. He smiles as he reads the paper, looking over to Kate once more.

On the note are three small words. A doorway that he has not seen opened before him in so very long.

Patrick leans over and kisses Kate, her hands coming to his cheeks as he does so. A love that he hasn't felt before sweeps into him like a river that has no end. And for the first time in so very long, he steps out of the doorway and into the sunlight to feel the wind blow across his face.

"I love you too," he says to her.

"I wasn't sure if you'd believe me, so I made sure to write it down, so you have it in writing," she tells him, holding back the tears that she can't understand.

"Thank you," he says, folding it and placing it in his inner pocket. As he does so, he feels the envelope of his son's letter to Santa Claus. Slowly he pulls it out and looks at it.

"What's that?" Kate asks.

"A letter my son wrote to Santa Claus." Patrick turns the envelope over and opens it to reveal the contents inside. Carefully he pulls the paper out and opens it.

"What's it say?" Kate says excitedly, but changes as tears form in Patrick's eyes. "Are you okay??"

Patrick nods once, and hands the letter to Kate. She takes it from him and looks down to begin reading it.

It reads as follows:

Dear Santa,

I'm sorry for bothering you on such short notice. I know I sent you my letter earlier asking for the new gaming phone, but I spoke with Terri and she said I could change my mind if I got this to you in time. Terri helped me write this. She is better at spelling than I am, so if I did spell something wrong, it is because she told me to.

Santa, I have been thinking lately about why my dad always looks so sad when he comes home. He smiles whenever I say something funny, but he doesn't sound like the other fathers that I have heard when they laugh. His smile isn't like other smiles I see. So I asked Terri, and she said I should write you and ask you to help me.

I know you're busy, but if it isn't too late to ask, then I want to ask for a new smile for my dad. My dad always makes me smile for real. Since I can't make him smile for real, can you please help him find one?

Terri says that her mom lost her smile when they moved. She says that it is because her mom doesn't love her father anymore. Terri thinks that my father's smile broke when my mother died. I didn't talk with my mother, but I'm pretty sure she still loves my father, so I don't know if that would break his smile or not.

I don't know how to fix a smile, or if you can fix one, but Terri says if anyone can, it will be you. I don't really need anything for myself. My dad and my grandpa always get me enough to make me happy. So you can take my present and give it to someone else if that is what you need to do. Terri says it might cost more than this year's present, so you can use the money from next year's too if you want. If that's not enough, then you can take my savings. I'm not allowed to spend it anyway. You can also have any presents that anybody gives me too.

I love my dad more than anyone else. Terri says that's why my smile is so big. I think a real smile is more important than any gift that I can get from you or anyone. If you can fix it, or maybe give him a new one, then I'll pay you back whatever it costs. I'll sell all my toys if you need. He's a bit grumpy sometimes, but he's really worth it to me. I wouldn't trade him for anyone else's dad. He gives great hugs. If you meet him, make sure to give him one for me and you'll see.

Thank you,

Thomas James

The End